The Last Deceit

The Mercian Ninth Century
Book 10

MJ Porter

Cover and map design by Flintlock Covers

ISBN: Paperback 978-1-917374-13-2

ISBN: Hardback 978-1-917374-14-9

ISBN: Kindle 978-1-917374-12-5

ISBN: Ingram Paperback 978-1-917374-15-6

 Created with Vellum

Contents

GWYNEDD
POWYS
DYFED
GWENT
CHESTER
LICHFIELD
TAMWORTH
REPTON
TORKSEY
GAINSBOROUGH
BARDNEY
THETFORD
EAST ANGLIA
ELY
PETERBOROUGH
NORTHAMPTON
GRANTABRIDGE
WARWICK
WORCESTER
OFFA'S DYKE
HEREFORD
KINGSHOLM
GLOUCESTER
MERCIA
PASSENHAM
LONDON
KENT
WESSEX
WINCHESTER
MAP OF EARLY ENGLAND
0
50 Miles

Prologue AD875

Canterbury, the kingdom of Wessex

I focus on the rounded tower that suddenly doesn't seem to be getting any closer, urging Haden to reach it as soon as possible. I'm wary there might be others who've deceived me. I don't doubt Archbishop Æthelred's loyalty, but my thoughts turn to Abbot Kynebert. He didn't like me. Perhaps he's in league with Lord Æthelwulf and the man I assume is Ealdorman Sigehelm.

'My lord,' Rudolf's voice is urgent, filled with fear, dragging me from my thoughts. And this time, I do rein my mount in, eyes furrowed with confusion that only clears slowly as I try and make sense of what's happening before me.

'Fuck,' I glower, raising my arm in the air to alert my warriors they need to stop this time. In a clatter of heavily breathing horses, my eyes rake in what's happening ahead.

I swallow uneasily, aware that for the time being, we have the time to watch events ahead.

Canterbury's so close, it feels as though I could reach out and touch it, but it's impossible because the road is once more blocked. And not by Ealdorman Æthelwulf and his allies, but instead, by the enemy, engaged in a brutal attack against the force of Mercians I ordered to hold where the two roads diverge.

'Bollocks,' I huff, reaching for my seax and gripping it tightly, although what I'm going to do with it, I don't know.

'There are hundreds of them,' Rudolf announces, his voice brittle with fear.

'Shit,' Eadfrith huffs from beside me. I turn and glance at those following on behind. We're strung out along the road, those with lame animals even further away. We're entirely exposed. When I set us on this path my concern was to get to Icel as quickly as possible and away from the enemy force and then Lord Æthelwulf and his attempts to stop us. I didn't forget about the other half of the enemy force, coming towards Canterbury from Richborough, but I did forget something crucial. They were never going to have as far to travel as I did.

'Fucking bollocks,' I explode, unable to think of anything aside from my shock at finding ourselves surrounded. There are not one but two enemies behind us. In front, there's another one. I'm sure any moment now they'll realise we're behind them.

The fighting's already bloody and brutal. I hear the shrieks and grunts of warriors using all they have to better their enemy. Somewhere amongst all that, Icel, Kyred, Wærwulf and the rest of my warriors are fighting as well.

I can't see them. I'm not close enough to make out anything more than the heaving mass of the slaughter field, as though an animal in itself, rising and falling with some unseen force behind it.

'Fuck,' I shout, roaring upwards, eyeing the sky where holy men would assure me my Lord God is looking down on me. If he is, he means to make this a fuck sight more difficult than even I'd considered.

I glance around. To the east, there'll be more enemies before we could reach the coast. To the west, there's a flat landscape that would make an escape visible to all when our horses are already exhausted, and many of them lame or in danger of going lame.

'What do we do, my lord?' It's Hemming who asks the question everyone must be thinking. The fact it's not Rudolf, assures me he knows how fucked we are. He won't voice his concerns. He doesn't need to because he knows the answer. But Hemming isn't quite as battle savvy as Rudolf.

'I wish I fucking knew,' I allow myself to mutter. Then take a deep breath and try to focus on what I can control right now.

I have an idea, but it's really shit. It's my worst one yet. Even worse than allowing myself to be taken as a prisoner within Repton. Even shoddier than when I allowed everyone to reach Northampton ahead of me and Haden. Even more stupid than when I thought to rescue my horse by putting my own life in peril.

But. There really is no bloody choice.

I hold that tight for a moment, as more and more of my warriors come close, their horses tired and exhausted, but not my warriors. No, my warriors are fresh, but scared.

I look to Hemming, and then to Ælfgar, who's arrived on the back of Ordheah's horse. Ælfgar assesses everything quickly. Resignation flashes on his face, but he nods towards me, giving his approval.

'Right, warriors of Mercia,' I call, just loud enough so they can hear. 'Dismount, add your helms, bring your shields, your spears, your swords and your fucking stones.'

'My lord,' Rudolf squeaks in shock, already realising my intentions.

'Ælfgar and any others with lame horses, gather all the animals together. Take them to the west, there,' and I point to a scraggly outcropping of trees, the only high point for a long distance all around us. 'Take the horses there, and if there's the option, continue towards Canterbury.' Ælfgar nods, resigned to his fate, as I dismount from Haden and force my helm over my face so that for a moment, my instructions echo and fill my head with the final command I'm about to give.

'We fight our way through the bastards,' I order. 'Together, as one, shield to shield. We'll pierce them from behind.'

'Like a hot poker up their fucking arse,' Rudolf huffs to counter his fear. I offer him a smile when my helm's secured.

'Just like a fucking great big hot poker up their arses,' I confirm, and stride onwards, having given Haden a pat along his nose after tying his reins above the saddle. I hope it's not the last time I ever get to do that. I really fucking don't. His assessing glance at my parting shot, promises me more retribution if it is, than anything Icel or my aunt could offer me.

My warriors hurry to join me, Rudolf at my side, while Ingwald's at my left. I'm not used to fighting with either of them, but this is more about reaching our allies than killing the enemy. It's also about distracting those bastards behind so they'll think they can engage us, rather than those with the lame horses.

'How?' Rudolf questions, but then grins. 'You're going first, aren't you?'

'Yes. And you're to be at my side, and we'll truly form a wedge driving the enemy away from us. If we're lucky, they won't understand what's happening until we're through to Icel.'

This seems to settle Rudolf, although the increasing noise from the slaughter field tests my resolve. Perhaps, I reason, we should all have gone to where I'm sending the horses. But no. That wouldn't have been possible. I need to ensure I'm the focus of those behind. Maybe, if my luck improves, the enemy won't realise they're fighting their own allies.

As we draw closer, I test the hold on my shield, and on my seax. I've not brought my spear to this fight. There won't be the reach to use the weapons effectively. This is just as much about speed and shock tactics, as what happened with the horses. We've discovered time and time again the enemy never consider who's with them at the back. I also appreciate the road's liberally splattered with blood and the dead and dying. The enemy do seem to be overwhelming my warriors. Already, I see the Viking raiders have won their way closer to Canterbury, leaving the two branches of the roadway visible behind them.

Aware those crying for aid are the enemy, I turn to my warriors, and meet their gazes, evenly. Only then do I tighten the guards on my helm, and lift my shield before me, wincing at the memory of the ache in my left thigh.

'As one,' I command, not a roar, but a spoken order filled with resolve. I hear the crash of shield meeting shield, Rudolf and Ingwald as my companions, and move forwards.

The stink of the slaughter field wafts up my nostrils. Blood, shit, piss, and sheer fucking terror. I'm aware of the battle calm coming upon me the closer I get to the rear of the current fighting. This might be an unusual way to win, but win it we fucking will. I'm sure of it. The cost might be high. I'll consider that when the battle's won, and not before.

'Now,' I murmur to my companions, aware Rudolf and Ingwald share the words with those to either side. Hemming's behind me, hefting his shield over my head. Others protect his head with their shields. We're few, but in such a way, we can be mighty.

Ahead, I see the swaying backs of the enemy, and push into them. An angry cry, and even angrier shriek, and the first man is beneath my feet, someone behind me ensuring he's dead.

To either side of me, I sense others moving, effortlessly being jostled so that, here, where the shield wall facing my warriors isn't a layer of wooden shields, the men move with more ease. I keep my eyes focused on the way ahead, visible through my helm, and between the thin gap of the top of my shield, and the roof over my head, provided by Hemming.

My breath is already harsh, the pressure of holding my shield in place taking its toll on my shoulders and back.

An angry shout, and another of the enemy thinks to look behind him. Before he can alert anyone, pugnacious face red and sweating, mouth open, I lift my elbow and slide my blade into it. He gargles and falls dead. Rudolf's also killed an enemy. No doubt, we all have by now. We're in the middle of it. The warriors ahead are more tightly woven together with shields, but on we go. No one's yet deciphered what's happening. That won't last long. When we're discovered those at the rear will close the open arrow head we're forging and the fighting will get fucking nasty.

I feel pressure against my shield as the next warrior refuses to yield. Like the last dead man, he turns to shout angrily at whoever knocks him. The raucous cry ends with a plaintive shriek.

'*Skiderik*,' he hisses, as I stab towards him with my seax.

'Same,' I retort, wishing he wasn't able to bat aside my attack so easily. A further string of Norse words pours from his mouth, before I can land another blow on his byrnie, but already, more and more of the enemy are turning, heeding his caution.

'Come on,' I shout, no need to hide the language we speak any more. From behind, I feel Hemming pressing into me, eager to continue onwards. We're close to the fighting face of the shield wall. I see red-sheeted blades flashing beneath the late afternoon sun as though burnished stalks of hay.

'Fucking come on,' I repeat, more to myself than the others because I'm at the front. I'm the one who can't defeat our enemy. I'm the one that must punch a hole through this wall of iron and wood. It's my place to do so, admittedly with my warriors' aid, but I'm the first to meet the backs of the shield carriers.

Hearing my cry, more and more of the enemy turn in surprise, even those who should be protecting their allies who form the shield wall. I realise our attack might just have an unexpected result.

A string of words, angry, and I sense the scrutiny of more and more of the enemy, although my focus remains on cutting a hole through their defence. But now they come against us. It's as though I've been hit by the tidal bore rushing along the River Severn. The force of the attack almost takes my legs from beneath me. Only Hemming's strength stops me from buckling as my left leg falters. It's done well to last as long as it has.

I wince, and struggle upright, Hemming's free hand holding my shoulder upright, while Rudolf and Ingwald ensure my shield stays in place. I redouble my grip, plant my left foot behind me to secure my failing balance, chest heaving with the effort, as spears and seaxes slide over my shield. I'm grateful Hemming held onto his shield as he aided me. In fact, I'm indebted to all of my men.

As the heat and shouting and heaving intensifies, I realise this is fucking madness. What was I bloody thinking?

My seax arm is busy, slashing and banging against any part of my enemy I can reach because I can't lift my head over my shield to sight the next attack. It's all I can do to risk extending my seax arm. Perhaps, after all, I should have had my men bring their spears. The enemy are using enough of them against us. Where the shields don't quite join, blades slip their way through.

'Ware,' I roar to Hemming because he doesn't have a shield to protect his legs, too busy ensuring my head stays on my neck.

Angry voices grow even angrier. I've got fuck all idea what's happening ahead of us. Our progress has been halted but I don't believe we're being forced backwards. Instead, we hold in place, trying to kill the enemy, but it's almost impossible. Hemming's trying to protect the heads of me, Rudolf and Ingwald, his breath harsh in my ear. We're so close together, I can feel him pressed against my back, his heat making me even hotter. I'm surprised I can't hear the thrum of the blood in his body.

Rudolf shrieks. I feel a weight to my left, trying to drag my shield down.

'Rudolf,' I cry, fearing for him, but like me only moments ago, he manages to regain his feet and recover himself, ensuring the shield wall stays in place.

'This is fucking madness,' I hear Ingwald roar, the clash of his seax arm frenzied. I'm minded to agree with him. Finally, I manage to worm my seax over my shield wall, stabbing forward, but angling the blade down, exposing my elbow in the process and hoping my byrnie will keep me protected. When I retract my weapon, the blade flashes redly. I allow a slow smile to touch my tight cheeks, sweat stained and itchy with the heat.

I repeat the motion, stabbing and jabbing, retracting and then doing the same. Hemming's steady behind me now, some space between us so I don't have to worry about elbowing him in the face. Ingwald has his rhythm as well. Even Rudolf's managing to hold his own.

I strain to hear my allies in front and behind, but it's impossible. The voices of the enemy, furious at finding themselves under attack from such an unexpected position, flood the air. I can't quite determine who shouts. I feel I should know the names of the jarls, but it's impossible to determine more than the hum of voices above the crash of wood and iron.

'Fucking come on,' I urge myself. My left leg's growing weaker now, forced to absorb the impact of keeping me upright. My right leg's no better, but I'm not giving up. I'll fight until my body can take no more.

The movements of my enemy show no intention of slackening. I risk a brief look over the top of my shield, unable to make sense of what I'm seeing. A shimmering blade veers alarmingly close to my head. I duck down to avoid losing my eye, or being smacked on the head hard enough to lose all sense. That would be most unfortunate.

I stab with my seax, adding more of my weight to keeping my shield upright.

'Advance,' I bellow, unsure if it's even possible. Hemming steps closer. I sense Rudolf and Ingwald doing the same. It's impossible to risk looking at them. My head is low, the smell of such a confined space fetid.

'Advance,' I cry once more, forcing my left leg forwards, trusting my right one to hold firm even though its shaking with the strain.

'Again,' I bellow, hoping my warriors can do what I demand from them.

My right foot lands on the churned and bloodied ground. I test my footing, and then force my left leg to do the same. The most worrying moments are when all my weight rests on only one leg. I could be unbalanced by anything, but my left foot lands in front of my right. I repeat the motion. Rudolf and Ingwald stay with me, as does Hemming, and the others who are behind us.

It's a fucking monumental effort, but I have to press on.

Chapter One

A few weeks earlier

'Get him inside,' I growl, not that Hereman and Goda aren't already busy with him. I glance from Gardulf's slumped form to King Alfred's perplexed expression. A moment ago he was joyful, now I'm unsure what he is. He hardly astounds me while taking to his knees and beginning to pray loudly, hands clasped before him, eyes uplifted.

I growl and shake my head at his display.

He's kneeling, in the mass of dead Viking raiders, the air rife with the smell of their innards, the metallic tang of blood making me want to grimace. His warriors watch on, bewildered, and I fear I've committed too hastily. Again. Will I never bloody learn?

'Get Gardulf inside. Icel,' I roar, only to startle, as he appears before me, a grimace on his blood-streaked face, his iron-rimmed beard splattered with the stuff as well. He's removed his helm. His eyes and upper cheeks are pale on his lined visage.

'My lord?' he offers in his deep voice, with a quirked eyebrow. He growls on passing King Alfred. I almost think he might shove him over. I'd like to see that. I consider ordering him to do it, but no. Icel's attention must be for Gardulf and Goda.

I hobble. Now the battle joy's left me, I feel tired and achy. My wounded left thigh pulses as though I've only just taken the savage cut that has been plaguing me.

'Fuck,' I mutter, realising Haden's no longer here, as he's transported Gardulf inside. I need to know where Gardulf's been and how he knows about the approaching attack on Canterbury, the home of Æthelred, the Archbishop of York. I suspect I know what he's going to tell me, and I'll be fucking angry with him. I really bloody will.

Scarred Kyred comes to me next, again, casting an appraising eye over the praying King Alfred, and in doing so, revealing the full extent of the scar on the left side of his face. We could be doing much more useful things than begging forgiveness for killing a man who threatened our lives. King Alfred's a stupid fucking arse.

'Kyred, you're well?'

'Aye, my lord king. A good few wounds. I'm sorry we were overwhelmed by the other force. They ploughed through us.' I nod. I'd wondered about that.

'Any other enemy seen?'

'No, my lord king. Shall we retrieve the horses?'

'Yes, they're still in the woodlands. Sæbald's also there. He's wounded. Bring him back, carefully. But be alert. There could be more of the bastards hiding, determined to take their chance when we've relaxed our guards. You did well. Thank your men. Pillage where you will, but bring any severely wounded here. We need to ensure injuries are cleaned. Kill any of the enemy yet living.'

Kyred nods, continuing to breath heavily from his exertions. I eye him. He seems hale, but the bruises won't show until his byrnie's removed.

'My thanks,' I offer more softly. 'It was a difficult task. It went well, considering our lack of planning.' Kyred grins then, his face splitting wide open to show the pink of his tongue.

'Aye, my lord king. Better to see how it goes, than stake everything on having minute control over what happens. The mark of a true warrior.' With that, he turns his back on the loudly praying King

Alfred and shouts his men to join him. I notice the sluggish few who might be hurt. I hope they know themselves well enough to seek aid rather than amble around, bleeding their last, when the battle's won and the enemy vanquished.

Ealdorman Ælhun comes to my side. He's already ordered his men to similar tasks. Now he stands and watches King Alfred, an unfathomable expression on his ice-rimmed bearded face.

'What do we do with him?' he murmurs. I shake my head once more.

'Leave him to it. Look, his guards are coming to protect him.' A collection of six men dressed as warriors take themselves to King Alfred's side, where he remains kneeling. I narrow my eyes. Not one of them has so much as a blood splatter on their byrnie or blades. I'm sure they've not cleaned themselves up already. These men have played no part in the fight to defend their king. Their arrival now, shimmering beneath the sun in so much protective equipment, is ludicrous.

I observe my warriors. Tall Icel's leading Haden within Old Sarum, Hereman beside him, the first and second gateway open to allow them and Goda inside. Rudolf and Pybba are combing through the dead. I hear young Rudolf exclaim as he finds something of value amongst the pickings. Old Wærwulf's speaking roughly to the few Viking raider survivors using their tongue, while slow Osmod and hobbling Ingwald keep them guarded. Ingwald does well despite the loss of one of his toes some years before. They growl whenever one of the enemies thinks to move, or breathe too deeply. The foemen all bleed. Osmod's byrnie has a gaping hole in the side of it but I see no blood. I hope he's unwounded. He's bled enough for Mercia in his long life. Like Icel, he's been a warrior of Mercia for a long time. There's much he could tell me, if I asked him. Sometimes, I'm tempted, but other times, not so much.

In the absence of wounded Sæbald, nine-fingered Gyrth and the almost-toothless Leonath share accounts of the fighting, both talking too loudly and too fast as they try and outdo one another with tales of how many of the bastard enemy they killed.

Scarred Hemming and bent-nosed Eahric converse with some of Ealdorman Ælhun's men, while they move through the mass of dead bodies, kicking them for good measure to make sure they're really lifeless.

Other than King Alfred and the six Wessex warriors who surround him, there are no West Saxons to be seen. No one comes through the double gateway to survey the carpet of white and grey bodies. No one thinks to pilfer valuables from the dead. No one thinks to bring us water to quench our thirst, or food for our hungry bellies.

'Fuck me,' I mutter, wobbling on my injured leg, surveying the scene before me.

'Aye, my lord king,' Ealdorman Ælhun concurs. I assume his thoughts mirror mine.

'Are you injured?' I question.

'No, just some bruises. I lost two men, though.' His face sours at the news. I grimace. I didn't want good Mercians to die defending a man who'd rather pray on his knees than fight.

'They were good men. They died fighting for Mercia.' I console, even though the words burn my throat.

'They were, my lord king. We'll have them buried and their families will be honoured.' I wince to hear they had families. I hope they weren't fathers to small children. Fuck. It breaks my heart to hear the wailing and sorrowing of the widows. I swallow a lump of grief that lodges in my throat. My gaze once more rests on King Alfred. I can see the top of his head. If he wore a helm, he's removed it. I hope my hair's not as thin as his. I can see the outline of his scalp easily, as though he's a tonsured monk.

'What do we do with the dead?' nimble Rudolf calls, standing and jutting his hips forward, indicating he's got a sore back. I'll show him a bloody sore back.

'Leave 'em for the West Saxons,' I call, bracing myself and

walking through the spread of lifeless bodies with an assessing gaze. I circle around the loudly praying King Alfred and take myself towards the only entrance inside Old Sarum, even if it's protected by two gateways, one outside the other. I'm curious to see what it's like inside. I limp, but decide I can't do much about that with Haden already gone on ahead. The other horses are yet to return with Kyred. It'll take them some time to get here, and I'm not inclined to wait.

Loyal Ealdorman Ælhun dogs my steps. He's as curious as I am.

I eye the defences at the first gateway that kept the interior safe from the enemy with dismay. They're hardly permanent, but instead, almost anything the daft bastards could find to put between the gap separating the two sides of the first earthen bank, high up on the steep grassy mound, including casks of ale and what looks to have once been a wooden cart, although it's far from intact. It'll only be good for burning after this.

My eyes trace the first enclosing turf wall. I imagine it being a void, but I can't see any means of getting into it if it is. Instead, I'm greeted by the second, even steeper bank of turf wall. These grass-covered walls stretch far into the distance, curling around, although I can't see that from here. Instead, there's a building in the way. It's not the church. There is one, though. I see the squat wooden tower from where I am, to the rear of the settlement. This should be such a fine place within which local people could find protection. It should be. And yet, I don't believe it is.

I turn, surveying the surrounding landscape. We're quite high up, and Old Sarum is even higher yet. I can see a good distance. Not as far as Winchester, admittedly, but here, there are gentle hills and one or two places that shimmer with fresh growths, and others dark with oak trees. These would be good places to live, but of course, lack the walls that guard Old Sarum. But, within Old Sarum itself, they would find shelter, should it be needed. Really, this place is akin to our defences at Northampton, and those being constructed at Hereford and Worcester.

Frightened eyes look my way from inside the doorways of wattle and daub buildings as I stride inside the second turfed embankment. Roofs hang low to the ground, and are resplendent in rich greens.

'Mercian,' I shout, just in case one of the fuckers thinks to do something other than cower in fear. 'We need food and drink, and somewhere for the wounded.' No one meets my eyes. I grimace as they scurry away, some even slamming reasonably robust looking doors on us. I can't imagine everyone in Wessex is this useless, but perhaps they are. Maybe, I should have some sympathy for King Alfred. Perhaps he's merely the best of them all. I fucking hope not.

I look to Ealdorman Ælhun. His eyes are busy, but I can't determine whether he's impressed or not.

'Like Northampton,' he informs me having assessed Old Sarum for himself.

'It is, I agree, 'but substantially older.'

'Yes. We could consider making the walls surrounding Northampton as permanent as these. And forcing a much deeper trench outside it'

'It would take a lot of effort. Almost as much as killing the bastard Viking raiders.'

'It would, yes. But once done, it need not be done again, as can be seen here,' Ealdorman Ælhun indicates the sets of enclosing embankments. 'These aren't new, are they, my lord king? No. These have been here since before Mercia was Mercia, I assure you.'

I grunt. I've found a barrel containing water. I hurry towards it, hooking a wooden drinking cup from a table close by, and drink the stale tasting water thirstily. Turning aside, I scoop more water and throw it over my face before handing the cup to Ealdorman Ælhun. He drinks as well. No one seems to be hurrying to see to our comfort, which pisses me off. Perhaps they'd all sooner be dead.

I follow the familiar sound of Icel's rumbling voice to a small workshop. I wince as I realise it's a blacksmith's. But, at least the hearth fire's burning fiercely. Gruff Icel and Rudolf have Gardulf and Goda on the ground. I know what they're going to do, as they rip free clothing to reveal the deep wounds the pair carry on pale flesh.

'Do you have everything you need?' I call.

'No, we bloody don't,' Icel moans. 'These West Saxons have nothing prepared. There's not a healer to be found in this arsehole of a location.'

'What do you need then?'

'Honey, clean linen, and some pottage, for now.' Rudolf shouts his orders, not Icel.

The blacksmith's watching with frightened eyes. It surprises me. A man of his size, scared of Icel and Rudolf. Perhaps it's the menace they exude. I confess, I hardly notice it any more.

'Good man,' I call to him. 'Can you aid my warriors with what they require? I don't know where the cooking's prepared.' I shrug my shoulders, making a thousand hurts felt, and wish I hadn't.

'My lord, my lord king,' he mutters, cowed by my presence. I sigh softly. A woman shoves past him, casting him a downturned look.

'My lord king, excuse him. He's big and strong, but not one for thinking. Where's King Alfred?'

'Praying,' I reply with a growl, taking in the sight of her. She's younger than me, I believe, with long hair, intricately plaited down her shoulders, and a collection of many objects hanging from her girdle.

'And we're to obey your orders?' she asks archly, meeting my gaze frankly.

'Until he tells you not to do so. Of course, if you're not happy, I'll just resurrect the dead enemy, and allow them within,' I taunt.

'No need to be like that, my lord king,' she offers with a flash of iron. 'You don't rule here.'

'And you do?'

'No, my lord king. I do not, but I owe my oath to my king.'

'Then I suggest you bloody go and ask him.'

'I don't think that'll be necessary,' she determines, eyeing the groaning men on the ground. 'Can't you take them to the hall?' she directs to Icel.

'There's no fire within the great hall. It's colder than the grave in there. Heat must be used.'

'Very well,' and she marches from the building, mumbling under her breath. I try not to listen to the litany of complaints. She swears like a warrior. I find I like that. I watch her go and then turn to the blacksmith.

'Charming woman. Is she your wife?'

'Sister,' the hulking man offers.

'Not so bloody bad then,' I mutter. 'At least you can sleep alone. Can you build the flames up? We're not here to hurt you, just to tend to our men.'

He bows and moves to obey my request. I see he has a huge store of wood and pile of small pieces of charcoal to fuel his furnace. I turn and admire the orderly state of the workshop. Hammers and tongs hang from large nails fixed into the wood of the posts holding up the roof and walls. Perhaps, when I return to Kingsholm, I might think of a similar arrangement for my sword and seax. Not that the bloody things are ever far from me. One day, perhaps I'll be able to put them down. But no, I know I wouldn't like that. It's better to keep my blades and shield close to my body.

Finally, I sense something else happening outside and stride through the doorway to see King Alfred making his way back inside his settlement. His six warriors escort him. His face is pale beneath his receding hairline, which I should probably stop noticing, but I can't. I run my hand through my sweaty head of hair, smirking to myself.

'My lord king,' I call to King Alfred, astounded he shrieks on hearing my voice.

'I must. I must,' he mutters, eyes frantic, hands still clasped in prayer, as he sweeps a look at me.

'You must fucking lead,' I inform him harshly. 'Lead your men and earn their regard. You've accomplished a great thing today. You fucking killed a man.'

At my blunt words, his entire body judders. I fear he might take to his knees again. I'm sure his trews are wet. Has the arsehole pissed himself? I suppose that shouldn't surprise me. But it does.

I stamp my way to his side. He smells foul. I think he's shit himself as well. All the same, I grip his weak forearms, my hands encircling them easily, and hold him steady. I lean in to him.

'Don't fuck this up. Your men have no respect for you. They fight in your name because they pledged their oath to your brother, King Æthelred, or so it seems to me. Take this as your due, or you'll never protect your kingdom. The Viking raiders will traipse over it, and trap all of you. You need to fucking understand that.'

I stand back, but I realise it's worthless. Without my hands to hold him upright, King Alfred sways. I shake my head, puffing air through my sweat-dry cheeks.

'You need to order your warriors to move the dead, or before the sun sets, and it won't be long, you'll be fighting off the denizens of the woodlands, streams and rivers nearby. Not to mention the carrion crows. You don't want that. You really don't. We bury the dead when we kill 'em. Do the same.'

'I,' King Alfred stutters once more.

'For fuck's sake, you're the damn king. Now, be kingly.'

'I must pray,' he mutters instead. I step back. He really is a bloody lost cause. I can't see he'll survive this. From the blacksmith's, I hear a shout of pain, and turn back to aid my men. King Alfred isn't worth my time. I know that. I sense everyone here perceives that. What then, are we to do with him? I can't remain in Wessex. I've a kingdom to rule. But King Alfred, I'm reminded, isn't the only one with a claim to govern Wessex. Neither is he entirely alone. He has his ealdormen, provided they still live.

I don't watch him hurry on his way. Instead, I stride towards where Goda and Gardulf are having their wounds cauterised. Wounds they've gained defending a king who's worthless. But, the people within Wessex deserve protecting. They are, after all, Saxons, just like the Mercians. Well, I pick hairs. The Mercians are Anglians, the West Saxons are just that, Saxons. Admittedly, we're all the same, apart from that. Oh, and having the stones to defend themselves. That's certainly something the West Saxons don't have in common with the Mercians.

I scowl and kick aside a loose stone, as I make my way back to Goda and Gardulf.

There's much to think about. I need the advice of my warriors. I'll heed their words. No matter how dismissive they may be of all Wessex has to offer. Without my warriors, I'm nothing. King Alfred needs to take fucking note of that.

Chapter Two

I can hear voices when I finally leave the blacksmith's and stride once move through the entrance of Old Sarum which is now being guarded by some of Kyred's men. Unsurprisingly, my warriors have taken control of disposing of the dead. I eye Wærwulf, with his scarred nose that makes him look wonky, and one-handed Pybba as they instruct the few West Saxon warriors still capable of moving about their task. I also see the flash of a holy man's robes, as he bends to offer his prayers to the dead.

'What's this?' I stamp my way to my two trusted warriors.

'How are they?' Pybba asks first. I don't miss he runs his left hand over the stump of his right arm. I know where his thoughts have taken him.

'Sleeping. They should be well, provided they don't get the wound rot.'

'And Gardulf?'

'He has a story to tell, but we'll have to wait to hear it. What's happening here?'

It's self-evident, but I ask all the same.

'We're going to burn the bastards,' Wærwulf rumbles in his

distinctive voice. 'Too many of the fuckers to dig holes for them. It would take a week to make the damn hole deep enough and big enough. And where would we put it?' He lifts his arms wide while speaking. He makes a good point. To dispose of this many dead men would take a hole almost as big as the ditch encircling Old Sarum. We don't have bloody time for that.

Kyred's men on guard duty watch the West Saxons drag the white and marbled flesh to a growing mound of bodies far to the side of the entrance way. I heard Kyred and the horses return some time ago. Sæbald, with his lightly tufted face because he's not shaved for days, has been added to those who needed the aid of hot metal over sundered skin. My three badly injured men are now within the king's hall, being watched by a grumbling Icel and an equally out-of-sorts Rudolf, who've finally managed to encourage some of the West Saxons to build a fire and tend to it. I'll have to watch my warriors. They, like me, must sense we're still a long way from Mercia. It's not right. Not at all.

'And the Mercians?'

'They'll be buried,' Pybba hastens to reassure. It'll soon be dark. Brands are being lit to keep the darkness at bay and then thumped into the ground to light the space without someone having to hold them aloft. When they set the bodies aflame, there'll be a beacon that'll be seen from far distant Winchester. Possibly. I just hope the bloody fire gets hot enough to incinerate the fleshy parts of the dead. If not, even after the inferno, we'll still need a bloody big hole and the fuckers will be blackened and even more disgusting to move.

'Have we sent our scouts? I don't want to be trapped within Old Sarum should the enemy come again.'

'Ingwald and Osmod have gone to check the road to Winchester. Kyred said he hadn't seen more than the smaller party that overwhelmed them, but it's best to check.' I nod in agreement.

'Bloody hell. How many dead?' I ask.

'Over three hundred of 'em,' Wærwulf's quick to reply. The number astounds me. Our force was so much smaller.

'How many did you kill?' I question. He smirks, eyes lighting up at my question.

'More than you,' he offers with delight.

'And you, Pybba?' I growl, wanting facts not bragging.

'A few of 'em,' he grins.

'You'll look like seven shades of shit in the morning,' I warn, because his face is vibrant in the last rays of the day.

'Well, at least I'll be able to walk without looking like I've got a wonky leg,' he retorts. I look down, keeping the smile from my face. I enjoy these moments with my warriors after a fight. It's good to share the calm after the storm.

'Where's shit for brains?' Pybba questions. My chuckle deepens.

'Crying his eyes out while he prays,' I reply quickly. I've had trusty Eadfrith check on what King Alfred's doing.

'What now?'

'Now that, my friend, will depend on what Gardulf tells us, and also, on what Ingwald and Osmod discover.'

'So, you don't plan on helping shit for brains take back Winchester then?'

'I bloody don't, no. Although, I'd be curious to know how many more Viking raiders are within it. We've seen none of the Repton jarls, but they must be behind this. Why else would those men have converted to Christianity?'

'I doubt they converted,' Pybba muses. 'It'll have been a ruse. Almost all of the men had some sort of cross emblem around their necks. Many of them had not one, but two, the other showing Odin's wolf. Their faith and Christianity. They were hedging their bets.'

'Even so, that took some bloody thought.'

'Perhaps,' Pybba concedes. Wærwulf's left us. I watch him with a lit brand, making his way to the first pile of bodies. I grimace at the gruesome task, but these mortal remains need to be disposed of or, as I warned, shit for brains, as Pybba's taken to naming him, they'll bring other predators, ones that are more difficult to drive away than Viking raiders. And possibly more dangerous with their sharp beaks, teeth and claws.

Selecting where he thinks the flames will catch quickest, Wærwulf lowers the brand into a pile of bodies, and quickly, there's a bright flare, lending a strange glow to the marbled whites of the dead, as the clothing and hair is the first to set alight. I stand and watch. This needs to be witnessed, even though the stink is already noxious.

I watch the priest or monk, whatever he is, stand before all the dead, his hands busy while he intones prayers. They end in a choking cough.

'Daft fucker should have stood out of the wind,' I inform Pybba.

'Aye, as far away from the bodies as he could get.' Both of us watch with amusement as the man bends over, coughing, his intentions forgotten. I wince as he stands and skips away, only to fall over the flailing arm of a body from the second pile of dead. There's too many to fire them in one go.

A most un-Christian shriek erupts from his mouth. I shake my head, while Cuthwalh, perhaps reinvigorated now he's back as a permanent member of my warrior band and not growing fat at Kingsholm, stamps his way to the priest and hauls him upright. It's done with little ceremony, and we all see it, while the flames leap higher to drive back the encroaching darkness. The sizzle of burning hair and stinking grease used on byrnies and perhaps, also on hair, mixes with the uncomfortably hunger-inducing smell of crisping flesh. I wrinkle my nose while Pybba chuckles darkly.

'This could have been us,' I mutter sourly.

'It couldn't. You're not a damn arse,' Pybba retorts. It's not reassuring. It's probably not meant to be. 'Anyway,' he continues, 'We wouldn't have put ourselves in such danger. We're not lackwits, unlike some.' His tone darkens. No doubt he speaks of shit for brains.

Wærwulf moves to the next collection of bodies, and then the next. Soon, there are four blazing piles of corpses, stretching across the road. They've been piled so as to not be too close to Old Sarum, or anywhere near the stream or roadway. The heat of the flames is fierce. I realise more and more of my men have stirred themselves to witness this. I don't miss that few West Saxons are there to watch their enemy burn. I consider if King Alfred's summoned them all to the church. It wouldn't surprise me. Equally, it's a wasted opportunity to reassure his people the enemy are mortal and can be cut down with the right blades and correct tactics. He should be here, taking pride in what we've accomplished, as opposed to babbling to his God for forgiveness for doing what any man or woman would do to protect the people they love.

'The bastards burn well,' Wærwulf offers with approval, as he returns to my side. I realise Kyred and Ealdorman Ælhun have also joined our small party. We all bear witness to this, as is only right.

If our situation were reversed, I'd hope the Viking raiders would be respectful enough to watch our bodies consumed by flames.

'They'll see this,' Ealdorman Ælhun comments.

'They will. And they won't know who burns.'

'They might come to look.'

'I'd expect them to,' I confirm. With that announcement, I hear the familiar sound of hooves, and look up. The horses shy at the leaping flames. Ingwald and Osmod bring them around behind the inferno, closer to Old Sarum's wall.

'Anything?' I question, noting their unconcerned return.

'No. But, this will bring 'em out, if they're close,' Ingwald concedes unwillingly.

'It will. It'll be interesting to see who it is, though, won't it?'

The pair lead the horses within Old Sarum, but I stay, stand and watch. I'm tired, my leg hurting once more, but we killed these men. Now, we watch them consumed by the flickering flames. In the morning, I hope Gardulf will have more to tell me about the enemy's intentions towards Canterbury.

If what he says is true, then, just like the dual emblems worn around these men's necks, Jarl Guthrum has fastened onto an idea that'll cause uproar amongst the holy men and women on this island, regardless of the kingdom they live within.

It's one thing to threaten isolated nunneries and monasteries, steal their priceless treasures and kill their inhabitants. But the Archbishop of Canterbury? Now that's a real target. I consider if Jarl Guthrum realises he'll face the might of every kingdom, and not just Wessex if he does intend to attack Canterbury. I wonder if that's his plan. He's never struck me as a man lacking in ambition.

I snarl, watching the smoke curl blackly into the increasingly dark sky.

Somewhere, Jarl Guthrum and the other Repton jarls are plotting. I thought to divert them to Wessex, and that's worked, but if they turn their sights on Canterbury, I don't imagine Bishop Wærferth will share my joy in how well the ploy's worked. He'll probably be pissed at me, and he'll expect me to defend the archbishop as I have Wessex. I've been lucky he didn't force me to aid the Archbishop of York. I doubt the same will apply to Canterbury.

I consider all this long into the night, as the smoke curls, and changes from grey to white while the bodies crumble to ash, leaving little but the odd missed metal object to glow red in the embers, and some white bone, most often skulls or leg bones.

I watch, and I think, and only with the coming sunrise do I return inside.

I must speak to Gardulf.

And then, I'll have to contend with bloody shit for brains, King Alfred. Again.

Chapter Three

Gardulf wakes slowly. I wait as patiently as I can. I'm brought a meaty pottage and also a jug of water by a servant who bobs, and taking a chance, leans forwards and whispers, 'thank you,' to me. I nod and open my mouth to speak, but she rushes off, as though too embarrassed to remain. I shake my head. What sort of place is Wessex? It doesn't appear to function as Mercia does.

Eventually, Gardulf rouses and eyes me with his too-familiar face. Just like his father would have done, he tries to stand, staggers, and I rush to aid him.

'Take yourself for a piss,' I urge, 'and then we need to talk.' He nods. I notice that while he's tired, his eyes are sharp. On his feet, he clutches his wounded belly. I wince in sympathy. It's a long wound, but not deep. With the aid of Icel and Rudolf, well, more Rudolf than Icel, I'm sure he'll be well in no time. After all, he recovered from the injuries he and Hereman took last year. He's young, and fit. And if he ails, I'll send him to my aunt, or perhaps summon Werburg from Kingsholm. She knows much of my aunt's knowledge now.

By the time Gardulf returns, Rudolf at his side, casting me a censorious look, no doubt for allowing Gardulf to venture outside alone, I've been joined by Icel, Hereman and Pybba alongside others. Ealdorman Ælhun and Kyred are also there. I notice, without surprise, that King Alfred's not to be seen.

I've been told he's praying once more. A man such as him should spend more time learning to fight than repeating words to a Lord God with fuck all interest in who prevails in this war against the Viking raiders. I know my aunt would be horrified to hear me say that. But I suspect Bishop Wærferth would simply give me a knowing look. He's a man of God but also has some sense. I admire him for that.

'Have you eaten anything yet?' I ask Edmund's son. In the dull light from the fire, his father's features are etched clearly into his face. I feel a stab of sorrow, but don't allow it to take hold of me. I mourn Edmund, but there's a time and a place, and this isn't fucking it.

'A few mouthfuls of pottage last night,' Rudolf answers for him.

'Can you manage more?' I question Gardulf directly.

He nods. I move aside to let him sit beside me. Rudolf watches his patient carefully. I hear Gardulf needed stitches to sew him shut as well as the heat from the blacksmith's forge. I know both those pains far too well.

'Are you ready to share all you know?' I ask him.

'Aye, my lord. Everything. Where shall I start?'

'At the beginning, when we left you, for which you have my sincere apologies. We intended to return and look for you.'

Gardulf's eyes are far away. I know he's seeing what happened to him. I don't push him, despite the sense of urgency rippling along my spine. Gardulf will tell us when he can put words to his experience.

He coughs, and begins to speak, his voice husky. 'I moved through the trees, at the back of the fight. I was wounded, but I thought I'd be able to come at the enemy from behind, or something like that. I don't really know what I was thinking. At some point, I lost all sense. When I woke, it was the next day, the battle won by you, as I discovered, and you were all gone. You left a right old fucking mess,' he complains. 'It's not like you to leave the dead behind.' I almost chuckle at that. As last night's activities show, I don't like to leave a mass of decomposing bodies for others to find.

'I stole some Viking raider equipment from the dead, and set off for Winchester. I thought you'd either be there, or somewhere close by.'

My eyes narrow. 'We did go to Winchester, but we were chased away.'

He nods. 'Aye, my lord. I saw that as well, but I couldn't get to you in time. My wound was too painful to risk running.'

'Bollocks,' I exclaim softly, frustrated. 'We were looking for you.'

'Aye, my lord. I know that. It was one of those things. So, I decided to sneak into Winchester, alongside those who chased you. It was an effort to walk as the Viking raiders did, and of course, apart from knowing how to call them bastards and to fuck off, I know bugger all Norse.' Despite his evident discomfort, Gardulf chuckles as he recounts this.

'I should have been fucking terrified, but I wasn't. The men on guard duty were there, not because they had the sharpest eyes, but because they'd done something wrong. It was a punishment, and they couldn't give a shit about who they allowed inside.'

'So, if you didn't understand their words, how did you discover their plans?' Wærwulf questions. I've not realised he's also joined us. Looking around, I see all of my men have come to listen to Gardulf. They sit or stand, but all watch our young friend carefully.

'You're jumping ahead,' Gardulf says without any rancour. 'I need to tell this in the right bloody order.'

Wærwulf subsides with a rueful grin. Gardulf takes a moment to recollect his thoughts.

'Apart from Icel, has anyone ever been to Winchester?' Gardulf questions. I look at my collection of men and realise everyone's shaking their head. 'Well, it's not worth the effort, I assure you. The walls, as you were told, aren't very tall and they don't stand complete in many places. There seem to be hundreds of gates, allowing people in and out. The Viking raiders might have taken control of it, but I assure you, if someone put half a thought into beating them from there, it would be easily done.'

'Not the most defensible then?' As I say this, I gaze at Icel. A flicker of something covers his face, and I consider what that might mean, but know better than to ask him.

'No. But, those living within hardly put up much defence. So, it's easy to overwhelm, and the residents have fuck all idea how to defend it, anyway. It wasn't the most difficult of places to snatch from the king of Wessex, I can assure you of that.'

'So, you got inside,' I prompt because Gardulf can dwell on Winchester's lack of defensive stone walls but we need to understand the plans concerning Canterbury.

'Yes, and I ambled around, well, limped, following where the others went. I'd collected a shield and a few other items from the men you'd killed, a few trinkets.' He pulls them from around his neck and beneath his tunic. They glint dully, and look much like any other Viking raider sigil. Perhaps it's a wolf, or maybe a raven. Or even a hammer. The thing's so poorly cast I can hardly tell, and I'm not about to ask what it is. Hereman has other ideas.

'What the fuck's that supposed to be?' he questions Gardulf. 'It looks like a bloody piece of shit.'

Gardulf, used to his uncle's humour, shows the sigil again.

'A piece of shit or a damn raven?' Gardulf suggests.

'A piece of bloody shit,' Hereman declares, but now I can tell it's vaguely bird shaped. It must be a raven. Gardulf, with a shake of his head, drops the sigil and continues to speak.

'I ended up in some big hall, within which the Viking raiders were eating and drinking. Those who'd chased you had to report to that worm, Jarl Anwend. He looked fucking furious at whatever they said. I ate and drank and generally kept myself to myself. When I slept that night, I kept my blade to hand. No one seemed to pay me any heed, however. But when I woke, I was in pain. I needed someone to help me with my belly wound.'

I sense this is how Gardulf found out all he knew, but I allow him to speak as he wants without prompting him now Hereman's infuriating questioning has subsided.

'I made my way outside and took a good look around. No one seemed to be aiding any of the wounded Viking raiders. I didn't really know where to start. I thought the best thing to do was pretend to be one of the bastards, but all I'd managed to decipher was that they were arrogant enough to put disgruntled men on guard duty because they didn't anticipate being evicted from Winchester. I needed a healer and someone who spoke our language. I went to one of the many churches,' he offers, holding Icel's gaze.

'I bet you got fuck all help from the monks?'

'The monks were all dead, or fled. I don't know which. I never did find out. The place felt hollow, as though no one had been inside it for weeks. I was really weak, and in a lot of pain. I must have thought to pray, or just collapsed. When I came round, I was in another building entirely, one with a low thatch roof. It smelt similar to when Lady Cyneswith makes her lotions and potions.'

"Ah, you're awake,' an old, cracked voice said to me. And I opened my eyes to see a milky eye peering down at me. 'Saxon?' she'd questioned, and I'd nodded, apprehensive. 'Nothing to fear here,' she'd reassured me. 'Now come, we'll get some food into you.' The woman wasn't a healer, but she knew enough to pack my wound with honey and to give me some comfrey to seal it as well. I'm grateful to her. She also knew much of what was happening within Winchester. It was she who told me about the plans to take Canterbury. She saw Jarl Guthrum arrive to speak with Jarl Anwend. While I sweated and slept, she kept me in water and made sure no one knew I was there. She worked out I was from Mercia.'

'How?'

'She said I talked in my sleep, mumbling about Coelwulf, or some such,' Gardulf admits, looking uncomfortable at the admission.

'Why was she allowed to walk around without being beaten by the Viking raiders?' Icel questions, no doubt to stop me from asking more questions, or Hereman from teasing his nephew.

'She told me she'd persuaded them she was a wise woman and they were scared of her. She'd laughed as she told me. She'd gabbled some nonsensical words and convinced them if they did anything to her, they'd face punishment from one of their Gods. She was fiery to the Viking raiders.'

'A clever woman?' I suggest.

'Aye, she was. I was there for three days. Only when I could walk unaided did she allow me to leave her hut, and even then, she bid me stay away from the Viking raiders. It was she who walked amongst them and heard all they had to say. She spoke their language as well. To be honest, I think she was probably Norse herself. She didn't exactly speak with a West Saxon drawl.'

'So how did you come to leave Winchester and be close to Old Sarum?'

Here, his face contorts into a grimace.

'She told me that was where King Alfred would be found. I didn't know where you'd gone, so I thought it best to start there. But leaving Winchester wasn't as easy as getting into it. The gate guards were too suspicious. They'd allow no one to leave, on the orders of Jarl Anwend, unless as part of a foraging party.'

'So, you were trapped?'

'I was, yes. I was stronger, but I couldn't do much about it. I didn't want to be discovered by Jarl Anwend, so I had to stay hidden. I had no idea who of his warriors might be within Winchester alongside him. The woman knew of their discussions because she strode brazenly amongst them, shaking a stick at them, which they all feared. It was something she used to keep the door open in the summer months,' he chuckles at this and then winces, hand reaching for his belly wound.

'How did you get out then?'

'I had to wait for them to move towards Old Sarum. Then I slipped through the northern gate with them. But I was weak. I quickly fell behind, and fearing discovery, I left the main road she told me to take, the one that would take me to the Portway, and somehow ended up slightly to the west of Old Sarum, where I found Haden.'

'So, she's still alive?' Icel surprises me by asking about the woman Gardulf encountered.

'Aye, she was fine when I left. As I said, the Viking raiders fear her, although the people of Winchester show no such concern. What few of them there were.'

Icel nods, a smile playing on his lips. I'd like to know his connection to the woman, but I hold my tongue. That's not important right now. Instead, the news of the intended attack on Canterbury is.

'So, is it Jarl Guthrum's idea to take Canterbury?'

'Yes, she told me as much.'

'And when will they do that?'

'I don't know. There were no dates. No doubt what's happened here will either encourage them to move on, or will delay them.'

'How many within Winchester?'

'It's impossible to tell. Jarl Anwend and his warriors. And then Jarl Guthrum and his. I don't think there was another Repton jarl, but there were other jarls, men I don't know.'

'Did Anwend and Guthrum remain within Winchester?'

'Yes, they weren't part of the attack on Old Sarum.'

I fall silent now, considering all Gardulf's told me. I can understand the desire to take Canterbury, sort of. I know Mercia and Wessex have argued over it for decades, or rather, the whole of Kent, so why not the Viking raiders as well? Still, there remains the problem of Winchester and Wareham which remain besieged by the enemy.

'How far is it from Winchester to Canterbury?' I question Icel.

'At least four days travel, if not more, overland. We'd need to go to the south of London via the Portway and the Devil's Causeway before joining Watling Street. By sea, I don't know. But Canterbury is still some distance from the sea, so they'd need to travel overland to reach it, if only for a day.'

'When did you learn the names of these bloody West Saxon roads?' I ask, astounded.

'I've always known them, my lord. You just never asked about them before.'

I shake my head, pleased Icel's being as difficult as always. If he was being more helpful, I'd suspect we were all about to meet our deaths on enemy blades. 'So, what will the Viking raiders do?'

'They have ships. They're shit at riding,' Hereman interjects.

'And we're good at riding and shit on ships,' I smile while replying. He nods and grunts. My thoughts settle on Winchester. That was what we came to do, secure Winchester for King Alfred. If we do that, will the enemy be encouraged to go to Canterbury? If we just go to Canterbury, will the enemy remain within Winchester? I've known the Viking raiders to settle for a winter in a settlement. At Repton, they lingered. At Torksey they did the same. Grantabridge was similar until we mostly destroyed it.

But it's not winter. Yet. Winchester, it seems, has little to offer, and so far, they've lost men fighting us in the woodlands to the east of Winchester and many more outside Old Sarum. Will they take the defeat and leave, or will it make them determined to succeed? I wish I bloody knew.

If this was Mercia, I'd know what to do. But this isn't Mercia. I find myself in Wessex, with King Alfred, who's just killed a man and has spent the time since praying for forgiveness. The Archbishop of Canterbury is someone for whom I hold far more respect. I'd sooner aid him than King Alfred, but I've pledged to help both of them.

'What does everyone think?' I question, looking from Ealdorman Ælhun to Kyred, and then settling on Pybba and Icel. They always provide good counsel.

'Fuck knows,' Hereman growls. 'Go home to Mercia and leave the bastards to fight it out amongst themselves.' I chuckle as he speaks.

'We'd all like to do that, I'm sure,' I confirm.

'But we need to get rid of the enemy.' Ealdorman Ælhun is calmer and more reasoned with his response.

'But which one?'

'All of them,' Hereman interjects.

'We don't have the men.' I admit, unwillingly. That's the problem. This isn't my kingdom. We don't fight for Mercia. I've a limited quantity of warriors I can call upon to fight away from Mercia. If it were Mercia, and I needed them, I could summon the fyrd, although no one would thank me for doing that when the harvesting work needs doing. But here, in Wessex? King Alfred doesn't have what I would classify as a good fighting force. Whatever losses the kingdom has faced, and I suspect there have been many over the years, Wessex is decimated of its warriors. There are few who could counter the enemy.

Again, I recall that I've agreed to this alliance with King Alfred.

'We need to train the men of Wessex,' I announce unwillingly. 'We can't do this alone. We're too few, and the number too vast.'

I see Pybba nodding, while Icel violently shakes his head. Ealdorman Ælhun looks pensive and Kyred unhappy.

'We can't fight their battles for them,' I reinforce. 'Here, at Old Sarum, where their king was, they would have been entirely overwhelmed had we not been close. Winchester is in the hands of the enemy, as is Wareham. The enemy threaten Canterbury. That would stretch us far too thin, and King Alfred, it appears, has fewer men. What numbers did he tell us there were?'

I look to Rudolf. He furrows his forehead and rubs his nose.

'Just about two thousand, I think. There'll be fewer than that now, though. In fact, where are they?'

And this is another problem. We don't know where King Alfred's alleged warriors are. Ealdormen Cuthred, Eadwulf, Garulf and Wulfhere are surprisingly absent. Lord Æthelwulf, who should show his allegiance to me, and not King Alfred, is also missing. And while King Alfred said he had a thousand men, we've witnessed their worth. They have the equipment, but not the ability to fight. Not that

I'm surprised. King Alfred isn't a warrior king. He lacks all the qualities such a man needs to lead his warriors to battle. If I were one of his warriors, I'd be running to Mercia not defending Wessex.

'So, the Wessex force is too small, and potentially, already overwhelmed. We have who is already here. Thankfully, our fatalities have been small, though we'll mourn our men. The only thing we don't know is the size of the force under the command of the Archbishop of Canterbury.'

'Similar to mine?' Kyred questions, after all, he's a warrior serving one of Mercia's bishops.

'And the enemy?' I nod as Kyred answers the question. 'They vastly outnumber us, or so it appears.'

'So, we have too many bastard enemies, not enough bloody warriors, and no others to call upon, and half of the ones we do have are sodding missing anyway.' Icel's summary is far from welcome, even if it is accurate.

'My thanks for stating the bloody obvious,' I mutter. Icel's face is thunderous. I sense it'll take very little else to appear unsurmountable, and he'll be riding back to Mercia. I'll probably be at his side.

'We need to understand how vast their force is,' Pybba suggests calmly. He's often a voice of reason when all else fails.

'Even Gardulf doesn't know and he's been inside Winchester, and you travelled to Wareham and assessed the size of the fleet there.'

'We did yes, Archbishop Æthelred said he thought there were more warriors than ships.'

'We bloody know there are more warriors than ships,' I counter.

'I know we know that,' Pybba comments, his patience fraying. 'But we need to get greater clarity. At the moment, you want to start a fight without knowledge of the terrain or the numbers arranged against us. We can't do that. We can't make bloody decisions when we lack such important information. I'm all for rushing in, as you know, but in this, we need to be more bloody sensible. If not, we'll achieve nothing and leave Mercia, Wessex and Canterbury with no one to protect her. The Saxons will fall beneath the wave of the enemy, and from now on, the Saxon people will cease to exist as they currently do. None of us want that. None of us.' I bite my lip to prevent arguing against his logic. Pybba's correct. That no one else disagrees with him proves we all think the same.

'How?' I ask. His grin has no humour in it.

'How we always do these things. We need to find the answers by any means possible. Send Gardulf back to Winchester. Send Icel and me to Wareham. Have someone travel to Canterbury. Others need to journey along the southern coastline to find all of the enemy ships, along whatever roads Icel named.'

'That'll take a long time,' Rudolf complains. 'And Gardulf's too injured.'

'It'll take a long time, yes, but rather a long time to find the information we need to formulate a plan than a long time bloody dead.' Pybba crosses his arms as he speaks, and my eye is drawn to his missing hand.

'Fuck, I don't like this,' I reply quickly. 'But Pybba's correct. We need to retreat to a place of safety, where we know we can hold firm, and in the meantime, some of us must risk ourselves to discover all we can about the enemy.' Grunts and nods greet my words.

'I'm not going back to Winchester,' Gardulf complains.

'No, you're fucking not,' I agree quickly. 'That would be a great risk for you, and one I can't allow.'

'Who then?' Pybba questions.

'I don't know that yet. But you're right. We need people in Winchester and Wareham, but before all that, we need to decide where to base ourselves. Where's the place of greatest safety?'

'London,' Icel speaks without hesitation. I open my mouth to argue. He holds up his hand to forestall me. 'Trust me, my lord. London is the answer. It's the closest to Wessex, and from there, it's quick to travel to Canterbury and to Winchester. All we need do is get across the River Thames, which can be done using the shallows at Laleham Gulls if there are no ships. And, if we need to, we can also quickly reach Northampton or Gloucester, should the bastard enemy think to attack us there. We know the landscape. We can use it to stay alive even if we're entirely overwhelmed.'

'You'll be far from Old Sarum and Winchester.' I suppress a sneer as King Alfred finally appears and joins the conversation. At his shoulder is the priest from last night and more monks trail behind them. It's as though he has a train of holy men at his skirts. I don't like the image that forms in my mind.

Icel continues as though King Alfred's not spoken.

'There's also room to train the West Saxon warriors to know more than which ends the bloody pointy one.' I look down at my hands, hiding my smile. Icel has such a way with words.

But I consider Icel's wisdom before replying. Is he correct? Would London be the best location? The walls around the ancient fort are tattered in places, but could be rebuilt. There's no replacement bishop there yet, so I could have one of my ealdormen or even another bishop in overall command. Being there would give us time to discover the strength of the enemy. My aunt, I'm sure, would appreciate me being back within Mercia. Fuck, I'd quite like it too. I'm uneasy in Wessex.

Yet, I realise, I can't send my men to do these deadly tasks alone. Can I? Should I be crawling through Winchester and Wareham? Should I be risking myself on the southern coast hunting for the enemy? No, but neither should my warriors.

'We'll ask Archbishop Æthelred to meet us at London, or if he doesn't want to leave Canterbury, we'll inform him of the danger. King Alfred, you'll need to discover the size of the force at Wareham and Winchester, and scout for ships along the southern coast. It'll take time, but only when we know all there is, can we devise an effective means of defeating the enemy.'

'You promised an alliance,' King Alfred replies angrily. I notice absentmindedly that his face is still stained with the blood of his dead foe. Does he think it makes him look warrior-like, or is he ignorant of the decoration?

'And I'm not reneging on that. But we need to be sensible.'

'You mean to protect Mercia, not Wessex.'

'I did mention the fucking Archbishop of Canterbury,' I counter angrily.

'And me and my men?'

'Will be welcomed within London when you've discovered the size of the enemy. You've been so bloody determined to get your hands on it, I can't believe you're arguing when I've sodding invited you.' This stops King Alfred in his tracks. He snaps his angry mouth shut in a thin line.

'This isn't what I expected from the mighty King Coelwulf, the second of his name, of Mercia.'

'Then be assured, King Alfred, the first of his name, I anticipated finding a man capable of fighting for his kingdom and people, a man who would commit the worst possible things against his enemy to accomplish that goal. You can't imagine my disappointment at finding someone who vomits after taking a kill and who must pray for an entire day for every life he takes. If that's how you mean to protect your kingdom, you'll fail, and I'll not be the one to pick up the bloody pieces. So, you have a choice. Accept the suggestions, or fight alone. Quite frankly, I really don't give a shit either way.'

Chapter Four

He stands there, breathing heavily watching me, eyes narrowed. King Alfred, I realise, was born to the ruling line of Wessex. Unlike me, he's never been anything but obeyed with every command given. I want to label him a spoiled arsehole. I want to say it to him. I don't. I've done more than enough damage, I can see, from questioning his abilities. Not that I've said anything that isn't true. He's fuck all use as a warrior.

What he does now will reveal what sort of man he is.

'We fought…'

'No, you didn't,' I counter aggressively. I know he's going to talk about Nottingham. I don't give a fuck about Nottingham. That was his brother, King Æthelred, not him. The stories I've heard of the West Saxon force don't portray them well, no matter who was leading the force.

'We fought…' King Alfred tries once more. I can sense all eyes on him. My men, who know nothing about ruling and everything about fighting observe him with barely concealed disgust.

'Was that man you killed outside your first kill?' I demand. I remain sitting. I'm not going to stand up and face him. I won't pain my leg for this fight.

'I.'

'It's a simple yes or no. Have you killed men before? Or women? Anyone? Other than when you order people to fight on your behalf, have you ever bloodied your blade before yesterday?'

'No,' King Alfred announces, chin raised with defiance. At last, we might be getting somewhere.

'Then you need to learn to fight. If not, the Viking raiders will slaughter you with ease. They nearly did yesterday.'

'They won't get close to me,' he counters aggressively, rage pouring from him, aimed at me and not the enemy, of course.

'How can you guarantee that? If we'd not been here, outside Old Sarum when the enemy came, do you think you'd be standing here now? Or would you be little more than ashes, or a rotting corpse?'

'I have my warriors. They have excellent equipment. They're good men.'

I don't reply. I don't need to. This isn't about his warriors. This is about him.

'If they're so good, you don't bloody need us, do you?' I murmur.

Again, there's silence, other than the noises coming from outside of horses, chickens and any other animal in the vicinity. I don't break it. I won't speak into it. King Alfred must understand I know how weak he is. He must understand this alliance has fuck all use for Mercia. This is about his frailty, and his kingdom's weaknesses.

'We do need you,' King Alfred mumbles unwillingly, eyes watching me, fiery with humiliation. 'We need Mercia to aid Wessex.' He swallows so I see his Adam's apple bob up and down, reminding me of his weakness all over again.

'Then you'll do as I bloody say, and while you're doing it, you can also learn to fight. No man can protect his kingdom without lifting a blade. You learn to fight and you do as I say and then we'll triumph against our enemy.'

My quick words are once more met with silence. I don't look

away from King Alfred. As I watch him, I try to dampen down my dislike of him. I know not all men can be warriors. King Burgred of Mercia, my predecessor, hardly wrapped himself in battle glory. But King Burgred is nothing to me other than the man who gave away Mercia to the bastard enemy. He named me as the only viable threat to the Repton jarls, setting the events of the last eighteen months in play. I consider if King Alfred would do the same to save himself. I wouldn't be fucking surprised if he did.

'I'll do as you suggest,' King Alfred acknowledges. 'I'll have my warriors teach me to fight. I'll send men to Winchester and Wareham and along the southern coast.'

'Good, but you won't ask your men to train you. No, you'll be taught by the warriors of Mercia, as will your men. I don't know who's been showing them how to wave their swords in the air, but you need to learn to fight dirty. The Viking raiders are vicious bastards. You'll become a vicious bastard, honed as sharp as a seax. You'll learn to kill, and glory in it, in the name of your Lord God, if that's what makes it acceptable for you. But you'll learn to do it, and do it without compunction or fear of what will happen to you when you die. And regardless of whether the men you fight are pagan or Christian. You'll be as lethal as any one of my fine Mercian warriors. And that way, you might stand a fucking chance of beating these arseholes. And I know just the man to perform that task.'

I turn then, and see Icel shudder, but I'm not that much of a bastard. No, there's another who taught me to fight, who taught almost every single one of my warriors how to wield his blade.

'Pybba,' I state. He nods, lips pensive, shoulders tight.

'I'll not be tutored by a one-handed warrior,' King Alfred decries, offended by my decision.

'If a one-handed warrior can still live after all the battles we've fought in the last eighteen months, then I assure you, he's the man to show you how to do the same when you have two fucking hands. Pybba will stay with you. He'll be your commander when you train.

You'll obey everything he orders, without complaint. You'll become Pybba's squire.'

A chuckle swells from amongst my warriors. I look to Hereman who grins widely before speaking. 'And he's not as harmless, or 'arm-less' as he looks. Pybba's a fucking bastard and I tell you now, my lord king, there's no finer man to teach you how to kill our enemy. Pybba's the master of all.' With such a ringing endorsement, Pybba eyes Hereman with surprise, his lips curling upwards as well. I feared I might have offended him by not asking him first to perform such a task, but it seems not.

'You were a useless turd when you first took up a practice shield and seax,' Pybba reminisces, beaming widely. 'And to be honest, you're still shit with a spear.' Now Hereman cackles as well. King Alfred looks from me to Pybba to Hereman, and I think he'll piss himself with fear. Hereman's not exactly shit with a spear. He's a lucky bastard. Every. Single. Time.

'Now, we'll discuss the deployment of your warriors once Pybba's given you your first lesson.' And with that, I turn away from King Alfred, and nod towards Pybba. He holds my gaze, perhaps questioning whether I really want him to inflict the same on King Alfred as he has on every one of my Mercian warriors, me included. I nod. Pybba inclines his head, and the next words out of his mouth make me wince with the sharp memory of his tactics.

'Right, lose that embroidered tunic and all your bloody finery. Meet me outside wearing a plain tunic, trews and boots, nothing else. Bring your warriors with you. We'll start with a bit of physical exercise.'

I think King Alfred will refuse Pybba's orders. I wait for the sound of footsteps moving away. I observe Rudolf, who watches what's happening, his mouth open in shock, and eventually, he snaps it shut and strides towards me.

I think he'll question me, but sometimes, and it is only sometimes, Rudolf knows better.

'I might just go and watch that,' he mutters as an aside. He's not alone in following Pybba. Eventually, only Ealdorman Ælhun, Kyred, Gardulf, Sæbald, Goda and Icel remain.

'Is that fucking wise?' Icel's the one to finally speak.

'Do you want to bloody do it?' I retort.

'Fuck no,' he offers with a broad grin. 'I don't want to train that arsewipe to do anything. I'd fucking kill him.'

'Which is why I didn't order you but rather Pybba. You can get your hands on him if he ever works out how to stand and fight.'

'No thank you. You can leave it to Pybba. He knows how to forge the roughest shit into something remotely useful.'

Ealdorman Ælhun's face is pensive.

'You mean to embarrass him into fighting?'

'No, I mean to make him realise it's fucking hard work. Someone should have done this when he was no older than my nephew, young Æthelred.'

'No one thought he'd ever be king,' Ealdorman Ælhun muses.

'So, they let him spend his time praying. I mean, have you seen him? If the sun touches his face, he'll be bright pink in no time at all. I doubt he's ever spent more than a morning or afternoon outside. The bloody wind will terrify him.'

From outside we all hear Pybba shouting his relentless string of instructions.

'Get your arses over here. Come on. We'll run round Old Sarum five times, more if you're too damn slow. And if you're still slow then, it'll be another twenty times. You'll be sweating like a blacksmith forging iron tips before a battle by the time I'm done with you.'

I look to Kyred. He smiles.

'I remember that well,' he sympathises.

Ealdorman Ælhun glances from me to Kyred.

'Remember what?'

'Pybba, the slower you go, the more you have to do.'

'Running?'

'Yep, running and that's only the start of it. Pybba knows what he's doing.'

'He does. I think only Icel, Osmod and Cuthwalh didn't have to endure Pybba's training. Is that right?' I question the others.

'I had someone worse than Pybba to teach me how to fight,' Icel offers with a raised eyebrow. Any moment now, I know he'll come out with one of his tales. 'In the reign of King Wiglaf,' he'll start and I'll know it's all shit. 'I had to prove myself, just as King Alfred will have to do.' I startle at the admission, on the cusp of asking for more details. But Icel stands, and holds his finger to his nose, tapping it. 'Never you mind, you nosy sod,' he informs me and strides outside. My mouth drops open in surprise. This isn't at all what I was expecting to hear from Icel.

'You mean,' Gardulf winces. 'That Icel wasn't born with a seax in each hand, headbutting anyone who got in his way?'

I chuckle. I imagine Edmund thought the same about Icel.

'Are you coming to watch?' Ealdorman Ælhun questions. He hasn't been taught by Pybba. It intrigues me he's interested enough to actually take himself outside.

'No, I'm resting. I don't need to watch to know how shit it'll be. I don't want to feel any sympathy for bloody King Alfred. If he's got half a thought in his head, he'll realise the way to win the true loyalty of his men is to persevere no matter how much it hurts. I think that'll take him a while to grasp.'

'Perhaps,' Ealdorman Ælhun muses.

I stretch my arms above my head, easing the tension from my back and neck.

I can't say the task I've set King Alfred will be easy. But nothing in my life has ever been easy. He needs to learn that, or the Viking raiders will overwhelm him. I can't protect his bloody kingdom. I need to return to my beloved Mercia. After all, this is where my current endeavours began. I can't abandon it. Not when we've achieved so much already.

Chapter Five

Pybba eventually finds me, seeing to Haden. My horse needs grooming. I find it a restful experience despite the nips from sharp teeth and stamping hooves that force me to dance out of his way, not at all an easy task with one leg almost useless. Our bickering is far from silent despite the fact only one of us can talk. I've been aware that Pybba's distant shouting has been missing for some time.

'My lord,' he announces himself. He's freshly washed, his face glowing with the cold of the water he's no doubt dunked himself with. Perhaps he's been to the nearby stream outside Old Sarum. I've discovered, from talking to those within Old Sarum, that the water supply relies on a single source. That's a terrible weakness should the enemy ever realise.

'That took a while.'

'It did, my lord. He's got the stamina of a newborn babe. He bloody cries almost as much.'

I grin while he chortles darkly. Pybba's older than me. King Alfred is my age. We all know it should be Pybba who struggles and not the other way round.

'It felt good though, to get some exercise. Most of the Mercians joined me eventually, running around the inner embankment. The West Saxons who live here didn't. They didn't know what to make of it all.'

'Did King Alfred get to hold a weapon?'

'No, it took too long for him to finish the run. I was bloody hungry.'

'Where is he now?'

'No idea. Probably lying on his bed or praying. Perhaps if he prays hard enough, he'll be able to run faster than a headless chicken.'

I continue to laugh, but Pybba's face grows serious.

'It could be time to seek an alternative to him. I can't see he's going to survive for long. Not with the Viking raiders already in Wessex.'

'His nephews?'

'Perhaps one of his ealdormen?'

'I'm not here to decide who should be king,' I muse. 'I don't want to be involved in that. That'll be for the ealdormen to decide, not me. Whoever's king, Wessex needs to commit to protecting Canterbury.'

'Aye, my lord. I realise that. Still, just a thought.'

I don't miss that Icel's joined us. I know he'd be happy if all the descendants of King Ecgberht of Wessex and his son were dispensed with, but the problem would remain of who would become king afterwards. While the nephews are a possibility, neither of them are old enough to rule in their own names, although their lack of warrior prowess is more understandable than their uncle's.

'I take it they have no 'spare' claimants, as Mercia did when King Burgred fucked off?'

'No bloody idea,' Pybba shrugs, clearly not having considered it.

Icel shakes his head. 'No, the ruling line, aside from the sons of King Æthelwulf is distinctly lacking in future generations. Alfred's older brothers weren't that concerned with producing sons. They were too busy undermining their father, and then, when he was dead, one another. And, we don't want any more of the bastards, anyway.'

'So, we're sodding stuck with him, or one of his nephews.'

'Seems that way,' Pybba acknowledges.

'Will you be able to make him into a warrior?'

'Not quickly. He's not the most coordinated, and he lacks upper-body strength. He might be able to ride better. But whether he could ever ride with shield and spear at the same time, I wouldn't like to commit.'

'Perhaps,' I muse, flexing my leg. My wound still pains me. It's healing, but not quickly enough. 'But we don't do much fighting from the back of a horse, do we?'

'He might be able to command.'

'Command who?' Icel interjects fiercely.

'And that, of course, is the problem,' I sigh, running my hands over my left thigh, wincing at the movement, but aware I need to do something to keep my strength in the leg. Hobbling will not do that. If anything, it'll make my other leg and foot hurt, and then I really will have the wonky leg Pybba accused me of having yesterday. The bastard.

'We can't remain here for much longer,' I acknowledge what I've been considering. 'So, we have to decide whether to do anything about bloody Winchester and Wareham or just take ourselves to London.'

'It would be fraught with difficulties, despite the shit walls, to fight for Winchester. The Viking raiders have been there for a while, as they have at Wareham. While Gardulf doesn't know the exact numbers, from what we saw, there are a lot of the enemy inside Winchester. And if we do fight for Wareham, there's not really much to hold on to if we did get it.'

'I know that. But, do we want to allow the Viking raiders the permanence of having such a possession on Wessex land? It's not many days walk to Mercia from there. It's less if they ride. Even if they ride about as well as bloody King Alfred,' I add to stop one of the others making the comment.

'They could just as easily make the journey by ship.' Icel

comments. 'It takes much less time than you might think, especially with calm weather and skilled shipmen.'

In the midst of continuing my thought, I look at Icel, feeling my forehead furrow.

'When did you sail to Winchester from Mercia?'

He offers me a rare smile. 'A long time ago, my lord. A very long time ago. And it was to Southampton. Winchester isn't on the coast.' Again, he astounds me.

'Why?'

Now he taps his nose in that infuriating way of his, and seals his lips once more.

'Fine. So, Winchester?'

'It must be akin to the bastards taking Repton,' Pybba muses. Rudolf's come to see what we're doing. He runs his hand along Haden's nose, and my bloody horse is gentled by the touch. Bastard git.

'Avoiding someone?' Rudolf questions.

'Me, never?' I smile.

'This has healed well,' he announces, inspecting the wound Haden took at Gloucester.

'It has, yes. My thanks.'

'Always happy to help your horse,' he chuckles, the implication that aiding me doesn't make him happy. 'Now, why are you hiding in here?'

'Pybba came to report on King Alfred.'

'Bloody arsehole,' Rudolf complains. I realise now he's got wet hair as well. It seems all of my men have taken the opportunity to clean themselves. 'He's got about seven left feet. I'm amazed he can sodding walk in a straight line.' There's no sympathy in Rudolf's complaint.

'Pybba says it'll take a while.'

'A while? It'll take him until his children are grown men and women. Really, my lord, how can he lack even a modicum of skill? How can he be Wessex's king when he's so shit?' I confess I laugh at the outraged expression on Rudolf's face. It's refreshing to hear him say everything we're thinking.

'I assure you, there are those in the witan who wish I had the political acumen of King Alfred instead of brute strength and an ability to kill our enemies. Different places. Different requirements.'

'Well, all I can say is, it's not as though the Viking raider attacks are a new thing. It's been years, decades even, but no one thought to train a possible future king. It's bloody crazy.'

'King Æthelwulf was always an arsehole,' Icel murmurs. 'More likely to be looking at Mercia than events in his own kingdom. It doesn't surprise me his youngest son is shit at fighting. His older sons were all rebellious bastards. No doubt he thought it best not to teach every single one of them to fight him.' Again, this is a telling statement, but I stop myself asking him outright how he knows so much about King Æthelwulf who was Wessex's king for nearly twenty years.

'So, Rudolf, in your opinion, will he ever make a warrior?'

'No,' the reply is immediate and damning. If even my former squire says King Alfred will never amount to anything, I know to heed his words.

'So, should we eject the enemy from Winchester or go to London?' I'm not truly so uncertain I need my warriors to tell me what to do, but I'm genuinely interested.

'Depends if you want to kill some of the bastards anytime soon. If you feel the need, then Winchester. If you don't, then London.' So spoken, Rudolf meanders away to check on Jethson. I watch him, shaking my head.

Pybba asks the question. 'So, my lord, which one will it be?'

I sigh heavily. I'd really like to go to London as planned, but I'd also like to kill some of the enemy. 'Winchester,' I glower. 'But only if King Alfred's ealdormen and their warriors put in an appearance in the next few days. If not, it'll be London, and King Alfred can bleat about it all he fucking wants.'

With the decision made, I turn back to Haden. Now he's clean, my horse needs to be exercised. I reach for his equipment, ensuring the saddle is firmly in place, and mount up.

'A little canter around Old Sarum,' I tell my oldest friend. 'And we'll see what else we can find out about the West Saxons.'

Pybba and Icel step aside as we emerge into the bright daylight, and I direct Haden towards the only means of entering and leaving Old Sarum. As we ride through the double gateways, I appreciate once more just how steep the twin embankments that protect the ground within Old Sarum are. It would be almost impossible for anyone to devise a means of attacking over the embankments. They can only come through the gateway, and now it's heavily guarded by Mercians, and a few of the West Saxons. I don't acknowledge Rudolf keeping watch on me from behind. Every so often, he does know to shut up.

Although my leg pains me as I ride a full circuit around Old Sarum, I enjoy being with my horse when we're not fighting the enemy or battling for our lives. His gait is steady, and I feel my tight shoulder relaxing. Not that I really discover much about Old Sarum or the West Saxons, well not until Lord Æthelwulf calls for me to stop from atop his horse when I'm in sight of the entranceway once more.

I eye him with surprise.

'I didn't know you were here.'

'Well, I am,' he replies, stating the obvious. 'I would speak to you about your intentions towards King Alfred.' His tone is far from deferential.

'What's it got to do with you?'

'He's my brother by marriage and my king.'

'Is he now?' I respond, my voice low and menacing.

Immediately, Lord Æthelwulf realises he's erred.

'Yes, he is, as are you, of course.'

'I find it strange you name him before me, but as I said, my intentions towards King Alfred aren't your concern.'

'You embarrass him.'

'So, not being able to lift a sword and defend himself isn't bloody humiliating?'

'Well,' he begins, and then pauses. 'He is a king.'

'And he's under attack. He should be able to fight to defend his kingdom. Would you not fight to defend Mercia and Wessex?'

'Of course I would,' Lord Æthelwulf snaps.

'So why is King Alfred any different?'

'He wasn't raised the same way.'

'That's not an excuse. If he doesn't wish to remain king, then he needn't be a warrior, but if he wishes to be king, he needs to be able to perform that function. His coronation oath demands it from him, doesn't it?'

Lord Æthelwulf doesn't immediately respond.

'There's no need to embarrass a man who can't fight. He has other skills.'

'All of which are fucking irrelevant if he has no kingdom to rule. Lord Æthelwulf, I'm sorry you're here, trying to berate me for something King Alfred has already accepted. If he wishes to have this discussion with me, then I'll speak with him. But, you're not him, and so, respectfully, fuck off.'

Swift fury covers his face. Haden, unhappy with being brought to a halt for so long, shuffles beneath me. I know it would take but a slight squeeze of my knees, and we'd be gone from Lord Æthelwulf. Yet, his words in support of King Alfred anger me.

'If I wasn't a warrior king, your land in Mercia would be in the hands of the Viking raiders. You'd be a lord without land, and your sister would have no value either. You'd be no use to King Alfred. He keeps you close because of what you and your sister represent, his alleged alliance with Mercia, remember that.'

Now I do move Haden away. I'm considering what I could do to Lord Æthelwulf. I could have him renew his oath to me, and make him beholden to me alone. He shouldn't even be in Wessex. His sister has been wed for years. He could leave her with King Alfred. That he doesn't speaks to me of a man who's too comfortable allowing others to govern in his stead, and too comfortable with being the brother-in-law of a man who's a king. Perhaps Lord Æthelwulf thinks he should be a king? They say there's some distant claim to the kingship of Mercia in the family line, and that's what made the match with Wessex possible. I doubt the truth of that. I think King Burgred was content to allow Alfred to marry a woman of good birth, not a woman or royal birth. I consider if King Alfred knows that.

I shake my head, frustrated by these thoughts. I need to ruminate on the coming fight with the enemy, not whether or not Lord Æthelwulf is happy with how I speak to his bloody brother by marriage.

I encourage Haden to greater speed. The interior of Old Sarum is only lightly filled with dwellings and other buildings. It's not difficult to canter through the space back towards the stables, but as I do the realisation floods me that being angry with Lord Æthelwulf will do me no good. If he holds himself more loyal to King Alfred then who am I to argue with that. However, Lord Æthelwulf can't tell me what to do. I will say it, and say it again, remembering Pybba's words to me, King Alfred can either learn to fucking fight or he can give up his kingdom and leave it to another.

From what little I know of King Alfred I don't believe he'd ever want to do that. That would offend him. And so, I can embarrass him for being unable to fight, or he can learn to fight. I don't much care for his feelings on the matter.

I bring Haden to a halt, directing him back towards the stables, and dismount quickly, ensuring his saddle and reins are removed and stored where he can't stamp on them. Then, I make my way to where my warriors are gathered together in a corner of the hall.

I eye them, running a careful eye over those who were wounded fighting for Wessex. We've already given enough. I've no need to secure Winchester for King Alfred.

'We're going home,' I inform my men, contradicting what I said about Winchester but not caring. I eye Pybba meaningfully, because yes, we're going home, but Pybba isn't. He, and whoever wishes to remain with him, will need to stay close to King Alfred. When I see him again, in London, King Alfred needs to be able to fight. If he can't, then I'll be bloody fervent in my desire for a warrior to lead the West Saxons against the enemy.

If I'm going to risk myself, then Wessex must do the same.

A murmur of conversation greets my words, Pybba nodding to show he understands what I have planned for him. Ealdorman Ælhun and Kyred also bow in agreement.

'We leave tomorrow,' I inform them before anyone can argue with me.

I'll travel to London. I'll call my ealdormen and bishops to me, and I'll tell them of what we need to do.

We can help Wessex, as long as it bloody helps itself.

In the meantime, we'll prepare Mercia's border defences. Only that way can we be assured Mercia's sacrifices of the last year and a half haven't been in fucking vain, and that the men, almost brothers in all but blood, haven't died for nothing. I won't allow it to happen. I really bloody won't.

Chapter Six

I don't speak to King Alfred before riding away the following day. It's a wrench to leave Pybba behind, but he knows what's expected of him. And, should anything terrible befall King Alfred and his forces, Pybba will survive. A man such as him doesn't simply give up and die. Unlike others. He has one hand. He's been held captive by the enemy. That he still lives and breathes speaks to me of a warrior who's skilled and fucking determined to stay alive.

We don't turn towards Winchester as we ride through the twin turf embankments and outside Old Sarum once more, but north, retracing the steps we took to reach this place. The sooner we're once more in Mercia, the better I'll feel.

Gardulf, Goda and Sæbald remain unwell, but are mounted. Just about. I don't push my warriors northwards. The enemy have been surprisingly absent since we killed so many of the damn bastards. The funeral pyres still smoke, and I'm aware, white and grey bones remain requiring concealment beneath the earth. At least, I reason, the hole that's needed won't be anywhere near as big if we'd not tried to burn them first.

There's been no sign of movement from Winchester. I take it to mean we're not being chased. That's not the comfort it should be but serves to reinforce Gardulf's assertion the Viking raider jarls mean to attack Canterbury, the home of Archbishop Æthelred. I almost wish I'd never met the man at Lechlade and then I'd not feel such concern for his person. But I have met him, and now I must do all I can to aid him. The first step of that involves reaching Mercia and then turning towards London. I'll then send word to my aunt, Bishop Wærferth and Alfred's wife, Lady Ealhswith. I consider if she'll be pleased her husband lives. I know Lady Wulfthryth, his sister by marriage, won't be. That amuses me. I think Lady Wulfthryth is a stronger woman than Lady Ealhswith. She'd never have raised a son as useless as fucking King Alfred. I hope her fatherless sons will become fine warriors.

Icel leads us once more. We travel through one of the rings of stones with thick slabs in random placements, which I truly can't make sense of. They didn't just form like that. But what their purpose is defies me.

'What are they?' Rudolf muses in the bright daylight, taking Jethson through the stones, and even beneath the heavy looking slabs resting on top of two other upright pieces of stone.

'Fuck knows,' I retort, not that interested. I don't know why they're here. I don't really want to know. Admittedly, I'm curious as to how the horizontal upper stones were placed over the vertical ones. I don't think it was done merely by man or beast.

'It must have been the work of Giants,' Icel muses, surprising me. It's not like him to speak in such a way.

Whatever led to this collection being constructed in such a way is lost to us. It clearly was nothing to do with defence because there's no embankment. Just the stones. And, I don't think anyone could have constructed a house there. Could they?

'The view's not bad,' Rudolf continues, turning Jethson to gaze the way we've come, and then back the way we're going. 'Lots of hills, so why not put these stones on one of those? They'd be visible from a much further distance away then,' he questions.

'It wasn't the bloody Romans, that much I do know,' Hereman announces decisively. 'They made roads and walls. Not bloody stone monuments with so much air between them, they could blow down, if it was very, very windy. It looks to me like a game the Giants started playing and then forgot about.'

'Gives me the fucking creeps,' Gardulf mutters, his voice tinged with pain, and I notice he keeps his distance. Of course, I realise, he wasn't with us when we first came this way.

Hereman's dismounted. I chuckle to see him leaning his considerable weight against one of the vertical stones. 'They don't move at all,' he mutters. I shake my head, but we have places to be. Quickly, we're on the way to the second collection of stones Icel mistook for these in the dark. I'm not entirely sure how. They're very different, this second set being remarkably concentric and consisting of many more of them. But then, Icel's not the sort to remember such details. He's all about fighting, blades, and as we've recently discovered, knowing the names of roads built by the Romans. Aside from Watling Street and Ermine Street, and some of the others, I don't know them all. I've often mused on why the roads don't terminate at the borders between Mercia and her neighbours. Perhaps then, the Romans ruled the much larger territory of the whole island of Britain.

As we continue on our journey, my thoughts return to Old Sarum. It's a fine place. Well defended. Perhaps we should instigate more permanent changes within Mercia. If we ever get the bloody time to do so. But we'd need to decide on locations where a water supply was more bountiful than at Old Sarum. I realise the very reason it's only home to so few people is because of the poor water supply.

The following day, I breathe a sigh of relief as we reach the River Thames at Lechlade and cross once more into Mercia through the narrow fording point. The weather's been dry and the water levels are hardly above Haden's knees. A weight seems to lift from my shoulders as Haden steps onto Mercian land to the northern bank. I'm not alone in allowing myself to enjoy being home. Mercia thrums in my blood. I am Mercian. Those stupid fuckers from Wessex are really just that.

'Now we turn towards London,' I call as though the others don't know my intention. One of Kyred's men rushes northwards. His task is a thankless one, but my aunt must know of my whereabouts. If not, she'll probably ride to Old Sarum and demand answers from King Alfred. I don't doubt she'd get them as well.

I survey the landscape, marvelling as the River Thames twists and turns, slowly widening before bursting into its fall width, which will run all the way to London. I squint into the bright daylight, reassuring myself there are no Viking raider ships. I am aware the width of the river allows easy access into Mercia, if the enemy sneak past London. I can't allow that to bloody happen.

'Tell me Wærwulf,' I call to him as we settle for the night once more. 'Will those wolves of yours we found to the east of London recognise you?'

'I fucking doubt it,' he mutters darkly. 'Sooner eat me than know I ensured they lived.'

'Perhaps,' I muse, unsettled once more. Do I risk that happening if I teach King Alfred all I know? Will he turn on me and leave me as nothing but bones for the carrion birds?

'The mother might,' Wærwulf offers eventually. 'She'd have more reason to recall me than the pups.'

Once more, I consider King Alfred and all I'm doing for him. I know he won't appreciate it, but I wonder if there's one who might? His daughter interests me. She already seems to possess a stronger personality than her father. And her mother. She's also half-Mercian, something King Alfred seems to remember only when he wants something.

'Why, my lord?' Wærwulf breaks into my musings.

'I'm just reminded of the last time we were close to London,' I offer.

'It was bastard cold,' Wærwulf complains. 'And Bishop Smithwulf was as welcoming as rotten fish.'

I chuckle at that vivid image. I can almost smell it.

'Well, he was a corrupt fucker,' I retort as we settle to sleep. I'm expecting a message from my aunt at any moment. No doubt it'll be filled with fury and complaint. Until then, I allow my mind to consider the wolves and the snow, and London itself. I know London was attacked by the enemy during King Burgred's reign. I didn't bestir myself to defend London. Not then. My focus was only on the land beholden to Kingsholm. I consider if I'll find others who were involved. I'll have to ask when I reach London.

Whether there are people who were there or not, I must make the settlement more secure. It'll be my means of protecting the vast expanse of Mercia that stretches to the north and west of it. How exactly I'm to do that, I'm unsure, but there'll be a solution. It defies me for the time being.

'I hope Pybba's well,' Rudolf huffs as he wraps himself in his cloak close to me. 'He's too old to be left alone with shit for brains King Alfred.'

'As I said to our erstwhile ally, Pybba has stayed alive with only one hand. I think he can take care of himself.'

'Like he did in Wales?' Rudolf shatters my confidence with his angry question. I prop myself up on an elbow.

'Shall I send you bloody back to aid him?' I ask hotly, watching Rudolf's lips tighten with agitation.

'It's too bloody late for that, isn't it. Who knows where he'll be?'

'Winchester?' I suggest, but I doubt King Alfred will go anywhere near Winchester. Not until it's gifted to him by one of his ealdormen or the Mercians.

'He won't be there. King Alfred will be hurrying to follow your orders so he can get to London. He won't want to be parted from you for long. Mark my words. He might even be there already,' Icel mutters.

It's not a fucking comforting thought.

* * *

Our arrival in London is met with no fanfare. There's no bishop in overall command, and while Ealdorman Ælhun came this way to reach us within Wessex, he didn't have time to do anything else. I've been remiss since Bishop Smithwulf's murder, but his death is too closely connected with Edmund's. I allow myself some respite from such personal recriminations.

My eyes take in the settlement along the river bank, vibrant with trading vessels as the season starts to turn to winter, when the river is more, not less, passable. I take us towards the ancient white stone walls, and then through them. The walls are more fallen down than upright these days, but they'll provide some sort of protection from the enemy, I hope. Evidently, that's what the people who make London their home also think. Few live amongst the wooden buildings to the west of the River Fleet these days. The old place is more ruin than habitable.

I see Rudolf deep in conversation with Icel as we ride into the bishop's complex, close to the southern walls, but I'm too busy dismounting and handing Haden's reins to young Hiltiberht to give it more than a passing moment of my attention.

'My lord king,' one of the monks who must be in command here in the absence of any bishop, bows low, flustered by my arrival. I pity the poor sod. Perhaps I should have sent advance warning. 'I am Brother Matthew,' he introduces himself.

'Yes, yes, now tell me, who leads here?'

Brother Matthew sweats, pale face wobbling as he picks up his brown skirts and hurries to join me as I stroll through the former home of Bishop Smithwulf. It's a fine establishment, if built of wood in a sea of stone roads and stone ruins, smoke blowing merrily in the stiff breeze aiding the sails of the ships on the river, although I can't see them from here. However, I hear the shouts of men and women as they direct the small ships. The voices are a mixture of every tongue imaginable. No doubt, there are some who speak Norse. Hopefully, they're not bastard Viking raiders.

'No one, my lord king,' Brother Matthew pants as he catches up with me, where I've circumnavigated the many buildings that form the bishop's complex and found a small vantage point to survey the River Thames through a gateway giving access to the quayside. Well, gateway might be too elaborate a word for what seems to be more a broken-down section of the wall through which people now climb carrying their goods. I squint against the low sun and strong wind. 'No one yet. The archbishop hasn't reassigned London, and neither have you, my lord king.'

'Hum,' is all I offer, aware Hereman has been tasked with keeping me safe. He's as out of breath as the damn monk as he comes closer. I offer him an arched eyebrow. He offers me a sardonic bow. God, I love Hereman. He's such a shit, but he's my shit. I'm astounded Rudolf has stayed away.

'Then who collects the taxes?'

A blanched face and I realise no one's collecting the taxes. Or if they are, they're not doing it in my name. That'll need to be resolved. I shouldn't have abandoned London as I have. I must correct that. An ealdorman will need to make his home here, one with many warriors just as eager as me to keep London out of the grasping hands of King Alfred, and the bloody Viking raiders. I think King Alfred both the greater and the lesser threat. He doesn't have the warriors, but he's bloody determined. The Viking raiders have the warriors, but lack the commitment. They just want to piss me off. If they did have the determination, they'd never have been ejected from London in the past.

'I'm here now. I'll resume control until I appoint another. If you'd be so good as to arrange food for my many warriors. Perhaps,' I realise, noticing the shocked expression on Brother Matthew's face at the thought of feeding so many. 'I should have sent prior warning.' The poor man swallows heavily and hurries away. I can already hear the outraged shrieks of those who cook for the monks as they try and determine what they can produce and quickly. There should be plenty of excess at this time of the year.

'It's a good thing the harvest has been freshly collected,' Hereman offers, humour rippling through his voice. 'I could eat a bloody haunch of venison alone.'

'You always were a bloody great big pig. And terrible at sharing,' I offer.

'My brother stole my food. I had to get very good, very quickly, at keeping it all to myself.' I grin at that, finding comfort in being able to speak in such a way about Edmund without actually naming him. 'So, now we're here, what bloody next?'

'A message to the archbishop. Some work on these walls. They're in a terrible state.'

'Indeed, my lord,' and Icel appears, filling the space with his height and girth in a way that surprises me when Hereman and I are already there. We're not exactly reedy. 'The place is a mess. We need people on the walls. We need the old fortress made habitable.' The way he speaks makes me think this isn't Icel's first experience of securing London against the enemy. Not that he was here a few years ago when the Viking raiders attacked. No, this must be from another of those events Icel only ever alludes to in passing.

I turn to gaze at the remnants of the ancient fort to the north. I'm not sure I've ever been within it. It looks like it might collapse at any moment. Still, it rises above every other dwelling within London. I wait to see if Icel will say more. For once, he doesn't disappoint.

'Even in my lifetime, the fortress was habitable and the walls strong enough to keep out the bastard West Saxons.'

'And since then?'

'Well, it's fallen to bloody ruin, hasn't it?' he huffs, eyes glinting fiercely. I consider all he's seen here. I'm aware there were many battles over Londonia, as it was then named, when Icel was a younger man. Surely, he didn't fight in them all?

'My lord,' he offers, bowing slightly. 'I'm happy to ride to Canterbury. I know the way.' But I shake my head.

'No. I need you here. I've already lost Pybba to King Alfred.' If he's pleased to know how much he means to me, he expresses it by grimacing. Fucking charming.

'Then who?'

'Someone slight and quick.'

'I'm not going,' Rudolf calls from somewhere nearby. Are all my bastard warriors within listening distance?

'I didn't ask you to,' I retort, but I was going to. Now I'll need to think of someone else.

'Perhaps one of the monks?' Icel suggests instead. 'The Viking raiders with their new found faith won't want to kill one of God's warriors, should they meet him.'

I think to argue with him, but actually, it's a bloody good idea.

'Find me the most likely monk,' I decide. 'And the fleetest horse,' I conclude, but I'm considering the surrounding walls once more, including the improvised gateway that gives access to the River Thames. We could make something of the walls, built of either huge slabs of stone, or more often, pieces of almost slab-like structures held together by force of will more than anything else. But first, we need to assess the walls thoroughly with more than a cursory glance. I know to whom I'll assign that bloody tedious task. He might even bloody enjoy it.

Chapter Seven

Icel takes my command the next morning with ill grace. None of us are exactly pleased with the sleeping arrangements the previous night, or the food, which was both burnt and raw. Quite an astounding skill. Hopefully, today will be better.

'You're the only one who knows what's possible,' I glower at him while he scowls at me. 'Don't bloody deny it.'

'We don't have time to do what's possible,' he retorts quickly, turning to stride away. Quickly, I follow him. I'll at least see where he goes. Rudolf also hurries along with me, his breathing far more even than mine. I'm still limping and it slows me down. With a wry smirk, I notice Icel's marching towards the furthest point of the settlement. I thought he'd go to the crumbling walls close to the river bank, but no. I admire the bloody arse and his contrary nature.

I'm aware of others watching us, as I hasten over the uneven ground. It seems there were once roads here, in some places. In others, not so much. I narrow my eyes, trying to decide if the houses follow the roads or are built over where they used to be. A sharp stab of pain, and I wobble precariously, and wince. I've kicked a slab of stone with my foot. I hop around, and quickly, Icel's out of sight. Rudolf, however, stays at my side, a smile on his face, which he quickly replaces with a look of concern when he senses me watching him.

'Well, that went bloody well,' he offers, while I grimace, and find a discarded piece of half-tumbled down wall to sit upon while I rub my foot.

'It'll bruise,' he states, sitting beside me. He too is looking all around him. We've been to London before, not that long ago, but it was winter, with snow lying thickly on the ground, and we could see very little of what actually remains of the old settlement, and it is very bloody old.

'He'll give you a list of sodding problems as long as your arm,' Rudolf offers conversationally. 'Probably as long as both of your sodding arms,' he reconsiders.

'And he'll expect me to fix those problems as well,' I admit, feeling the sharp stab of pain slowly receding. I can feel a shimmer of cold sweat on my face. I'm working on releasing my tense backside. 'Bastard thing,' I complain, eyeing what tripped me with loathing. Rudolf leans forward and collects it into his hand.

'What is it?' he questions, running his hand over what look like patterns on the piece of white stone. I look around me, and then up. There are some random pieces of stones near to us. I consider what they were for.

'They came from one of those,' I call, nudging my head to where I can see similar patterns on the stone.

'But what were they for?'

'I've no fucking idea,' I mutter, standing and gingerly putting weight on my foot. It hurts, but not as bad as I feared it would. Rudolf moves towards the pieces of stone, and I hobble after him, trying not to wince at the discomfort.

Rudolf runs his hands over the flattened tops of the stones. 'They were to put something on,' he suggests, eyes narrowed, his head moving from side to side as he considers.

'What would you have put on those?' I question, 'and more importantly, why?'

I turn, surveying where we are. There are some dwellings here, and I realise they're perhaps built into the standing remains of something much older. I turn full circle, eyes narrowed as I consider. It's not as though London is the only place to survive from our long-ago ancestors, but it's unusual in not having been inhabited much in the intervening time. I know traders long preferred the settlement slightly to the west, that abutted the river front more easily without the walls inhibiting easy access. In recent years, people have begun to move back into the dubious safety of the surrounding walls, which themselves are not above tumbling down and trapping any unfortunate enough to be beneath at the time.

'Statues,' Icel mutters, appearing from ahead, forehead furrowed. 'Why are you bloody here? I thought you were following me.'

'I hurt my bloody foot,' I counter quickly, infuriated he expects me to trail him when I set him the task, and amused he's annoyed when I stopped.

'On what?' he demands.

'On a bloody great big piece of stone.'

'Well watch where you're sodding going,' he glowers, no sympathy in his barking voice. 'Come on. We don't need to look at the ruins of this place. Wherever the statues are, they're long since gone.'

'Statues of what?' Rudolf asks the question I'm eager to hear the answer to as well.

'People, Gods, who knows. They were still here when I was a young man. A strange collection of a lost people caught in obscure poses, and with the odd arm, foot and nose missing.' He sounds angry but then a grin touches his cheeks.

'I can assure you, young Rudolf, most of them had their cocks and stones on display. I believe they preferred to exaggerate those attributes.' Rudolf chuckles, but now my eyes narrow.

'So, they made naked statues of people?'

'That they did, Coelwulf. The male and female form. It was quite an education for a young lad.'

'Why?'

'Who cares. Now come on. Hobble if necessary, but this task must be performed, and immediately.'

I grimace, test my left foot with the pulsing toe, and decide I can walk, but I'll be tottering on both legs now. For a moment, I debate returning for Haden but dismiss it. I need to see this from the height of a man, not the back of a horse.

Icel leads on once more, and now I'm more careful where I step. These statues that Icel spoke of make themselves noticed now I know to look for them. And indeed, Rudolf's giggle assures me he's found something on the ground which he proudly displays as a huge stone cock. It's unmistakable. Even I find myself chuckling at the length and girth of it.

'Did that belong to a damn horse?' I question, bending to collect what I'm fairly sure must be the stones that fit with the cock.

Together, Rudolf and I slot them together, giggling, while Icel watches on, shaking his head at our childish display.

'I imagine he had the longest spear shaft as well,' Icel mutters sourly.

'Why would they make such things?' I question. I've seen the odd headless stone statue before, usually broken up into just as many pieces as these. 'And why are there so many in one place?'

'The ancients were keen to immortalise themselves,' Icel suggests. I accept that. Still, I'm astounded.

'You should get one of yourself,' Rudolf suggests, keeping the two pieces of stone in his hands. No doubt he means to share our findings with the others.

'How? Our stonemasons can't bring forth cocks like this?' Icel retorts, but there's a flicker of amusement in his voice, as Rudolf and I hurry to catch him.

'Why are we starting at the bloody furthest part of the walls?' I question, when I'm tired of limping and we still haven't encountered it.

'Because you wanted me to check them, and lazy men will only go so far around them when set the task. It's best to get the worst part over and done with.' But I sense there's something else here. Despite the jutting walls of stone, and collapsed roofs of grass that have evidently been used in more recent times to make the buildings we pass habitable, I sense Icel recognises the way unerringly well. He knows where we're going.

Finally, the wall ahead grows larger in my vision. I look up and up, coming to a halt first so I don't stub my toe on anything else, while Icel continues onwards. He moves better than I do. Watching him, I think I'm the one who has so many more winters to his name.

'Here,' Icel calls with some triumph. 'Here is where the wall was weak when I was no older than Rudolf. But,' he continues, 'it appears the heavy masonry has done the work of securing it for us. There was once a space here. There isn't any more.'

I look where he points, eyes narrowed.

'What was it?'

'A drain, sending waste water through and down to the outside of the wall.'

I walk towards the standing wall, considering his description. The wall here remains tall, although it's clearly slumped. There are taller sections to either side of it, but the same number of stone pieces.

'Who was the king then?' I question, just to see if he'll answer. He doesn't. I shake my head.

'The damp,' Rudolf suggests, with the wisdom of someone who has much experience with stone walls, which I highly doubt. I eye him with exasperation at such a statement.

'The ground's damp outside, and the weight of the stone pushes it down.' How Rudolf knows such things, I'll never know.

'So, what, you think the enemy could climb up the walls?'

'I bloody doubt it,' Icel calls from where he's clambered up far above head height to survey the exterior of the wall. 'There's a bog out there, almost a river really. Can't you smell it?'

I'd like to climb up myself to look, but I leave that to Rudolf and Icel, as Rudolf hands me his precious stone cock and balls and hurries up alongside Icel. I watch them both, the one twice as broad as the other, but with more than enough strength to maintain his hold on the handholds and footings he's discovered. The two speak to one another, while I, with an immature glee, slot the two pieces of stone together and then pull them apart again. I confess, I'm astounded by the ability of these ancients to bring such detail to the stone. Only the fact it's so damn cold, assures me it's not the flesh and blood of a living man.

'Have you fucking finished?' Icel questions, eyebrows high as he watches me. I'd not realised the two had made their way down the wall.

'Yes, yes,' I mutter hastily, thrusting the pieces of stone back into Rudolf's hands.

'We should go this way a little further,' Icel informs me. 'The boggy ground continues, and I'd like to see how far. Evidently, it's only really wet after rain or during the winter. It could dry out enough to allow the enemy to climb over the wall, if they brought ladders to aid them.' I follow Icel as he strides out once more, Rudolf staying at my side.

'You can still see the River Thames from up there. I didn't think you'd be able to,' he offers conversationally. 'The enemy will surely be able to discern the wall dips lower there. They'll think it might be a way inside.'

'And what can we bloody do about that?' I question. I can't have men and women outside the walls draining away the wet ground. If they did that, I fear the entire bloody structure might fall down.

'No bloody idea,' Rudolf offers with a shrug of his shoulders. 'But you need to know. I wonder if the rest is as wet?'

'Well, we are by a damn river.'

'We, are yes, aren't we, my lord,' Rudolf states slowly before sprinting away, laughing as he goes. I follow slowly. There are more dwellings here, built into the ruins, but not all using old stonework. Some of them have been erected using wooden posts and completed with wattle and daub walls. The cries of those living here fills the air, the banging of a woman cleaning clothes on a rock, the wailing of a small child, the sharp yips of dogs bickering over a twisted ball of twine. It interests me they stay away from the sinking wall. They've thought carefully about where to make their homes.

Rudolf speaks to those he comes across, no doubt informing them of who I am, for I'm greeted with bowed heads and curtsies, which I really don't need to see while hobbling along looking about as far from kingly as I usually do. Unless my aunt's managed to convince me to wear the finery she's produced.

All the same, I call greetings, and ask them about the wall.

'We get our water from the river,' one woman informs us. 'Not that one,' and she points towards the Thames. 'There's another, over there,' I look where she indicates. I can't see it from here, but I accept her word for it. After all, she'd know.

'The water's clearer from the Walbrook. The Thames is a turgid mess of waste and dead bodies. When the tide's low, it stinks,' she complains, wrinkling her nose. 'And then it's no good for the bloody trading ships either.'

'Have you always lived here?' I question, because the interior of London could certainly fit many more people within it.

'No. My father was a trader. Over there by the waterfront,' and she points to where Lundenwic once stood. 'He lost everything in an attack from the bastard West Saxons. We moved within when I was about to marry. I've been here ever since.'

'And your father?'

'Dead for many winters now. But this was his home,' she acknowledges, eyeing it with a glower. 'It could do with a new roof, but the garden to the rear is on good ground. I grow many herbs and vegetables. It's the same for most here. It looks like nothing, but at least there's soil. Many of the later arrivals have to force the ancient stones from the ground to clear the way to reach the earth to plant crops.'

'My thanks,' I acknowledge, realising I'm going to learn more from speaking to the inhabitants, than from staggering after Icel.

'Here, my lord king,' and she offers me a beaker of water. I swig it gratefully. It appears my preference for water is well known.

'If your man is looking at the walls here, he must realise they're weaker. We stay away from them. Every so often, the masonry drops into the damp ground to the far side. It's a pity,' she acknowledges, reclaiming my beaker with her careworn hands. 'The ground's good for growing, but poor for living on.'

'Come on, my lord,' Rudolf's head reappears from behind a wattle and daub fence demarcating two dwellings. I'm grateful he doesn't just shout 'Coelwulf,' as he normally would.

'My thanks again,' I acknowledge the woman, and stagger onwards. As I go, I see the settlement through the eyes of someone who lives within it, as opposed to someone who needs to protect it. The ancient buildings and structures that must have once dominated the space are falling to ruin. Some have been propped up with wooden posts. Others have been allowed to tumble and then the pieces taken away, perhaps to repair buildings elsewhere. There's a distinct lack of open space where food could be grown, although there are any number of animals, grazing on what they can find. A collection of goats is almost halfway up the wall where Icel has been following it. The grasses are certainly greener there, benefiting from the damp ground that underlies them. I imagine it can become a muddy quagmire when it rains.

Icel's far in the distance now, visible, but outside my ability to catch him unless he stops his rapid gait.

'What was all that about?' Rudolf questions.

'Domestic arrangements,' I offer.

'Not your usual area of expertise,' he offers with a cheeky grin, moving onwards and then slowing when he remembers I can't walk as fast. 'Why didn't you bring Haden?' he questions.

'What, and miss all this?' I indicate the cock and balls in his hands, and he laughs, the sound joyful. I join him, taking pleasure in the wind in my hair and the strong walls behind me, even if some of them are in danger of falling. Would the enemy know that from a cursory glance? I can't see they would.

Eventually, we catch up to Icel, who's standing, hands on his hips, peering upwards at a section of the wall. I look around me, considering why this has arrested Icel's attention so much. It looks no different to the other parts of it. I've realised it's not entirely continuous, although it looks that way. Some sections, have I think, been added later than others. Or repaired at different times.

'What is it?' I question. Icel turns to me, and points upwards. I realise he's not looking at the wall at all, but higher up.

'That eagle,' he mutters. 'I was just watching it hunt. A pity we can't look down on ourselves from the air. It would certainly make it a quicker task to discover where the walls are weakest.'

I hold my hand above my eyes and also watch the eagle. It's little more than a shadow against the sunlight, but its shape is unmistakable. With dazzling speed, it plummets towards the ground. Rudolf, caught in the moment, clambers up the side of the wall to see where it goes. I stay grounded. The wall, I realise, has abundant hand and footholds.

'You see it too?' Icel murmurs. I nod.

'Is it the same from the exterior?'

'I'll need to assess it. It could be a problem.'

'It could, yes,' I turn, considering where I've walked. I'm aware I can't see the River Thames from here. I can see the dwellings and workshops of the people who live here, including the hall where the bishop of London should be in residence, if he weren't dead and buried. The bastard traitor.

'These walls have been neglected of late. But then, they've not been called to use for many summers before the last attack by the enemy. Perhaps you might find a good stonemason to repair them.'

'Perhaps,' I muse. 'It seems easier to maintain turf ramparts and ditches, as we have at Northampton and Worcester. And soon at Hereford.'

'Yes, but they won't last as long as these. And they need constant attention. The ditches cleared, the walls checked for weaknesses. These walls have stood for hundreds of years.'

'But why did they need them?' I muse. 'I thought the ancient Romans had no enemies?'

'I suspect they had many. If not, they needn't have constructed defences such as these.'

'And now, we need to make use of them as well.'

'We do, Coelwulf. We do. Let's be grateful they knew how to build them so tall. Now, we must merely ensure they don't fall down. Perhaps not the easiest of tasks.'

I narrow my eyes. 'Could we build an embankment to protect them from the interior?'

'We could, yes,' he acknowledges. 'It'd take a long time though.'

'It would, wouldn't it?' I agree. 'But, it's not a bad idea.'

Icel nods quickly. 'It's not. I bid you good luck in encouraging men and women to bring so much mud within the walls. It'll not be a simple task.'

The words aren't quite the agreement I'm looking for.

'Bollocks,' I exclaim. 'Why is nothing ever bloody easy?'

Chapter Eight

Our tour of the walls of London continues, and my wounded leg begins to ache. I'm aware of Rudolf watching me. I'm even more grateful when Hereman appears with Haden. My horse looks outraged to have been made to travel with Billy. I suppress a smirk, although I don't mount because we've made it as far as the old fort. Here, I'm pleased to see the exterior walls facing into London itself remain strong and true. Inside, the fort it's another matter entirely.

'Why has no one ensured this remained bloody habitable?' I complain. Icel offers me a sharp glare. 'I'm not criticising you,' I glower, frustrated to find London, which King Alfred and the Viking raiders have been so keen to take from me, is not at all the stronghold I thought it was. 'We'd have more luck keeping the bastards out at Old Sarum.'

'Then, my lord,' and Icel offers me a cursory bow, 'I suggest you get it bloody sorted out.'

'Thanks for stating the fucking obvious,' I glower. I look aghast at the tumbled remnants of what must surely have once been a set of stone steps, leading upwards, to where I'm sure a walkway rounds the top of the fort building proper. It's out of reach now, only a few steps clinging to one another, where they hover, perilously close to joining the rest of the rubble where the stairway must once have started.

'Be careful,' I order the others, although it seems unnecessary. I duck my head through a doorway, although the wooden door has long since fallen from its ancient hinges. I see where something's been nibbling at the wood, perhaps insects, and squint into the gloom. The room I'm within is large, although the edges of it can't be seen.

'The main hall,' Icel informs me. I nod, scuffing my feet over the stone floor only to sneeze as I kick up dust that's lain dormant for a long time. 'I ate many meals within this room,' Icel informs me, a tantalising glimpse into his past, which Rudolf and I share a glance about. Neither of us asks for more details just in case Icel's feeling chatty again.

'And through here,' Icel leads on through the darkness without fear of stumbling or walking into a wall. I hurry to catch him because I don't share his confidence, 'Is where the warriors used to sleep, and through here, is where we kept our weapons store.' Now he indicates another room, this one entirely lacking a door. The smell of damp and rat shit makes my eyes water. I veer backwards, almost knocking into Hereman.

'And down here.' Somehow, we're once more in the courtyard but close to another set of steps leading into the black depths. Above the walkway beckons enticingly, but without the means to reach it. 'Is a series of small store rooms which don't allow access outside. They've been used to imprison people during my life.' I follow him down the steps, my hands out to either side to stop from tripping in the greyness, and face a small corridor with other doors leading from it. The smell's even more noxious. Icel walks towards one of the rooms, and peers inside, as though he seeks a ghost. I'm almost desperate to ask him why this one room is the one that attracts his attention, but I don't, although I have to bite my lip to stop the words escaping. Rudolf's nearly dancing with his desire not to show his interest either.

I sense Icel appraising the pair of us. He must know what we want to know. For once, he surprises us.

'There was once nearly a terrible calamity for Mercia played out in this very room,' he offers conversationally. 'It's never been written down, and there are few alive who would remember it,' he murmurs, and I consider how many men and women he's known in his long life who are no longer living. I would suspect a great many. 'And one day, no one will recall what happened. Which is both good and bad. Now, outside again. The smell's making my bloody eyes water.'

He strides up the uneven steps with the grace of a youth, leaving me to hobble behind, although I cast a final look at the doorway through which he peered. It seems Icel did indeed see a ghost, but whether it was of what happened here, or of him as a young man, with his life before him, I don't know. To distract myself from the discomfort I'm feeling, I consider what Icel thought his life would be when he was Rudolf's age, or near enough to it. I doubt he foresaw decades of violence with the Viking raiders, and Mercia's enemies. Or perhaps he did. Little seems to surprise him.

Outside, I breathe in deeply. Icel once more strides across the courtyard area, peering upwards.

'Some ladders to begin with,' he suggests. 'That way we can determine if rebuilding the steps is worth it or if we can just scamper up and down a ladder.'

'Scamper?' Rudolf complains, 'with byrnies, swords, shield, spears and whatever else you think we should have up there.' Icel rounds on Rudolf quickly, his face as implacable as usual, his earlier genial conversational tone gone.

'Yes, Rudolf, scamper, like rats from a bloody burning ship. Scamper up the damn ladders.' I shake my head, leaning heavily against the wall. I'd like to sit down, but if I do that, I don't believe I'll stand again, not with ease.

'Are we done here?' Hereman questions. From outside, we can both hear Haden's querulous nicker.

'Yes. But there's much to consider,' Icel confirms, appraising me before striding through the small dank tunnel we used to enter the fort building. I imagine there used to be doors to block it.

'But we do need to consider the main gate,' Icel's words echo back to me. I stagger to Haden and delight in not being forced to stand on my wounded thigh any longer. I turn my horse towards the gateway. I already know the wooden gate is ancient, but here at least, someone has thought to take care of the huge hinges. While the doors are open, held back by a piece of fallen masonry on one side, and what appears to be a stone torso on the other, they can be opened and closed, because I've seen them shut before. The doors don't hang at an odd angle. Admittedly, I see there are some places where they must scrape over the remnants of the roadway.

'It looks well enough,' Rudolf suggests, which pleases me, because I was thinking the same, apart from a few pieces of replacement wood needed at the bottom. But, again, Icel rounds on Rudolf, shaking his head as though he can't believe Rudolf spoke in such a way.

'No, it'll keep out big hungry wolves in the winter, but little else. It needs new bars to hold it shut, and hooks to hold them in place.' As he speaks, Icel forces the stone torso away from where it props the gate open and works to close it. I admit, the hinges do creak alarmingly with the action. Those trying to come inside, peer upwards from where they're crossing the bridge over the River Fleet, fear on their faces, others looking around them as though the enemy might appear at any given moment.

'Just inspecting it,' Rudolf calls as worried faces gaze all around, and some start to almost run.

'See,' Icel pays no heed to the people of London and the terror he's placed in their hearts. 'This side needs a new hook to hold the wooden bars in place. And this hole also needs fixing.' There's a large piece of wood missing at about head height. How that happened, I've no idea. 'And of course, the bottom of the doors is problematic. See, here and here, a child could make their way inside.' He's pulled the door across half of the opening. Now he instructs Rudolf and Hereman to do the same to the other side. The two doors come together in a horrible shriek of wood over stone. Haden shuffles backwards, unsettled by the noise.

'They do join,' Rudolf states.

'They do, yes, but they need to do more than just bloody join together. They also need to keep sodding people out.'

'Well, a child won't be able to lift the bars,' Rudolf argues.

'A child could tell those within to open them if they were traitors to Mercia. Anyway,' and Icel appraises Rudolf carefully. 'I imagine you could get through there if you wiggled enough,' Icel points to the ground, where there's a jagged hole in the wooden gate.

'Let us in,' a voice calls from outside.

'Just a moment,' Rudolf replies, but Icel's far from done.

'Go on, I want to see you bloody try,' Icel states.

'What?' Rudolf looks to me, his eyebrows high as though asking if he should do it or not.

'Go on. Let's see if Icel's correct, and if he's not, then you can win, and if he is, then you lose.'

'Bloody bollocks,' Rudolf huffs, but slips through the gap between the two sides of the gate. I can hear him talking to those outside, and they're far from quiet in demanding to be allowed entry. Then Rudolf's face appears between one of the gaps close to the ground. He's on his back, shuffling from side to side. Quickly, he wiggles his shoulders through, and then the rest of him and it is, as Icel stated, too easy.

'We're not doing that,' a furious voice calls from outside. There are also those waiting to exit.

'We don't expect you to,' Rudolf shouts, getting to his feet and brushing dust from his tunic, with a scowl on his face. 'Happy?' he directs to Icel.

'Not particularly, no. Even the damn gate's weak,' Icel retorts, but he does swing his side of the door open, replacing the stone torso and now those who've been temporarily halted stream inside or outside, Haden moved to ensure he doesn't take a nip of anyone's ears.

'What you buggering about at?' an angry voice spits towards Icel.

'I'm with the king,' is his quick reply, and now the man who speaks turns and peers at me.

'My lord king,' he bows low. I hear him muttering as he walks past me. I smirk, but Icel's not as amused.

'We need to get these doors reinforced, and we must ensure the river gates are as well guarded, and that bloody impromptu gateway sealed.'

'It seems there's much we must do,' I consider darkly.

'There always is, Coelwulf. There always bloody is.' I lean over Haden's shoulder and pat him calmly as a collection of yapping dogs comes inside. I eye them aghast. A good hunting hound isn't to be sniffed at, but these are small things. I can't imagine they're useful for anything but shitting in the house and yapping all night.

'Good ratters, my lord,' the woman who leads them calls. 'I could have that place cleaned out pretty quickly,' and she points towards the fort building. I look to Icel. He nods.

'See it done, good woman, and then, present yourself at the bishop's complex, and I'll ensure you're recompensed.'

She nods, and directs the dogs through the tunnel we used to gain entry to the fort building. Almost immediately, we can hear them barking and the scurrying of nails over the stone floor.

'Well, that's one problem solved,' I suggest, but Icel's not happy.

'Rats are the least of your problems.'

I'm really starting to wish I hadn't agreed to come to London. Maybe, if we'd gone straight to Canterbury, Icel would have vented his frustrations on the defences there, not here. But I must admit, he doesn't exactly point out things that aren't needed. London has long been a battle ground between Wessex and Mercia, and on occasion, the Viking raiders. We must ensure it can fulfil that purpose in the future.

'What would you suggest is most urgent?' I ask Icel for his advice as we begin to make our way along the western extent of London towards the bishop's complex. The walls above my head are tall and seem to be in good repair. I also see where the people of London have driven nails into them to allow clothing to dry.

'Clearing the walkways and rooms within the fort should be the quickest to accomplish, once the rats are gone. Then, we need to ensure the gates at the fort, and down at the waterfront, can withstand an assault, and only then need we worry about the rest of the circuit.'

'So, a few rooms and two gates?' I summarise.

'You'll need wood for the gates,' Icel continues. 'And for ladders within the fort. And the bladesmiths to produce more blades. Everyone within London should be able to protect themselves.'

'Anything bloody else?' but none of my men detect the bite of my sarcasm.

'A store of food and seeds, should they become trapped,' Rudolf continues. 'Then they need not fear being starved into submission.'

'And more wood for fuel,' Icel adds.

'And hay for the horses,' Hereman adds. I sigh at these demands. They're far from unreasonable, but I'm frustrated it must fall to me, the king, to make these adjustments. Just what has Bishop Smithwulf been doing with his taxes? Aside from fuck all, that is.

I don't blame the people of London for using what they could to make their lives easier. The walls do imply safety, compared to the all-but abandoned market settlement of Lundenwic, which is open on all sides, apart from where it faces the river. However, it would have made London even more defensible if they'd not stolen away stones from the walls and used them to build other things. Certainly, they could have made sure the walls were free of holes. As well as the bloody gates.

At the bishop's palace, Hiltiberht rushes to tend to Haden. He eyes the horse easily. The two have become friends of late, which pleases me. I can't be the only one, aside from Rudolf, Haden will allow near him.

'There's a good beef pottage,' Hiltiberht informs me with the joy of youth, when only hot food was a requirement.

'Did you leave any for your king?' Icel questions. I didn't push Haden or Billy to great speed. Icel and Rudolf have kept pace as we've journeyed here.

'Of course, Icel, of course.' I chuckle at Hiltiberht's outraged tone.

'Don't let him bother you, Hiltiberht. The old grump means nothing by it.'

I wince on dismounting, and then follow my nose to where my warriors are eating, while some of the monks look on aghast. I call Brother Matthew to me.

'Tell me, good man. Why's the fort building fallen to ruin?'

'Well, my lord king. Bishop Smithwulf said he lacked the funds to maintain it. He said there was a request for funds from the previous king, but they were denied. And it is rat infested,' he adds with a grimace, and as though that makes abandoning it to the vestiges of rain and storms an acceptable thing to have done.

'Were they now?' I muse, grateful for the overflowing bowl of pottage presented to me, thick with chunks of beef.

'And tell me, how many bladesmiths does London boast? And moneyers? They could aid us as well.'

'My lord king, I think three bladesmiths and only one moneyer.'

'Then have them summoned for the morning. I must speak to them about weaponry.'

'Will there be war, my lord king?' Brother Matthew worries at the girdle around his tunic.

'Undoubtedly,' Icel grumbles so that I don't need to answer.

'And we also need to hear from the woodspeople, and those who bring food into the settlement.'

'Of course, my lord king,' Brother Matthew bobs, and I wish he wouldn't. It's making me feel quite unwell while I eat.

'And anyone else who believes they can aid us in restoring the settlement and the walls. We must make it impenetrable.'

'Yes, my lord king,' Brother Matthew bows a final time, and

moves away, already ordering servants and slaves to him to relay such messages.

'You trust the bastard?' Icel questions with his usual charm.

'Not yet, no. But he knows this place better than we do. No doubt, when these craftspeople present themselves to us, others will quickly follow suit if they believe they've been slighted.'

'You mean to remain in London?' Hereman asks. He's already eaten two bowls of meaty pottage and now slathers butter onto bread using his eating dagger. The bread's so warm the butter melts, making my mouth water.

'I mean to make it as defensible as Northampton and Worcester, and as strong as Hereford will be when the bishop finishes his defences. Provided it's possible. I didn't realise so much of it was derelict. The snow that covered the place during our last visit was deceiving.'

'And after that?'

'I suspect what happens after that will be more to do with what the Viking raiders do, but I'll send word to my aunt, if she's not already on her way here. There are many more settlements in need of protecting. While we know the enemy are to the south, we should take advantage of the respite to reinforce those places with half decent defences and order that others are built.'

'We should, yes,' Icel agrees, doing his best to show his surprise that I can plan something, as opposed to react to it. 'But what of Canterbury?'

'I've sent a messenger to warn them. Once Alfred's come here, we can move towards Canterbury.'

'You really believe King Alfred has left Old Sarum?' Icel chuckles darkly.

'If he hasn't, Pybba will be making his displeasure known.'

'He is but one man.'

'He is, yes. But we know he can bloody guilt the best of us into doing what he wants us to do.'

'But King Alfred?' Icel still questions.

'Aye, I know. But I gave my word. He killed a man. If he kills more of the enemy, he might have some value as an ally.'

As we speak, I'm aware of the appraising gazes of those within the hall. I consider if any of them were involved in Bishop Smithwulf's treachery. I imagine someone must have been his go-between, but how to weed that arsehole out, is, for the time being, beyond me.

'So, tomorrow, we meet the men and women of London, and determine what can and can't be accomplished in a short space of time. And, hopefully, we'll hear a report from the archbishop as well.' I allow myself to relax, good food in my belly, and a plan in my mind. Of course, I expect none of it to happen as I hope. It never bloody does.

Chapter Nine

'Coelwulf,' my aunt's strident voice reaches me, even where I sweat and train with my warriors later that day. I close my eyes briefly, and then affix a smile to my face, while Hereman sucks his teeth in sympathy, only to land a final, lucky blow against my turning body so that I land too heavily on my wounded leg.

'Always be aware of your enemy,' he trills, as I growl at the bastard.

'Thank you for that. I would change that to always being aware of your damn allies,' I mutter, while he chuckles darkly, and moves to shout derogatory comments to Rudolf who's fighting Wærwulf.

'Aunt,' I bow slightly, fighting for balance, but she makes no such deference to my position, but rather scowls at me.

'What have you done to yourself now?'

'Hello, Aunt,' I counter. 'It's healing,' is all I state, and it seems I'm to escape her wrath. For now.

'That woman is a trial to me.' For a moment, I've no idea who she speaks about, but then see Lady Ealhswith and her children out of the corner of my eye.

'Why are they here?' I question, rather than ask her why she is. She's travelled here very quickly, perhaps, she was already leaving Kingsholm for Lechlade, and has merely redirected her destination.

'She demanded to escort me when she knew I was coming to meet you.'

'And why are you here then, dear aunt?' She stands alone, the rest of the Mercian warriors giving her a wide berth, while behind her, I see horses being tended to after a long journey. 'It doesn't seem you've travelled lightly?'

'No. I've brought what I could with me. Extra food, as you mean to reinforce this place. I've come to aid you,' she offers, as though that's a good enough excuse to risk her inside London.

'And why do I need your aid?'

'Oh, you know. You usually do, and it seems you have a wound,' she offers airily. I narrow my eyes.

'Were you bored within Kingsholm and came for the excitement?' I offer with a glint of iron in my voice.

'Not at all,' but her response is too quickly given. I leave it there. Better to conclude the subject as it is rather than questioning her if it's because she misses Edmund at Kingsholm. The place does feel empty without him.

'You can be put to good use aiding me ensure the walls are reinforced, bladesmiths are found and whatever else we need.'

'Healing supplies,' she immediately castigates. 'For you, Gardulf, Goda and Sæbald.' She misses nothing.

'And those as well,' I agree easily. I might want her at Kingsholm, but if she's here, I can keep a close eye on her. No doubt she means to do the same with me.

'So, you aided King Alfred?' her lips curl. 'And agreed to an alliance with him?' Her tone is haughty.

'I did. He killed one of the enemies. If he hadn't, I could have walked away, but he surprised me.'

'So where is he now? I saw no Wessex warriors.' My aunt is perhaps trying to be conciliatory but she just sounds aggrieved.

'He's supposed to be finding out what's happening with the enemy and then coming to meet me here. He has Pybba with him.'

My aunt looks astounded at this, evidently deciphering my intentions. 'You mean to have Pybba train him as a warrior?'

'I do, yes. King Alfred was lucky with his kill. He almost bloody did for himself first.'

'Poor Pybba,' she muses, taking an offered beaker of water or wine, I don't know which, and drinking deeply.

'And what of Lady Wulfthryth and her sons? Didn't they come to Kingsholm as well?'

'Oh yes, they did. Lady Ealhswith wasn't happy to see them.'

'Where are they now?'

'Lady Wulfthryth requested to remain behind. I mean, I hadn't invited her anyway, but she made it clear her intention was to stay with her sons. She believes Kingsholm is the safest place at the moment.'

'She and Lady Ealhswith are far from allies. Men fight with blades, and women with their even sharper tongues,' I comment, only to receive a slap on my shoulder for my efforts.

'Werburg has set her to tasks to do with preparing healing potions. It's the right time of year to be harvesting roots. The boys are being trained in the arts of swordcraft, alongside young Æthelred.'

'Then you thought to leave him behind for once.'

'I did. Bishop Wærferth's arranging his education. He's ensuring all is well in my absence. Anyway, I like Lady Wulfthryth much more than I do Ealhswith.'

I smirk at this admission.

'What did the poor woman ever do to you?' I joke, but she doesn't smile in return. It seems there are darker truths there that I don't need to know about. 'I'm pleased Bishop Wærferth takes such care of my nephew,' I veer away from my previous comment. 'It seems strange still to name him as my nephew.'

'I'm sure it does,' my aunt huffs softly, but there's sympathy in those words. 'I've always known about you, since your birth. It's a pity your brother didn't think to share his son with us. It would have made much of his premature death easier.' I fall silent at that. Remembering my brother is tinged with mixed emotions. He was always better than me. Better to the people of Kingsholm. Better with the politics of the king's court. Even, I would hazard, more loved in the eyes of my father. For all that, it was never him that I resented, but what he represented. What would he think of me now? He'd bloody laugh, I know that much.

'At least it means I don't need to tie myself to a woman,' I offer instead, arching my eyebrows towards my aunt. She nods quickly, a trace of sorrow on her familiar face. My mother died birthing me. I've never wanted to revisit the same. Such thoughts remind me of Icel. 'Icel,' I begin, but she's shaking her head before I've completed his name.

'It's not for me to tell you anything of Icel. He's your warrior. You can command him, or continue to be curious. It's his life and his to share, if he wishes to do so. Your brother knew less than you do. Think on that, nephew,' she smiles to take the sting from her words.

'Now, I'd welcome some good food and rest. And an explanation as to why you're walking like that. Tomorrow, it seems, there's much work to do. And, as usual, you stink, and aren't fit company for a lady while you sweat and play with your friends.' Her words are censorious but tinged with wry amusement.

'They are my warriors,' I counter.

'They are your friends, and loyal to a fault. Now. Get back to it. We can't have others questioning the abilities of Coelwulf, warrior king of Mercia.' And with that, she stalks from my presence and inside the bishop's complex. I take note of Rudolf, Icel and Hereman, all watching my aunt with varying degrees of trepidation. I wish I could instil that within the bastards.

Chapter Ten

‘Coelwulf,’ Icel wakes me with his gruff shout.

‘What?’ I blink sleep from my eyes and look at him. He’s flush of face and already dressed.

‘Get up, you lazy sod. There are people to see you.’

‘Fuck’s sake,’ I growl, rising stiffly and hunting for my clothes of yesterday.

‘Here,’ he thrusts my trews towards me, and eyes my messy hair aghast, even as he veers aside from my bad breath, which I blow towards him.

‘How long have you bloody been awake?’ I question, yawning around the words.

‘Since before daybreak. There’s much to be done. We can’t all sleep as though there are no enemy to battle.’

I hardly think that a fair fucking assessment, but hold my tongue. We’re used to waking with the daybreak. A roof over our heads is something of a novelty. I’m not sure if I like it, if I’m to be woken by Icel instead of sunlight.

With a swig of water flavoured with mint to sweeten my breath, I stumble into my boots and follow Icel to the main hall, where I anticipate seeing the monks breaking their fast, but am instead greeted with a swell of people.

'The bladesmiths and moneyers,' Icel informs me, pointing to a small group of men, some even wearing their leather aprons to protect their legs from stray sparks, as though they've rushed here mid task.

'The stonemasons,' he directs me towards a slightly larger collection of men with white faces, as though the stone dust is ingrained in them.

'The traders and carters,' is a larger group of men and women, all richly dressed and showing how much profit they make on every transaction.

'And of course, the farmers.' This is the biggest group of all. I see where many have kicked the mud from their boots, although there are still trails of the stuff, and already some of the fastidious monks have directed the servants to clear away the muck with buckets of sloshing water. I'll need to be careful. The wooden floor will be bloody slippery when they've finished.

'Good morning,' I call as the hubbub of conversation drains away. My aunt, I see, is within the hall, as are most of my warriors. I stifle another yawn, blink once more, and settle myself onto the waiting chair before them all. My aunt's to my left. Icel stands behind me, a threat, if one were needed, which I don't think it is. Unless, of course, he means to threaten me to be attentive to these people.

'Good morning,' I start once more.

'Just about,' my aunt offers slyly beneath her breath.

I inhale against that complaint. 'It's good of you to make yourselves available today. I would speak with you all about making London's walls firm, her blades sharp and plentiful, her food abundant, and perhaps grown within the walls, and whatever else we need to set in motion to ensure we can withstand any assault from our enemy.'

'Wessex?' a deep voice calls the question.

'Alas, no, not Wessex. But the Viking raiders. We have word they mean to attack Canterbury. We might soon play host to the archbishop as well. But I hope not. All the same. London must be made as impenetrable as Northampton.'

'Impossible,' a shrill tone calls. I seek out the female voice in the crowd. She's shoved forwards by those close to her. 'London lacks good soil. And the walls have more holes in them than my embroidery.' She laughs raucously. I observe a tall woman with wide shoulders and the stance of a warrior, although I think she must be a farmer from the ingrained mud on one cheek. The thought of her embroidering anything is incongruous. It would be like watching me stitch a tunic. I find I like her already.

'We'll repair the walls,' I confirm first.

'And what of the soil?' she retorts.

'We can bring soil in?' I suggest, looking at the farmers to see if we can do that.

'It'll take much labour,' she counters. 'No one would do so without payment.'

'I didn't suggest people need work without recompense,' I state calmly, aware I need to stop her rejecting everything I say. My appreciation for her is starting to dissipate.

'Where would it come from?' someone else asks, a squat man whose green tunic strains at his overflowing belly.

'That's why you're here. To provide advice on what's needed,' I offer an incline of my head.

'There's good soil to be found to the west of here. We already cart some of it in,' yet another voice suggests. I allow myself to relax. It seems there are solutions, if you ask the correct people.

'We get our wood from there, and it's where the charcoal burners labour as well.'

'Then we need to speak with the charcoal burners,' I turn to Brother Matthew, aware he's here to make notes of what must be done.

'They're a funny lot,' the first woman counters. 'If you go in there with your swords and shields, they'll hide. They can hide better than anyone I've ever met.'

'But there must be someone here who speaks to them. If not, how do you trade with them?'

'That's the task of Egbalth. He's the only one they'll talk to, and he's not here. He's got the hump,' the man who spoke informs me. 'He wasn't included in the summons to present himself before the king of Mercia and he's not happy when slighted.'

'Then, if you'll point us in the right direction, I'll remedy that,' I confirm warmly.

'Grumpy sod won't like that,' another calls. I narrow my eyes.

'So, he doesn't like not being summoned, but he won't like being summoned either.'

'That's the right of it, my lord king. He's a contrary bastard. Not much different to the charcoal burners themselves.'

'Nothing like a bit of reasonable behaviour,' Icel huffs from beside me.

'Does he particularly like anyone here,' I question, 'who could aid us in this?' As I speak, a divide opens up before me. I'm left facing a woman of indeterminate age, who stands, chin raised, entirely bald, but dripping in rich fabrics. Her skin's the colour of autumn chest-nuts, her lips wide and curling with disdain. She has an erect bearing wrapped beneath a fine dress and even better cloak.

'My lord king,' her voice is musical. 'Egbalth is a man of no words. He has no tongue. It was taken from him for some unspecified crime when he was no more than a boy. He speaks to me using his hands. There's nothing wrong with his hearing though.' I nod at this, perplexed why Egbalth is the only one who talks to the charcoal burners. Or rather, communicates with them, if he lacks a tongue.

'He was born in the woodlands. He's one of them,' she offers, determining my thoughts.

'Then I'd welcome your aid,' I confirm. 'Perhaps, you'll escort me after this audience?' I question.

'Perhaps I will,' she muses, and disappears amongst the others between one blink and the next. For all I can see, she might have left the hall altogether.

'And speaking of woodsmiths, we need good timber to repair the gates.'

'We can provide that,' a tall man steps forward, his arms bristling with strength. He holds his hands as though about to chop into a tree. 'We have good oaks, not far from here, but for the gates, you'll need seasoned wood. The only seasoned wood is currently for building Egbalth a new ship. So, maybe ask him if you can use that, and then I can replace what's lost.'

'My thanks,' I call to the ruddy-haired axe-wielder. 'And the bladesmiths,' I turn to those men with bulging forearms to rival Hereman's. 'Do you have the means to make more blades, and to repair those we have?'

An older man bows his head towards me, before meeting my eyes.

'We have the skills, and we also have an agreement with the charcoal makers, but it's only as much as we need to produce what we would normally do. We need more to place London on a war footing, if that's your intention.' I absorb this information.

'It seems in all this that the charcoal burners are the ones who hold all the answers.' There's a smattering of laughter at my rueful tone.

'My lord king,' now a woman presents herself to me, white neck exposed to show a thick rope of twisted beads and shells around it. 'To do all that you suggest, we'd also need to secure a better source of water. The Fleet is far from the walls. The Walbrook isn't always fruitful. The River Thames water is putrid and tastes of ash and feet.' As she speaks a murmur of agreement ripples through those in attendance. 'And cheese,' she adds with a grimace.

'It seems to me,' I muse, loud enough for them all to hear. 'That aside from its walls, London has very little to offer those living within it.'

'That's not the case, my lord king. There's trade and that's profitable. We can buy all we need when there's no war or enemy to threaten us. Admittedly, there are times of hardship. The fish are not always plentiful, and neither are fresh vegetables, but we survive. Most of the time.'

I consider all this. 'We must do more than survive. I'll speak with Egbalth, and communicate with the charcoal burners. With their agreement, we can provide more charcoal, hopefully, and also bring good mud within London. But, where should it be placed? Where's the best place to grow more crops?'

Silence falls. I hold my tongue. I see I've laid a huge task before me. London has its walls, but these people who live within them, have learned to rely on other means to feed their families. The protection of the walls compensates for much that's lacking. I consider why I've never truly realised this before. Perhaps, I've been too busy thinking only of Mercia's survival and the next man to face his death on my blade.

'To the north eastern corner,' a voice finally suggests. 'We don't live there.'

'But that's where the witch lives.' A male voice complains.

'She's no witch, you bloody fools. A woman who lives alone isn't a witch,' a female voice snaps. 'If anything, she's wise to live alone. Men are nothing but empty-headed fools who think only of their cocks.' I grin at that, while my aunt chuckles softly.

'Then, good people, it seems I must speak with a witch and a man who can't speak, and then we'll be able to, hopefully, ensure London can withstand the worst our enemy can launch at us.'

'But what of warriors?' A single voice calls above the more general murmur of agreement and good cheer.

'Mercia has good warriors. She might need more. If there are men here, or youths who wish to become warriors, make them known to my men, or those who serve the bishopric, or the ealdormen.'

'And what of now?' the same voice demands. I can't see who speaks, which frustrates me.

'For now, the king is here, with his fine warriors, and many others beside. I'm here to aid London, and only then to protect the archbishop.'

'And Wessex,' someone interjects before I can conclude. I hold my rapidly evaporating good cheer in place.

'And other Saxons as well as Angles. We're one people,' I inform them, allowing iron to inflect my words. 'If Wessex falls, Mercia will be next. Never forget our borders aren't high walls that deny access. We rely on rivers and the sea. And we must ensure they can't be breached by keeping our enemy from defeating those who share our language, if not our king.' The hall rings with the conviction of my words, but I see I've not won everyone over to my endeavours. I don't blame the people of London. It took me a long time to find any value to an alliance with King Alfred of the West Saxons, but I know I speak the truth.

If I ignore King Alfred, and think of the people of Wessex, I can find conviction for what I've done. I only hope King Alfred does the bloody same.

Chapter Eleven

'So, we go to find Egbalth?' I ask the tall, bald woman. She nods, and goes to stride out. 'But I'd know your name as well, and thank you for your assistance.'

'My name's Cata. I'm pleased to meet you, my lord king.' I'm aware of Icel and Hereman lowering behind me. I'd tell them to stop, but Cata looks entirely unimpressed by them. 'Come. Egbalth's a man of routine. He'll be at the quayside at this time of the day. He likes to hunt out anything that washes ashore with the high tide. He's an interesting creature. Be wary of drawing conclusions from his appearance.' I swallow down any further questions I might have at her direct way of speaking, and set out to follow her. Icel and Hereman remain with me. My aunt's mingling with those men and women of London who are less keen to be about their tasks for the day. I almost wish I could remain with them, but I've set myself an undertaking and I'm not going to shy away from it.

Cata walks quickly, her footsteps sure despite the state of the roads and trackways we follow. Her route to the quayside is quick, and soon we're through the gate that allows easy access to the riverside. The smell of the river is pleasant enough; although I imagine that's because the tide remains reasonably high. Those things left to fester in the wake of the waters retreat have yet to make their presence known.

'Egbalth,' she calls to a squat man sitting with his legs dangling over the wooden quayside, stretching into the water for quite some distance, although the end of it is slowly sinking or being eroded away. I eye it uneasily, and then follow where Cata leads, trying not to worry my foot might sink through the rotting wood if I'm not careful.

Egbalth turns to face Cata, a welcoming smile on his face, revealing a mouth filled with only one or two teeth. The smile drops quickly as he sees me, and he turns aside, evidently agitated.

'I bring King Coelwulf to see you, and to apologise for his oversight in not inviting you to today's meeting.' She inclines her head towards me.

'Indeed,' I struggle for words, not realising I'd be called upon to apologise in person. 'I'm sincerely remorseful for the terrible oversight. Alas. I've not spent much time within London.'

Egbalth doesn't react to even the king of Mercia offering an apology, but Cata holds out her hand, as though ensuring my silence and urging me to be patient. I peer towards the far bank of the River Thames, to Wessex-held land. It seems incongruous that such a small obstacle separates land which is beholden to Wessex and that to Mercia. But then, while the river looks inviting this day, on stormy days, or in the height of winter, with snow on the ground, I know that such a divide seems insurmountable. None would wish to risk swimming in its cold embrace.

'My lord king,' Cata reclaims my attention. I realise Egbalth's stood, or at least, it appears so. He's, perhaps, the shortest man I've ever met, coming up only so far as Icel's waist. His hands are busy. I don't understand what he's doing, but Cata speaks quickly.

'He says it's not unusual to be overlooked. A man such as him, lacking his tongue, is always taken to be devoid of all reasoning.' I almost swallow my own tongue at such a statement. But I'm not needed to reply. Cata continues to speak.

'I know what you want me to do. I will of course, do what I can, for a good price.' Eyes gleam as his hands are busy. I listen with half an ear, more intrigued by Egbalth. Some would say he's been punished to be so small and lack a tongue, but perhaps he's triumphed. Those who are overlooked can often accomplish much, all unseen.

'The charcoal burners are his family. They'll welcome patronage from the king, in exchange for protection from those who would denounce them their way of life, and think to take from them without payment.'

I nod, absorbed by the way Cata can interpret Egbalth's hand actions. I watch carefully, to see if his eyes betray Cata's words, but it seems not. They're a bizarre pair, but again, that must work to their advantage. None would imagine they knew one another so well. None would perhaps even think Egbalth was capable of complex thoughts, with his tongue missing, and his short stature.

'I'll ensure all charcoal burners are protected,' I confirm, but my curiosity gets the better of me.

'Can you tell me who ordered you to lose your tongue? I would punish them, if I could.'

Egbalth's eyes glitter dangerously, and Cata sucks in a sharp breath.

'My lord king, you shouldn't ask such a question.'

But Egbalth nods smartly, and his hands are busy once more.

'He was a small boy, half the height he is now, which admittedly, isn't very tall,' and Cata smiles at the description. 'He was hungry and stole from the bishop's bread oven. Unfortunately, the bishop was in attendance. He demanded the most terrible of punishments.'

'But you were a hungry boy,' I counter, angry to think of such occurring within Mercia. I know it can't have been Bishop Smithwulf who ordered the penance. Egbalth must be my age. It can only have been his predecessor.'

'Egbalth says you need not fear, he took his revenge against the man, when he was able.' Now I allow a slow smile to play on my lips.

'I take it, it was most unpleasant.'

Egbalth nods his head vigorously, his lips split wide with amusement.

'My lord,' Icel says from behind me, but I don't take the admonition.

'As long as you feel you attained justice for this, I confess, I'm pleased. And I'd welcome all you can do to help me with the charcoal burners. We must make London prepared against any attack from our Viking raider enemies.'

At this, Egbalth emits a low growl, his eyes furious.

Cata turns to me, forehead furrowed.

'Egbalth has no love for the Viking raiders either, but that's a story for another day. Now, my lord king. Egbalth will send word to those he knows. They'll come to London in five days' time. Does that suit?' I nod. 'And, of course, you may also have the wood for the gate, I've asked him about that.'

'It does suit, my thanks to you both. If either of you ever have need, come and seek me out. Ask for me, or my aunt, Lady Cyneswith. We'll always help you.'

Cata inclines her head and Egbalth reaches over to grip my hand. I shake his hand, aware of the roughness of his skin, and the firmness of that grip.

'Good day, my lord king,' Cata dismisses me, and I'd be offended, as Icel seems to be, but I'm shaking my head in wonder. For too long, I've thought only of Mercia's warriors, and her warrior enemies. But there are many within Mercia, such as the woodland dweller who aided us last year, who also work to ensure Mercia remains free from her enemy. I need to remember that. Mercia's warriors are the visible image of those who protect Mercia. Her people are the backbone of the creature that keep the warriors fed and it seems, in sharp blades as well.

'Coelwulf, you really shouldn't encourage,' Icel begins, but I speak over him.

'These are my people, Icel. It's for these people we fight our enemy, and it seems, they're working just as hard to aid us, as we are to aid them. We must learn to respect that and offer them our thanks.' A grimace touches his lips, but then he turns it upwards.

'You constantly amaze me, Coelwulf.'

'Why thank you, Icel, that's high praise from you.' He chuckles, but the sound is ominous.

'It is, Coelwulf. I'll be more careful next time. I don't want you to think you're pleasing me with what you do. Now. We need to see about the witch woman.'

'I'm sure she's not a witch,' I counter, my thoughts turning to my aunt. If she weren't the king's aunt, and indeed, a member of an ancient line of ruling Mercians, I'm sure she'd be thought of as a witch with all her healing knowledge.

'We'll see,' he states portentously, as I hurry to keep pace with his long stride, and my uncooperative leg, as the path slopes upwards.

'Have you met a witch before?' I question him.

'That would be telling,' Icel states blandly.

'Yes, it would. It would be telling your bloody king,' I complain.

'Is that a command?' His reply is as reassuring as a wet fart.

I falter, the iron in his voice impossible to ignore. 'No,' I say slowly.

'Good. Now hurry. We need to meet this woman and see what all the fuss is about.'

Chapter Twelve

Icel leads me onwards with his unfailing ability to know where he is. Perhaps, I reason, he does know London well. After all, it's been here for bloody centuries. So, almost as long as Icel has stomped around on this earth, I grin to myself.

'What's so bloody funny?' he questions, catching me.

'Nothing. Just stretching my lips,' I rise my eyebrows as I reply. He continues to watch me, and I fear he'll walk into the jutting stone wall ahead, but once more, with his instinctive ability, he manages to evade it.

'A pity,' I mutter too softly for him to hear. I hope.

As we draw nearer to the eastern corner of the walls, I realise the quantity of lived in dwellings is rapidly diminishing. While Icel seems determined to dismiss the accusation of 'witch' levelled on the woman, others seem less prepared to do so. But, it's also evident that mud and grasses are reclaiming London for themselves. There are fewer pieces of visible road. Indeed, it's so muddy it's boggy with the recent rain. The smell is rich and inviting if I were a cow or ox. For now, it reminds me of the summers I spent toiling for the payment of a few coins, determined to outrun my inheritance. It does mean, I appreciate, that I know surprisingly more about good locations for crops than others might suspect of a man who strides everywhere with a weapons belt glistening with menace.

'Here we are,' Icel stops before a squat building, with no stone evident in its structure. It's well sheltered, almost abutting the stone wall behind it, but with enough of a gap that I can see a huge pig grazing there. I wince. If we startle it, I fear it might crash through the wattle and daub wall and out the other side. I can see how we missed this location on our first inspection. We didn't follow the wall as closely as we could have done. And, at this point, I was distracted by the men and women I met and spoke to while Icel ploughed on ahead.

A column of blue-tinged smoke rises through the rafters. I hear a rhythmic chanting coming from inside. Icel holds out his arm to stop me entering. I had no intention of doing so. Not without being invited within.

'Good day,' Icel lifts his voice to call. It's not a shout. Indeed, it's almost softly spoken for him.

'I'll be with you in a moment,' a surprisingly firm voice replies. Icel nods. I suppress a huff at being made to wait by the witch. Icel offers me a grin, no doubt determining my thoughts. Any moment now, he'll call me an arrogant bastard. I might term him the same.

Instead, I turn my back on the dwelling and survey London from here. I realise this isn't truly the eastern corner, but perhaps more towards the east than the west. There's a slight rise ahead. It shields us from any breeze from the River Thames, and means I can't see the river itself. I would hazard the thought the ground might also be boggy, but perhaps, beneath the piles of soil and mud, the old stone foundations of the abandoned buildings work to keep the ground clear from water.

Aside from the old pig, there are also a handful of goats, standing on a tall pile of discarded hay. I suspect there's either a horse nearby, or more likely, the inhabitants of London think nothing of depositing their shit-stained stable leavings here. I sniff, but I can't smell anything aside from the richness of soil and mud.

'I knew you'd come,' a soft voice says close to my ear. I startle, hand reaching for my seax, as I turn and face a woman, standing tall and straight, with long white hair trailing down her back, and not at all the wizened old crone talk of a witch had me imagining. I release the grip on my seax while Icel laughs softly behind me. Damn the arsehole.

'Good day,' I bow towards her, expecting something similar from her.

'I bow to no king,' she informs me in an arched tone. 'Especially not one such as you.' My mouth drops open in shock, and Icel's deep chuckles continue.

'King Coelwulf, the second of his name, meet Gayadore, the wise woman of London.' I should have realised the bastard knew the woman.

'Well met, Gayadore,' I continue to be my usual pleasant self.

'That remains to be seen,' she mutters, fixing me with a firm gaze. Her eyes are a deep hazelnut shade, as is the colour of her skin. I consider if Cata is a sibling of this woman. Or is it just that they're both confident in their position, and have adopted the same arrogant tilt of their chins.

'Oh,' I expel, unsure what else to say.

'Hello Icel,' Gayadore moves towards the warrior, and they embrace. As I thought, they know one another.

'Well thanks for letting me know I was going to be meeting one of your few friends,' I jibe.

'Oh, we're not friends,' Gayadore is quick to rebuff. 'Alas, I've known him for long enough that I'll account him an acquaintance.' Now I'm smiling, while Icel looks offended.

'I'm a busy woman. Why are you here? I'm not aiding you with any magik potions, if that's what you're after.'

'No,' I quickly reply. 'We hope to bring more crops within

London, to grow. The people say this land is the best but fear you as a, well, as a wisewoman,' I suggest.

'Witch, more like,' she rebuffs my attempts to be polite. 'I know what they say about me. Never fear, my lord king, I act as I do to keep them away from me. Smelly lot.' She states with a glint of amusement on her face, a pointed look towards Icel assuring me she includes him in that.

'So, you'd have no problem with this area being cultivated?'

'No, none at all. You'd have to make sure the fools would eat the food, though. They're a superstitious lot, something to do with ancient spirits and long-dead giants, or some nonsense like that.'

I grin. I'm enjoying Gayadore's dismissal of such concerns, and also Icel's obvious discomfort. It's not often he's not entirely sure of himself. I'd like to ask more questions.

'Perhaps,' and Icel speaks hesitantly. 'We could have the monks come and pray here, assure the people all such spectres are banished and there's nothing to fear from you.' He ends almost on a quivering note as Gayadore fixes him with a dismissive look and shake of her head.

'No. They must fear me, or the work I do to aid them will become suspect. It is,' she directs towards me, 'important for some to fear me. I'm sure Lady Cyneswith would say the same.' I'm astounded she knows the name of my aunt, and now Icel appraises me with delight.

'You know my aunt?'

'Of course. She's a woman who understands much and uses her position well to aid those who need some assistance in healing, or other matters. I would suggest, that if the men fear me, you ensure the women are the ones to tend to the crops and soil. They don't dread me as mortal men do. After all, they're my customers, most of the time.' I swallow down all my questions I'd like to ask because Gayadore has a solution for me.

'I'll see if that can be done,' I confirm.

'And make sure they stay at least twenty horse lengths to my right. If they don't, the soil will slip beneath the surface. There are old holes there. People have been trying to fill then for centuries, but it appears impossible. Somewhere, down there, are the labours of people from a bygone age.'

'And you'll not curse the crops?' Icel asks, but it seems he does so just to regain some equilibrium in this conversation.

'I'll curse them if they need a bloody good cursing,' she arches an eyebrow. 'Otherwise, I'll say what must be said at each stage of the planting, growing and harvesting, to ensure the plants are strong and healthy. Those fools need not know about it. I know how to conduct my own affairs. If they must be under the darkest of nights, then so be it. Now, my lord king, if you'll excuse me from speaking of other matters, I'd warn you against your enemy. They're not to be trusted. They never have been.' Her lips curl as she speaks.

'The Viking raiders have never been my most trusted of enemies.'

Her eyes sparkle at my tone. I think she'll assure me I'm a wise man, and one who knows the personality of their enemy well. Her next words disabuse me of that.

'I speak not of them, damn fool, although they acknowledge a good healer when they see one. I speak of Alfred of Wessex and his damnable ambitions. No matter what, my lord king, he's your enemy, and will remain so, until his death, or yours.'

With my mouth open in shock, she turns her back on me and disappears within her workshop. The door shuts on my stunned face as Icel rounds on me, his expression impossible to read.

'She's not one to shy away from giving such warnings. She's not often bloody wrong, either, more's the problem.' And with that cheery thought resounding in my mind, we walk back towards the bishop's complex, my thoughts turning to Pybba now that Gayadore has mentioned King Alfred. I hope he's well. I really bloody do, or I'll kill him myself. And King Alfred. If he's allowed my warrior to be wounded or captured, I'll have no compunction in severing his head from his body, and placing one of his nephews in his place.

Chapter Thirteen

'Have we heard anything from Pybba?' I question Rudolf as soon as we return to the bishop's complex. He's with Hiltiberht and Haden. I eye the collective men and horses appraisingly as I recover my breath. My leg still pains me, so that walking, while good for it, also makes me sweat when something so simple really shouldn't. My horse seems much recovered even after just a few days within London. I wish I could say the same for myself.

'No. Why? What do you know?' Rudolf demands, worry lacing his words.

'Nothing,' I reply too hastily. His expression is assessing, as he looks to Icel for confirmation. The grumpy bugger shrugs his shoulders and moves away.

'There's a messenger from Archbishop Æthelred,' Hiltiberht offers, rising from where he's inspecting Haden's front hooves. Haden offers me a snarl of his upper lip as though it's my fault Hiltiberht's meddling with his hoof.

'What does it say?'

'No one tells me stuff like that. He's within,' he informs me, jutting his chin towards the hall. I sigh, and with a pat for Haden move my way through the collection of busy monks and servants, as well as warriors and horses. There are a lot of people in a very small space.

'Ah, there you are,' Hereman's eyes alight on me from where he sits supping ale with an individual I don't recognise.

'This is Nothbalth one of the archbishop's messengers.'

'Well met,' I offer, sitting as well, but reaching for the jug I'm sure contains water. I look for my aunt, but she's absent.

'My lord king,' the man sounds aghast at me helping myself.

'He does it all the bloody time,' Hereman offers conversationally, wiping the remnants of the drink from his top lip.

The messenger's glance flickers between the two of us, evidently trying to determine if Hereman speaks the truth or not. I nod, to show he does.

Nothbalth visibly swallows and then inclines his head towards me.

'Archbishop Æthelred sends his thanks for your message. He's as concerned as you suggest he should be, but refuses to leave Canterbury.'

I suppress my sigh of frustration. I can't say I expected him to leave Canterbury undefended and open to the Viking raiders, but it's another thing to hear that confirmed.

'But he does assure you he has many warriors, and has summoned aid from all who owe their oaths to him, the ealdormen and their warriors.'

'And how many warriors does that total?' I question, aware Rudolf's slunk his way inside to listen. He's a nosy arse.

'My lord king?' the man squeaks his reply in surprise.

'How many warriors does the archbishop have? It's not too diffi-cult a question, is it?'

But Nothbalth clearly doesn't know the answer.

'I'm unsure, my lord king. There are those who owe him warriors, and others who owe him foodstuffs. I'm not one of his clerics to have the information to hand.'

This worries me.

'King Alfred has a very small force. It numbers barely in the thousands. To defeat the enemy, which we believe could be much more than that, despite the many we killed and defeated outside Old Sarum, he'll need many, many warriors. A force at least as large, if not larger. I worry he perhaps underestimates the requirements.'

'My lord king, like London, Canterbury has strong walls.'

'Not like these walls,' Icel interjects quickly. I'd glower at him, and ask him how he knows such things, but there'll be time for that when Archbishop Æthelred has been informed of his peril.

'The walls surrounding Canterbury don't include the monastery, only the inner core of the settlement. Those who live outside would need to come within.'

'The walls have been much repaired,' the messenger muses, finally considering what we're saying. 'But, you're correct, my lord,' he inclines his head towards Icel. I bite down on the fact Icel is no lord, for as I've learned recently, the bastard actually is a lord. 'The walls lack the height, and width of London's defences. And, they're not as expansive, either, but they're mounted on an embankment.'

'Can you return to Archbishop Æthelred and inform him of our concerns. Tell him, London's going to begin growing food within its walls, to support it should the enemy come and try to besiege us. We're also encouraging the bladesmiths to have charcoal and iron-stone and bog iron to hand, ready for forging blades and repairing those that are broken. Our offer still holds. He's welcome to come to London. He can bring the people of Canterbury with him as well. But I'd suggest he hurries to make use of the shallows at Laleham Gulls before the water level rises with the winter storms.'

The messenger's pensive, but nods, and bows his head to me.

'My lord king. You speak with wisdom many say you lack. I'll inform the archbishop of all you've said. But, my lord king, you've implied you'll protect Canterbury, alongside King Alfred of Wessex.'

'I have, and I will, but the enemy may well reach that location before us. They might be there now. I suggest it's better to abandon the place than risk dying for it.'

'But my lord king,' the shocked voice of Brother Matthew who welcomed us to London interjects into our conversation. 'Canterbury's the home of Christianity on our island. It's there that the true word of God was first brought amongst the pagan Angles and Saxons.' I suppress a huff of frustration at the interruption. Icel's less reticent.

'That's only what some believe. Others suggest Northumbria was the first to convert, and of course, the Welsh were Christian long before the Saxons and Angles. You don't demand the king defends Northumbria and the bloody Welsh as well, do you?' Icel dismisses with contempt.

Brother Matthew's face shows confusion, his forehead furrowing and then he opens his mouth to argue further.

'We talk of war and the Viking raiders, not of the origins of Christianity,' I state quickly, already bored of the tediousness of a debate that's irrelevant to the current difficulties.

'My lord king,' Nothbalth inclines his head and moves aside, evidently keen to return to Canterbury and his archbishop.

I watch him leave.

'Why do these people never do what I bloody say,' I eventually announce. Icel offers me an appraising look. Rudolf chuckles darkly.

'Because, my lord, they don't know you as well as we bloody do.' I bark a laugh at that. Rudolf's correct. Perhaps, I should do something about that, although not now.

Hiltiberht comes to my side.

'Lord Æthelwulf asks to see you,' he murmurs. I roll my eyes so hard, I swear they risk popping from my face. I can't say Lord Æthelwulf is a welcome addition to the men who are gathering at London. Hopefully, he'll have news of how King Alfred is faring. And more importantly for me, Rudolf and the rest of my warriors, Pybba.

* * *

'Lord Æthelwulf, what a pleasant surprise,' I state, as he comes closer, bowing his head low, even as he tries to appraise the bishop's residence within London. I wince to hear how insincere I sound. I mean, I intended to, but I've not masked my words well. At all.

'My lord,' he mumbles. He's windswept from the breeze outside. No doubt, outside the high walls of London, the wind's more troublesome than within. His boots are muddied by the road, his clothing askew. He seems relieved to have arrived. He must have used the shallows at Laleham Gulls to cross into Mercia from Wessex.

'You bring word from King Alfred?' I ask, but then change my mind. 'First, assure me my warrior, Pybba, is well.'

'Pybba is well, I can guarantee you of that. He's lucky to be well with how he speaks to King Alfred.' I smirk at that, pleased Pybba's being as much of a contrary bastard as he needs to be. I wouldn't expect him to show any deference to King Alfred. He never did to me. Admittedly, I was no king when he taught me in the ways of the warrior. I don't think it would have mattered if I bloody had been. Pybba's a hard bastard, but for good reason.

'And King Alfred?'

'Growing stronger every day,' Lord Æthelwulf answers confidently and arrogantly. I doubt that, but I bite my lip, while Rudolf smirks at the thought, evidently more content now he's heard Pybba is well. Icel's thankfully silent. Sometimes, he does prove himself worthy of being my closest confidant.

'Why are you here?'

'To inform you of developments with the enemy.'

'And they are?' I say when he pauses and offers nothing else. A servant has brought him ale and food. He drinks thirstily although he doesn't eat. I also note his sister has appeared. She hovers within eyeline. I'm curious as to whether she's concerned about her husband, or whether she's just pleased to see her brother.

'Still within Winchester and Wareham.'

'They don't move along the coast?'

'Not by the roads, no.'

'So, they take their ships into the sea?'

'They do yes, heading east.'

'But some remain to hold Winchester and Wareham?'

'They do. They know what happened outside Old Sarum. Those who linger are happier to stay in the settlements they have.'

'And what of the jarls?'

'We've no news of them. It's assumed they remain with their warriors at Winchester and Wareham.'

'So, who leads the ships then?'

Here Lord Æthelwulf shrugs his shoulders, and fixes me with a bewildered look.

'We don't know the answer to that.'

I sigh, wishing I could tell him exactly what I bloody think of him, but taking note of Icel's demeanour, I try not to do so.

'No one has thought to find out?' I ask with barely suppressed impatience.

'How would we do that, my lord?' Now I try not to puff my cheeks out. Does he need me to tell him how to wipe his fucking arse clean?

'By sending someone to ask the question.' I suggest, barely holding onto my fraying anger.

'We suspect it's someone unknown, a new jarl.' Lord Æthelwulf replies quickly. I see his cheeks growing flush. I consider how much he hates being the one to have to tell me of events in Wessex.

'Why would it be a new jarl? Why would someone other than the jarls we know wish to travel to Canterbury? Think about it,' I offer, some heat to my words, but not as much as I'd like to add.

'My lord,' he gasps, as though sudden comprehension has taken hold.

'Really, Lord Æthelwulf, I didn't take you to be a man who lacked wit. Perhaps King Alfred, yes, but not you.' The faint blush grows pinker. I'd like to pretend it was there because of the wind outside London, but that's not the reason.

'And so, you see this is where the problem lies, Lord Æthelwulf. To survive against our enemy, you need to think beyond the end of your nose. The ships are being led by someone. If we knew who that was, we'd know enough to pre-empt what they plan to do next. King Alfred, with his lack of forethought does more to endanger his own kingdom than the Viking raiders do with their blades and violence.'

For a moment, I think Lord Æthelwulf will react angrily, but he nods, perhaps unwillingly.

'You're wiser than any gives you credit for, apparently,' he murmurs.

Twice in one day I've been told the same thing. It's good to know that because I'm a violent bastard, determined to do anything to protect my kingdom, people somehow think it makes me as intelligent as a fucking donkey. They say the same about my language. Do they expect me to be all 'please' and 'thankyous?' I doubt they'd be so worried about it if I were the only thing between them and certain death.

'He might be,' I hear Icel mutter, and fix him with a furious glare. A smirk plays on his lips at that.

'So, assuming that it's *our* jarls making their way along the coast, do we at least have a decent count on the size of the force and when they're likely to make landfall?'

'They were halfway between Southampton and Richborough when I left, so, perhaps even closer now. Richborough is the closest port to Canterbury,' he explains, and I'm grateful for that although not about to admit it. Instead, something else has caught my attention.

'Perhaps?' I question, confused. Lord Æthelwulf's eyes flare with the belief he knows something I don't.

'The wind, my lord. It's been blowing for days. The ships will struggle to make much headway when the wind is against them. The men won't wish to row, I'm sure of it. Not when they'll be so poorly rewarded.'

'Ah, I see,' I murmur. 'Then we may have more time yet to determine what will happen at Canterbury?'

'King Alfred will make it to London soon and can inform you in person of all he's seen of the enemy.'

'And when will that be?' If he's so bloody close, why has Lord Æthelwulf come here?

'By the end of the month.' I consider this. I could continue to tarry within London, waiting for King Alfred to join us. But I can't help thinking it's counterproductive to have Alfred come here. If he's on the southern coast, he's closer to Canterbury than we are. He could reach Canterbury before we do.

'I must return to my king,' Lord Æthelwulf states, although I'm mindful of his interest in the changes being wrought within London. His eyes are everywhere. He's too interested in London, just like his pestilent brother by marriage.

'No, you remain here, with your actual king. We'll send a fast rider to King Alfred and have him redirect his steps to Canterbury, not London.'

'But,' Lord Æthelwulf begins. I look at him then, and really see the man he is.

'Your sister's here, and your niece and nephew. Go and see them. Inform Lady Ealhswith of how her husband fares, and then ensure your warriors are prepared. You must be ready to ride out at a moment's notice in support of your king.'

'But,' he still persists.

'Lord Æthelwulf,' I speak sternly. 'You're a lord of Mercia, it's about time you fucking remembered that.' And without pausing, I stride from his presence, my mind considering all the possibilities.

Outside once more, Icel states what I'm thinking with unerring accuracy. 'A ship army would get rid of the bastards once and for all.'

'It would, yes, but we don't have one sufficiently large to send against the Viking raiders,' I mutter, shuddering at the thought of fighting from a ship. The promise of death in the watery depths would be all too present. And it would either be that, or risk being cut down by the enemy if I didn't wear my heavy byrnie. It would be risk sinking, or swimming, and neither thought is any comfort.

'What do you plan to do?' Rudolf queries instead, as I stand and survey the activity taking place in the courtyard of the bishop's palace.

'We go to Canterbury. I'll order King Alfred to meet us there. We have to tidy up the fucking mess we made,' I state. 'We must return to bloody Wessex, and this time, we know it'll be to face more of the enemy.'

Couldn't Archbishop Æthelred just come to London and then I could remain here as well, but I don't say that out loud.

'Canterbury might not have the defences of Northampton or London, but it should still be possible to defend it.'

My eyes narrow at that. I tilt my head towards him.

'Icel, my old friend, tell me what you're thinking?'

'I could, my lord, but that really would spoil all the fun, wouldn't it,' and with that Icel inclines his head and takes his leave. I watch him go. Now it's Rudolf who knows my thoughts as well as I do.

'Well, from the way he talks, it seems highly possible the Viking raiders might be somewhat overconfident in their attempts to take Canterbury.'

I turn to face him, noticing how his eyes crinkle in amusement.

'Let's bloody hope so,' I echo. 'I really bloody do.'

Chapter Fourteen

I take leave of my aunt two days later. It's taken that long to prepare everything we need, and to ensure the work to keep London secure will continue in my absence. She doesn't try to stop me. I'm pleased she's learned when it's worth fighting me, and when it's not. Lady Ealhswith has already bid me farewell, with all the warmth of a shard of ice down my naked back. I've forced Gardulf to remain in London. He accepted it with as much grace as his father would have done. But my aunt has warned me Gardulf needs more time yet. The wound that he took isn't to be quickly healed. If he's not careful, I was told, he might never fight again. Goda and Sæbald are in a much better condition and so they have insisted on joining us. I've had another messenger sent to King Alfred. One of Kyred's men. Someone he trusts and so I do. Better him than bloody Lord Æthelwulf. The messenger took ship across the River Thames, but we can't risk doing that with such a large force.

'Ensure the work within London progresses,' I charge my aunt. 'Try and be conciliatory where we all know I've failed, and make sure the gates are the priority.'

'I will. You've made some good progress,' she offers, grudgingly. 'In your absence, I will, of course, do more than you've accomplished.' She angles her chin towards me as though challenging me to deny her words.

'Very well,' I offer, biting down on my desire to argue with her. 'Ensure our new friends are treated well. They have a great deal to offer us, and sometimes, their input is more needed than blades and warriors.'

'How wise you've become,' and she dips her head, as I growl from atop Haden.

'Take care of Gardulf,' I reaffirm. My friend's son watches me with twisted lips and the angry stance of someone who'll be on his horse and following me as soon as he's sure I can't stop him. I know that. My aunt knows that. I also know who'll win the coming altercation between the pair of them.

Haden's fractious. It remains windy, the breeze rushing down every available street and bringing with it, dust that makes me blink, as well as the taste of salt on my lips. The wind's truly blowing from the sea towards the west. The autumn's clearly going to be wild this year. I don't welcome that, but, if the wind stops the snow from falling too soon, that would be a bonus, as will it holding the enemy at bay.

'If Archbishop Æthelred comes in my absence, make him and his people welcome,' I offer as an afterthought.

'He won't leave Canterbury,' she muses. I know she's probably correct to say that.

'All the same. And,' I pause, and bend lower to her, 'should King Alfred come here, deny him entry. Send him on his way to Canterbury.'

She nods, grips my forearm as I right myself.

'Stay well,' she urges me. 'It would be just like you to do something stupid and irreversible when the enemy are so determined to make inroads into Wessex.' I grimace and nod. This is our pact. We make it every time I travel to war.

With a clatter of hooves, my aunt steps back, and watches me ride from the bishop's complex towards the gate that even now is being repaired. The sound of men and women moving through the fort building can also be heard. From the gate, we'll cross the River Thames at Laleham Gulls shallows, provided the water's low enough, and if not, we'll return almost to Lechlade in order to find somewhere to cross the River Thames more safely. Icel's suggested we swim it. I've told him he's bloody welcome to try it.

Outside London's walls, I shudder as the cool breeze ruffles my clothes and hair, noting as I do there are people coming in and out of the fort building, which has a new wooden door, and the gates could now be closed thanks to some reinforcement work, but the gaps still need to be properly sealed. There's even a pile of wood I suspect is to block the gaps at the bottom of the gate which Rudolf crawled through. There's a buzz of activity. I pull my hood over my head, and narrow my eyes to prevent even more debris from landing in my eyes.

'Come on men,' I call to them when I'm sure we've left London behind, using the bridge to crest the River Fleet and ridden through the few dwellings still within the market settlement of Lundenwic. 'Let's get this done.' A few groans and complaints greet my words, but the horses are wild to be free from the stables, with the wind in their manes and tails. I can't see this will be a slow passage with the wind pushing us onwards to our destination. It doesn't need to be.

Ealdorman Ælhun, and Kyred, with their warriors, also escort us. They've been to Wessex before. They know what to expect.

Lord Æthelwulf is also with us. He shows far too much enthusiasm at returning to Wessex when I'd initially ordered him to remain at London.

Our journey's accomplished quickly, but not without some protests.

'In the reign of King Wiglaf, I swam the River Thames with my horse on multiple occasions,' Icel's quick to state after a rough's night sleep on the hard ground, forced to lie on everything we own to stop it from blowing away.

'And in the reign of King Coelwulf, the second of his name, we're taking the sensible river crossing,' I retort. He shakes his head, with such an action implying I'm not a true warrior, or even a man. I growl, while Rudolf chuckles, but then his forehead furrows.

'So, it's just for warriors who used to be squires then, all this bloody swimming in rivers?'

I hear Icel's dark chuckle, as I face Rudolf, outrage evident in the pink of his cheeks.

'Yes, because sometimes the only way to get a rest from their constant bitching, is to plunge them into cold water,' I argue. He snaps his mouth shut audibly, but I hear him muttering, even when we make it to the shallows at Laleham Gulls, and begin to cross the river because the water's just about low enough. A rain storm has raised the level of the water at the crossing, according to Icel, but not enough that we need to travel further to reach Lechlade before attempting the crossing.

'We're going to get as bloody wet as if we'd swum,' Rudolf complains, standing in his stirrups so the water doesn't pool over his Jethson's back.

'Did you want to swim the River Thames?' I round on him, trying not to wince at the cold influx of water into my boot. 'I'm sure that can be arranged.'

Icel chuckles, but then, he enjoys shit like this. Hereman's far from happy.

'We could have saved ourselves all the travel if we'd known we were going to get this bastard wet.'

I realise we could have risked taking a ship over the River Thames, but I knew Haden would be a pain in the arse. Still, I'd be drier, I hope, than I am now.

'Stop bloody complaining,' Icel calls, his voice high, as though this is enjoyable. I shiver as Haden makes contact with the bank to the south of the River Thames. I pull my cloak tighter around my shoulders, and wish I was anywhere but here.

'Now what?' Hereman huffs. I wince to see the dark line where water's flooded along his legs, almost to his crotch.

'You should have stood up,' I offer him. He growls, doing so now to peel the cloth away from his legs, only to grimace.

'We could stop in the ale house,' Rudolf suggests, scenting the air like a hound. I smell the promise of warmth. I turn and survey my warriors, and those who are still making their way across the churning water.

'Fine,' I huff, appreciating it's a good idea. If we ride damp, we'll get cold, and probably sore legs and the horses will suffer as well, the leather of their saddles rubbing on their chilled flesh.

'Really?' Rudolf squeaks in surprise.

'Really. Come on. I imagine they'll be surprised to be playing host to the king of Mercia,' I suggest with a smirk for the chaos that will ensue. But of course, there's no fuss at all.

'You again,' the man standing behind a bank of wooden casks nods towards me. I swallow down my surprise at such a response, and then realise the man's looking at Icel, not me at all.

'Indeed, good man,' Icel replies.

'Most sensible men would have waited for the water levels to lower,' he suggests, his accent somewhere between a West Saxon one and a Mercian one. 'You'll be dripping all over the bloody floor now and my wife will complain for a week.'

'The king of Mercia isn't known for being the most sensible of men,' Icel offers, and if the innkeeper's surprised to note me, as Icel jerks his head in my direction, where I stand at his side, he gives no sign.

'Well, I've heard he's a bit headstrong,' he mutters instead, and then calls over his shoulder.

'Wife, get that fire piled high. We've got some damn fools to dry off after crossing the shallows.' A querulous voice emerges from somewhere behind him.

'In this bloody weather? Why didn't they wait, the arseholes.' Now all of my warriors are chuckling, even Hereman who was so damn angry about getting wet. A head pokes from a doorway I've not noticed, bright eyes in a wide face, assessing me. She's some indeterminate age between about thirty summers, and perhaps fifty, grey hairs starting to make themselves seen in her dark hair. She has sharp eyes, as she wipes her hands on an apron tied over her dress.

'Who the bloody hell are you? The damn king?' she asks, raking in my fine clothing, as I stand, dripping onto her precious floor.

Now all of my warriors are laughing, as is the innkeeper, his eyebrows high into his hairline. The woman must sense something is off. She appraises me, and then stamps to her husband's side.

'It is the bloody king, isn't it?' she questions, although there's no deference in her voice.

'Indeed, my lady. I'm the king of Mercia.'

'So, you're the sensible one then. Although, not to be crossing on a day such as this. Didn't they tell you to wait on the other side? The surge only lasts a day after such heavy rain.'

'The sensible one?' I ask instead of answering that.

'Yes, not the damn fool we're saddled with, King Alfred. He's less sense than a day-old foal. Always getting himself into trouble with the Viking raiders. They say he came here not long ago, and I did see some arsehole all done up in glittering tunic and byrnie, but if that was him, then Wessex is bloody doomed. Not like in the days of his grandfather. Now, King Ecgberht might have been an arsehole for other reasons, but at least he knew how to fight.'

More and more of my warriors are entering the hall. Already, the heat has increased and steam hangs in the air from our damp trews. The goodwife watches them all and then shakes her head.

'Well, perhaps you're not the sensible one after all. Now, mind out of my way, or even better, you two lugs,' and she points to Hereman and Rudolf, 'can help me bring in more wood. 'We'll get you warmed up and then we can talk about some food for you as well. Now, don't be serving them the swill from last night,' she directs to her husband, while Hereman looks about to argue, but Rudolf, with a martyred sigh follows the woman outside. Rudolf knows enough to do as he's told.

'I'd do as she says,' the innkeeper suggests. 'Or you'll get nothing but spit in your dinner.'

In the sudden silence that falls, and through which I can hear the goodwife directing Rudolf and Hereman as though errant children, the innkeeper offers me a grin.

'She's a fine woman. Provided you do as you're told, and when you're bloody told to do it.' And with that, he reaches behind him and pulls a round metal pot onto his board. 'Now, I can make you all something hot to drink first, and then she might relent, and let you have ale.'

'My thanks,' I offer, feeling put out the woman thinks so little of our arrival. On any given day, I'd welcome it, but, not today.

I look at Icel. He continues to grin, amusement dancing in his eyes.

'A good woman,' he reiterates, while I grimace and take myself closer to the fire. I consider Hiltiberht, outside tending to Haden. I'd get a warmer welcome from my temperamental mount than I do here. I've half a mind to force my warriors outside once more, but that does seem cruel now the warmth of the fire is beginning to make itself felt. I need it because right now, my wounded thigh is making me limp. At that exact moment, a huge gust of wind ripples through the tavern. I'm not the only one to look upwards as though the roof might take flight.

'Shut that bloody door,' the woman shouts from outside. I've no idea how she even knows it's come open.

Icel hurries to hold the door closed, while the tavernkeeper busies himself with producing something warming for us to drink.

Ealdorman Ælhun and Kyred have found seats and also warm themselves in the glow from the hearth. Rudolf and Hereman call to be allowed within, and Icel opens the door wide, so they can bustle within, accompanied by the woman. As she bends before the fire, she slaps Rudolf's hands aside.

'There's a knack to it,' she remonstrates. Rudolf steps away from here, his hands to either side of him, making it clear he won't interfere any more.

'Tell me,' I ask the tavernkeeper when he brings me a beaker smelling of warm spices, which I cup in my cool hands. 'Has there been any news from Wessex?'

'No, nothing. I'm grateful we don't trade with anyone from Southampton. The last we knew it was impossible to reach the place. The Viking raiders have been sighted everywhere, if you listen to those who come here. There's been a flood of people trying to reach Mercia. They think it'll be safer there.'

'So, no news of your king?'

'None at all.' As he replies, I sense his words faltering, and turn to see Lord Æthelwulf has also entered the tavern. For all his keenness to return to Wessex, he and his men have been the last to cross the River Thames. He looks like he's been up to his neck in the water, and I'm looking forward to the comments he'll receive from the innkeeper's wife for bringing half the River Thames within. 'Ah,' the tavernkeeper's voice trails away.

'You know this man?' I murmur, curious despite myself.

'Yes, a regular visitor. He's always sticking his nose into affairs in Mercia, even though his sister's wed to our king.' In this moment, it's almost as though he's forgotten that I know this. 'We hear things, you know, about his plans. I'd watch him, my lord king.'

'Thank you for the warning,' I reply, while Lord Æthelwulf scowls in my direction.

'Why have we stopped?' he demands.

'To give you time to bloody catch up,' Icel rumbles, saving me from answering.

'It's still days until we reach Canterbury. We need to hurry. If only there was a bloody bridge over the River Thames. There was one, once, you know,' Lord Æthelwulf stamps towards the fire, bringing with him the pong of the river and the reminder of how frigid the water was.

'Get to the door,' the woman shouts, Lord Æthelwulf finally coming into her field of vision.

'Do you know who I am?' Lord Æthelwulf all but shrieks.

'You're not a bloody king,' she retorts, not to be dissuaded, and I suspect, absolutely aware of Lord Æthelwulf's identity. 'You can't be bringing all that water in here.'

'Well,' he huffs, looking to me as though I'll gainsay her.

'You heard what the good woman said,' I state.

As Lord Æthelwulf turns his back and once more stamps his way towards the door, trailing water along the floor, I hear my warriors chuckling. I've no qualms about joining them. He really is a bloody arse.

Chapter Fifteen

'You know,' I turn to Icel the next day, the wind still blowing fiercely and now hindering us as opposed to aiding us. 'It might be a good idea to have a bridge over the River Thames at London. For all Lord Æthelwulf's an arse, he might be right about that.'

'It would make it too easy for the West Saxon bastards to get to London,' he dismisses.

'Yes, but, and hear me out here Icel, it would also solve a small problem for me.'

He looks at me. His forehead would be wrinkled in consternation, but it's covered beneath the hood of his cloak. It's bloody cold. No one's enjoying this trip, not even after our night in the tavern.

'Well, tell me then.' I pause to consider my next words.

'You know King Alfred is desperate to have a toe-hold in London.'

'I do, yes. And it's never to happen.'

'Bloody wait for it,' I comment. 'If we built a bridge, then the Wessex side of the bridge would need protecting, wouldn't it.'

'What?' But he doesn't say anything further. I see him thinking frantically. 'So, you'd agree to build a bridge, and then allow the West Saxons to take control of the bridgehead on the southern bank of the River Thames.'

'That's it,' I announce, smiling broadly, and then regretting it as I cough on a leaf blown into my mouth. 'Bloody hell,' I growl. It's such slow going. It's hard to ride into the wind, let alone be the horses who are being asked to canter at a steady pace all day. At least we've finally finished retracing our steps to the southern bank of the River Thames opposite London. We're now making some progress towards Canterbury. If all we had was ourselves, we could have chanced taking a boat across the expanse, as most people would do. But, with the horses, it's always a risk, and with the wind so bad, it wasn't one worth taking. And, Haden would have been most aggrieved as well.

'Who'd pay to have the bridge built?' Icel queries. I'm delighted he's not dismissing it immediately.

'A joint venture, or just the Mercians?' I question.

'The Mercians,' Icel decides quickly. 'A bridge,' he muses. 'A bloody bridge.'

'What's wrong with a bridge? There's once at Gloucester, and further along the River Severn as well. It means Mercia extends to either side of the River Severn, and the River Trent.'

'A bloody bridge,' Icel continues to marvel. 'Why has no one ever built a bloody bridge before?' Now I understand why he's so astounded.

'Surely, one of your other kings thought of a bridge?'

'No, not that I recall. It was always boats or ships, and the shallows at Laleham Gulls or Lechlade,' and he fixes me with a firm look, despite the wind.

'So, do you think it's a good idea?'

'Who would build it? Who knows how to build it?'

'Well, the people of Gloucester. Maybe some of the Welsh.'

'No,' and Icel's reply is too quick. 'No. That bridge has ancient stone pillars, probably built by the bloody Romans as well. We don't have anything like that at London.'

'Are you sure?'

'Am I sure about that?' he replies hotly.

'Yes. The road, Watling Street as you call it, goes to London, and then it stops. But this road here could be an extension of it.'

'An extension of it?'

'Yes. London has ancient walls. Canterbury has ancient walls. I don't think the bastard Romans could fly over the water. They needed to get from one place to another.'

'Bloody bollocks,' Icel exclaims, still watching me. 'You really do think about things. I'm astonished. All these years, and I've never even considered it. A bloody bridge. Coelwulf, I'm stunned. And yes, why not. A bridge. That would make it easier for us to get about. It might even make it easier to stop the enemy from getting to London.'

'What?' Now I'm the one who's confused.

'We could throw things down at them if they came in ships. We could make the stone struts, because we'll need them to support the weight of the bridge, so narrowly placed together that only the favoured traders can get through. You could have people in ships moored to the struts. It's a bloody brilliant idea.'

I'm taken about.

'Are you taking the piss?' I query, but Icel shakes his head, his lips stretched in a broad smile.

'I assure you, my lord, that I'm truly not taking the piss. Now, all you need to do, is find people who can do it. And get King Alfred to agree to it.'

I sense my good mood evaporating, but I stop myself from worrying about King Alfred too much. 'I think he'll agree to it,' I assert confidently. 'There'll be no marriage with me or anyone within Mercia, and he won't get his claws on Mercian London, but he can be close to London, almost. I'll give him everything he wants, in my own way.'

Icel's continuing to nod. I can tell his comments are genuine.

I lean towards him. 'Honestly,' I question, just to be sure. 'Not even you, the mighty Icel ever considered this before?'

'Absolutely not, my lord. Absolutely bloody not.' And he's still shaking his head in amazement.

* * *

With the weather so spiteful, we see few people as we continue towards Canterbury. I take it as a good sign there are no frightened people streaming towards Mercia.

'We should get there soon,' I assert as we continue our journey two days later.

'We should yes. The wind is certainly helping us,' Icel comments.

'It has to change eventually,' Rudolf interjects. Now we no longer ride towards the east, but instead south, the wind isn't as awful as it has been, but I'm fed up of listening to the constant whine and occasional crash of something heavy falling over nearby. I'd also like to have a nose not quite as red from the constant cold.

'Only when we reach Canterbury,' Icel states. 'Which, won't be much longer now.' His voice rings with conviction. I share a glance with Rudolf. We still don't know about Icel's trip, or trips to Canterbury. I'd like to understand a lot more.

We've seen no sign of Archbishop Æthelred heading for London. That frustrates me, but my aunt was adamant he'd never leave. She's been proven correct in that regard.

'I, for one, will be pleased to get out of the wind,' Kyred calls from nearby. He and his men have been responsible for scouting ahead. Icel's taken himself off once or twice as well, and I've not missed his assessing gaze as he tries to make sense of where he is. I've no idea. I've never been to Canterbury before.

'Are we nearly there?' Rudolf's cry is plaintive.

'By this evening,' Kyred informs. A mild cheer ripples through my warriors. I sense even Haden would welcome being out of the wind. It's been blowing fiercely for days, really weeks, now.

'What will we find when we get there?' I ask Icel.

'Somewhere that's not easy to defend,' he suggests.

'And?'

'And?'

'And what else. When we spoke before, you alluded to something else.'

'Ah, well. We'll have to see, won't we,' he smirks, and then encourages his piebald horse to greater speed. I watch Samson's tail swishing from side to side.

'Do you know?' I question Kyred. 'Have your scouts said anything?'

'No. Nothing at all.' Kyred turns pensive. 'Maybe there's nothing and he just wants to keep morale up.'

'No. Icel doesn't care about morale. There's something else. I'm sure of it.'

'You'll know soon enough, my lord king,' Kyred chuckles, and I realise he's correct. I will know soon enough even if I don't like being kept ignorant.

Chapter Sixteen

'Is that it?' I question, my surprise making it impossible for me to mask my disappointment as Canterbury comes into view before me. The skyline is sporadically dotted with puffs of grey smoke from cookfires, but it's the entire settlement that fills me with disappointment. 'This is the home of Christianity?' I question Icel.

'It is, my lord. For some people. And Archbishop Æthelred is the preeminent holy man on this island.'

'Is he?' I mutter, too astounded to mask my true thoughts.

I look at Rudolf, just ahead of me. We've all reined in, keen to absorb our first view of Canterbury.

'It's not very big.' I mutter.

'It's big enough to cause us problems,' Icel offers darkly.

'The walls aren't very high,' Rudolf continues.

'Not from here they're not. No,' Icel agrees flatly.

'So, what, they're taller close up?'

Icel's grimace assures me they're not.

Beside me, Ealdorman Ælhun's as stupefied as I am. Even Kyred looks suitably unimpressed with Canterbury. Lord Æthelwulf's not joined us. I'm grateful for that. No doubt, he'd try and impress on us how magnificent it all was.

'Bollocks,' I explode softly. Canterbury looks like nothing. It's small. It looks small, at least. And what there is, seems to be mostly church-related. 'Bloody hell,' I continue to murmur. 'Why hasn't the bastard just come to London?'

The fact no one answers my questions assures me they're all thinking the same.

I scratch my neck. The wind has finally stopped being so fierce, and there is, instead, a bright sun overhead making the day uncomfortably warm.

'Come on, my lord,' Icel calls to me. 'Let's get this over and done with.'

I encourage Haden to follow Icel. 'You're not bloody wrong,' I agree. Indeed, all of my warriors mutter uneasily to one another. I feel a tightness in my neck and back. I don't like being within Wessex at the best of times. Now, faced with a settlement that looks as though it's got more holes in its walls than a leaking bucket, I feel all of my enthusiasm drain away. Perhaps, if it weren't for the church, the enemy would be welcome to this place. It would certainly make it easy for us to overwhelm them if they were within.

And yet, as we do draw closer, I'm in for a pleasant surprise, and scowl in Icel's general direction. I can see more now. And yes, some of it is old, perhaps not as aged as Old Sarum, but old all the same, and I also see the walls are built on an embankment serving to push the remains of the walls even higher. From a distance, it looks unimpressive. Up close, it might have some unexpected advantages.

'Perhaps it's not all that bad,' I try to console myself, while Haden rides through a gateway. To the right of me, I see a church, with a curving tower, hidden behind another wall, this one certainly not as tall as the one surrounding us.

'What's that place?'

'The archbishop's church,' Icel states, his voice revealing his frustration with all our questions.

'And there's one outside the walls as well?' I question. 'That's not the archbishop's?'

'Yes, my lord.' His next sigh is audible to me, even here, and I realise why. Archbishop Æthelred has made an appearance. He's all broad smiles, and a beckoning welcome.

'Come within, my lord king. Welcome to Canterbury,' he continues effusively, fixing his gaze on me.

'Well met,' I dismount, handing Haden's reins to Hiltiberht while moving to greet Archbishop Æthelred. He's wearing clothing similar to mine, comfortable for being in the saddle all day, which assures me he's not all about pomp and splendour.

'King Coelwulf, ah, and Lord Æthelwulf.' The archbishop also welcomes Ælhun and Kyred, while a handful of his monks and servants stream outside the walls of the church complex, and quickly start to try and organise the arrival of so many horses and men.

'Come this way, my lords. It will be a bit of a crush if not.' I turn to find Icel in the melee. He remains mounted and offers me a wry grin I can't decipher. Either way, he makes it clear he's not going to join us as we step inside the walls of the church complex and are greeted with what was probably a tranquil spot mere moments ago.

'Welcome, welcome. We had word of your impending arrival. There'll be food for all your men, and horses, at least for today.' We're led towards a long wooden building, with low hanging thatch. Behind it, I realise the church is constructed of stone, but not much else, aside from the walls.

I consider all this while I smile and nod to everything the archbishop says to me. Luckily, Ealdorman Ælhun picks up on cues I miss as I'm assessing where I've brought my men, horses and much of Mercia's warrior strength, under the command of Ealdorman Ælhun and Kyred. My aunt will have to hold London for me, in case of problems.

Canterbury's walls, I admit, are better than I first suspected. Still filled with holes, but quite high up, when the banks and remnants of a once deeply dug ditch are taken into account. What concerns me more is the glimpses I've had of many openings into the walls. London has the main gate, but the majority of the others have been blocked up. There's one that opens onto the quayside, but no others. And, there's also the matter of the fort which does provide a means of getting a good view of any who think to attack. By the time I return to London, I hope the old fort building will be in a fit state to be garrisoned. On first inspection, I don't see a fort forming part of Canterbury's walls, even a decrepit one. Unfortunately.

'Come, come,' Archbishop Æthelred hurries, seemingly excited to have me here. All thoughts of any impending danger from the Viking raiders is far from his mind.

'I'll arrange a tour of Saint Saviour Christ Church. Of course, there are always repairs being undertaken. At the moment, the tower's out of bounds while they fix the roof. One of my men had a nasty scare when part of the thatch blew almost on his head. Admittedly, Father John does like to make a fuss about nothing. Perhaps, on this occasion, he was right to scream his head off until others came to see what was happening.'

I nod, a faint smile on my lips at the image Archbishop Æthelred presents. It's a pity he didn't retreat to London, but perhaps I might forgive him. He's evidently incredibly proud of his church. It must be akin to my love for Kingsholm, although I'm buggered if I'm ever able to spend any time there.

'Here we are,' Archbishop Æthelred sweeps into his hall, little different from my own at Kingsholm, although it does lack the collection of dusty shields and spears affixed to the wall. Instead, there are bright tapestries hanging from equally dusty rafters, and a fierce fire blazing at the centre. It's warm inside, and I shudder, remembering the chill of crossing the River Thames when the water was really too high to risk the fording point.

'Now, I'm grateful you're here. I didn't wish to abandon Canterbury.'

I nod, and settle on a stool close to the fire, allowing the warmth to turn my cheeks pink and to ease the ache in my left leg. It's persistent. Not even my neck wound was as niggling as this. I know it's the cold that causes it. I'll have to consider how I can counter that. Dismounting with a hop to spare my left leg isn't how I intend to spend the rest of my life.

'What reports do you have from King Alfred?' I question, accepting a beaker of water eagerly, and drinking deeply. I can smell sweet herbs in the air and hold out the hope there might be something warm coming soon to sample.

'King Alfred?' Archbishop Æthelred looks at me with furrowed brow.

I catch sight of Lord Æthelwulf hurrying to join us, and wait for him to sit, a slight bob of his head towards the archbishop. I'd welcome even that too-quick obeisance from him. I'm never to receive it. I'm not bloody fool enough to not realise that.

'So, you've heard nothing from King Alfred?' I repeat the question. Archbishop Æthelred's bright enough to understand why.

'No, nothing. Only from you, my lord king.' I watch Lord Æthelwulf's flushing face.

'Wouldn't you expect your brother by marriage to have sent word to Archbishop Æthelred about his findings? He sent you to London,' I query.

'Well, yes,' Lord Æthelwulf's already spluttering. 'But, of course, you've ridden through parts of Wessex that are peaceful. My lord king must evade the Viking raiders.' I manage to hold onto my fraying temper, grateful to see Icel, Rudolf and Hereman have managed to seat themselves within listening distance. I smirk at that, but luckily the movement's hidden beneath my growing beard and moustache. I scratch it while I listen to Lord Æthelwulf.

I turn to Archbishop Æthelred, who listens with a fixed expression on his face.

'Tell me, my lord bishop. Have you heard anything from the local ports or traders? Have they reported any Viking raiders causing difficulties. I've been assured the wind will have delayed the enemy, but still, I'd expect someone to have seen something.'

'In all honesty, my lord king,' and Archbishop Æthelred stresses that added word with a slightly contemptuous glance towards Lord Æthelwulf. 'We've had few traders these last few days. Most people have simply stayed in place rather than face the wind. It's caused damage to many of the homes. At one point, many who live within Canterbury were here, sheltering beneath the roof. It's well protected from the wind with the other buildings surrounding it.'

'Then, at the moment, all we know is that ships have been seen to the south.' I surmise quickly, my thoughts tumbling. My sudden worry for Pybba is pricking at my usually iron resolve. 'We'll need to send scouts south.'

'I'll arrange it,' Lord Æthelwulf states, but I shake my head.

'Perhaps it's best if we send some of the archbishop's men with a Mercian. After all, my warriors won't know the landscape well. If we're to have success in our commitment to protect Canterbury,' at this I incline my head towards Archbishop Æthelred. 'It'll be important to understand exactly where we are in relation to where the enemy are.'

'Perhaps,' Lord Æthelwulf admits grudgingly.

I focus on Archbishop Æthelred and Ealdorman Ælhun rather than Lord Æthelwulf.

'Tell me, my lord bishop, have you seen the ealdorman who rules here recently?' I don't know the man's name. The archbishop will.

'Ealdorman Sigehelm. Alas, not in a few months. He's not often to be found within Canterbury. He prefers to keep to his holdings at Cooling alongside his brothers.'

'Cooling?' I question, because I don't know where that is.

'North from here. Not that far, in all honesty. A day's good travel. Two if they don't wish to push the animals.'

'Back towards London, or more to the east coast?'

'Both,' Archbishop Æthelred suggests, but then shakes his head. 'He'll have a view of the estuary to the River Thames. I'd suggest that's why he's so determined to stay there. If he's heard reports of the enemy, he'll want to ensure they don't go near his holdings.'

'Hum,' I muse, not liking to hear that. 'Another man keen to protect his own possessions, but not the peoples of Kent.'

'Perhaps, my lord king,' Archbishop Æthelred acknowledges in a brittle voice. I'd like to ask him more about that. But as ever, Lord Æthelwulf, the man who can make excuses for anyone, interrupts.

'He's a wealthy man. A good warrior, and he has a young family he'll want to protect, and ambitious brothers who stand at his side. He'll be doing what King Alfred demands from him and them.'

'I doubt that,' I mutter, and then raise my voice. 'How will he know, if King Alfred has sent no instructions since the storm struck? We need to know more,' I feel my legs jiggling beneath where I rest my arms on them. Only the arrival of a warm and fragrant drink stops me from becoming even more agitated.

'Right, as I'm here and King Alfred isn't, I'll make plans, if that's acceptable to you, Archbishop Æthelred. If you continue assessing any damage from the storm and at the same time, I'll ask Icel to take a look at the walls. I assure you he's done the same within London, and he doesn't spare anyone's feelings in giving an honest opinion. And we'll also send four sets of scouts, three to the south of here to find King Alfred, and another to have Ealdorman Sigehelm summoned to Canterbury. We need to know how many men he has loyal to him, and what his abilities to protect Kent amount to. I won't keep him for long. I'm sure he can leave one of his brothers behind to command his warriors,' I speak quickly over any complaint Lord Æthelwulf might have. 'And, I assume he'll obey a summons in the name of Archbishop Æthelred, if I can take that liberty?' I question, but the archbishop's already nodding.

'I can go and find him,' Ealdorman Ælhun offers. 'Like for like, and all that. I'm sure with Kyred here, you'll be protected in my absence.' I nod, pleased with the man's ability to aid me with the tricky situation.

'Of course,' Archbishop Æthelred interjects. 'These lands were once beholden to Mercia. You might be surprised by those keen to return to that status.' As Archbishop Æthelred speaks, I watch Lord

Æthelwulf from the corner of my eye. His lips are twisted in outrage at such a statement. He really is as loyal as a bull in season.

'Then we have our plans for the next day or two. We'll gather together all the information we know and ensure the people of Canterbury are prepared for what might happen. But, Archbishop Æthelred, I'd welcome an assurance from you that should the enemy numbers be too vast for us to even contemplate overwhelming, you'll abandon this place and retreat to Mercia. I understand how important the symbol of Saint Saviour Christ Church is, but equally, buildings can always be repaired or rebuilt. Alas, a man such as yourself can't be easily replaced.' I startle myself with my almost sycophantic comments. I hear hastily stifles chuckles from my men, but I hold my nerve. A slow smile spreads across Archbishop Æthelred's face. He leans towards me, lowering his voice.

'Your aunt does you a disservice when she says you lack all political acumen. And you have my word, on the holy relics buried here, should the attack be catastrophic, I'll order all here to abandon the settlement and seek sanctuary elsewhere. It'll be a terrible day but I'll do it. As you imply, some battles are worth fighting when victory can be guaranteed but not when I'd be sending good Christian men to die on heathen, and admittedly, other Christian blades.'

I nod, pleased with his easy acceptance. I'm sure, if it should come to it, which I bloody hope it doesn't, he'll argue more.

'I would recommend, my lord bishop,' Ealdorman Ælhun comments. 'That you have your relics made portable, if they're so very valuable. We can always take bones in sacks. Not exactly an honourable way for such saints to travel, but better to keep them than leave them for the enemy.'

A flash of surprise crosses Archbishop Æthelred's face but he nods sagely.

'Again, you're correct. I'll instruct some of my most loyal monks to have the relics gathered together, where possible. We must always protect St Augustine and others of his ilk. And of course, the priceless books as well.' Now I startle. Books? Archbishop Æthelred's quick to explain.

'My lord king, they contain knowledge gleamed over centuries, and written in the hands of some of the most eminent scholars this island has ever known. They must also be protected, or we'll fall back into an age without knowledge.' He shudders at even contemplating such an event, and I nod once more.

'Portable is the word, then, my lord bishop. Make everything as portable as possible, and ensure you have good horses and riders you trust. If we have to leave here, we won't all be going the same direction as we'll need to cause confusion amongst the enemy.'

'Of course, my lord king,' Archbishop Æthelred acquiesces. I lean back, the pain in my leg easing as I drink the warm, summer berry-infused drink. It's pleasant.

'But for now,' I incline my head again. 'I think a tour of this fine church would be in order, while we rest from our journey. I think we can afford to take off the rest of the day.' None of us miss the outraged grunt from Icel. But we all decide to bloody ignore it.

Chapter Seventeen

I'm not really the correct man to appreciate an old building, or the shrines for men who've long been dead, but for the sake of Archbishop Æthelred, I pretend to be interested. I force Rudolf to escort me, alongside Ealdorman Ælhun and Kyred. Lord Æthelwulf makes his apologies and hurries away. I watch Icel trail him. He trusts no one. Not that I trust Lord Æthelwulf either. He'll be up to something. We just need to determine what that something is.

'Here,' Archbishop Æthelred leads us through the church, well, it's quite elaborate for a church. There's nothing simple about it. 'Is where we have some of our most valuable silvers in storage.' We've been taken into the depths of the church, beneath the building. It smells of damp, and I also suspect, slowly rotting corpses. That said, Rudolf is all wide-eyed and fascinated. I'm not sure he's paused from asking his near-constant questions. The archbishop is evidently pleased to have such an avid audience. I take the time to speak with Ealdorman Ælhun.

'I'll leave tomorrow,' he informs me. 'I've been assured it's not difficult to find Cooling. I just need to follow one of the roads that leads through the eastern gate and then north.'

'You'll take your men with you,' I order him.

'I would sooner,' he begins, but I'm shaking my head.

'No. You take at least twenty of your warriors with you, on the strongest and fleetest horses. If you discover anything isn't as we believe it, I want to know as soon as possible.'

'My lord king,' he confirms. I'm pleased he doesn't argue with me. Although, I do suspect our often-close association means he's learned when he can and can't reinterpret my instructions to do what he wants. After all, he has more than enough experience of what Icel, Rudolf and Pybba get away with. And, of course, he also knew about Edmund's ability to do exactly as he pleased. I'm a little aggrieved. Perhaps this is how my aunt often feels regarding her instructions to me.

'And you?' he questions, while Rudolf eyes the collection of slightly tarnished silver as though it were the most fabulous thing he's ever seen. I might advise Archbishop Æthelred to check Rudolf's pockets to ensure he's not helped himself to something small and easy to transport. And valuable.

'I'll remain here. I'm concerned for Pybba. I'll rest easier when I know he's well, and that King Alfred is coming this way and not trying to reach London, as we originally agreed.'

'Of course, my lord king. And you'll be staying, here, within Canterbury?' I fix him with a fiery glance and he surprises me by laughing. 'I've instructions from your aunt,' he informs me, holding his hands up as though to ward off blows.

'I just bet you bloody do,' I concede. 'For now, I plan to linger here. I need to ensure Canterbury's protected, and for once, I'm not about to dash around without any idea what the enemy are intending. I trust Gardulf and what he told us. If the plan is to come here, I'll stop them.'

'And here,' I listen to Archbishop Æthelred, nodding as he focuses mostly on Rudolf but with a sly glance towards me to ensure

I'm paying attention. 'Is where one of our most notable saints lies.' I grimace away from the finely carved wooden coffin, trying not to wrinkle my nose at the cloying scent of incense which I'm sure covers something must less pleasant.

'Do you open it often?' Rudolf queries.

'Open it?'

'You know. To make sure he's still holy and all that stuff. I thought saints could only be saints because they were incorruptible,' he stumbles slightly over the word, 'even in death. You know, they don't rot like people who aren't holy, or get eaten by worms.'

'Well, yes, of course that's correct,' Archbishop Æthelred replies quickly, surprised by Rudolf's knowledge and no doubt, his irreverent tone. 'But I don't believe we have a tendency to routinely inspect them to make sure they remain holy once declared holy.'

'Why not?'

'Well, once they're a saint, they remain a saint. We don't strike them from our Daily Offices.'

'Why? It might make it easier to squeeze a new saint in. There's always someone to pray to,' he comments, while I smile at Archbishop Æthelred's perplexed expression. Rudolf does have a way of asking questions no one else ever even considers.

'And then, you'd have room for someone else here. Like you, for instance. In many, many years' time, I mean,' Rudolf's hasty in offering some qualification to his statement. Kyred makes no secret of his amusement, and even I'm laughing aloud.

'Perhaps I should mention it in our Chapter meeting,' Archbishop Æthelred stutters, while Rudolf nods enthusiastically.

'I think you should. It's important to plan these things, or so I understand it.'

I offer the archbishop a wink. He recovers his poise somewhat, but then his forehead furrows.

'Are you suggesting we no longer revere the man responsible for making our island Christian?'

'Well, if he's all rotten, and it smells like he might be, I would think it might be a good idea.'

'He's been dead for hundreds of years.'

'Yes, but if he's only just started to rot, perhaps it's time for someone else to take his spot.'

While the archbishop's face reveals his shock, the rest of us laugh even louder so that Rudolf turns to face us.

'No idea why you're laughing so much, my lord. I think it's time you thought about such things as well. You're not going to want to be buried at Repton, are you, not now you know the enemy have pissed all over the tombs of those earlier kings of Mercia. I mean, it stinks in that crypt as well, but not as bad as here.'

And now I'm chuckling, my eyes streaming with water and even Archbishop Æthelred's stance has relaxed as he joins us.

'My thanks,' I turn to Rudolf. 'I'll certainly give it some thought.'

'I suggest you do, my lord,' Rudolf's all wounded and haughty pride. 'I won't be visiting you any place where the enemy have been, I can bloody assure you of that.' And just like that, my humour evaporates as I truly consider his words.

'Well, we're just have to get my aunt thinking about that,' I murmur, while Rudolf nods almost happily at my changed expression.

'Aye, my lord. She'll know what to do with your bloody heavy bones when this is all over.'

I don't find his words very reassuring. I really bloody don't.

* * *

'I want to go,' Rudolf approaches me the next morning. I've already seen Ealdorman Ælhun on his way. Now I'm organising my warriors to escort some of the men the archbishop's commander think will be good scouts.

'No,' I announce quickly. I knew this would be a problem. But I have men who are good scouts and who can look after themselves if things get nasty. Those men are Oda, Lyfing and Wærwulf. The three of them are arranging themselves and their horses, and trying not to listen to the argument Rudolf and I are about to have in the middle of the stable.

'Pybba's very bloody dear to me,' Rudolf continues. For once, he's not paying much attention to my reaction to his words.

'And he is to me, Rudolf. But I need you, Icel and Hereman here, along with the rest of my warriors. Oda, Lyfing and Wærwulf know what they're doing.'

'And I don't?' he demands angrily.

'Maybe,' I equivocate, watching the men of Canterbury preparing. The stable's very full. Many of the animals are being kept outside, in a corner of the archbishop's grounds that's not given over to growing crops and herbs for treating ailments, or flavouring the pottage. Already, some of the monks have complained about allowing the animals onto consecrated ground. I'm not far from telling them the horse shit is just as much a gift from God as everything else in the garden.

'Rudolf,' Icel's welcome rumble distracts my young friend. 'Stop bloody arguing and let everyone get on with this. The sooner we know, the sooner we'll send you to join Pybba.'

'I,' Rudolf continues to argue, but then stops, his shoulders slumping as he nods unwillingly. 'He better be well is all I'm bloody saying,' he finishes, stalking away with wounded pride. Icel glances at me.

'Why didn't you just let him go and save yourself the argument, and sulking?'

'Because if he found Pybba wounded, or even worse, we all know Rudolf would be inconsolable. We love Pybba, but Rudolf more than most. I didn't want to take the risk.' Icel nods, as though that's acceptable as I turn to Oda, Lyfing and Wærwulf. The three have food enough for a week, but I hope they'll be back much quicker than that. The season's advancing quickly. I'd welcome returning to Mercia for the winter months.

'You know what you need to do?' I question them. The men who'll direct their paths wait outside.

'Seek the enemy, or find Pybba, or better, both of them,' Lyfing replies quickly. He's got possibly the most difficult task of travelling south and then west back towards Winchester and Southampton on the coast road that Icel knew so much about.

'That's it. Don't engage with anyone, unless there's no choice. It's information I crave, not dead warriors.'

'My lord,' Wærwulf bows his head towards me, and Oda follows quickly. The three are eagle-eyed. 'Don't do anything bloody stupid in our absence,' he announces, flashing me a lingering glance, before ducking his head and guiding Cinder outside.

I watch him go, as well as the others, and then turn to Icel.

'Right, let's get this over and done with,' I announce.

'No need, my lord,' Icel replies quickly. 'While you pissed about yesterday, I surveyed the walls and informed the archbishop's men this morning what needed resolving, as well as keeping an eye on Lord Æthelwulf. There are a few gaping holes in the defences, and quite frankly, there are far too many fucking gates.'

'What do you mean to do about the gates?' I question him, striding outside, aware there are people waiting patiently to clean out the horse shit behind us. I imagine they'll be adding it to the herb gardens, no matter the monks complaints.

'Do about the gates?'

'Are we blocking them up?'

'No. But I've asked for a collection of bricks and masonry to be made available if needed. It's to be hoped the ditch and embankment stops them from attacking. I've suggested the scaffolding be put to better use than holding up the roof.'

'Better use than repairing the roof?' I can't deny my voice squeaks as I speak.

'Yes, providing platforms to fight from by the gates. There are no towers and there's no fort. I've also made it clear we won't be protecting the monastery beyond the walls.' Icel's response is remarkably calm.

'Ah yes. Why is that outside the walls?' I ask again.

'No bloody room in here for two sodding churches, is there?' he amuses me by stating. 'And, it means they get to bury the dead who weren't bloody archbishops out there, rather than in here. Keeps the smell down.'

I chuckle, squinting against the bright sunlight. It's cold but bright. Winter isn't far away.

'Show me,' I suggest and together we walk away from the archbishop's complex and into the streets of Canterbury. I look around me. It's all well and good Icel giving me his assessment of the place, but I'd like to consider it as well.

There are streets filled with wattle and daub walled houses, some with turf on the roof, others with thatch. Some are large, some small, and all of them have wide wooden posts outside holding up the walls and the roof. Smoke rises into the air, the scent of good wood burning reinforcing my belief that it's cold today. Small children run hither and thither. A large number of cats have found spaces to spread themselves in the sun, often on roofs, while dogs bark at them. I see the odd scurry of a rat and overhead, there's the raucous cries of birds looking for something to eat as well.

The words these people use are known to me, but roll. There's a thriving bakery along the street we take, the smell of baking bread making my belly grumble even though I've already eaten and from nearby is the clang of a blacksmith and the unmistakable scent of metal being heated. It's a busy place. Not thriving. But busy.

'When did you first come to Canterbury?' I question Icel, while Rudolf follows on behind. Hereman's been distracted by the smell of baking bread. He'll catch us when he's finished in there.

'During the reign of King Wiglaf.' I furrow my brow at that. He doesn't offer anything else, but Rudolf and I have learned to hold our tongues if we want Icel to tell us more of his youth. For Rudolf, it has taught him some patience. For me, it's taught me not to demand answers from him. Icel only offers them when he's well and good.

'I was older than Rudolf. Much younger than you,' Icel adds, walking through a gateway and outside Canterbury, where I see another church and a collection of buildings attached to it. In fact, I realise quickly, there are two churches. Maybe three.

'A man had been murdered, and we brought him here to be buried,' Icel indicates the monastery complex. 'They took him and buried him for only a small payment. It was good of them. After all, he was a stranger.'

'Who murdered him?' Rudolf can't help asking. 'It wasn't you, was it?'

'No, Rudolf, I only murder the enemy. That man was sick and dying anyway. But he might have lived for some years yet, if he hadn't been deceitfully killed.'

'So, why was he murdered?'

'A story for another day,' Icel offers softly, but his assessing gaze unnerves me. Sometimes, I can't help thinking he's testing me. 'But this is it, the monastery outside the walls of Canterbury.'

I turn and look back the way we've come. I'm still perplexed as to why the monastery doesn't benefit from being inside the walls. Instead, they stretch upwards, almost shadowing the collection of lean-to shacks propped up against the wall, also high on the embankment. There's a deep ditch, filled with detritus but not much water.

'It's high,' I agree, assessing it myself. 'But the gateway's wide.'

'It is. One of the main passages in and out of Canterbury,' Icel confirms.

'Who was he?' Rudolf persists in asking, and we both know he's speaking of the murdered man.

'None of your business, Rudolf. Keep your thoughts on what we're here to do.'

'But why was he murdered?'

'By a traitor to Mercia,' Icel rejoins quickly. But if he thinks that's going to stop Rudolf's questions, he's badly underestimated Rudolf's persistence.

'Why was he in Wessex then, if he was Mercian?'

'Did I say he was Mercian?' Icel retorts, the pair of them following in my wake, as I circumnavigate Canterbury's walls, assessing everything I see, somewhat astounded to realise how much of Canterbury isn't within the walls. I'm aware the old market settlement close to London was outside the walls, but that makes sense to me. With the tall walls in the way, the traders couldn't access the river front. Here, there's no such problem.

'No, you didn't,' Rudolf admits unwillingly. I turn as a stone kicks its way past my feet, and see Hereman's found us again. His face is sticky and berry juice drips down his chin, marring his beard.

'How sodding old are you?' Icel complains.

'Bloody delicious,' Hereman ignores him, licking his fingers.

'And where's mine?' I question.

'Ate it. Too good to share. If you'd waited, I wouldn't have had the chance to eat them while I found you. You can only blame your bloody selves.'

I shake my head, considering whether I really needed to eat more.

'You'll be the size of a bull if you eat like that,' Icel comments acerbically.

'Like you then?' Hereman quips, but my attention wavers as I continue to survey Canterbury. Ahead, I've caught sight of Lord Æthelwulf, bending low as he speaks to three men dressed, I suspect, to look like warriors, but lacking the stance of fighting men. I hold up my hand to caution the others.

'What's he up to?' I ask.

'Buggering about,' Icel retorts quickly. But his eyes also narrow. He's as suspicious as I am. 'Yesterday he busied himself walking around but didn't seem to speak to anyone in particular. This looks different.'

'Lord Æthelwulf,' I raise my voice to shout. He startles, turning guilty eyes my way.

'My lord,' he stutters, quickly dismissing the three other men and striding towards me, along the way settling his cloak and striving to lose his guilty countenance. I sense Rudolf skipping away, Hereman as well, but Icel remains with me, growling low in his throat.

'I didn't expect to see you outside the archbishop's complex,' Lord Æthelwulf comments, not quite meeting my eyes.

'Why's that then?' Icel demands.

'Well, you know. Archbishop Æthelred is very demanding.'

'Is he? I hadn't noticed. Who were those three?' I direct my chin to where he was standing when I first saw him.

'Just some of my warriors.'

'Really, they looked like thieves to me,' Icel continues with his sarcastic conciliatory approach.

'What would I have to do with thieves?'

'No idea. That's why I'm asking. I'd also like to know why you've dressed them up as warriors.'

'Well, I never,' Lord Æthelwulf attempts to bluff.

'We'll find out. You may as well tell us,' I ask with smiling menace.

'Well, if you must know. I'm sending them to seek King Alfred.'

'Why, we've already sent scouts. Are you hoping to get to him first? And if you are, why?'

'Of course not. I just thought it better to be doubly certain we find him. We've not heard back from your other messenger. We don't want him going to London, as originally agreed, when you're in Canterbury, do we?'

'A likely story,' Icel muses, the threat palpable in the air.

'They're local. They know the roads well.' Lord Æthelwulf bluffs.

'As do Archbishop Æthelred's men,' I add.

'Yes, of course they do, but well, it pays to trust no one.' I muse on that, as I shake my head and leave Lord Æthelwulf to his business.

Has he just stated he can't be trusted? I've a feeling that might very well be it.

'We need someone to watch him all the time,' I muse to Icel. He nods, and then grins.

'I know just the boy.'

'Boy?' I gasp.

'Yes, my lord. Someone that an arse like Lord Æthelwulf wouldn't even look at because he's so beneath him. A boy. Not a man.'

I grunt in agreement, but I'm not happy about it. Not at all.

Chapter Eighteen

Hiltiberht hops from foot to foot in excitement as Icel lays his new instructions before him. Rudolf looks offended at being overlooked. A quiver of unease threatens to have me refusing to allow Icel's commands. But I close my lips tightly, determined not to voice my fears.

'If there are problems, come to us, immediately,' Icel informs the younger man. 'If you have to beg for forgiveness on being discovered, ensure you name your king and explain, in great detail if it helps, just what Coelwulf will do to anyone who lays a finger on you.'

'Yes, Icel, my lord,' Hiltiberht's so busy bobbing and nodding, his legs jiggling beneath him, he reminds me of a small child, about to piss himself.

'Just be fucking careful,' I glower at my squire, and then I pause, assessing Rudolf's tight face. 'We all know Haden only tolerates you or Rudolf, and Rudolf will kill you himself if you balls this up.' A swift look of fury from Rudolf and then he makes an effort to look less affronted at being overlooked.

'Aye, Hiltiberht, be bloody careful or I'll be cursing you for the rest of your days, or your bloody death.' So spoken, Rudolf stalks from my presence, and while Icel shakes his head muttering, 'bloody youths these days,' I grip Hiltiberht's shoulders with my hands.

'I want a vow from you that you'll not put yourself in unavoidable danger.' He bobs even more, and I drop my hold on his shoulders, for fear of overbalancing.

'Yes, my lord, you have my vow. On my, on my. On Haden's head,' he eventually announces.

'It's hardly set in stone, unlike a promise to God,' Icel mutters, but even I can tell he's trying not to chuckle at the earnest look on young Hiltiberht's face. I swear the boys are getting younger. It's nothing to do with me getting fucking older.

'Now, take this, and remove your tunic. It's too well made. Have this cloak, this tunic, and this seax as opposed to the one your king gave you. Every night, you come and sleep in the stable, close to Haden. We'll seek you there. Other than that, try and keep hidden.'

'I'll cover my hair with mud,' our over enthusiastic young friend announces confidently.

'It'll make you itch when it's dry. Don't do that,' I reject. 'We want you in disguise, not giving yourself away by scratching all the bloody time. People will think you have lice.'

'Do I start now?' he questions.

'Yes. This afternoon follow Lord Æthelwulf. If he's in the arch-bishop's hall, just come to the stable, or watch from a distance. Only shadow him when he's not here. Now, I saw him next to the bakers,' and Icel directs our young man towards Haden's stable to get changed, all the while shaking his head as though regretting his deci-sion now.

'Are you confident about this?' I ask, just because I do feel like making him really consider this outrageous suggestion of sending my young squire to keep an eye on someone who should be my ally. It was one thing to send him to get drunk with the West Saxons at Lechlade. I'm far from convinced at this.

'He'll only be within Canterbury. How much trouble can he get into?'

'Now that, Icel, we both know is a weighted question. A great deal.'

'I'll ensure the others know to look out for him. Hereman can always make an arse of himself and distract any unwanted scrutiny.'

I bite my lip, rubbing my hand through my beard and moustache, before shaking my head from side to side with indecision.

'It's not like you can bloody do it?' he snaps, and also strides from my presence, following Hiltiberht who's already made his escape. Unease prickles down my spine once more. I turn, as though some-one's stood behind me, but there's only me, and no one else aside from the horses. All the same, I'm driven to check all the individual compartments before I accept no one's heard our latest plan. Despite that, I'm uneasy. I wish I'd stayed in London. I really bloody do.

* * *

That night, Icel bends and whispers in my ear while I'm speaking with Archbishop Æthelred.

'Nothing suspicious this afternoon,' he informs me. I offer a smile, and restore my attention to the archbishop.

'All is well?' he asks, eyes tracking from Icel's retreating back to me.

'Yes. Icel's always keen to ensure I know my horse is well before sleep,' I equivocate, aware if my aunt was here, she'd chastise me for lying to the archbishop. I feel no remorse. He doesn't need to under-stand how wary I am of Lord Æthelwulf. I don't think the archbishop would be surprised, but it's best not to reveal the discord in this alliance already.

'Your horse?' Archbishop Æthelred surprises me by asking. 'He serves you well?'

'If you call being a bloody-minded arsehole serving well, then yes. He's feisty. It's thanks to him that we couldn't take a ship over the River Thames. He's not a fan of water. He didn't really even appre-ciate the fording point either.'

'I don't know many horses who love to swim,' he smiles. Like me, the archbishop drinks water, although he insists on it being boiled and then cooled. I'm not sure I appreciate it, but he's spent much of the evening telling me such drives away any foulness from the water. I've not asked why he fears his drinking water so much. It tastes palatable enough when not boiled. It's more refreshing.

Then Archbishop Æthelred turns serious. 'I'm aware you inspected the walls today, and the exterior of Canterbury. Will it be very bad if the enemy come here?'

'For those in the monastery and living outside, it will be terrible. They'll need to come within, or flee so the enemy can't be arsed to follow them. If not, they'll either be killed, or taken for the slave trade. It won't be pretty.'

'Hum,' Archbishop Æthelred muses, unhappily. 'There's some unease between my establishment, and that of the monastery. It might be politic if you visited the abbot.'

'Don't you command in both places?'

'Alas, no. There have been some, let's say, long running difficulties. I must warn you that while there are saints buried within this great church, in the buildings over there are the graves of many archbishops of Canterbury, including Theodore, as well as kings and queens. Should the enemy get their hands on those, it'll be similar to what your young enthusiastic friend mentioned happened at Repton.'

I grunt, the word Repton still reminding me of my temporary captivity there.

'It was besmirched by the enemy,' I confirm, thinking of all the ways I might describe what happened if I wasn't talking to the archbishop. *Fucked it up*, would probably be the most apt description.

'I'll visit with him tomorrow,' I confirm, wishing King Alfred was here to contend with the concerns about bones and bodies. I'm sure it's more his sort of thing with his love of praying.

'My thanks. And now, I'll retire. There are prayers to be observed throughout the night. I'll lead them tonight and into the morning.

You're, obviously, welcome to join me.' I assess the man before me, and then his eyes alight, and he bows swiftly.

'I thought it worth a go.' His words reach me as he departs the hall, leaving me with those of my men who've not been sent about their business. Ealdorman Ælhun's absence is also telling although those of his men who remain are behaving themselves in his absence. A pity my own bastard fools don't care whether I'm here or not.

While they're not drinking heavily, there's a heated game taking place, and the piles of coins to either side of Wulfstan and Rudolf, assure me there's much at stake. I collect my wooden beaker, once more surprised by the choice of tableware the archbishop employs, although perhaps I shouldn't be, and stand beside Hereman.

'What's all this, then?' The large man is watching avidly.

'My money's on Rudolf,' he answers quickly, 'but that Wulfstan's a tricky bastard.'

I shake my head, smiling at the tightness of his words. I swear this means more to him than his own horse. No, perhaps not his horse. Something else. Maybe his nephew.

'What are they doing?'

Now he huffs and flicks a glance my way.

'A game of chance and bluff. You'd expect Rudolf to be the best at it.'

I see there are pieces on a board, but they don't look like *tafl* pieces, or the Norse game.

'What is it they're playing?'

'Like *tafl*, but both of them have the same number of pieces, so it's both easier and much harder to win. Now, my lord, shut up because I'm concentrating.' I take the complaint with good humour, and only moments later, Rudolf growls, as Wulfstan takes the victory. A succession of coins trade hands, amongst other things.

'I didn't realise you lot liked to gamble so much?'

'It's a wager, not a gamble,' Rudolf sulks, stalking from my side to slump in the corner of the hall where some of the Mercians already sleep.

'He's still got the huff, I see,' Icel comments. 'Young Hiltiberht's taken himself to the stables. He says he must be about early tomorrow, because Lord Æthelwulf has an early meeting arranged with someone. He doesn't know who, but he heard the message being delivered.'

'We've an early start as well, my friend. It seems we must an ally of the abbot because he's no friend of the archbishop.'

'These holy men bicker more than women.'

'Surely not?' I counter.

'Yes, my lord. Women bicker. Men or rather warriors, fight, and holy men, well, they throw biblical quotes at one another and generally, get their robes in a tangle.' I chuckle at the image in my mind, and slap him on the shoulder.

'Time for some sleep,' I lift my voice to call the Mercians to order. There are some complaints, but we're not here to indulge as though it were a feast. No. We're here to defeat the enemy. If they ever make it to Canterbury. And in the interim, it seems I've some ruffled feathers to smooth. I doubt the abbot will be as forgiving as Egbalth was in London.

Chapter Nineteen

'Abbot Kynebert' I greet the other man warmly, despite the chill in his small office just off the cloister. The night has been cool, and the first sign of frost has turned the roadway crisp.

'My lord king,' the man mutters. He's younger than I anticipated, perhaps even younger than me. I assumed he'd be older than the archbishop. I was wrong about that. I always think monks and priests should be old wizened men.

Hereman, Icel and Rudolf wait for me outside, not allowed within by the monks, but not prepared to leave me either. We've examined the three churches here. The first is smaller than the second. The second is smaller than the third. I can easily see why there are so many gaps in the walls surrounding Canterbury. They've been put to good use in building these bloody churches. I mean, people only have so many knees to wear down with praying. Surely they can do it in the same place all the time.

'Thank you for welcoming me within your abbey.'

'You took your time,' is his heated reply.

'Alas. I didn't realise the abbey wasn't part of the archbishopric.

That was an oversight on my part, and one I hope to put right now.' He doesn't reply, but I can hear him inaudibly muttering. I already don't like him.

'Why are you here? We're part of Wessex.'

'I understand your concerns,' I decide to attempt a conciliatory approach. 'King Alfred and I have reached an accord to defeat the enemy together. I hope you've been told about that. But we have reason to believe the enemy mean to attack Canterbury.'

'They won't succeed, even if they do come here. Our Lord God will protect us,' he announces arrogantly, chest puffed with pride. I observe him with jaundiced eyes. How does he think to stop them? With his bloody woolen robe?

'What with? Does he have warriors, swords and shields?' I question, mainly because he's annoying the hell out of me. 'And anyway, haven't you heard some of the Norse have converted to the one true and righteous religion of Christianity?'

'Why would they do so?' Abbot Kynebert demands, his eyes alight with horror.

'Doesn't that please you?'

'Why would it please me? Only the virtuous are to be Christians.'

'Not every Norse man and women is an enemy,' I find myself commenting, reminded of young Knut and his grandmother. He's a brave boy, even if he did cause me some problems in Gloucester. In time, I hope he'll fight on behalf of Mercia.

'They're not to be trusted, and not to be taught the one true faith.'

I snap my mouth shut on my immediate denial, and instead return to the task at hand. I can't deny a small frisson of delight that I've instigated this conversion. It might cause me problems, but it's annoying the holy man. That's alright with me.

'If the enemy come, your establishments will be at risk. I've instructed Archbishop Æthelred,' and I don't miss the look of fury on his face at mentioning his close neighbour, 'to have his relics and manuscripts removed to portable sacks or wooden boxes, so they can be rescued quickly should the enemy attack.'

'Well, he would do that, wouldn't he. He has no faith in our Lord God, for all he's the archbishop. Should never have been allowed,' Abbot Kynebert complains. I can tell it's a phrase he often mutters.

'As I said, from my experience, our Lord God isn't likely to send heavenly warriors to protect churches and monks. I'd highly recommend you prepare the same. And, be ready to retreat within Canterbury's walls should the enemy be sighted.'

'We have our own walls,' he retorts, still arrogant, and evidently not enjoying being forced to listen to my advice.

'You do, and I see somewhat liberal use of the masonry from Canterbury's walls has been used to build it. However, your walls lack a ditch and embankment, and most people could hop over the top of them if they were no taller than a donkey's back.'

'We'll remain here,' Abbot Kynebert rejects fiercely.

'Then the Mercians can't promise to protect you. And just to make it clear, by staying here, you're prepared to be sold into slavery and have your relics thrown around without care, and probably burned.'

'Why would they do that if they're Christian?'

I puff my cheeks out in exasperation. He's the worst of all holy men.

'I didn't say they were all Christians, just that some of them might be.'

'Well, if they are, they won't damage a house of God, or they're not really Christians, are they?'

'Maybe not,' I admit unwillingly. 'Still, Christian or not, they'll come armed with seaxes, swords and shields. They'll mean to kill and overwhelm this place, taking control of the most important Christian site on this island. Are you happy for that to happen?'

'Of course I'm not happy for that to happen. I'll send word to my king and demand protection.' I stand at that and incline my head towards him.

'I wish you luck, my lord abbot,' and stride to the door, thinking nothing of allowing the wood to crash shut loudly. I note even these walls have been formed from part of that which surrounds Canterbury, it doesn't take an expert to realise that.

From behind, I hear the abbot's complaints, but I eye my men and urge them to hurry at my side.

'Went well, my lord?' Rudolf quips.

'About as well as shitting yourself in your sleep,' I retort.

'So, what now?' Icel questions.

'I've done what the archbishop asked me to do. The abbot wants bloody King Alfred, not me.'

'Ah,' and now Icel understands my frustration and holds his tongue. But, Hereman was never going to let that one go without a retort.

'Bloody hell. What's that sack of shit going to do? Order them all to pray and hope the enemy doesn't sever their heads from their necks. Fucking arseholes.' His words, hardly softly spoken, ring with great conviction from the surrounding stone walls as I direct our path to where I'm sure we entered the cloisters.

'This way, my lord,' Icel directs me, as I shake my head, confused by where I actually am. He opens another door, and on the other side of it, I see a matching door, opened at the moment, and which gives out onto the path we took to reach here.

'Why are these places so bloody confusing?' I complain.

'If you spent more time within them, you might know the way out,' Icel offers, but I'm aware he spends as little time as me praying.

'We have monks for that shit,' I state, turning to cast a lingering glance over the complex of churches and monks' accommodation. 'If the Viking raiders do come, they won't have a chance.'

'No, they won't. But you've said what needed to be said. The rest is up to them. I assure you, my lord, in my experience, they'll be banging on the gate to gain entry inside Canterbury with just the faintest sniff of one of the enemies. They know what happens to holy men who the Viking raiders don't like, and it isn't pretty. They know what happens to holy men the Viking raiders do like, as well.'

I shake my head and work my anger free.

'Anything from Hiltiberht this morning?' The smell of the bakery has reminded me of another of my men who's doing something that might place him in danger.

'Oh yes, my lord, there certainly is. Lord Æthelwulf met with a man in fine livery. From what Hiltiberht saw and heard, I suspect its someone loyal to this ealdorman Ælhun's gone to communicate with at Cooling.'

'Really?'

'Yes. They spoke of how they'll keep Canterbury safe when the enemy come, and that they don't need, bloody King Coelwulf of Mercia to help them.' I stop abruptly, incensed by Icel's singsong tone as he simulates the conversation, and my experience with the abbot.

'I really fucking wish I'd stayed in London,' I mutter. Hereman grunts his agreement. 'If only King Alfred would hurry up and arrive,' I continue, but I perceive, as do my warriors, that wherever he is, and whatever he's doing, he's not likely to be any help. After all, a man can't become a warrior in a matter of a few bloody weeks. We all know that. There's not a single man here, and I include myself in that, who's not been training to be a warrior since they could hold a bloody wooden stick and bash it against a small, replica shield, while shouting incomprehensibly at the top of his voice.

The thought sparks a memory in me. I close my eyes, and look to Icel. He meets my gaze calmly, not smiling, but not angry either. I blink and look away, the memory fragmenting. And yet, I'm sure there's something there. Who, after all, did hand me my first sword and shield? Despite recollections of my father being ineffectual and unable to fight because of his terrible limp that plagued him, I've always assumed it must have been him. But was it? I breathe deeply, dismiss the idea as I exhale. Here, at Canterbury, with the threat of the enemy attacking at any moment, is no time to be considering my childhood, a period in my life that's lost to me through the drunken haze of my later years when fury drove me from Kingsholm. Perhaps, I realise, I lost a lot more due to that than just recollections of my father.

'We need to know exactly what the bastards are planning,' I muse, kicking a stone in frustration. 'It's always the damn way. If only we knew.'

'Hiltiberht knows what to do, and the rest of the men are alert to any tricks Lord Æthelwulf might be up to. What we need, my lord, is news from Ealdorman Ælhun or our three men you sent south. If we knew where the enemy were, we could act accordingly, or retreat to Mercia.'

I grunt, but I agree with Icel. This not knowing is making my skin itch. It's not like me, not at all, to be worried about the bloody Viking raider enemy. But here, deep within the ancient kingdom of Kent, now part of Wessex, and therefore beholden to King Alfred, I know I'm not the one in control. And I don't fucking like it. Not at all.

Chapter Twenty

'My lord,' a hand on my arm rouses me during the night, and my blade is in hand, before I recognise Rudolf's voice. Luckily, he knows me well, and has a shield before him to keep him protected.

'What the fuck?' I glower.

'Wake. Hurry. Come quietly,' his words thrum with worry, and from years of experience, I bite back all my questions, and simply follow him, as he demands.

He takes me through the archbishop's hall, where I'm convinced the majority of the Mercians still sleep. The archbishop really shouldn't have served pork for last night's meal. The smell makes my eyes water. Outside we walk towards the stables, as I shrug into my cloak to keep the cold air away from my skin, I'm convinced I'll see Hiltiberht there, no doubt with some fresh evidence of Lord Æthelwulf's betrayal. But, it's not Hiltiberht who awaits me. Well, he does, but he's been woken from sleep, hay in his hair as he stands, yawning and blinking in the light from a single candle, which Icel holds to illuminate the figure of Lyfing, one of the men I sent to scout.

I startle on seeing him, and even more when I appreciate his clothing is filthy and blood mars his cheek.

'What the hell?' I question, my voice too loud.

'Shush, my lord. Listen, and ask questions later.'

Hereman's also there, but no one else. There are only six of us, Lyfing, Hiltiberht, me, Icel, Hereman and Rudolf.

'My lord,' Lyfing speaks quickly. His voice is firm. I consider whether it's his blood on his tunic, dark in the candlelight, and then I realise he's alone. Where's the man who went with him?

'I travelled south and then west, using the coast road, along with my ally. He was a good man.' I swallow heavily at that. I don't welcome telling Archbishop Æthelred one of his warriors is dead. 'We were seeking the enemy. I fear to tell you we were set upon by a scouting party.'

'Viking raiders?' I interject.

'My lord, let me speak. It'll be quicker. We were set upon by a scouting party,' Lyfing's words are respectful but firm. I bite my tongue. 'They killed the archbishop's man, but I managed to escape, with both horses, thankfully. They followed me throughout the night, but as the sun rose, they'd not found me. I left the horses in a grove of trees, and sought out those who'd attacked us. And they were the West Saxons. They'd not even asked if we were friends. Arseholes.'

I growl, but give no other sign of my anger.

'I returned to the horses. There'll be time for recrimination when King Alfred arrives, or so I thought. I'd not yet found the enemy, only our alleged allies. I continued to seek the enemy. Travelling further west, following the trail of horse shit left behind by their passage. I saw the enemy in their ships. A lot of ships. They're coming this way. I would say at least fifty ships.'

I look to Rudolf. His eyes are a little glazed. I know he's working out how large the force is.

'About two and half thousand men,' he murmurs, and I notice he doesn't get bollocked for speaking. It's good to see who can and can't offer their thoughts.

'That's a fucking lot of the enemy.'

'It is, my lord. I came straight back to tell you, evading the West Saxon force this time. I didn't think it worth the effort of trying to get King Alfred's attention.'

'My thanks, Lyfing,' I comment, lips twisted in consternation.

'But where will the enemy make landfall?' I muse.

'I don't know the answer to that, my lord. But I'll depart again when it's daylight, and keep track of them. I'd welcome another to escort me,' he states, although I notice his voice cracks with grief as he does so.

'Of course. We'll arrange it.'

I look from Lyfing to Icel to Hereman to Rudolf, and even young Hiltiberht.

'Well, we knew the bastards were coming this way. Now we know they definitely are. And also that King Alfred does intend to come to Canterbury and not London, which is good. Did you see Pybba?' I remember and ask the question.

'No, my lord. I stayed away from them. The bloody fools stab and then ask if they should have done so. They suspect everyone is the enemy.'

'I suppose we should be pleased some of the scouts are capable of killing,' I muse, but I'm not happy about. Not at all. Killing your own allies is a sure way to find yourself alone.

'Cocks,' Lyfing glowers. I fucking agree with him.

'Right. Get some sleep. We'll meet back here at daybreak.'

'Will we, my lord?' Icel questions.

'If someone wakes me, then yes. You know. Some of us do like to get some bloody sleep. We're not all as old as you and needing to piss five times a night.' If Icel's offended by my words, I can't tell. He merely shrugs.

'It won't be that long, my lord, and you'll be doing the bloody same.'

'Bastard,' I huff, turning my back to stalk back into the hall, only to walk straight into one of the bloody posts holding up the stables in the dark.

'Fuck,' I glower, shaking my head to clear my vision.

'My lord,' Hiltiberht's all outraged honour on my behalf, and takes the candle from Icel before hurrying to aid me. The rest of the bastards laugh, but I don't berate them. If I wasn't trying not to cry from the pain, I might think it bloody funny as well.

* * *

I'm awake before it's fully light. I've not actually been back to sleep, my mind too busy playing with all the unknown variables we face.

We know King Alfred's coming. We know the enemy are coming. What we don't know is if King Alfred will arrive before the enemy, or where the enemy plan to come ashore. Canterbury's not a coastal location, but it's not that far from the coast. Neither do I know what Lord Æthelwulf's up to, and I'd like Ealdorman Ælhun to return as well with news about Ealdorman Sigehelm. What news he'll bring will tell me a great deal about my alleged allies.

Grumpy, I stamp through the great hall, wincing again at the terrible smell of so many men's farts, not helped by the hearth fire being brought back to life so the heat makes the stench almost visible.

'Bloody hell,' I complain, taking some pleasure in knowing my loud stamping wakes those who think to sleep. I greet the night guard as I reach the door. Kyred's men incline their heads towards me.

'All quiet, my lord king,' one of them comments. 'Aside from the visitor you know about,' he leans forward to whisper.

'Get some sleep,' I urge them, 'and you have my thanks for taking the worst of the watches.' The men almost preen at my praise. I smirk as I hear their complaints on entering the hall. For men who've spent the night outside in the piercing cold, that aroma is going to be very far from pleasant.

Rudolf hurries to join me, still trying to secure his boots and run at the same time. I shake my head at his antics.

'Just secure them,' I come to an abrupt stop. 'Better than tripping over.' I run my hand over my face. I can feel a bruise has formed on my chin during the sleepless part of the night I've been awaiting daylight. Hopefully, my beard will stop others from seeing it. I wouldn't like to have to explain I gained it from walking into a bloody wooden post.

When we arrive inside the stables, Hiltiberht's already left and Lyfing waits impatiently for me. Icel's also there, as is another man I don't recognise.

'This is Ælfric's replacement.'

'My lord king,' his tone is formal.

'My condolences on your loss,' I murmur. He nods, absorbing the words as though a blow.

'He was a good man.' But he offers nothing else. I swallow, and look from Icel to Lyfing.

'He knows your intentions?'

'Yes, my lord. Now, we should leave.'

'Go then, but be careful. I want no more of these avoidable deaths.' I stutter and manage not to say 'stupid' but it's a close thing.

'My lord,' and the two ride out, ducking below the lintel of the door and emerging into the growing daylight. I turn to Icel. He looks as though he's enjoyed a full night's sleep.

'That looks nasty,' he juts his chin towards me, and I appreciate my bruise can be seen.

'Well, we should all look where we're bloody going, shouldn't we. Let that be a lesson to you all not to let me walk around in the bloody dark again.' I sigh heavily, and fix my men with a frustrated glance as Hereman bumbles through the doorway, lacing his trews and looking like he's half asleep.

'Did I miss it? Bollocks. That pork took it's time exiting the building, as you might say.' I grimace at his graphic description while Rudolf grins.

'Plans for today, my lord?' Icel questions.

'I think two of you should ride out and see if you can waylay

Ealdorman Ælhun. We need to know what he's learned.' Icel makes it clear by looking at Rudolf and Hereman it's a task for them.

'And?'

'And, we wait and see what Hiltiberht discovers today, and if none of the others return during the day, tomorrow, we'll scout south. I must know where the enemy are.'

'You heard him,' Icel again directs to the other two, and I think Hereman might refuse the command but his stance relaxes and he nods.

'I could do with getting away from here,' he murmurs. I mirror that thought.

I feel as though I've been at Canterbury for weeks, not just days. I can't say I find the place appealing, the stink of pervasive dampness never far from my nose.

'Be careful,' I instruct the two as they lead their horses outside.

'Always, my lord. Always,' Hereman retorts. We all know he's talking shit, but I let it go. After all, he's the one riding towards a huge force of the enemy, if they've come ashore since Lyfing last saw them. I don't envy him that task.

Chapter Twenty-One

I regret feeling frustrated with the lack of information very quickly.

'My lord king,' I turn and see Ealdorman Ælhun hailing me from where I'm grooming Haden in the absence of Hiltiberht. He rides through the gateway, and I look for Rudolf and Hereman but fail to see them.

'Ealdorman Ælhun. I take it you're well?' I walk towards him, realising at the last moment I still have the hoof pick in my hand.

'Aye, my lord king,' if he's aghast at finding me doing such a task, he masks it well. He dismounts, hands his horse to one of his waiting men, and walks with me back towards Haden. There's a cool breeze but the sunlight's bright enough I can convince myself it's warmer than it is.

'Tell me, how was Ealdorman Sigehelm?'

'Evasive, my lord king. He's evidently hiding something.'

'Did you learn anything?'

'Perhaps what you already suspect as I saw your young squire hiding behind some casks and listening to a conversation taking place between a man dressed as one of the ealdorman's retainers and Lord Æthelwulf, who looked very furtive.'

'Ah, yes. Hiltiberht's following Lord Æthelwulf around. He's bloody up to something.' We're talking quietly, but there's so much noise from the horses and squires I doubt anyone could hear us unless they were hiding between Haden's four legs, and no one would be fool enough to trust my difficult horse not to crush him with four heavy hooves.

'Ealdorman Sigehelm assures me he answers only to King Alfred, and has no interest in coming to Canterbury or listening to anything 'that bastard' from Mercia might have to say.'

'Charming,' I smirk, pleased to be known as a bastard by a man who might or might not be slightly terrified of me.

'And what do you suspect?'

'He and Lord Æthelwulf are in something up to their ears. Bastard,' Ealdorman Ælhun growls, running his hand through his salt and pepper beard with resignation. 'They'd sooner stab themselves in the foot than accept you might know what you're talking about.' Now I laugh, startling the ealdorman.

'I'm sure there was a time you thought as they did.' He shakes his head, but then nods slowly.

'Perhaps, my lord king, you might be correct there. Now, what of events in my absence?'

'First, where are Rudolf and Hereman?'

'What?' Concern touches his cheeks.

'They left this morning to try and intercept you. Didn't you see them?'

'No, my lord king, I didn't.'

'Bollocks,' I huff, my amusement leaving me immediately. 'What are those fuckers up to?'

'I don't know. We saw no one other than the locals on the road. There wasn't even anyone we suspected of being an enemy.'

'I'm sure you're right. They'll have dashed off to meddle in something. Whatever it is, there's no point worrying about it. They'll come back when they're good and ready. In your absence, one of my men has found both the enemy, in ships, as many as fifty of them, and King Alfred, who it appears, is slowly making his way to Canterbury. But I've not heard from the other two. And,' I lower my voice even more. 'One of the archbishop's men was killed by the West Saxons. My man only just escaped. The stupid arseholes asked no questions, and now we're missing a good fighter.'

Ealdorman Ælhun looks suitably speechless, and then his face darkens.

'That's a huge enemy force.'

'It is, yes. We don't have the numbers to counter that, especially if Lord Æthelwulf and Ealdorman Sigehelm are unlikely to bestir themselves to action. Oh, and I met another charming man, Abbot Kynebert. I didn't know the two religious establishments were separate. He didn't like being excluded, and when I attempted to apologise and inform him of the danger, he assured me his Lord God would protect him from the enemy. So, he's a fucking dead man as soon as the enemy do arrive.'

'Should we not be on the offensive? Take ourselves to meet the enemy?'

'If we knew where they were, then yes. But, as so often the case, they're as restless as a dog on a windy day. Who knows where they mean to come ashore, even if they do intend to do so.'

'Hum. Yes. It's a problem,' Ealdorman Ælhun muses.

'There's time yet,' I try and comfort, aware this is all far from reassuring. 'I'm sure King Alfred will arrive soon and he'll have knowledge of the enemy.' The look Ealdorman Ælhun fixes on me convinces me of his thoughts on that. 'Get some food in you. Have a rest. I'll summon you when Hiltiberht returns. I'm sure between the pair of you, you'll make sense of what Lord Æthelwulf and Ealdorman Sigehelm are involved in. Then, we can at least counter that.'

'Aye, my lord king.' Ealdorman Ælhun leaves me to Haden, who nudges my hand with his long nose.

'I know. I know,' I grumble, but it's better to focus on such a simple task rather than worrying about what exactly's going to happen. Not that I'm alone for long.

'My lord,' Icel's boots materialise before my eyes. I'm unsure what he's been up to since early this morning.

'Icel.'

'I have news.'

'Tell me it then,' I complain, not looking up.

He huffs softly. 'I've been talking to last night's guards.'

'Yes.' I prompt when he doesn't continue speaking. This is more difficult than getting Haden to stand still.

'I suspect someone else left Canterbury last night, heading south.'

Now I do stand, and meet his angry eyes, dropping Haden's hoof at the same time. Beside me, I sense him testing the weight of it.

'Who?'

'Someone under Lord Æthelwulf's command.'

'Bloody hell,' I growl. 'Seeking King Alfred?' I question. Icel shrugs.

'I don't know, my lord. I would suspect it. Or perhaps, something less...welcome than that?'

'What, the enemy?'

'Why else would someone sneak out after dark?'

'Look, I know we don't like the bag of wind, but do we think he'd rather ally with the enemy than me?' The fact Icel doesn't reply, or show any shock at my heated comment, is about as comforting as Haden stamping on my foot.

'Really?' I hiss. 'You think he'd prefer an alliance with fucking Jarl Guthrum or another one of the bastards?'

'I don't know, as I said, my lord. I do think him capable of anything.'

'Why didn't anyone speak up?' I ask, angry that near enough a full day has gone by and this is the first I'm hearing about it.

'They came to me in confidence, bedevilled by the idea.'

'Fucking bollocks,' I exclaim, my eyes looking all around, as though somehow that will give me the answer. And then I see Hiltiberht hurrying towards me, a bloody nose marking him, despite his furtive movements.

'What's all this?' I ask the youth, who's not far from crying. I gentle my tone, as Hiltiberht reaches out to touch Haden, evidently taking some comfort from my petulant mount, who, of course, immediately stills at his touch.

'Who did this?' I ask very softly, already thinking of the joy I'll take beating seven shades of hell into them.

'They saw me, and set upon me.'

'Who?'

'The man in the livery, and the one with him. It wasn't Lord Æthelwulf,' Hiltiberht sniffs, rubbing his sleeve over his nose, both coming away bloody.

'You need to hold it, at the bridge of your nose, here,' and Icel places my squire's hand on his nose, slightly tilting his head back. Hiltiberht's Adam's apple bobs as he holds back his tears. I share an angry glance with Icel. He's furious as well. For a moment, neither of us speak.

'I heard them. They were talking about that ealdorman Ealdorman Ælhun went to see, at Cooling. They were saying everything was in place and King Coelwulf of Mercia wouldn't be causing them problems for much longer. I tried to get closer, to hear exactly what they had planned, my lord, but the wooden bench I was standing on collapsed under my weight, and they came after me. They punched me, and then the baker intervened. He didn't know what it was all about but he told the bastards to fuck off, in no uncertain terms.'

I nod, already considering how I'll reward the man who's saved my squire from a nasty beating.

'You did well, Hiltiberht. Now, take yourself inside. Get some hot food in your belly, and stay with those you know. I don't want you getting caught by anyone else. Your task is at an end.'

'I'm sorry, my lord,' Hiltiberht looks a pathetic figure. I confess, I feel paternal pride take over.

'You did well,' I confirm. 'It was a difficult task. You were the only one who could do it. No need for apologies. If anything, Icel should be saying sorry for placing you in danger.' Icel grunts at those words, and then astounds me.

'The king's right, young man. You shouldn't have been in such peril. Now, do as the king says, and I apologise. I assure you, your nose will stop hurting in a day or two. It'll give you your first battle scar as well. No warrior worth his salt ever had a straight nose.'

Hiltiberht's young face breaks into a grin, and with a final stroke for Haden's nose, he darts to the hall, feet fleeing beneath him, the thought of hot food cheering him.

'Bloody hell,' I huff, wishing I was as young and easily reconciled to getting in a fight.

'Indeed, my lord. Now what do we do?'

'We suspect deceit from everyone, I take it?'

'Yes, aside from Archbishop Æthelred. He at least, is on our side, although, he'd make it a lot easier on us all if he'd just leave bloody Canterbury for London.'

I run my hand through my beard, forgetting the growing bruise, and wince as my fingers touch the delicate flesh. Haden knocks me, and I almost lose my balance on my weaker leg. Icel catches me, and I growl low in my throat.

'I have had fucking enough of this,' I growl. 'We need to know more. We need to know where the enemy are.'

'My lord,' a voice hails me. I turn to see Wærwulf riding into the archbishop's complex, escorted by the archbishop's warrior. 'I bring tidings,' he shouts, directing Cinder to my side.

'I know where the Viking raiders mean to come ashore. There are already ten ships docked there.'

'Ten?' I exclaim, trying to determine if that's an additional ten to the fifty that Lyfing saw, or part of that number.

'Aye, my lord. And they're to the east of here, no more than a day's journey.'

'And?' Wærwulf hesitates and I realise he knows more.

'And, they're already doing so. Half of the ships are held tight, and their men have disembarked. It's our old friend, Jarl Guthrum, who leads them.'

'Did they see you?' I ask quickly.

'No, my lord. But we heard them. They're coming to Canterbury. They're coming, and more of them will follow on behind. Jarl Anwend was named, as was Jarl Halfdan, and a few others I don't know. They intend to take Canterbury, and Archbishop Æthelred as their own.'

'Fuck,' I mutter. Could the day get any worse?

And then it does.

Chapter Twenty-Two

'**M**y lord,' I look up and gasp at the figure before me, brought to my attention by three of Kyred's men. It's evident they know who the bleeding ruin is, half slumped over an equally bloodied horse, almost unrecognisable to me.

'What the?' I explode, and soften my words. 'Pybba, is that you?'

As though summoned, thundering hooves can be heard from nearby. I glance to see Rudolf and Hereman hurrying to my side, not even bothering to dismount, so both horses kick up a spray of mud to land as high up as my mouth. Even Haden shies away.

'What the hell?' Rudolf explodes, seeing Pybba.

'The enemy,' Pybba gasps. It's only his so-familiar eyes that assure me I'm talking to my warrior.

'What of them?'

'They took the king's force by surprise. I fought my way clear.'

'Fuck,' I explode.

'They were told where to find them,' Rudolf spits into the heated silence.

'Hiltiberht,' Icel roars over his shoulder, which brings Ealdorman Ælhun running as well.

'My thanks,' I call to the three men who've brought Pybba to me. 'Please return to your position, but my thanks for allowing Pybba to enter.'

'My lord king,' the lead man bows smartly, a look of unease on his face.

'What happened?' Ealdorman Ælhun demands, while Icel and I try to aid Pybba in dismounting.

'You smell like shit,' Icel grimaces.

'Needs must and all that,' Pybba states with exhaustion.

'I'm sorry, my lord. I was away from King Alfred at the time. I knew I couldn't get him back alone. Instead, I fought through the enemy, and rushed to find you.'

'Pybba, don't apologise,' I berate, my mind working quickly to try and make sense of everything I've been told today.

'I thought the enemy were to the east?' I direct to Wærwulf.

'They are, my lord.'

'But they're also to the south?' this I direct to Pybba, standing between me and Icel, but swaying alarmingly from side to side.

'Get him water,' Icel barks to the still bleeding Hiltiberht, who dashes to do as he's told, while Rudolf rushes to examine Pybba.

'You're too old for this shit,' Rudolf berates, worry making his voice sharper than normal.

'No, he's not,' Icel retorts quickly. 'No one younger than Pybba would have had the stones to come here. They'd have tried to rescue the useless arsehole, and gotten themselves killed in the process. We'd have had no warning, then.'

'Who told the enemy where King Alfred would be?' I direct to Hereman, as we allow Pybba to rest on one of the stools the squires use. I still stand beside him, Icel to the other side. Hiltiberht's given him a beaker of water, but as he tries to swallow, Rudolf's busy patting him down, checking for injuries because Pybba's sheeted in blood.

'Hiltiberht, can you see to the horse, please?' I speak quietly. Brimman's in a terrible state, lame on the back leg, but also bleeding from a cut on his shoulder. His coat is matted with dust and blood, much of it, I fear, from Pybba.

'My lord,' my young squire bows, but when he's upright, he winces.

'Don't do that until your nose doesn't throb,' I scold him, aware Archbishop Æthelred has also been summoned to join us. Kyred dogs his steps. I feel as though all eyes are on me. I need to make decisions. I said I wanted to know where everyone was, and who was involved. Now, I have all my answers but I'm still unsure what the best next step is. And, while I've spoken with Lyfing and Wærwulf, Oda has yet to report in.

'How did they know where to find the king?' I ask Hereman, because Rudolf's entirely consumed with tending to Icel.

'We went to find Ealdorman Ælhun, but instead, we came upon two other fast riders, avoiding Canterbury. We could hear what they were shouting to one another. It's evident they betrayed King Alfred to the enemy.'

'Whose men were they?'

'We don't know that. They evaded us and we came this way to inform you with all speed.' This, Hereman directs to Icel meaningfully. Hereman's not an arse either, to try and solve the problem alone. I'm again grateful for that although it feels as though our position in all this is being squeezed ever tighter from all directions.

'Fucking bollocks,' I growl. 'No one wants us to beat the bastard enemy. There are too many arrogant bastards thinking to benefit from those aggressive fuckers.'

'So, it seems,' Archbishop Æthelred's response is quiet and composed. Silence falls, aside from Rudolf muttering under his breath and Pybba drinking deeply. I'm watching Pybba. He is bloodied, but I'm beginning to suspect his wounds have merely bled a lot, not that he's in mortal danger.

'How far away?'

'A day, at most,' Pybba replies quickly, words edged with exhaustion. 'I rode all night,' he confirms.

'And Wærwulf, those to the east?'

'The same.'

'They mean to join up,' I surmise quickly. 'Both forces. One of them with King Alfred as their prisoner to force the issue and take Canterbury from us.'

'It seems probable, yes.' Wærwulf doesn't shy away from confirming my thoughts.

My heart thuds in my chest, the sound of my breathing is harsh in my ears. I allow a moment, and then another two to compose myself. Then, I turn to Archbishop Æthelred.

'My lord bishop, we're betrayed. Take your monks, and your treasures. And those from Canterbury you can convince to escort you. Follow the road north. I'll send twenty Mercian warriors with you. You must avoid becoming embroiled in this. We'll move outside Canterbury, to the south. We'll intercept them before they can get any closer, I hope, and try to win back King Alfred from their hands. But I'll not shy away from allowing them to keep him if we can't overwhelm them. Ready your men,' I order Kyred and Ealdorman Ælhun. 'Archbishop, I must ask you to leave your warriors behind. They'll hold out against the enemy, should we be overwhelmed.'

'It's to be hoped it won't come to that,' Archbishop Æthelred comments quickly, nodding to show he will obey my instructions.

'Take as many of the people who live here as you can. The fewer left to protect, the easier it'll be for us, should they break through our forces.'

'My lord king,' Archbishop Æthelred bobs his head once more. I'm aware of some of the monks watching, horror on their faces. The archbishop breathes deeply, and then asks the question I hope he won't.

'What of Abbot Kynebert?'

'He won't leave. He said as much.'

'My lord king,' he confirms, and then asks an even more unwelcome question.

'What will you do about King Alfred?'

'What I can, as I said. If he's a prisoner, I can't be confident of rescuing him, but we'll do our best. If not, there are his nephews, I believe, who could rule in his place.'

'They're but children,' Archbishop Æthelred protests, and a horrible thought begins to form in my mind, aided by Lord Æthelwulf's absence.

'Or, of course, there's his brother by marriage.'

'The fucking cock,' Hereman grumbles, and not a single one of us berates him. If Lord Æthelwulf has betrayed his brother by marriage, although how I'm unsure, then Lord Æthelwulf will need to die. He's as far from being a loyal Mercian as I thought possible. If, I accept, it is him trying to direct these matters, and not Ealdorman Sigehelm of Cooling.

'Kyred, your men will follow the road towards the east. I want you to supplement your force with ten of the archbishop's men. They'll know the landscape well. Wærwulf, you'll escort him, as will another five of my warriors. The intention is to stop them. If it's impossible, don't engage them. Withdraw to Canterbury and we'll work together. Ealdorman Ælhun, I want you to remain in Canterbury. I need a man I can trust to try and hold the settlement in the absence of me and the archbishop.'

'My lord king,' he's already trying to argue. I reach across and grip his forearm, stopping him from speaking further.

'Ealdorman Ælhun. You and your men are as loyal to me as those within my warband. I need you to do this for me. But, alas, I'll have to take the vast share of your warriors with me, and another ten of the archbishop's men. If this all goes wrong, you're to retreat to Mercia, with the archbishop. Tell my aunt of what's happened. She'll know what to do.'

Ealdorman Ælhun takes a deep breath, and I'm convinced he's

going to debate with me, but instead he puffs out his cheeks, and nods unwillingly.

'I'll do as you request,' he confirms formally, his unhappiness at the command adequately conveyed.

'Icel, decide who'll go with Kyred. Five of the best. Nasty bastards, if you will, not that any of my warriors aren't vicious, of course.' I nod towards him, and look to Pybba. With the aid of more water, Rudolf's managed to reveal what on Pybba bleeds and what doesn't. He has a nasty wound on his forehead that needs stitching, but it's bled a great deal, and much of the rest of him seems almost intact, aside from a collection of bruises on his chest, and a deep gash on his single, remaining hand.

'You need to stay with Ealdorman Ælhun,' I inform Pybba. 'You've done enough. And if you argue with me, I'll bloody send you with Archbishop Æthelred to London and my aunt,' my voice cracks forcefully. He opens his mouth, and snaps it shut again.

'My lord,' he confirms.

'Now tell me, how many of the enemy were there?'

'At least five hundred. They didn't match King Alfred's force. He had found two of his missing ealdormen, but the enemy were sneaky and knew where to attack him, lying in wait for him while a large part of the force was stretched out behind the West Saxon king. I tried to stop them from endeavouring to save their king, but they didn't heed my orders.'

'And we're sure King Alfred still lives?'

'No, my lord, I'm not. But I heard his shrieks as I evaded the enemy. After these few weeks together, I'd know his feeble cries anywhere.'

'So, at that point, he lived?' I'm keen to ascertain this.

'He did, my lord. Yes.'

'Right. Then our endeavour is to try and get King Alfred back, and also beat back the enemy.'

'Sounds bloody easy,' Hereman grumbles, swaying his hips from side to side, as though to ease back pain.

'Aye, my lord. We've done this sort of shit before,' Rudolf offers with a glint in his eye.

'They won't stand a fucking chance,' Wærwulf comments, but all of those words ring hollow.

I gaze at those loyal to me, and meet Archbishop Æthelred's perplexed and fearful expression.

'This is going to get nasty, quickly. Ensure you've dealt with your worldly affairs. I make no guarantees of success, but if a single one of you fucking dies, I'll hunt you down and bedevil you in Heaven. I bloody swear it.' My words land harshly, jagged stone against stone, reverberating through the space we occupy. Haden gives an answering nicker, giving his voice to the matter, and I don't miss that this time, my warriors all look worried. All of them. Even Icel. And Icel never looks bloody worried. Never.

'Get to it,' I bark. 'We all have our bloody orders.' And with that, I turn to Haden and eye my monstrous horse affectionately.

'And I count you in that. You leave me, and I'll come for you.' Haden's silence assures me he knows exactly what I'm saying. In an assessing glance, he offers me the same. Fuck, I love my horse. He's such a shit, but that doesn't stop me from caring for him. I have to hope, that once more, we live through the crap we must contend with to ensure the future of Mercia, and of course, Wessex.

Chapter Twenty-Three

I cel orders the recovered Sæbald and Goda, Beornstan, Leonath and Cealwin to go with Wærwulf. They're all firm men. I know they'll do what needs to be done. Kyred inclines his head towards me, as he moves with his warriors swiftly outside Canterbury and along the roadway leading towards the east.

The rest of us are quickly on our way as well. We ride light. There's enough food for three days. I don't think we'll need it. We either counter the enemy quickly, or we'll need to fall back to Canterbury, and then, north, towards Mercia. There's been no time to make Canterbury a safe refuge. Archbishop Æthelred, I know, is already busy encouraging everyone to leave with him. Those warriors who'll accompany the archbishop are far from happy about it. They know, as I do, that getting people and their animals to move quickly is going to be fraught with difficulty, even with the threat of a blood-thirsty enemy hunting them down.

Ealdorman Ælhun and Pybba watch us ride out and then have the gateway blocked up tightly behind us. All of the many gates are to be closed as soon as Canterbury's deserted. Abbot Kynebert has been informed of the impending attack by Archbishop Æthelred.

I'm grateful he took responsibility for that. I'd have been more likely to smite the damn arse myself when he refused to heed the warning, sanctimoniously stating his bloody Lord God would keep him safe.

I eye my warriors, wishing I knew where Lyfing and Oda were. I hope they've not been captured by the enemy. I also hope they're not desperately trying to rescue Pybba from the clutches of the Viking raiders when he's within Canterbury, for the time being, safe from the enemy.

'Where will this road take us?' I call to Icel.

'Dover,' is his quick reply. Outside Canterbury, we've quickly passed where the road splits, half of it veering towards the east.

'And that way?' I point towards where my other warriors are going, with Kyred.

'Richborough, my lord.'

'And this is all Watling Street.'

'It is, my lord, yes.'

I absorb that, the temporary distraction doing nothing to ease my worry and fear.

I agreed to an alliance with King Alfred. I consented to work with him to overwhelm the enemy and drive them from our shores. I didn't anticipate I'd once more have to rescue the ineffectual fucker.

Before we left, I asked Pybba about King Alfred's warrior training. His pained expression, for once not caused by Rudolf coating him in a stinking healing salve, told me all I needed to know. King Alfred can't help himself. He won't be able to fight his way out of this. If anything, he's probably trying to reach an accord with the enemy. Perhaps, he'll make an agreement with them, similar to the one his brother by marriage, King Burgred, enacted at Repton before abandoning Mercia to the enemy, and informing the fuckers that I was the only threat they needed to counter. If King Alfred does that, I'll have no compunction in placing one of the two nephews in his position. Or, of taking the whole of Wessex under my command as well. I sense it might be the only way to keep Wessex safe from the enemy. I wouldn't welcome it. I've got more than enough to do keeping Mercia secure.

I gaze along the road heading to Richborough. I see no sign of my Mercian warriors, and they left only a short time before me. Neither do I see the enemy heading this way. I hope it remains that way until I can prevent the Viking raiders surging along the road from Dover.

A cool wind continues to blow. I wish it would turn as wild as earlier in the month, stopping the enemy from using the sails on their ships to travel east around Wessex and Kent, but, of course, to capture King Alfred they've come ashore. The wind will do nothing to help me unless it gets strong enough to blow the fuckers away. I don't even know if that's possible. Perhaps I should have asked Abbot Kynebert. It sounds like the sort of thing God should be able to enact at the snap of one of his ethereal fingers.

My warriors are sullen. I consider lifting their spirits, but in this, it's perhaps better if we all fear what's to come. Then, I hope, we might get a pleasant surprise when we beat the enemy and rescue King Alfred.

King Alfred. I can't help blaming him for all of this. He should have been better. At everything. He just should have been. I wouldn't allow myself to be captured. I just fucking wouldn't, aside from obviously, when I did. Anger drives me onwards, and I appreciate I'll have to combat it if I'm to be successful. Being fucking angry never won a fight. No, skill and precision did that.

Mounted, I test my wounded thigh, wincing slightly as it twinges. I've not had the opportunity to work strength back into it. I'll be relying more on my injured left leg than I'd like, when this gets to face to face combat. I hope my skills will keep me safe. If I die in Wessex, my aunt will be the one to track me down and make my afterlife hell. She'll never forgive me. Fuck, I'll never forgive me. And I really don't wish to be haunted by a vengeful Icel, either. When I reach the afterlife, if I do, I'd hope there'd be less people there to argue with me.

'My lord,' Icel rides close to me, but it's still hard to hear him over the thunder of so many horses' hooves. 'What do you plan to do?'

'Counter the enemy,' I shout back to him.

'But how?'

'I need to know more before I can devise a plan.'

Ahead, Eahric and Osmod are on scouting duty. They're taking it in turns to ride on and then return to me and tell me they've seen nothing yet.

That pleases me. The further we get from Canterbury, the more time we have to stop the enemy from claiming the sanctuary for themselves. I'm perplexed by their decision to take it. It lacks walls that'll keep them safe, and is nowhere near as good a location as Old Sarum, or even Winchester. I realise I might have erred in making Jarl Guthrum a Christian. If I'd not done that, he'd not even know what Canterbury signified. He's certainly not understand the symbolism of what he plans to do.

As I consider all this, I realise Osmod's racing back towards us, and this time, he's accompanied by Lyfing, the archbishop's warrior and Eahric.

'Ahead,' they all shout. 'No more than half a day.' I lift my hand and call a halt to our headlong dash.

'Did they see you?' I question Eahric and Osmod, nodding towards Lyfing and his companion. He offers me a smile but it doesn't touch his eyes as he realises how much of Mercia's strength is behind me, with the jangle of harness and shields.

'No, my lord, no.'

'Lyfing, what can you tell me?'

'They have the majority of the West Saxon force. There are few who weren't captured. Those who remain free follow on behind, dogging their steps and occasionally, trying to forge a path through to King Alfred which usually ends in more dead men added to the trail the enemy are leaving behind them. The two Wessex ealdormen seem determined to rescue their king, even though they have fuck all idea how to go about it successfully.'

'King Alfred lives?' I clarify quickly, surveying where we are. Icel's taken Samson forwards, but I listen to the report from my warriors.

'He did this morning. I saw him with my own eyes,' Lyfing asserts. 'Where's Pybba? I've not seen him with King Alfred.'

'He escaped and made it to Canterbury. That's why we're here.' Swift relief covers the other warrior's face. I consider if he was thinking of trying to rescue Pybba. I hope not.

'Where's everyone else? Ealdorman Ælhun?'

'The ealdorman will hold Canterbury. Archbishop Æthelred's evacuating it. Wærwulf and Kyred have taken the road to Richborough.'

'Another force?' Lyfing surmises quickly. I nod unhappily. 'Fucking bollocks,' he explodes, and I grunt my unease.

'Do you have suggestions?'

'Not really no. This land isn't filled with places we could use to ambush them,' Lyfing complains. I glance at Icel. He's surveying the landscape as well, his expression pensive.

'What now?' Lyfing asks the question I'm not yet prepared to answer.

I move towards Icel, seeing what he does. There's a band of smoke on the horizon, evidently caused by the Viking raiders on the move. The road we're following stretches onwards towards where I assume the coast is. I see nowhere we can hide from the enemy, and no slope that might give us a tactical advantage. Nothing.

'We either return to Canterbury, or at least where the road splits towards Richborough, or we use one of the small valleys,' I summarise. Icel nods, unwillingly.

'We do, my lord. This is a mess,' he mutters. 'A great big bloody mess. And all the fault of the fucking Wessex king. Again,' I hear him expel more softly. I don't know what that means, but don't question him.

'There must be something else,' I growl, but there really isn't. I look once more at the smoke rising into the air close to the horizon, and then turn back to face Icel. I have an idea, but it's shit. And I don't want to do it. But perhaps there was only ever going to be one way to counter this.

'I want you to take half of the men back to join Wærwulf.'

'No, my lord,' Icel immediately denies.

'Yes, Icel. I'll keep half of them. We'll show our faces. Taunt them, until they hurry to catch us.'

'And then what? You risking being fucking captured.'

'Then, you and Wærwulf, and Ealdorman Ælhun make the road secure and we fight them there. Ensure we can make it through whatever blockage you employ.'

'No, my lord,' Icel repeats, his words already ringing with resignation.

'Jarl Guthrum will only be taunted by me. He knows who I am.'

'He knows who I am as well.'

'Yes, but he's not going to bloody chase you, is he?'

'And what if he captures you?'

'He won't,' I announce arrogantly.

'But if he does?'

'Then leave me. Return to Mercia. Protect it.'

'No, my lord, I can't do that.'

'You have to. I'm ordering it.'

Icel winces, a slight movement but I know him too well not to notice it.

'It's very fucking foolish.'

'It is yes. And if you can, I want you to send a quarter of the warriors to join up with the West Saxons to the rear.'

'That's even more dangerous,' he complains.

'It is, yes. Send Hereman, and whoever else is as half cracked as he is. If I'm captured, they'll know to come and get me, no matter what.'

'There must be another way,' Icel huffs, blowing out his cheeks.

'I'm all ears, Icel. Tell me what else we could do.'

'Fuck it all off and go to Mercia, together. Then we could force the enemy out of Canterbury and Wessex.'

'With what army of warriors? Half the West Saxons have no loyalty to their own king, let alone to me.'

'Coelwulf, there has to be another way.' The fact he uses my name is worrying. It speaks to his desperation. It hardly fills me with confidence in my decision.

'But I can't determine what that is, and why we're arguing, the fuckers are just getting closer.'

'Fucking bollocks,' and in that, I know Icel agrees with me. 'You can have Rudolf,' he adds. 'I can't have him asking all those bloody infuriating questions of his.'

'And you can contend with Pybba,' I barter.

'I'd forgotten about him,' Icel complains.

'And I'll also have Ordheah, Ingwald, Eadfrith, Ælfgar and Hemming. You take the rest with you.'

'As you wish, my lord,' but Icel brings Samson close to Haden. The two horses show no sign of unease with one another. A surprise in itself. Perhaps, then, they sense what's at stake here. 'If something happens to you, my lord, your aunt will string me up by my stones and not let me down until you make some sort of miraculous return. So, my lord king, Coelwulf, you better not fucking let me down, or I'll come after you. I promise you that.'

I smile, despite the unease permeating every part of my body at Icel's unwilling acceptance of my ploy. I reach out and grip his forearm, holding his gaze with my unflinching one.

'Icel, you're a good man. I'm sure my aunt will forgive you, in time, but I promise you, I've no plans on being captured like fucking King Alfred. I'd never live with the shame.' Icel nods, and then grips my forearm as well.

'And we'd make very fucking sure you never forgot it, either.'

Chapter Twenty-Four

Rudolf's full of questions, as my small band of warriors continues south. Ordheah, Ingwald, Eadfrith, Ælfgar and Hemming don't speak, perhaps content Rudolf will ask all the questions they have on their behalf.

'So, we're facing the enemy alone?'

I glance behind me, along the horse-shit splattered road. It does feel as though we're very alone, I don't deny that. Even though we still have half of the main force with us as well. With Icel gone, Hereman as well, and even Pybba missing, I'm strangely bereft. It reminds me Edmund's not here, or Gardulf. I really have stretched my resources thin in an effort to hold true to my alliance with King Alfred. I already know he wouldn't do the same. He has no idea of the honour a man who's beholden to his people should have running through him. I mean, he has no idea about most things, but most especially that.

'Well, I have you,' I retort.

'But,' Rudolf starts, only to think better of it.

'So, we're to entice them back towards the others?' This perhaps makes more sense to him.

'We are, yes. They'll be keen to have two kings as their captives.'

'But you're not going to get captured?' I know where his thoughts have taken him.

'I assure you, I've no plans on being captured. That would do no one any bloody good.'

'Why have you chosen us to aid you?'

'You all have fast horses, as do the others with us.'

'Bollocks,' Rudolf expels slowly. 'You think they'll have horses?'

'No doubt, they have King Alfred's horses. I assume, even as slow as his progress was, that he wasn't walking to Canterbury from Old Sarum.'

'And Hereman's to attack them from the rear?'

'He's to ensure the enemy don't think to leave anyone behind. We want all of them to crash against our combined forces outside Canterbury.'

'And how will we rescue King Alfred?'

'Fuck knows. That's the part of the plan I still haven't worked out,' I offer confidently. 'So, we'll see what happens.'

'See what bloody happens?' Rudolf muses, warily. 'And this 'what happens' won't involve me in a river or facing the enemy alone?'

'How do I know? We'll show them our arses if we must, but we have to get them to come this way. And, preferably before they can join with the other force at Richborough.'

'So, you're hoping Icel and Wærwulf will already have encountered that half of the enemy?'

'In my wildest dreams, yes, I do. But I'm rarely that fucking lucky.'

'I think,' Rudolf starts only to snap his mouth shut. If he's going to say I'm lucky, he's changed his mind.

'Best not to think about it too much,' I offer. His lack of response, has me turning to gaze at him. We've slowed our pace, to try and give everyone else the chance to get where they need to go. I'm not at all convinced Hereman will get far as he attempts to lead some of my warriors by a circuitous route to join up with those of King Alfred's who've not yet been captured, but maybe he won't need to get far. After all, if everything happens as I hope it will, which I already strongly doubt, he needs only get so far and then come to find the road when he hears the great big fucking fight taking place. I hope he'll also find Oda. I'm concerned about my missing scout.

'Aye, my lord,' Rudolf agrees unwillingly. Hemming's close to Rudolf. I imagine the two youngsters are the most worried.

Ælfgar, Ingwald, Ordheah and Eadfrith are older men. While they might not want to risk injury and death, they can be confident they have the element of experience to aid them. Rudolf and Hemming have learned fast, and they're good. I don't know if they're the best they'll ever be, but I do hope they live to become grumpy old bastards like the other four.

The thunder of horse's hooves fills my senses, even though we're moving at a slower pace. I'm forced to reconsider the wisdom of what I have planned. Icel's correct. If my aunt were here, she'd not allow this. She'd think nothing of abandoning King Alfred to his fate. I should perhaps do the same. Maybe we should open a dialogue, offer the enemy something in exchange for having King Alfred returned as opposed to thinking we can overwhelm a much larger force with so few Mercians.

But, fuck it. I'm not one to make treaties. The one with Jarl Guthrum has hardly bathed me in glory. And, it's brought this about. No. We need to stamp on the enemy as hard as we did outside Northampton. We need them to leave the shores of this island, and consider never, ever returning. But King Alfred has royally fucked that up. Again, I'm astounded by him, I really fucking am.

'My lord,' Rudolf recalls me to the here and now, and not a moment too soon. We're close now, the scent of smoke rippling through the air, and not from someone's hearth fire. The enemy are burning as they go, a battle tactic I've never truly understood. The harvest will be in grain stores by now. If they burn those, they'll have nothing to eat come the cold weather, and neither will the people they hope to have control over. They'll all fucking starve just because they're incapable of considering whether burning everything is a good idea or not.

Ahead, there are five enemy scouts, shimmering beneath the afternoon sun, ensuring we know their shields and spears are to hand. They're not mounted, which does surprise me. I'm sure scouts should be mounted. I feel my forehead furrow. Perhaps, then, they're not scouts after all. As I watch, more and more of the enemy join those five men, with their shields before them.

'The shields all have different emblems on them,' Rudolf comments quickly. 'The raven, the wolf, the owl with a winged dove, the boar and something else. Fuck, it might be a bloody cross.'

I nod. I'm not surprised by this. I'm stunned the enemy aren't mounted. My own force has come to a halt in a jangle of iron and wood, snorts from the horses, and gasps of dismay from the Mercians. I don't turn to look at them. I don't want them to see my face. I might give away some of my concern and that's not what these men need to see right now.

'That means Jarl Guthrum has King Alfred,' I confirm, unsure who the rest of the jarls might be, but sure we'll discover their identity soon enough.

'It does, yes,' Rudolf agrees. Ælfgar's moved forward to the other side of me. Poppy, his horse, is quiet beneath him. Indeed, all of the horses are placid. None of them shows any sign of unease. Not even the smoke is upsetting them. I wish I was as calm as them.

'Once we've seen King Alfred,' I inform my warriors, 'we retreat.'

'Fast?'

'Making sure they keep up,' I state confidently.

'So, you're going to show your face as well, so Jarl Guthrum knows you're here.'

'I think he'll know that anyway,' I mutter. 'He knows as well as I do that no other fucker will bestir themselves for King Alfred and Wessex, not even Wessex itself.'

There's a divide between us, which makes me squint against the bright light. Rudolf and Hemming can see better than I can. I watch the force swell around those five shield holders. I'm sure Rudolf's quickly trying to work out how many of the bastards there are, but my focus is on what's happening behind them. I wish I could see more. I'd like to see the part of the Wessex force that hasn't been captured. I'd like to know where the bloody horses are, because at the moment, the enemy are only on foot. But, like me, the enemy are on a slight rise. While my force is arranged behind me, the bastard foemen are only showing as many of the force as can be seen from my position.

There are many things I'd like to know right now, including how I'm going to beat the fuckers. But, of course, I'm not to get those answers. Until I do, and then I really wish I hadn't been trying to work out where the horses were.

It's the rattle of harness that gives the mounted enemy force away. Despite thinking there was nowhere to hide, the bastards have found somewhere.

My head swivels at the sound that comes from behind and not in front. My eyes narrow. My focus has been wrenched away from the enemy shields, even though I've not yet seen King Alfred. Even before I can make sense of everything, I'm turning Haden quickly, kicking his wide sides to do my bidding.

'Retreat,' I roar. 'They're hiding behind the hedgerows.'

Rudolf and Hemming are quick to do as I command, but the others all waste precious time, as though doubting my words. I'm halfway through the line of Mercian mounted warriors before I hear most of them encouraging their horses to follow. I bend low over Haden's neck. I don't want to leave my warriors to face the coming attack, but Icel's words ring loudly in my ear, and he's correct. I can't be captured. If I'm apprehended then the Viking raider jarls will have accomplished far too much and far too easily. As much as I've placed myself in danger, it was to taunt the enemy, not to be fucking imprisoned.

'Retreat,' I roar, slapping the backsides of those horses only slowly turning as I emerge through the end of the line of mounted Mercian warriors.

I feel as though we've not long separated from Icel, but half a day has gone by. We have a good distance to travel to meet up with Icel, Kyred and the others, and we've been caught unaware. I should have realised the crafty bastards would have the horses, rather than worrying about where they were.

'Come on,' I bellow, listening for the sound of an impromptu attack taking place behind me, and grateful when it doesn't come. Instead, there's the din of hooves over stone. Rudolf streams ahead, Hemming close to him. Where my other four men are, I'm unsure. Perhaps, they, unlike me, protect the rear to ensure the enemy don't pick off my men one by one.

I hear the outraged cries of the Viking raiders, just, over the drumming of the horse's hooves. I risk looking behind me, confident Haden will strive to keep pace with Rudolf's new mount, Jethson. It's good he doesn't still ride Dever. Dever would never have been able to keep up such a fast pace.

What I see is reassuring, but also comprises of only a small proportion of my force. I have to hope the others are doing as well as the sweating horses, and confident riders, I can see.

'I should have fucking realised,' I rage, and then dismiss it. I can't dwell on my mistake. I must only concentrate on what will come now.

I saw a huge force of enemy warriors. They weren't mounted. I don't know how many do have horses. I should have questioned Pybba more carefully to discover how exactly King Alfred was seized. If I'd known the enemy only had a few on horseback, I could have made a different decision. Again, I dismiss it quickly. I must focus on what I now know.

The enemy force is likely split between those on horseback and those who must walk the same distance. That means, provided we manage to join up with Icel's roadblock ahead, we'll face a smaller force before a larger one. That doubles our chances of success. Better to face a split force, and triumph over it, than have to encounter them all in one go.

I keep my head down, straining to hear anything that should concern me, but there's just thundering hooves and nothing else.

The speed of our passage is so fast I'm forced to squint to shield my eyes from the dust of our earlier journey, still lingering in the air. I don't worry about Haden. I know he can maintain such a speed for a long time. I'm aware Rudolf is going faster than us. He keeps up a good pace, Haden striving to overtake Jethson. I'd find it amusing if I wasn't so focused on what we need to achieve.

I consider if Icel will have had time to forge the blockage we need. If Hereman has even taken his leave in an effort to reach the remnants of the Wessex force. I'd not realised how near the enemy were. I should have paid more attention when Icel spoke of how close Dover was to us, and of how near Richborough also was.

'Ware,' Rudolf's bellow rouses me from my thoughts, and from the tension of keeping my seat even when my left thigh is screaming in agony from clinging onto Haden's sides.

'What the fuck?' I glower. My head comes up, my eyes disbelieving everything I'm seeing, but perhaps, I should have anticipated this all along. I knew I was being deceived. I didn't realise who by. I really should have known, as ahead, stretched across the small roadway, with high hedgerows to either side making it impossible for us to go around the bastards, is a force I didn't want to see, but one which proudly displays the emblem of both Wessex and Mercia, with the bastard, Lord Æthelwulf, grinning broadly at me, and with other men at his side, men I don't know but who I suspect are led by Kent's ealdorman, Sigehelm. What have the arseholes fucking done?

Chapter Twenty-Five

'I don't have time for this shit,' I glower, refusing to accept it.

'Faster,' I call to Rudolf. His shocked eyes round on me, but he nods, and encourages Jethson to greater speed. The road's blocked between the two tall hedgerows, lacking much of their summer ripeness but impenetrable despite that. We'll have to go through the fuckers.

'My lord,' Lord Æthelwulf's gloating cry reaches me, but I lower my head, assessing the chances of this fool-hardly approach being successful.

'Faster,' I bellow, lifting my arm to encourage my warriors. The horses aren't going to like this. I'm not going to bloody like it, but I'm not going to allow Lord Æthelwulf and his traitor allies to better me. Not here. Not ever.

'Come on, boy,' I encourage my horse while ahead, Lord Æthelwulf and the man I assume is Ealdorman Sigehelm seem entirely oblivious to what I'm planning, waiting in the road way, shield holders before them, while they remain mounted. They must be working with the enemy, I'm sure of it. Was capturing King Alfred a rouse they agreed with the Viking raider jarls? Is King Alfred even in danger? Did Pybba escape because he was supposed to? I don't have time for such thoughts, but they rattle through my head, more regularly than Haden's increasing speed. My horse doesn't even falter, as ahead, Rudolf's the first to encourage Jethson through the shield holders.

The realisation we're not going to stop our headlong dash comes all at once. I see Lord Æthelwulf's mouth drop open in shock, the shield holders hurrying to evade us. Some of them almost make it, but it's impossible. They've wedged themselves in between two high hedgerows, almost denuded of leaves, but the branches remain tightly packed. They're jammed more tightly than onions in a jar of brine, and those at the back have no idea what's happening at the front.

I consider removing my seax and taking a quick swipe at Lord Æthelwulf, but don't risk it as Haden bunches his back legs and soars over the shield holders at the front. They have spears to hand. I momentarily fear for my horse as the surge of wind rustles my hair, but over the heads of men who should be my allies, I appreciate there are only two rows of shield holders and spears. Those at the front, unable to move aside, have taken to their knees, sprawling forwards. Haden's hoof clips something with a wooden bang, but he lands evenly, and I'm rushing past Lord Æthelwulf, mouth agape at what's happening to his careful plans.

The sound of men unexpectedly under attack floods the air, but my horse and I, with the rest of the Mercians not even halting their advance to take a run up against them, are already rushing through to the back of the force, many of them running to try and avoid being knocked over by the horses. These men are unmounted, foot warriors, with only a handful of riders, most of them Lord Æthelwulf's men, if the flash of their shields is anything to go by.

'Fuckers,' I roar as we pass, grateful when we're free of the blockage. I risk looking behind me. Others haven't had such a clean headlong dash as Jethson and Haden. I see Ælfgar, encouraging his horse, who's limping on its right hind leg, and also other animals with blood on their forelocks. I don't stop though. I'd like nothing more than to turn on my new enemy, but I focus on reaching Icel, who I hope has either evaded this or who Lord Æthelwulf purposefully hid from. I don't want to become separated from the vast majority of my force. Not when the enemy numbers we face have just increased.

'Bloody hell,' Rudolf roars, slowing Jethson to join me.

'Fuckers,' is the only word I reply. If Lord Æthelwulf and the man I assume is Ealdorman Sigehelm live through this, I'll be the one to end their lives. It'll give me great fucking pleasure. They're as loyal as a bitch in heat.

'What was all that about?' Rudolf huffs angrily, Hemming and Ordheah joining him. We've slowed the horses a little, to compensate for what they're just done. Here, I'm aware the gap between the two hedgerows lining the road is wider. There are even some gaps, allowing access to the fields beyond, brown now, without a crop in them, although there'll be seeds beneath the soil, waiting for the warmer weather.

'We knew they were up to something.' I explode. 'Bastards.'

'They weren't there to help us?' Hemming questions with all the naivete of the young.

'If they were, they'd have let us through,' Ingwald answers, saving me from doing so.

Ahead, Canterbury is growing closer and closer. I see the wooden tower of the church of Saint Saviour Christ Church just pocking its head upwards on the distant horizon. Only now do I consider how Lord Æthelwulf's force made it to their position when Icel and the others should have seen them. I can't imagine Icel's been overwhelmed, not by that pathetic excuse for warriors, but I'm still concerned for him. What if he hasn't made it back this way? My warriors better still fucking live. They really had.

I keep the pace steady, aware the warriors behind me are shouting of their experiences to one another. A few of the horses have gone lame, aside from Ælfgar's. Behind, but not too far away, those riders have dismounted, and now ride behind another warrior, leading the lame animals. It'll still pain the horses, but at least they'll evade the enemy as we hurry to reach Canterbury.

I focus on the rounded tower that suddenly doesn't seem to be getting any closer, urging Haden to reach it as soon as possible. I'm wary there might be others who've deceived me. I don't doubt Archbishop Æthelred's loyalty, but my thoughts turn to Abbot Kynebert. He didn't like me. Perhaps he's in league with Lord Æthelwulf and the man I assume is Ealdorman Sigehelm.

'My lord,' Rudolf's voice is urgent, filled with fear, dragging me from my thoughts. And this time, I do rein my mount in, eyes furrowed with confusion that only clears slowly as I try and make sense of what's happening before me.

'Fuck,' I glower, raising my arm in the air to alert my warriors they need to stop this time. In a clatter of heavily breathing horses, my eyes rake in what's happening ahead.

I swallow uneasily, aware that for the time being, we have the time to watch events ahead.

Canterbury's so close, it feels as though I could reach out and touch it, but it's impossible because the road is once more blocked. And not by Ealdorman Æthelwulf and his allies, but instead, by the enemy, engaged in a brutal attack against the force of Mercians I ordered to hold where the two roads diverge.

'Bollocks,' I huff, reaching for my seax and gripping it tightly, although what I'm going to do with it, I don't know.

'There's hundreds of them,' Rudolf announces, his voice brittle with fear.

'Shit,' Eadfrith huffs from beside me. I turn and glance at those following on behind. We're strung out along the road, those with lame animals even further away. We're entirely exposed. When I set us on this path my concern was to get to Icel as quickly as possible and away from Lord Æthelwulf and his attempts to stop us. I didn't forget about the other half of the enemy force, coming towards Canterbury from Richborough, but I did forget something crucial.

They were never going to have as far to travel as I did from the road to Dover.

'Fucking bollocks,' I explode, unable to think of anything aside from my shock at finding ourselves surrounded. There are not one but two enemies behind us. In front, there's another one. I'm sure any moment now they'll realise we're behind them.

The fighting's already bloody and brutal. I hear the shrieks and grunts of warriors using all they have to better their enemy. Somewhere amongst all that, Icel, Kyred, Wærwulf and the rest of my warriors are fighting as well.

I can't see them. I'm not close enough to make out anything more than the heaving mass of the slaughter field, as though an animal in itself, rising and falling with some unseen force behind it.

'Fuck,' I shout, roaring upwards, eyeing the sky where holy men would assure me my Lord God is looking down on me. If he is, he means to make this a fuck sight more difficult than even I'd considered.

I glance around. To the east, there'll be more enemies before we could reach the coast. To the west, there's a flat landscape that would make an escape visible to all when our horses are already exhausted, and many of them lame or in danger of going lame.

'What do we do, my lord?' It's Hemming who asks the question everyone must be thinking. The fact it's not Rudolf, assures me he knows how fucked we are. He won't voice his concerns. He doesn't need to because he knows the answer. But Hemming isn't quite as battle savvy as Rudolf.

'I wish I fucking knew,' I allow myself to mutter. Then take a deep breath and try to focus on what I can control right now.

I have an idea, but it's really shit. It's my worse one yet. Even worse than allowing myself to be taken as a prisoner within Repton. Even worse than when I allowed everyone to reach Northampton ahead of me and Haden. Even more stupid than when I thought to rescue my horse by putting my own life in peril.

But. There really is no bloody choice.

I hold that tight for a moment, as more and more of my warriors come close, their horses tired and exhausted, but not my warriors. No, my warriors are fresh, but scared.

I look to Hemming, and then to Ælfgar, who's arrived on the back of Ordheah's horse. Ælfgar assesses everything quickly. Resignation flashes on his face, but he nods towards me, giving his approval.

'Right, warriors of Mercia,' I call, just loud enough so they can hear. 'Dismount, add your helms, bring your shields, your swords and your fucking stones.'

'My lord,' Rudolf squeaks in shock, already realising my intentions.

'Ælfgar and any others with lame horses, gather all the animals together. Take them to the west, there,' and I point to a scraggly outcropping of trees, the only high point for a long distance all around us. 'Take the horses there, and if there's the option, continue towards Canterbury.' Ælfgar nods, resigned to his fate, as I dismount from Haden and force my helm over my face so that for a moment, my instructions echo and fill my head with the final command I'm about to give.

'We fight our way through the bastards,' I order. 'Together, as one, shield to shield. We'll pierce them from behind.'

'Like a hot poker up their fucking arse,' Rudolf huffs to counter his fear. I offer him a smile when my helm's secured.

'Just like a fucking great big hot poker up their arses,' I confirm, and stride onwards, having given Haden a pat along his nose after tying his reins above the saddle. I hope it's not the last time I ever get to do that. I really fucking don't. His assessing glance at my parting shot, promises me more retribution if it is, than anything Icel or my aunt could offer me.

My warriors hurry to join me, Rudolf at my side, while Ingwald's at my left. I'm not used to fighting with either of them, but this is more about reaching our allies than killing the enemy. It's also about distracting those bastards behind so they'll think they can engage us, rather than those with the lame horses.

'How?' Rudolf questions, but then grins. 'You're going first, aren't you?'

'Yes. And you're to be at my side, and we'll truly form a wedge driving the enemy away from us. If we're lucky, they won't understand what's happening until we're through to Icel.'

This seems to settle Rudolf, although the increasing noise from the slaughter field tests my resolve. Perhaps, I reason, we should all have gone to where I'm sending the horses. But no. That wouldn't have been possible. I need to ensure I'm the focus of those behind. Maybe, if my luck improves, the enemy won't realise they're fighting their own allies.

As we draw closer, I test the hold on my shield, and on my seax. I've not brought my spear to this fight. There won't be the reach to use the weapons effectively. This is just as much about speed and shock tactics, as what happened with the horses. We've discovered time and time again the enemy never consider who's with them at the back. I also appreciate the road's liberally splattered with blood and the dead and dying. The enemy do seem to be overwhelming my warriors. Already, I see the Viking raiders have won their way closer to Canterbury, leaving the two branches of the roadway visible behind them.

Aware those crying for aid are the enemy, I turn to my warriors, and meet their gazes, evenly. Only then do I tighten the guards on my helm, and lift my shield before me, wincing at the memory of the ache in my left thigh.

'As one,' I command, not a roar, but a spoken command filled with resolve. I hear the crash of shield meeting shield, Rudolf and Ingwald as my companions, and move forwards.

The stink of the slaughter field wafts up my nostrils. Blood, shit, piss, and sheer fucking terror. I'm aware of the battle calm coming upon me the closer I get to the rear of the current fighting. This might be an unusual way to win, but win it we fucking will. I'm sure of it. The cost might be high. I'll consider that when the battle's won, and not before.

'Now,' I murmur to my companions, aware Rudolf and Ingwald share the words with those to either side. Hemming's behind me, hefting his shield over my head. Others protect his head with their shields. We're few, but in such a way, we can be mighty.

Ahead, I see the swaying backs of the enemy, and push into them. An angry cry, and even angrier shriek, and the first man is beneath my feet, someone behind me ensuring he's dead.

To either side of me, I sense others moving, effortlessly being jostled so that, here, where the shield wall facing my warriors isn't a layer of wooden shields, the men move with more ease. I keep my eyes focused on the way ahead, visible through my helm, and between the thin gap of the top of my shield, and the roof over my head, provided by Hemming.

My breath is already harsh, the pressure of holding my shield in place taking its toll on my shoulders and back.

An angry shout, and another of the enemy thinks to look behind him. Before he can alert anyone, pugnacious face red and sweating, mouth open, I lift my elbow and slide my blade into it. He gargles and falls dead. Rudolf's also killed an enemy. No doubt, we all have by now. We're in the middle of it. The warriors ahead are more tightly woven together with shields, but on we go. No one's yet deciphered what's happening. That won't last long. When we're discovered those at the rear will close the open arrow head we're forging and the fighting will get fucking nasty.

I feel pressure against my shield as the next warrior refuses to yield. Like the last dead man, he turns to shout angrily at whoever knocks him. The raucous cry ends with a plaintive shriek.

'*Skiderik*,' he hisses, as I stab towards him with my seax.

'Same,' I retort, wishing he wasn't able to bat aside my attack so easily. A further string of Norse words pours from his mouth, before I can land another blow on his byrnie, but already, more and more of the enemy are turning, heeding his caution.

'Come on,' I shout, no need to hide the language we speak any more. From behind, I feel Hemming pressing into me, eager to continue onwards. We're close to the fighting face of the shield wall. I see red-sheeted blades flashing beneath the late afternoon sun as though burnished stalks of hay.

'Fucking come on,' I repeat, more to myself than the others because I'm at the front. I'm the one who can't defeat our enemy. I'm the one that must punch a hole through this wall of iron and wood. It's my place to do so, admittedly with my warrior's aid, but I'm the first to meet the backs of the shield carriers.

Hearing my cry, more and more of the enemy turn in surprise, even those who should be protecting their allies who form the shield wall. I realise our attack might just have an unexpected result.

A string of words, angry, and I sense the scrutiny of more and more of the enemy, although my focus remains on cutting a hole through their defence. But now they come against us. It's as though I've been hit by the tidal bore rushing along the River Severn. The force of the attack almost takes my legs from beneath me. Only Hemming's strength stops me from buckling as my left leg falters. It's done well to last as long as it has.

I wince, and struggle upright, Hemming's free hand holding my shoulder upright, while Rudolf and Ingwald ensure my shield stays in place. I redouble my grip, plant my right foot behind me to secure my failing balance, chest heaving with the effort, as spears and seaxes slide over my shield. I'm grateful Hemming held onto his shield as he aided me. In fact, I'm grateful to all of my men.

As the heat and shouting and heaving intensifies, I realise this is fucking madness. What was I bloody thinking?

My seax arm is busy, slashing and banging against any part of my enemy I can reach because I can't lift my head over my shield to sight the next attack. It's all I can do to risk extending my seax arm. Perhaps, after all, I should have had my men bring their spears. The enemy are using enough of them against us. Where the shields don't quite join, blades slip their way through.

'Ware,' I roar to Hemming because he doesn't have a shield to protect his legs, too busy ensuring my head stays on my neck.

Angry voices grow even angrier. I've got fuck all idea what's happening ahead of us. Our progress has been halted but I don't believe we're being forced backwards. Instead, we hold in place, trying to kill the enemy, but it's almost impossible. Hemming's trying to protect the heads of me, Rudolf and Ingwald, his breath harsh in my ear. We're so close together, I can feel him pressed against my back, his heat making me even hotter. I'm surprised I can't hear the thrum of the blood in his body.

Rudolf shrieks. I feel a weight to my left, trying to drag my shield down.

'Rudolf,' I cry, fearing for him, but like me only moments ago, he manages to regain his feet and recover himself, ensuring the shield wall stays in place.

'This is fucking madness,' I hear Ingwald roar, the clash of his seax arm frenzied. I'm minded to agree with him. Finally, I manage to worm my seax over my shield wall, stabbing forward, but angling the blade down, exposing my elbow in the process and hoping my byrnie will keep me protected. When I retract my weapon, the blade flashes redly. I allow a slow smile to touch my tight cheeks, sweat stained and itchy with the heat.

I repeat the motion, stabbing and jabbing, retracting and then doing the same. Hemming's steady behind me now, some space between us so I don't have to worry about elbowing him in the face. Ingwald has his rhythm as well. Even Rudolf's managing to hold his own.

I strain to hear my allies in front and behind, but it's impossible. The voices of the enemy, furious at finding themselves under attack from such an unexpected position, flood the air. I can't quite determine who shouts. I feel I should know the names of the jarls, but it's impossible to determine more than the hum of voices above the crash of wood and iron.

'Fucking come on,' I urge myself. My right leg's growing weaker now, forced to absorb the impact of keeping me upright. My left leg's no better, but I'm not giving up. I'll fight until my body can take no more.

The movements of my enemy show no intention of slackening. I risk a brief look over the top of my shield, unable to make sense of what I'm seeing. A shimmering blade veers alarmingly close to my head. I duck down to avoid losing my eye, or being smacked on the head hard enough to lose all sense. That would be most unfortunate.

I stab with my seax, adding more of my weight to keeping my shield upright.

'Advance,' I bellow, unsure if it's even possible. Hemming steps closer. I sense Rudolf and Ingwald doing the same. It's impossible to risk looking at them. My head is low, the smell of such a confined space fetid.

'Advance,' I cry once more, forcing my right leg forwards, trusting my left one to hold firm even though its shaking with the strain.

'Again,' I bellow, hoping my warriors can do what I demand from them.

My right foot lands on the churned and bloodied ground. I test my footing, and then force my left leg to do the same. The most worrying moments are when all my weight rests on only one leg. I could be unbalanced by anything, but my left foot lands in front of my right. I repeat the motion. Rudolf and Ingwald stay with me, as does Hemming, and the others who are behind us.

It's a fucking monumental effort, but I have to press on. I hope I saw what I think I saw in the brief gap.

'Again,' I roar, voice cracking with the effort, the sound taking all my air to expel.

And then I feel it on my next step forward. The shield wall ahead has broken apart, and suddenly my movements are no longer laboured, but so easy I almost stumble to the ground as the force against us disintegrates. I just keep upright, again, thanks to Hemming's hand on my shoulder. Then I hear a welcome sound.

'Well, you took your fucking time,' Icel roars, as a crash of wood and iron assures me our shield wall has reformed, but that my warriors, my brave Mercians have made it through the enemy line, and are now reunited with those men I ordered away or to protect Canterbury.

I turn slowly, astounded to see my warriors there, bloodied but hale, or so I hope. Rudolf sags to the ground wearily, head between his legs. I envelop Hemming in the sweatiest, bloodiest embrace I've ever given or received, and I don't fucking care.

'Come the fuck on, my lord,' Icel bellows from nearby. 'We still need to kill all the bastards.'

Chapter Twenty-Six

I growl, unsure I'll be able to do anything after all that effort, but I stand with one arm around Hemming's shoulders, trying to make sense of what I'm seeing.

We're away from the main brunt of the fighting, which sways as though a bough in the wind. The number of Mercians is far from huge, but I see Kyred, and Wærwulf, and others of my warriors, all working together to defeat our enemy. I grin with delayed pleasure at rejoining my men, casting an eye to where I sent the horses to the west, but if the enemy have spotted them, it's not yet obvious. For the time being they're safe. But I have something important to share with my warriors.

'Get some water,' I urge Hemming, bending to pull Rudolf upright. I slap the backs of my warriors who all try to recover themselves, knowing as I do, that there are more enemy coming this way. Amongst them are some of the fuckers who've betrayed us. Men of Wessex and Kent who should be fighting with us not against us.

I stride to Icel, testing my legs as I do so, feeling the strains and stresses as I slip in battle slime and only then find my sturdy warrior, standing back from the front of the attack, breathing deeply.

'That could have been a fuck up,' he growls. 'What possessed you?'

'We've been betrayed. Fucking Lord Æthelwulf and Ealdorman Sigehelm, I presume, tried to trap us on the road. We galloped through them, and then had to reach you,' I pant. Icel's already furious face, turns ever darker, although no longer directed at me.

'Fucking cock,' he growls. 'We need to warn the men not to allow any others through the shield wall.'

'I know,' I gasp, bending forward, my throat parched, grateful Hemming slips a waterskin into my hand.

'We're already outnumbered,' Icel informs me, quieting his voice so my good Mercians won't hear his announcement. I doubt they've not already realised. We're heavily outstripped.

'I know,' I grumble, my immediate relief at making it to Icel's side evaporating as the din of the battle seems to redouble.

'We should retreat to Canterbury's walls.'

'They're shit.'

'They are, but the turf bank and ditch will provide some protection.'

'They enemy surround us,' I complain.

'They won't think that far ahead,' Icel announces with far more confidence in his answer than I think is possible.

'Really?' I huff.

'Daft fuckers, all of them,' he asserts. I appreciate he's trying to convince himself of that, as well as me.

Another shout from the shield wall. A decision must be made.

I sight the shield wall, looking from one end of it, to another. In all honesty, we're already retreating, we're just perhaps not aware of it. The roadway here, so close to Canterbury, is wider than the place where we were trapped, but stubborn impenetrable hedgerows sit to either side, and they're helping us keep the enemy at bay. It won't be long though, I suspect, until the enemy devise a new tactic to force a way through our defences.

I shake my head. I really don't fucking like this.

'We do it,' I announce firmly. 'Hemming, rush to Canterbury. Inform them we're retreating. We need them to open a single gateway, and have a hundred men defending it so we can slip inside. Then, they're to follow us within and we'll hold against the enemy from there.'

'My lord,' if my instructions alarm him, he doesn't show it.

'Go now,' I urge him. 'As quick as you can. We'll be along soon.'

He bows quickly, and dashes onwards. I turn to Icel.

'Now, how the fuck do we do this?'

He shakes his head from side to side, considering this new problem. If we could just retreat that would be unpalatable but possible. But, if we sound the retreat, the Mercians will be overrun by the enemy who are determined to overwhelm us.

'We make it look like they're winning, and then we run for it,' he announces. I've drawn the same conclusion. I'm pleased he agrees with me.

Wærwulf staggers free from the shield wall. I beckon him towards us.

'We're going to stage an orderly retreat to Canterbury. We slowly allow the enemy to believe they're winning, and then, within sight of Canterbury's walls, where the hedgerows run out, we make a run for it.'

'My lord,' he gasps. I grimace. This is a problem. Everyone's knackered. It's taking all we have to stay our ground. If we also have to run with all of our warrior equipment, we'll be encumbered and in a perilous situation.

'I'll take the middle ground and spread the word,' I announce before I can reconsider. We're fucked. I have to do something, or we face breathing our last here, outside Canterbury, and much, much worse, at the hands of the bastard jarls of Repton and whoever they've brought along for the fucking ride.

'Icel, right, Wærwulf, left. Spread the word. We start the retreat after two hundred beats of our hearts, now go.' Without pausing, I stride to where Kyred's encouraging his exhausted men to fight more ferociously, and share my orders with him.

His nod is far from confident, but he slips through to those he can reach and I do the same. Not one of my warriors argues with me. We're in a damning situation. But, none of them look fearful, only resigned to what must be done.

I retrieve my shield and watch as the Mercians begin to give ground. It's unwilling done, but the mass of warriors almost moves as one, as though someone, somewhere, is banging a drum and forcing each step to take place in order.

I swallow my unease, glancing towards Canterbury, hoping nothing's befallen Hemming and he'll manage to pass on my instructions to Ealdorman Ælhun and Pybba. I know he'll be astounded. I hope he's not fearful.

Back and back we go, just slowly enough the enemy believe they're winning against us, and we're not conducting an organised retreat. For that reason, we spread the command by word of mouth and not in a roar of fury and despair.

'Come on,' I realise we must make this even more authentic. 'Come on,' I repeat, my warriors knowing I encourage them to fulfil my orders while the enemy must think I'm trying to counter the fact they're overwhelming us.

I walk backwards, my eyes all around me. It won't be long, I realise, until the hedgerows run out and we're fighting through the part of Canterbury unprotected by the walls. If the enemy are clever, they could defeat us there. We need to be quicker than them.

Icel, Wærwulf and Kyred are as alert as I am. Soon, the trickiest part of our retreat will be upon us. If we still had our horses, we could evade the enemy, but the animals have already been pulled back, a wise precaution I'm grateful the others have taken.

I strain to hear Wessex voices amongst the enemy, but so far, I'm confident, the forces haven't met. Perhaps, I consider, Lord Æthelwulf is, even now, trying to secure King Alfred, but I doubt it. He's proven to be a deceitful fucker. I can't imagine he intends for his brother by marriage to live.

A voice from behind, and I see Hemming, beckoning me onwards. As I commanded, there are fresh Mercians and the arch-bishop's warriors, already preparing to defend us as we rush through the open gateway. I see Ealdorman Ælhun, bedecked as a warrior in all his shimmering battle gear, Pybba beside him, and in only a few more steps, the roadway will open out.

I look to Wærwulf, Icel and Kyred, and to those of my brave Mercians who are behind the front face of the shield wall, and I roar the command.

'Now.' And I'm running, my shield banging against my leg, the rattle of iron and wood easy to hear, even as the enemy shout in triumph. My feet are sure footed, although the roadway is uneven in places. I look left and right as I rush into the collection of dwellings as the hedgerows run out. I'm desperate to reassure myself the enemy aren't also waiting there.

I run as quickly as I can, but still, others overtake me. Bloody younger legs. Fucking younger bodies. Lucky sods. I hear their hot breath as they gasp, and veer to the side, not wanting to slow them down. At the first of the warriors ready to protect our retreat, Wulf-sige, Ealdorman Ælhun's commander, I come to a halt, preparing to do the same.

'Get inside, my lord king,' Wulfsige orders me, his words harsh with fear. 'Please, my lord king,' he repeats, as I stand my ground, heart pounding, watching the majority of my warriors coming closer. Already, many of the Mercians are safely inside Canterbury, if that is safe, but those who faced the enemy in the shield wall are slower. I wince as one man stumbles, his ally bending to aid him, only to be knocked over as well by those rushing after him.

Those behind the collapsed group are more alert, moving around so they have time to gather their feet, but only just.

Caught a little by surprise, the Viking raiders are slower to catch us. I bite my lip.

'Get inside, my lord,' Icel bellows rushing to me, and grabbing my arm with very little respect and very tight fingers.

'I told him that,' Wulfsige growls angrily at my side.

'I must.'

'You must fucking live and think of a way out of this fuck up,' Icel growls, and unwillingly, as I see more and more of the Mercians enter the safety of Canterbury, I appreciate he's correct.

'Withdraw as soon as you can,' I order Wulfsige. He nods, but his gaze is on the advancing enemy. Any moment now, the fresh Mercians will have to block the roadway with their might, forging another shield wall of flesh and bone, as well as iron and wood.

I move quickly, bending to scoop dropped blades and to help an exhausted Sæbald to his feet. I scramble through the fetid ditch surrounding part of Canterbury and up the steep embankment to feel the walls enclosing me. I turn as quickly as I can to look back the way we've come. My fresh Mercian warriors under Wulfsige's command have closed ranks. I wince to see one of the original Mercians is about to be overtaken by the enemy. I urge him onwards and at the last possible moment, he slips through the shield wall, and the enemy butt up against it with a thundering crash.

Immediately, the front of the reforming enemy shield wall is forced backwards by the speed of the enemy approach. They take at least five backwards steps before they can reassert themselves.

My exhausted Mercians continue to make their way through the gate, and the shield wall retreats more slowly, more calmly, the enemy shouting angrily at being thwarted when they sensed imminent victory.

'Do we have any arrows?' I call breathlessly to Ealdorman Ælhun.

'Aye, my lord king, a few.'

'Prepare to employ them when the shield wall withdraws.'

My chest's tight. I fear for my brave warriors, and for those who're bent over, trying to breathe in enough air to calm their rapid hearts. I fear for everyone, including my horse and warriors abandoned outside Canterbury. The enemy are going to be fucking angry when they realise we've evaded them, even if we are stuck within the dubious safety of Canterbury's shit walls. It'll make them determined to exact their revenge against anyone who's not within. I consider Haden. He wouldn't have made it through the enemy shield wall, as we did on foot, but I can't risk losing him. Perhaps, I hope, my warriors will have found another way to lead the animals to safety. I certainly want that.

'Now,' I roar, and the thrum of arrows fills the air as my shield wall retreats, making use of the arrows to provide some much-needed protection.

The enemy roar with renewed assurance of their victory. My Mercians rush and run as quickly as possible. At the last possible moment, I hear the clatter of hooves, and turn astonished to see Icel and Wærwulf on Samson and Cinder, rushing through the gate to provide more protection for my warriors.

I watch, unable to tear my eyes away as they get between my Mercians and the enemy with their horses. Samson rears, front hooves snapping out and crashing into two different enemy warriors who drop as though struck by stones from a height. Cinder does the same, and momentarily, the enemy advance is stopped, giving those on foot just enough time to get ahead of the Viking raiders.

Icel and Wærwulf turn their mounts and rush for the gates, the horses making quick work of the ditch and steep embankment.

The last of my Mercians from the second shield wall are within, the thrum of arrows still resounds, and at the last possible moment, Wærwulf and Icel crash through the small space in the gateway just as its slammed shut to an angry cry from our enemy.

There are Mercians on the high walls, making use of the scaffolding that should be holding up the church roof, raining down whatever they have to hand on the enemy. I expect a thud against the gate. It doesn't come, and more and more heavy items are thrust in front of the wooden gate. The reinforcing bars, four of them, are slipped into position, the highest one needing the use of mounted warriors because it's too high. It must, I appreciate, be a new addition.

As each bar slams into position, my thudding heart eases and by the time the fourth and lower one is in place, I stand and breathe more easily, limping on my strained left leg, but able to walk amongst my collapsed warriors, some lying on their backs, chests heaving.

There are wounds and some cry in pain as well as frustration at finding themselves in this position, but when most of them can breathe, they shout in triumph.

I stride to Icel, furious.

'Why did you bloody risk Samson?' I glower, reaching out to touch the horse, noting a spot of blood high on his shoulder.

'We need all the men we have,' Icel replies, his voice devoid of emotion. 'It was the only way.' I snap back my angry reply. He's no doubt correct, as little as I like it.

'My lord king,' Ealdorman Ælhun's before me, worry on his familiar face. 'What happened?'

'We were deceived by Lord Æthelwulf and Ealdorman Sige-helm, well, I assume that's who the other bastard was. They tried to trap us, but before that, I realised we could do nothing to stop the enemy, so tried to withdraw. We used the horses to get through Lord Æthelwulf and Ealdorman Sigehelm's force, and then shields to join up with the others.'

'Your horse?' Ealdorman Ælhun questions, forehead furrowed in confusion.

'Hopefully safe. Some of the animals went lame. I sent them to the west. But tell me, is Canterbury secure?'

'As much as it can be. Archbishop Æthelred's gone. Most of the people have also left. Abbot Kynebert hasn't retreated,' Ealdorman Ælhun confirms. His expression is pensive.

'What now?'

'I don't know the answer to that. King Alfred remains captive, and his brother by marriage and the Kent ealdorman are both traitors.'

The rumble of the enemy beyond Canterbury's wall is slow to die down. I turn to view those watching, hopeful they'll inform me if something happens. I bite my lips, and remove my helm next, grateful to feel the wind in my damp hair, as I also pull the linen cap off.

'We should retreat to Mercia,' Ealdorman Ælhun argues hotly. There are those nearby who nod in agreement. 'We can't get King Alfred back from here,' he further asserts.

'Perhaps not,' I agree unwillingly.

Pybba joins me. He's cleaner than he was, but still pale.

'That went well, then?' he offers, but there's no derision in his voice.

'It was a fuck up because we were betrayed,' I state flatly. I'm pleased to see the Mercians and the archbishop's warriors aiding one another. It reminds me this isn't just about King Alfred, even if he'd like to think it was.

'I don't know the answers yet,' I reply. 'For now, we can recover from the attack. Well done', I turn to Wærwulf and Icel, seeking out Kyred, but he's tending to one of his men, still flat out on the ground. 'You did well,' I comment.

'The enemy were upon us very quickly. It's good Kyred hadn't gone too far,' Icel comments sourly. 'It was almost as though they knew we were coming.' I hold his gaze.

'You think they knew?'

'I suspect it, yes,' he comments sourly. He's bleeding from a cut on his arm, but it doesn't seem too deep. I inspect the others quickly, but my real concern is for Kyred's men as I realise more and more of them have slumped to the ground.

'Are they well?' I call to Kyred.

'They will be,' he shouts back. I know a moment of unease. I look carefully at the figure dispersing water amongst the tired men.

'Do we know that person?' I mutter to those near to me, deep unease welling inside me.

Icel's eyes narrow, and so do the ealdorman's. But it's a passing member of the archbishop's warrior force who answers.

'That bastard,' he strides towards the squat figure, and hauls the man upright, dragging him towards me, although not without complaints.

The figure quickly resolves itself into Abbot Kynebert.

'What have you done?' I demand, reaching for the water jug he carries. I sniff it, only for Rudolf to take it from me and really sniff it deeply.

'He's laced it with hemlock. The fucking bastard.'

'Why would you bloody do that?' I demand. Abbot Kynebert fixes me with a defiant expression. Hemlock, even I know, can be deadly, and it brings about a bloody cruel death.

'My Lord God told me to do so. There's no call for Mercians within Canterbury.' I growl to hear that. 'There never has been. Not since Kent became part of Wessex in the reign of King Ecgberht. God Rest His Soul.'

'Lock him up in the crypt,' I instruct Icel, and turn to Rudolf. 'Will they be well?'

'We need to make them sick and then they should be, provided not much was used. And he can't have used much. The smell is a real giveaway.' He's already hurrying about his business as Icel leads the suddenly pliant Abbot Kynebert away.

I shake my head, while Rudolf calls for Hemming to aid him, Kyred rushing to do the same.

'I'm bloody betrayed from all around,' I mutter angrily.

'Aye, my lord, you really fucking are,' Pybba confirms, and then, I suspect, before he thinks I'll allow myself to wallow in self-pity, he continues speaking. 'You wouldn't have it any other way, and you know it.' I grumble beneath my breath, listening to the sound of men retching to void the poison in their bodies.

'But it could be a fuck sight easier to resolve,' I complain, while Pybba chuckles.

'It wouldn't be a bloody challenge, then.' And he leaves me, hobbling on his way to help the rest of the warriors, those poisoned or too tired to move. I slump to the ground, too exhausted to think about more than resting my left leg.

I don't fucking like this. Not at all. But then, as Icel says, I rarely fucking do.

Chapter Twenty-Seven

I'm unsurprised when I'm summoned to climb the wooden scaffolding close to the gateway facing the enemy and look down on Jarl Guthrum's smirking face, his owl tattooed arms on display. Sunlight bleaches the sky to the grey of coming night but I can see him well enough. Nor am I particularly astounded to find King Alfred at his side, his pale face badly bruised, as far as I can tell, but aside from that, hail. Well, he's standing upright, at least.

'Ah, King Coelwulf, the second of his name,' Jarl Guthrum taunts, a huge silver cross visible around his neck, catching the dying glow of the sun. 'I think I have something you desire.'

Icel's at my side, as is Ealdorman Ælhun. It's uncomfortable balancing on the scaffolding without some protective barriers to keep us in place, aside from the face of the wall in front of us, but here, there's no buttress in which we could stand. Canterbury's walls lack a walkway along their tops. No doubt, someone, at some point, has robbed away the stone that formed the walkway and put it to what they consider to be, a better use. Fucking arseholes. I'm surprised they've not filled in the ditch as well, or indeed, demolished all the walls and allowed free flowing access. I mean, why wouldn't they have bloody done so?

I seek out Lord Æthelwulf and Ealdorman Sigehelm amongst the enemy force, but don't find them. I consider where they are. Hopefully, the bastards are dead.

King Alfred looks upwards, squinting, but doesn't speak.

'I don't want him,' I reply quickly.

'I thought you were allies now?' Jarl Guthrum mocks. I glimpse King Alfred shimmer with fury.

I shrug my shoulders, wincing at the tightness in them. Icel's there to try and determine the size of the force arranged against us. Rudolf's still busy with the men who were poisoned, and so I lack his ability to quickly access the strength of our enemy. Not that I really need either of them to advise me we're vastly outnumbered, with nothing but a steep embankment and a flimsy stone wall to separate us from the mass out there.

'I propose a treaty, as we forged outside Northampton,' Jarl Guthrum continues arrogantly, when I offer nothing else. I really hate the fucking bastard, but I listen all the same. 'We'll take Canterbury, and you can have back King Alfred, and we'll allow you to leave Wessex in our hands, on payment of five thousand pounds of silver.'

I keep my expression as blank as possible, not wanting King Alfred or Jarl Guthrum to realise how those terms impact me like physical blows. I came here to keep Canterbury safe from the enemy. I've no intention of exchanging a kingdom for King Alfred's life. I hope he's man enough to know he shouldn't expect such. He is but one man. He can be sacrificed for the good of others.

'Come, come, King Coelwulf. You'll get to live. It's better than when we met at Repton, and a reversal of what you did to me at Northampton. And, you've no choice. You have until this time tomorrow to make your decision. If not, I'll personally kill King Alfred here, before you all, and then attack Canterbury anyway. You'll lose your ally and Wessex.'

'Until tomorrow,' I call back, not trusting my voice to hold firm for any longer than that. The terms are appalling. They're a complete setback. If we'd remained in Mercia and not heeded King Alfred's call for aid, the terms would have been better. Fuck.

I descend the scaffolding carefully using a long ladder, arms and legs thrumming with exhaustion, so I'm pleased to jump the last few feet and land heavily, knees absorbing the impact with a wobble, my left leg complaining.

'Fuck,' Icel mutters. 'There are thousands of them, not hundreds. I didn't see Lord Æthelwulf, or the other bastard, though.'

'I hope they're dead,' I mutter, leaning against the stone wall to keep upright.

'We should retreat. We have a day on them,' Ealdorman Ælhun urges quickly. I'm half minded to agree with him. I came here to protect Archbishop Æthelred and he's already fled. I've fought for over a year to defeat the Viking raider jarls. It's infuriating that King Alfred's determination to force me from Mercia and into Wessex has failed so spectacularly. It's a reversal for Mercia as well as for Wessex. It's making me doubt myself. Within Mercia, I know my mind clearly. I know what I must do and who will aid me. Here, deceit is everywhere. Even the bastard abbot has tried to kill my men. Arsehole.

'No,' I announce, although I've nothing else to add to that. Not yet. I push away from the wall and walk amongst the Mercians and warriors beholden to Archbishop Æthelred.

There are too few of us. Far too fucking few. After Abbot Kynebert's appalling actions, the Canterbury men have gone amongst those who remain and reassured themselves any others within the walls are loyal to us. Those poisoned will, Rudolf hopes, recover, but it'll take time for their stomach cramps to resolve themselves. For now, they sweat and heave, stumble to the latrines, and generally look like shit. Poor bastards. At least, we're not within Old Sarum with a single water supply that if tainted could have killed us all.

Icel and Pybba keep me company. Ealdorman Ælhun wisely takes himself away to see to his men. Kyred's doing the same with his.

'We have how many men?' I murmur.

'Not enough,' Icel reassures me. I grin, but it's more like a grimace.

'Do you have any suggestions?' I ask them both wearily.

'Ealdorman Ælhun's right,' Pybba mutters, 'we should retreat. But we all know that's not going to bloody happen.'

His comment has me scowling.

'Perhaps this is one of those occasions when I should do the sensible thing.'

'Unlikely,' Icel offers conversationally. I feel my temper spark.

'I'm always supposed to find a way out of the most difficult of circumstances. What if this time, there's no other fucking way?'

Neither man replies. They don't look overly concerned at my outburst. They don't tell me to be quiet. They don't offer any reassurance either, the bastards.

'The Viking raiders always overextend themselves,' Pybba eventually announces.

'They do. And Jarl Guthrum's an arrogant arsehole,' Icel confirms.

Still, nothing comes to me. I look between the two men. The daylight's entirely gone. Dusk took a long time, but it's often the way as winter nears. Darkness, when it came, was immediate, like snuffing out a candle or dampening down a fire. Now we can only see thanks to flames from fires and brands. In the feeble light, my allies appear old and denuded of their strength, even tall Icel, who still overtops me. His broad shoulders suggest the strength within him is retained, and yet his arms hang limp to either side. He doesn't even stand with his legs apart, aggressively showing off his taut muscles. And Pybba? Well, Pybba's riddled with more scars than I have on my body. They've been at this game for longer than I have. It's evident on their very person. I've considered before how Icel can keep going. He's been fighting for his entire life, but so has Pybba.

'One suggestion,' Pybba murmurs. 'I've spent time with King Alfred and his warriors.'

I nod. I know this.

'I can tell you that while we didn't try to reclaim Winchester or Wareham, as we understand it, the enemy have abandoned both sites. They have their gaze firmly set on Canterbury. Jarl Guthrum has been most aggressive in his demands everyone follow him here, to the home of Christianity on this island, despite the weather so evidently being against them for much of the last few weeks. I suspect capturing King Alfred was never his intention. That it's happened is more to do with King Alfred being shit than Jarl Guthrum deciding to grab the Wessex king.'

'I don't see how that helps us,' I murmur.

'I don't believe it does. Not here, and not know, but, my lord, if we can somehow banish them from Canterbury, Wessex will be restored to its rightful ruling line.'

I consider this. I know what the bastard's trying to do. He's attempting to convince me besting Jarl Guthrum will resolve all the problems King Alfred's so far faced. And, yes, it might, but Winchester and Wareham are days away from here. I don't even know how I could get word to anyone else to hold those settlements for Wessex.

'King Alfred sent his ealdormen to hold Winchester and Wareham as soon as he realised that.'

I nod. It makes it a little easier. It means Wessex is held by the West Saxons, apart from here, where, as far as I can tell, Lord Æthelwulf and Ealdorman Sigehelm have compounded the issue by turning against me.

'So, Wessex is once more Wessex.'

'It is, yes. Jarl Guthrum's overplaying the current situation when he announces Wessex is in his hands.'

'And if he's overconfident there, where else is he overconfident?' Icel summarises neatly.

'Not fucking here,' I growl, but the pair shake their heads, far from convinced.

'I suggest we all get some sleep,' Pybba announces, yawning

widely and stretching his arms above his head. 'Everything will appear better in the morning.'

'I fucking doubt that,' I retort, but his yawn makes me yawn. With a final walk through the dwellings where the Mercians are seeking shelter, and after checking the gate to ensure its secure and the men on guard duty know what to do, I seek my bed. I tumble to the floor in the archbishop's great hall, determined to stay with my warriors, and wrap myself in my cloak. I ache all over, my body unresponsive aside from my left leg which throbs as though the brand used to seal the wound still adheres to the skin.

I sense we're properly fucked, but because Icel and Pybba refuse to accept that, I allow my mind to wonder, considering possibilities and thinking about how, in the past, we've managed to win free from the enemy in the direst of circumstances.

I consider when it was really bad, when only some random happenstance aided us, and my thoughts keep returning to the last time I slept in a church, with ancestors forever slumbering in their coffins beneath me.

As my breath slows, I realise there's always a way.

It's just fucking risky.

But, there's always a way. If I can convince anyone else of the worth of my idea.

If.

Chapter Twenty-Eight

'That's fucking crazy,' Icel roars as I offer my suggestion the next day.

I nod. I can't argue with him, but I'm determined to withstand his anger.

'I didn't say it wasn't,' I announce calmly, reconciled to his reaction and my decision.

'It won't bloody accomplish anything.'

'It might,' I counter.

'Aside from getting me strung up by my stones, no it won't.' Icel's very determined about all this. I knew he would be. But, so am I.

'I won't allow it,' Icel reiterates, voice a growl of menace that would have many others running for cover. I'm not these 'others.' I've been standing up for myself against Icel for many years now. I know how to do it.

'We'll see,' I murmur, pleased Hemming has found his way to us and stops the argument.

He's limping slightly, but aside from that, seems well enough after the exertions of yesterday.

'My lord,' he inclines his head towards me.

'Ah, Hemming. I've a difficult task to demand of you.' He stands taller, nodding swiftly to assure me he'll do as I request.

'You're to return to London, via the shallows at Laleham Gulls or by boat, and inform my aunt of what's happened here.'

'And?' he questions, when I offer nothing else.

'That's it. Inform her of our current, predicament,' I decide to term it. 'And that we'll return as soon as possible.'

'And?' Hemming repeats, forehead furrowed with confusion.

'And you'll stay there, with her. Assure her Winchester and Wareham are once more in the hands of the West Saxons. That'll please Lady Ealhswith, at least.'

'Of course, my lord.' I sense his gaze flickering towards Icel, as though assuring himself I mean what I say, or at least, that Icel agrees with what I'm ordering him to do. I should probably be annoyed by that, but I'm not.

'We'll see you safely through the northern gate, although, as far as we understand it, the enemy haven't encircled Canterbury. Have they?' I direct to Icel.

'No. They haven't. Jarl Guthrum believes you're too fucking honourable to abandon King Alfred to his fate.' From the way he explains, it's evident Icel would feel no such compunction. 'Also, inform Archbishop Æthelred of what the abbot's been up to, should you catch those fleeing to the north. Don't remain with them. Get to London as soon as possible.'

'My lord,' Hemming bows and marches away, shaking his head.

'What's all that about?' Pybba demands.

'Best to get him out of the way. A pity he's about the only one who'll take my orders without arguing against them.'

I hear the audible snap of Pybba's jaw and smirk at him.

'You'd send us all away?'

'I would, yes. Honour will only get us killed.'

'But we're not bloody going,' Icel menaces.

'No, you're not going. We'll hold out for as long as possible,' I declare. 'Fuck Jarl Guthrum and his demands. We'll react when we can hold off no longer.'

'Is that wise?' Pybba questions.

'Do you really think Jarl Guthrum will kill King Alfred? He thinks he has us in a predicament from which there's no solution other than to do what he says.'

'He's got you by the bloody stones, you mean?' Icel rephrases.

'That's it, yes, by the stones. But does he? Does he really or can we rely on his arrogance to convince him of that?'

Silence assures me they both agree, even if they don't want to admit it.

'Now, how are the ill men?'

'Much better, and Abbot Kynebert has been singing like a bird.'

'About what?'

'Ealdorman Sigehelm ordered him to poison the men, as he sees it.'

'Did he now? He really is a fucking cock. Hopefully, he's been killed by the enemy.'

'Isn't he part of it?'

'That I'm not sure. He meant to trap us, alongside Lord Æthelwulf and ensure we were killed by the enemy. Did they mean to betray King Alfred as well? I'm not so sure. It makes little sense. Lord Æthelwulf could never be king in place of King Alfred.'

'Then where are they?'

'That, I don't know. Dead or fled. I suspect fled. Perhaps, they're on their way to Winchester, or maybe, busy trying to work out how to free King Alfred.'

'With what fucking army?'

'No idea,' I shrug. 'As long as they're not here, within Canterbury, I'll be happy.'

Rudolf joins us then. He's yawning.

'How is everyone?'

'Better and sleeping, which is what I'm going to do.'

'Go on then, and my thanks for your quick actions yesterday.'

'Aye, my lord. The bloody abbot, luckily, dosed too lightly to kill the men. Whether he intended to or not, I don't know, but that's why they still live.'

'Small mercies,' Icel expels. 'Now, I need to eat, and so do you,' Icel directs to me. I nod. I'm hungry, and the smell of good food being cooked has me welcoming whatever the meal will be. At least, for now, we have plentiful food. Depending on how long we're within Canterbury for, that might change.

I decide to savour it. We'll not be rushed, no matter Jarl Guthrum's attempts to force us to respond quickly.

'What's your answer? Jarl Guthrum taunts at sunset from outside Canterbury. Throughout the day, I've periodically cast my eye over the encampment of the enemy from the scaffolding. The bastards are so confident I'll agree to Guthrum's terms they've not built tents and instead sleep out in the open. A brave decision to have made when the clouds are low and grey, threatening a deluge.

'Go fuck yourself,' I retort. The erstwhile King of Wessex is being held at seax point by four of the jarl's warriors. At my words, his face blanches and trembles suffuse his body. He really has about as much back bone as an eel. The seax blades waver but don't pierce King Alfred.

Jarl Guthrum nods, as though expecting my reply.

'Then I'll give you until sunset tomorrow, but now the price is six thousand pounds of silver.'

'As you will,' I reply, jumping down from my perch before King Alfred can communicate with me in anyway.

'He won't do it,' I exult. 'He really won't bloody do it.' I repeat, but Icel looks far from happy.

Hemming's gone to London. The poisoned men are almost standing once more. There's no sign of Lord Æthelwulf or Ealdorman Sigehelm. Admittedly, there's none of my lame horses either, and I have no idea where Oda is. And now, despite how much I hate it, we need to play a waiting game and see just how far we can push Jarl Guthrum. If he is, indeed, a new man converted to the same faith as me, then it should be a long time. No man, with a past as dogged with violence and murder as Guthrum's would surely wish to risk his immortal soul further by killing another anointed king. Would he?

* * *

The price increases daily. I offer the same responses as before. We're at an impasse. I know it. Whether Jarl Guthrum yet appreciates it, I'm unsure.

King Alfred's bruises slowly fade, as Jarl Guthrum's forced to present himself to me earlier and earlier to ensure I can see now the sunset is so much quicker each night. The weather turns cooler, and when the price reaches twelve thousand pounds of silver a week later, I'm aware there are now tents and canvases for the enemy to shelter within. They've made occasional sorties around Canterbury's walls, but really, they're waiting. I wish I could witness what was happening in Jarl Guthrum's tent every time I rebuff him. No doubt he believes at some point I'll capitulate. Perhaps he hopes our food supplies will run low, whereas they have much food, stolen from settlements south of Canterbury, probably, provided the fools didn't burn everything. If not, it's their own damn faults for burning everything in their path. I pity those West Saxon affected by it but they can blame their own damn fucking king for that. It's far from my fault.

Inside Canterbury, my warriors grow restless and bored with their confinement. When I walk amongst them, I know they eye me in confusion. This is most unlike anything I've ever done before, which, if they were quicker thinkers, they'd realise. I mean to frustrate my enemy. I hope it's working. I'd like to escape from Canterbury as well, but with King Alfred captive, and Lord Æthelwulf and

Ealdorman Sigehelm still elsewhere, I must remain in position. For now.

We're lucky the harvest has been recently gathered because there's much food within Canterbury. We can eat, and drink as much as we want. We can lay about and do little during the day, but I'm not idle. I'm planning and plotting.

I'm aware Icel, Pybba and Rudolf have devised some sort of timetable so one of them is always with me. Their lack of trust assures me they're rattled by what they think I'm going to do. I'm more concerned with how long I can continue frustrating Jarl Guthrum. For now, his warriors remain loyal. I'm not sure that will be the case for much longer. Admittedly, my men might consider revolting as well. What fun that could be.

'My lord,' it's Pybba who's given the delicate task of approaching me when the ransom has nearly reached twenty thousand pounds of silver, and we've been captive for two weeks.

'Pybba. How lovely to speak with you,' I offer as I descend from denying Jarl Guthrum once more. King Alfred has stopped glowering at me when I shrug off the latest round of demands. I consider if he'll yield and agree to pay the ransom himself and drive me from Canterbury. I doubt it, but I'm willing to be surprised.

'My lord, this can't continue. The number of enemies swells every day. They're coming from every port to lay siege to us at Canterbury.'

'And yet, they allow us the means to escape from the rear of the walls.'

'Do they really, my lord, or are they also there, waiting to attack should you attempt such a thing?'

'I hadn't considered that,' I shrug. I mean, I have.

'Is it not better to pay the ransom now, and then withdraw to Mercia?'

'Do you think it is?' I question.

'Well,' Pybba falters. 'I'm not Mercia's king,' he responds without heat.

'No, you're not, are you,' I announce jovially. King Alfred, when he's brought to stand before Canterbury's walls by Jarl Guthrum is no longer held at seax point. No doubt, he and Jarl Guthrum have found some common ground, the one boring the other with his religious convictions. I shudder at the thought.

'Coelwulf,' Pybba hisses at me, lips pressed together. 'Tell me what the fuck you have planned.'

'All will become clear, my friend. In time. And provided we get that time.'

The following day, Jarl Guthrum's alone, with no sign of King Alfred at his side. I'd startle at that, but those on guard duty have seen King Alfred during their duties so I know he's far from dead.

Jarl Guthrum doesn't increase his demand for payment. Instead, he shouts to me across the embankment and ditch.

'King Alfred's unwell. He's taken to his bed. Bad stomach or something. He stinks.'

'As long as he's not dead,' I reply, my thoughts already tumbling down an unlooked-for path.

'Is he like this often?' Jarl Guthrum shouts, some unease in his words. Does he fear what will happen if King Alfred isn't well within a day or two?

'No,' I reply confidently, even though it's a lie. There are reports of King Alfred's weaknesses.

'Hum,' Jarl Guthrum replies. 'Do you have someone who could aid him? A wise woman or a man of the faith.'

'He wishes a priest?'

'He's asked for one, yes.'

'I'll see what I can do,' I lower myself quickly, and stand, considering this new development. It's not at all what I had planned, but perhaps there's another way. It would be rare for two opportunities to present themselves, but perhaps I'm due a little luck.

'Is there someone aside from Rudolf who could treat the unwell king?' I question Pybba and Icel. Rudolf's absented himself.

'A few of the monks remained to tend to their shrines, despite the archbishop's request that they didn't,' Icel comments, but it's Ealdorman Ælhun who has the answer.

'There are two priests. They've been administering to the people of Canterbury within the archbishop's hall. They have much book law,' he informs me.

'Then, I need to speak with them. And you can all come along.' I may as well invite them. They'd only follow if I don't.

I find the men in the church of Saint Saviour, praying. It's a strange ceremony with only a few monks. They sound like mice scrabbling under the grain store. Their voices far from fill the huge church building. I wait patiently, as the daylight drains away, and the only light is provided by the candles. I wait for the service to finish, and for Ealdorman Ælhun to direct the two men my way.

I realise I've seen them about their work, but never spoken to them before.

'This is Father John and Father Jerome,' the ealdorman introduces them. 'They both have much knowledge of healing.'

'Well met,' I begin. 'I've a task, if you're tempted to it, although I'd quite understand if you didn't wish to be involved. It will necessitate some evasion and possibly, outright, lying to the enemy.'

The older of the men looks shocked, but the younger doesn't seem much concerned. In the way of all priests, they're well-fed and clothed in good brown cloth, even if they have tonsured heads and lack all facial hair.

'What is it you want us to do?' the younger questions. And so, I explain what this new development offers us. As I continue to speak, I sense the other Mercians settling as I detail my intentions. While the older man allows a look of horror to touch his face, the younger simply nods along.

'I think we can do that,' Father Jerome states quickly. Father John's agreement is much slower in arriving, but he does eventually nod, although his hands shake where they're clasped together.

'I won't send you alone,' I continue. 'One of my men will escort you.'

I don't look at the others as I say this.

'Not bloody you,' Icel growls, and I shake my head.

'No, not me,' I confirm, meeting his gaze evenly.

'He means bloody me,' Rudolf expels softly. 'It's always bloody me,' he states, although he doesn't refuse to go.

'It is always you, Rudolf. And this time, we're going to have to scalp you so you look like a priest as well.' He grimaces, but again, doesn't deny me.

'As long as it's not fucking you, I'll do as you command,' he confirms, and I know he will.

'Then that's settled. Prepare yourselves, for tomorrow, I'm sending the three of you into the lion's den, or rather, the owl's.' The statement quickly loses its menace and at the same time, the two priests look less apprehensive. And the bastards all think I'm shit at words and politics.

Chapter Twenty-Nine

I don't laugh at Rudolf when I come across him the next day, his hair cut short, and entirely missing on the sides. I don't even chuckle at the sight of his lanky body in priest's robes. In fact, I keep my expression entirely neutral although others are enjoying his discomfort. Bastards, all of them.

'You have everything?' I murmur. Rudolf nods, eyes bright, no trace of fear on his face. I don't like sending him without any blades, aside from an eating knife, but if we risk it, Jarl Guthrum will grow suspicious.

'I do, my lord, aside from joy in my heart,' he comments blackly.

I nod, pleased with the statement.

'Father Jerome will hold his nerve. Keep an eye on Father John, and don't let King Alfred change the plan in any way. If it's deviated away from, then we'll be in the shit.'

'I know what to do,' Rudolf reiterates.

'Remember to keep you face covered as much as possible. I don't want one of them recognising you. Although, you're almost unrecognisable to me, so don't worry too much about it. And I will see you again in three days. No more. Less if necessary, but not more.'

'Aye, my lord,' Rudolf confirms, and I reach out and grip his shoulders firmly, holding his gaze.

'You're a brave man, young Rudolf. A very brave man.'

'Or fucking stupid,' he complains, before grinning broadly. 'Now, let's get this done.'

And so, two priests and young Rudolf step through the briefly open gates, where they're met by a worried looking Jarl Guthrum, and taken to one of the tents.

We watch from the scaffolding.

'King Alfred's too stupid to realise what's happening,' Icel menaces.

'Perhaps, but he's been with the enemy for many days now. He knows I'll sacrifice him rather than pay up. That might have given him some wisdom.'

'Unless the bastard really is dying,' Pybba adds. 'Although, he's too fucking stubborn to do that.'

'Then, we'll have to let this play out,' I confirm. Either way, I think to myself, this is all turning in the favour of the few trapped within Canterbury. The Viking raiders might number thousands, but they're also confident of success. Soon, I hope, they'll be denied that confidence. And if not the confidence of overwhelmingly high numbers, then hopefully of keeping hold of their prized prisoner.

Three days pass, as I ordered, and then I'm summoned by a worried looking member of Archbishop Æthelred's warrior band to the wall.

'Jarl Guthrum demands you speak to him.'

'Does he, now?' I mutter, secretly pleased by the request.

'Open the gateway,' I call to those on guard duty, Icel and Pybba hurrying to join me, while Ealdorman Ælhun and Kyred watch on uneasily.

Just before the gate creaks open, I turn to the Mercians, and offer them a wink. They don't know what it portends.

For the first time in many days, I step through the gateway, rocked backwards by the stink of so many foemen living close by.

'They could have dug fucking latrines,' I complain, wafting my hand before my nose from atop the embankment.

I have my byrnie, but not my shield. Jarl Guthrum startles on seeing me, and hurries towards me, escorted by two of his warriors, pumping his legs frantically to reach me. I see how concerned he is. He doesn't even have his weapons belt on, much less a byrnie.

'My lord king, Coelwulf.'

'Jarl Guthrum,' I offer, and can't stop from adding, 'Blessings be upon you this day.'

His entire body shudders, and he crosses himself as the priests would do. Fucking arsehole.

'King Alfred's deathly ill. I must demand you allow him within to take succour from the holy place you occupy.'

'The priests haven't aided him?' I question, adding concern to my voice.

'No, he's become worse, not better. They assure me he's not long for this world.'

'Then, he'll be welcomed, of course, but he must come alone, with only the priests as escorts.'

'Of course, King Coelwulf. I declare a truce until....well, until King Alfred is departed from us.'

'Agreed,' I announce, perhaps too quickly. Jarl Guthrum, however, doesn't notice, and quickly he instructs men to carry a stretcher forward, with the priests to either side, intoning their prayers, while Rudolf walks behind, eyes downcast, no doubt so he doesn't see me and start to chuckle.

'We'll take him from here,' I confirm quickly, once I've let the enemy do the difficult task of climbing up the steep incline with a lifeless form between them. I do check it is King Alfred, and veer back from the smell of him. Rudolf bends to take hold of one of the wooden poles, while Icel, Pybba and I take the other three ends.

Brother John and Jerome continue with their prayers. I turn quickly, catching sight of Ealdorman Ælhun high above us, ready to attack if I call the order.

Head bowed, as though grief stricken, we shuffle through the gate, and wait for it to be closed and then barred against the enemy.

Only then, do I turn to Rudolf and the priests.

'Well done,' I exclaim. The priests are far from jovial. I look to Rudolf, and he winces.

'The fucker is genuinely unwell,' he comments, taking the edge from my delight at having King Alfred back with us.

'Are you?' I direct to the pale face, lying on the blankets. King Alfred opens one eye, and then the other. I see him take a huge breath and then force himself upright and then to his feet. He's a bit shaky.

'Not really. My thanks,' King Alfred inclines his head towards the priests, Rudolf and then to me. Rudolf and the priests look astounded to see Alfred upright.

'That was a risk,' King Alfred chastises me wearily. 'I began to feel much better two days ago. It's been an effort to remain immobile, but it seems I've managed to convince even your priests.'

'Then you have my profound apologies for having to lie down while all else were busy around you.' Of course, King Alfred doesn't detect the sarcasm. The priests startle at seeing their patient so much better.

'It seems to me, book learning is perhaps not the true path to healing,' I mutter to Rudolf.

'Nor to me,' he retorts. From within Saint Saviour's, the bells are being rung, as arranged. In that way, I intend for Jarl Guthrum to believe King Alfred is truly about to die.

'Where's Lord Æthelwulf?' King Alfred demands next, seeking him out.

'He turned traitor, so you tell me. Alongside some bloody ealdorman, Sigehelm.'

'Traitor,' King Alfred queries, forehead furrowed. We've walked to the archbishop's hall, better to have Alfred inside than risk the enemy realising our ruse.

'They tried to apprehend me, or rather, kill me when I went to find the enemy.'

'No, my lord king, you must be mistaken,' King Alfred is staunch in condemning the idea Lord Æthelwulf and Ealdorman Sigehelm could have become the enemy.

'I only wish that were true, but it's not.'

King Alfred sits abruptly, as though he lacks all strength to stand, while he shakes his head. 'No, not Lord Æthelwulf and Ealdorman Sigehelm. They wouldn't do that.'

'Whatever,' I murmur, looking to Rudolf again. Now I'm confident King Alfred is well I'm only concerned with the rest of Rudolf's instructions.

'Is it done?'

'It is, my lord, yes. It won't be everyone.'

'No, but a large proportion of them.'

'Hopefully, yes. And it won't last long either, so we need to be ready.'

I nod, and turn to the others.

'Tonight. We attack tonight, when Jarl Guthrum will be curled in pain from his belly, wishing he were dead, for all he won't be.'

'What?' King Alfred questions, trying to determine why he's no longer the centre of our attention.

'Tonight, King Alfred, you'll remain here, with the priests, and nominal command of the few people and warriors that will remain inside Canterbury.'

'What will you be doing?'

'That's for me to know, and you to find out,' I respond enigmatically, and as I stride from the hall, I allow a grin to touch my lips.

I believed I'd have to sacrifice myself to get King Alfred restored to us, but that's not happened. Indeed, King Alfred's illness provided us with an entirely different possibility, and it's one I intend to employ until every single last one of the bastard enemies are dead, or fled, but preferably dead.

I can hardly bloody wait.

Chapter Thirty

The noise from the enemy encampment gradually increases as night draws in. The bells from within Saint Saviour Christ Church rang for much of the afternoon, but now they're silent, because we need to listen to what the enemy are doing.

The growing swell of people being violently sick has me wanting to retch as well, but dressed for concealment, with my weapons silenced by the addition of wool to their sheaths, I wait impatiently. Soon, the vomiting will cease, I hope, implying the enemy are incapacitated. Once that happens, we'll slip into their encampment. Come the morning, I hope many of them will be dead and Jarl Guthrum, I pray, once more my captive, or dead. Either way, I won't be allowing him to walk freely from this place tomorrow.

I turn to eye my warriors. They're all here and dressed as I am. Even now, I sense Icel shaking his head, as though unable to believe what I've put into play. Or perhaps, more perplexed that it does seem to be working. I won't exalt yet, however. There's no way we could have poisoned all of the enemy force. No chance at all. We'll have an easier time escaping into the encampment, but we must still be wary.

What we need to do won't be easy, but nothing that's worth doing ever fucking is, or so I've discovered.

I turn to eye Ealdorman Ælhun. He nods in my direction. He's dressed for concealment, just as we are. Cloaks cover our byrnies and anything that might flash in flame light and reveal our intentions. One person who's not here is King Alfred. The craven bastard didn't even argue to join us even though I'd decided he couldn't. Despite our attempts, King Alfred is no warrior. At some point, I'll either reconcile myself to that, or he'll be killed and that'll put a bloody end to it. I know which one I'd prefer.

Time seems to drag. I blink grit from my eyes, tired despite everything. It's been no fun trapped within Canterbury, well, aside from annoying the enemy, that is. I hunger to be free of the place, and reunited with Haden and my missing warriors, but I can't be until the Viking raiders have been routed.

Rudolf's at my side. I pretended not to watch him and Pybba's interplay about who would have the dubious honour. Of course, no one has tried to usurp Icel from being at my other side. We are, I've ordered, to work in groups of three or four to accomplish what must be done. Icel, Pybba and Rudolf have glued themselves to my side. I'd sooner have had Wærwulf, so I could at least understand what the enemy were saying, but instead, he's with Eahric and Lyfing.

Kyred's with three of his warriors, Ealdorman Ælhun with three of his, Commander Wulfsige another three, and so it goes. Our numbers aren't huge, but there are twenty odd such groupings to infiltrate the enemy encampment. King Alfred's nominally responsible for what happens within Canterbury, but I'm not a fucking fool. I've ordered four of my loyal men to protect the gates. Even now, I wouldn't put it beyond Alfred's thinking to deny us entry back into Canterbury when the slaughter's over.

So, Hiltiberht, Gyrth, Wulfstan and Cuthwalh will remain within Canterbury. They've complained about it, well, aside from Hiltiberht who I'd not have sent to fight anyway, but they understand my concerns. There's little to trust about King Alfred. I'm taking no further chances that if we succeed in this endeavour we can return to the dubious protection of Canterbury.

Eventually, all is silence apart from the odd groan of pain, and the horrific sound of some poor bastard either shitting himself, or losing his guts out of his mouth. But, it's much quieter than it has been since the sun set. The dose of hemlock was intended to be larger than the one the abbot used, so as to incapacitate some of the enemy, even when they made themselves sick to void the poison.

Overhead, the moon's partially obscured by the odd cloud, but mostly clear. It'll be bright enough to see even with only a slither visible. After all, we need some protection. Already, the air's turning cold, my breath puffing before me. The first proper frost has been threatening for the last few nights, now it's upon us.

'Are we ready?' I mutter to Icel and look towards those on the gate. Earlier, when all was noisy in the encampment, we removed three of the huge iron bars so only the lowest one remained. The enemy haven't realised, and we've been protecting the gate in the interim just in case they decided to attack while we were weaker, but now it's time for the final bar to be removed.

We've oiled the gate hinges in the hope they won't give away our intentions. There was some complaint about using the holy oil for such a base task.

It's Gyrth and Wulfstan who lift the iron bar free and slowly open one side of the gate without any attendant shrieks, just enough for us to slip through.

Not that Icel allows me to lead the attack. Instead, with his huge hand on my arm, he indicates four of Kyred's warriors should go first. I see the flash of white from their necks, and then they cover their faces with the hoods of cloaks, and one by one, slip through the gate.

I don't breathe, straining to hear, wincing at the slightest sounds, which can only be the warriors walking down the steep embankment before merging with the tents of the enemy, scattered through the exterior dwellings of Canterbury.

When there's no sudden cry or call of alarm, Icel nods with satisfaction, and we're the next to slip through the gate. As I go, I turn to Gyrth, aware King Alfred stands in the shadow of the archbishop's hall, watching us leave. 'Do whatever must be done to ensure we can return.' He nods confidently. I've spoken to him about this. If he has to restrain King Alfred he will. If King Alfred is so difficult only his death can prevent him from revealing our actions, he's to do so. I've also taken Cuthwalh into my confidence. Like Icel, he has little love for the West Saxons.

Outside the walls, I don't consider how exposed we are, but instead, bend low, almost touching my arse to the steep decline so my feet don't run away with me. My left thigh twinges at the movement. I wince, but it's been weeks since I took the wound. It's almost healed. I doubt it'll ever stop protesting at such actions, however.

Level with the dwellings and tents, I wave aside the foul stink of vomit and shit, and move with confident steps to the left of the encampment. Everyone has been given a direction to take. The first men went to the far right. We move to the far left, Icel on nimble feet. Everything is shadows and black-edged, even with the moonlight, and the slowly crisping surface beneath my feet as the frost begins to settle on stray pieces of greenery and the dirt floor surrounding the dwellings.

The first tent we approach positively honks with the stink of vomit and shit. I grimace away from entering. Icel shows no such reticence, and neither does Rudolf. I remain outside, while from within, I hear the slight sound of sharp blades being sliced across throats or stabbed into hearts.

The two emerge quickly, the smell now overladen with freshly shed blood. Their blades are already sheathed once more, as Pybba and I silently make our way to the next tent. We dip into this although I rear backwards, overwhelmed by the smell and crash into Pybba.

He holds me steady as I wince at the slight noise, but then we're busy at our work. I feel my way as there's no candle within. The moonlight is bright enough to offer a faint glow, however.

I eye the first man, bent double on his bed, curled around his stomach. I slice my blade cleanly through his neck, although the angle I have to achieve is painful to my hand. With satisfaction, I hear the drum of blood onto the floor, and move to the next sleeping enemy. There are six of them in all who need silencing, and then Pybba and I join Icel and Rudolf. I glance towards the gateway, seeing the next group of men making their way through and down amongst the encampment.

I've heard no cries of alarm from the enemy, and now I've killed three men, I feel the tension in my shoulders relax. I don't like to kill like this, but there's no choice when we're so overwhelmed by enemy determined to exterminate us.

And so, we continue, moving through the line of tents, extending backwards towards the roadway, in a dog-legged fashion. In one of the tents we enter, the men are already dead. I realise we've become entangled in the line others are taking. But there's no other tent to the side, so I'm confident we're working our way through every tent.

In some, I'm convinced the poison has already done the work of killing our enemy. In others, there are restless warriors, not fully asleep, but in so much pain they don't realise our approach.

We kill everyone we encounter, stabbing those who are potentially already dead, but unprepared to take any chances. Just as I'm beginning to worry this is all too easy and we might manage to severely deplete the number of foemen, reach Jarl Guthrum and kill the bastard, a distant sound catches the edge of my hearing as I emerge from yet another tent.

I come to a stop, tilting my head as though that'll make it easier to hear, aware Icel's doing the same from where he guards us against an attack from behind. I look around, but can't see many details. I think Canterbury's gate is closed tight and my loyal Mercians outside, but in the reaching shadows I can't be certain.

'There,' Icel hisses, pointing. I see it. A flare of light to the middle of the encampment, perhaps close to where Jarl Guthrum has erected his own tent. And it's moving around.

I watch it pensively, unsure who's up and about at this dead time of the night, aside from the Mercians. I don't know if we've been discovered. If we have, quick action must be taken. We've not done nearly enough damage to enemy numbers, despite my confidence of moments ago. Not yet.

Abruptly, the flaming brand disappears. I blink the brightness from my eyes, seeking out where it's gone. I hear a slight scuffle and realise whoever it was has been stopped, I hope, by one of my Mercians, and not vice versa.

'Come on,' Icel whispers encouragement when he's convinced nothing else will happen. 'Bloody get on with it.'

I follow him to the next tent, and then we all pause. I hear a voice from within, someone who's awake and praying beneath their breath. This one is Icel and Rudolf's. Quickly, Pybba and I move to the doorway, and yank it open. Icel surges inwards so swiftly, a breath of cool air touches my face. A quickly gargled cry of shock rings out. I tense, aware it's the loudest noise I've heard since leaving the confines of Canterbury. I wait for someone else to mirror the cry, but then Icel and Rudolf join us and the danger passes.

'We must be moving beyond those who owe their oath to Jarl Guthrum. These men might not have partaken of the same food and drink.'

'We carry on until we know that for certain,' I whisper. But of course, it's more dangerous now. I've not appreciated the smell of vomit and shit has started to dissipate. Emerging from the next tent, Icel's heavy hand on my shoulder has me staying low, no word of caution needed.

There's something else out there, moving. I see whoever it is as shadow moving past the tents. I peer back the way we've come, astounded by how far we've travelled away from Canterbury's wall. With no respect for the fields and crops lying dormant here, the enemy have set their tents up, and there's a darker shape to my right, which must be the thick hedgerow. What's happening to the other side of it, I don't know.

I want to speak, and discuss what we should do next, but I dare not risk it. We've done much better than I thought we would but we can't face being discovered, not now. I bite my lip, forcing my hand away from my sticky blade in its sheath, which will be madder-red by the time daylight once more pools over the horizon.

Our path of destruction should continue, but our numbers are so small, I know it's not possible. Equally, we won't have such a chance again. I think we should press on, and do as much damage as possible to the enemy, but equally, while Jarl Guthrum's encampment had no guards, all incapacitated, here, further away from the walls, there must be warriors beholden to another, lesser, jarl, with more and more guards. Abruptly, firelight grows ahead, temporarily blinding me. I hear a voice calling softly into the cool night air.

'Bollocks,' I mouth. I know what this is. This's one guard shouting to another, and when he receives no reply from him, he'll wake others, because he'll be uneasy investigating alone.

I look to Icel, and he meets my gaze, nodding slowly. We've reached the limit of what we can accomplish. Now, we need to make our way back within Canterbury and wait for the others to join us. When Jarl Guthrum discovers what we've done, he'll be fucking angry, but he'll lack his own loyal warriors to exact his revenge, if he's not been killed that is.

I turn, unwillingly, but eager to evade detection, and using the canvases we've entered and killed the inhabitants within, we begin to scuttle back towards Canterbury, even as the voice grows louder, calling a name and something else. This is why we should have had Wærwulf with us, but of course, he couldn't be with every grouping of men.

I move swiftly, grateful and frustrated as cloud temporarily covers the moon overhead. I can't call to my other warriors to retreat, but I can detect other swift steps. Those to this side of the hedgerow are alert to the danger, although others aren't. I can't shout for a retreat. I can't even see many of the other Mercians. We make our way closer and closer to Canterbury's walls, their solid blackness growing as we move into the wider space, where Jarl Guthrum's encampment meets the homes outside the walls.

I turn as soon as the cloud moves, wanting to order my warriors back. From behind, the cry of the confused guard has grown louder, and been joined by others. Any moment now, everyone will be awoken and our nighttime excursion will be discovered.

'We split up,' I huff when we're almost close enough to make a dash for the gateway. I can't see others doing the same. 'Get everyone back inside,' I urge my three loyal men. Icel scowls, but nods, which thankfully prevents me from having to argue with him about it.

'We go in pairs. Icel, with me. Rudolf and Pybba take the left.'

We separate, me and Icel seeking out my warriors. It's difficult, all is shadow and gloom, and the shouts of the enemy further away are growing louder. I see movement, and grab Icel, dashing along one of the rows, close to Jarl Guthrum's tent. Icel's footfall is swift beside mine. We should have had some means of ordering everyone to withdraw. What that might have been, I don't bloody know.

I reach out and grip Kyred's arm. He startles, blade raised menacingly, but sees me before striking.

'Retreat,' I hiss. 'We've been discovered.'

He nods. I sense him grabbing his warriors, and urging them to return to the gate.

Icel's two rows over, his bulk illuminated against a pale tent, as he does the same to another group of warriors. I turn my head, determined to get everyone back within Canterbury. I see figures crawling up the steep embankment and a slight creak as the gate opens to allow them within, before closing again.

I move between a tent and a wattle and daub dwelling, and reach out to grab the next figure I see. At the last moment, I don't. The man isn't hooded so isn't a Mercian, and I move quickly around the wall once more, keen to avoid being seen. My warriors all wore cloaks, this must be one of the enemies. I listen, straining to hear, and then there's the sound of water hitting the floor. The man's merely gone for a piss.

I don't know why he still lives. Somehow, some of the tents must have been missed.

I need to kill him, and prepare myself to emerge once more into the open, blade to hand. I hear his steps returning, and wince at the distant cry I can hear. The man pauses. I sense him turning his head, trying to determine what's being said, but then he continues his path back to his bed. I emerge from behind the dwelling, seeking him in the pale glow of the moonlight. The ground is crisp and each step I take makes a slight crunching noise.

I hardly dare breathe, as I dog his steps. I'm not far from reaching out to clasp my hand over his mouth and plunge my blade into his back, when a huge flare of rekindled fire seems to envelop the encampment from ahead, blinding me and eliciting a bellow of shock from my target. But it's nothing compared to the roar of outrage from rudely woken men who've discovered their allies have been slaughtered in their sleep.

My enemy must sense my presence, and he turns, blade extended although I've not heard it being drawn, a grimace on his shadowed face.

'*Skiderik*,' he cries, but my body moves more quickly than my mind. My blade impales him with a quick jab sliding through his tunic, for although he's armed, he has no byrnie. He dies as more and more voices join the clamour, and flame spreads more quickly from campfire to campfire than I thought possible.

I turn, eyes scouting for Icel and the rest of my warriors, as the thunder of horse's hooves reverberates and realise the enemy mean to hunt down whoever has killed their allies.

I see Icel, looking for me, and I lift my voice, the time for stealth long over.

'Retreat, Mercians, retreat,' I roar, the sound echoed by others. I'm running through the encampment, here, where the men are all dead, strangely quiet and lacking all movement, even when Jarl Guthrum, the fucker, joins his voice to the outrage.

We should have ensured he was dead, we really bloody sure, but it's too late now.

I'm just about to surge up the embankment to the gate, grateful to see others are far ahead of me, when a new voice makes itself heard.

I stumble, turn back the way I've come, and clap eyes on the man I suspect is fucking Ealdorman Sigehelm, and somehow, he has Pybba at knife point.

'King Coelwulf, I believe I have something you desire,' he calls, taunting me.

Chapter Thirty-One

My view narrows, as more and more of the enemy emerge from wherever they've been hiding. I glance at Pybba, and despite the blade at his throat, he nods in my direction. It's obvious he's giving me permission to leave him, but I hesitate.

'My lord,' I hear Rudolf roar, from two rows over, also detecting Icel's growl of fury. I lift my eyes to glance at Ealdorman Sigehelm, and a smirking Jarl Guthrum behind him, illuminated by the succession of fires being rapidly lit. I'm curious as to where Lord Æthelwulf is. There's not much distance between Pybba and me, but it feels like there's a whole fucking world.

For a moment, I consider if we've been betrayed by one of the Mercians, or by King Alfred, but I don't know how. This is happenstance, I'm sure of it. I'm further convinced by it as Jarl Guthrum shouts for his warriors to rise, confusion evident when not one tent flat opens.

'Your men are dead,' I shout to Jarl Guthrum, enjoying the moment of understanding as his body jolts. 'And you're a fucking cock,' I inform Ealdorman Sigehelm. He shrugs, allowing the blade to graze Pybba's throat. I'm astounded Pybba's been caught. When we get him back, because we will get him back, we're going to enjoy teasing him about this.

'King Coelwulf, as a man of honour, you can take the place of your friend, and no one here need die. The Mercians can return to Mercia.' Ealdorman Sigehelm calls his demands, but I appreciate he voices what Jarl Guthrum wants.

'What have you done?' I question Ealdorman Sigehelm, my tone quiet so he has to strain to hear.

'I've ensured Wessex is safe from Mercian pretensions,' he retorts arrogantly.

'What, by siding with the enemy of both Wessex and Mercia?'

'No, by joining with men who'll protect Wessex from Mercia.'

I'd shake my head at that, but I'm busy assessing my next move.

'But they had King Alfred captive,' I splutter.

'He's inconsequential,' Ealdorman Sigehelm suggests. 'And anyway, he'll be dead soon enough if he's not already.'

'Will he?' I muse, but what I'm really doing is trying to extend this conversation for a little longer. I wish Hereman was here, now, with his spear ready to kill the impertinent fucker, but of course, Hereman's somewhere out there, behind the enemy. Or so I bloody hope. Along with the rest of my missing men, and my horse.

With Hereman's absence, I wish for someone else to strike with spear at the Kentish ealdorman. However, I hope Rudolf isn't considering flinging himself at the collection of men before me. If he does, he'll be dead before I can do anything to aid him.

'So, what, you'll rule Kent?'

'Of course,' Ealdorman Sigehelm retorts, but I see Jarl Guthrum wince behind him. No doubt, he's pleased there aren't too many nearby to hear this. I can't imagine that's truly what he intends. 'And the whole of Wessex, in time,' Ealdorman Sigehelm adds. The fucker is entirely mad. 'Now, come on, let's exchange you for this old bastard here, and we can all get some sleep.' Ealdorman Sigehelm sounds quite sane, but is far from it.

'Don't do it, my lord,' Pybba shouts. 'Let me die so you can live. I've lived a good, long life.' He sounds terrified, but he's not. If there was more light with which to see, I'm sure he'd offer me a crafty wink. Pybba's saying exactly what Ealdorman Sigehelm and Jarl Guthrum wish to hear. Both look suitably pleased. But there's something I'm missing here. I'd like to turn my head, and catch sight of what it is, but that would draw attention to it. There's a reason Pybba's shouting to me, distracting the enemy in the process.

'You must live, my lord. You must. Mercia would be bereft without you,' he continues to urge.

I keep my eyes on Pybba, aware more and more of the enemy are waking from their tents further away from Canterbury's walls and being drawn to the huge fires and tense conversation taking place.

'I might be a man of honour,' I reply. 'But my warrior here knows I'll sacrifice my men for the good of Mercia. So, you're welcome to him,' I retort, preparing to turn my back on Pybba, Ealdorman Sigehelm and Jarl Guthrum.

'You arrogant arsehole,' Ealdorman Sigehelm begins, but I'm finally aware of what Pybba seems to have known for some time. There's no one within Canterbury that could come to our aid, but I've forgotten something. I really didn't think I had, but I have. It's not like me. Not at all.

From nearby, the thundering sound finally begins to make sense. I don't know how he's done it, I really don't, but suddenly, a collection of horses appear, led by Haden, riderless, his trajectory bringing him towards me. I allow a smile to play on my lips, even as Rudolf dives towards Pybba, with Icel not far behind. I'd get involved in that, but instead, I stand my ground, catching sight of Hereman and Ordheah directing the horses this way, pleased to see Oda is with them.

While my Mercians surge towards Pybba and the enemy, Haden comes to a panting halt before me, kicking up a spray of blood-tinged mud.

'Hello boy,' I welcome him, running my hand swiftly along his nose in greeting and apology for abandoning him before mounting.

The cries and shouts of Jarl Guthrum and Ealdorman Sigehelm can be clearly heard, as the horses and their riders, all seemingly no longer lame, turn to face the enemy.

'Take them alive,' I call, directing Haden towards the tableau, relieved to see Pybba's already won free with the aid of Rudolf and Icel. 'Take them inside,' I further instruct, joining Ordheah, Oda, Hereman and the rest of my missing men on their horses.

'Good to see you,' I call.

Hereman grunts, mounting up with a spear in his hand.

'Now what?' Ordheah questions. 'We don't have the fucking numbers.'

'We don't, no, but we'll ensure our allies retreat within Canterbury before we do anything.'

I hear Ealdorman Ælhun ordering his men to drag Ealdorman Sigehelm and Jarl Guthrum within Canterbury. The enemy warriors look wild but are keeping their distance, those who did come closer reversing those steps because while they severely outnumber us, they still don't understand why Jarl Guthrum's men don't defend their jarl. Perhaps they're holding out for when they will. They must suspect Jarl Guthrum's men have something else planned.

'We retreat, slowly,' I call to my warriors, overjoyed to be reunited with them. 'Slowly,' I repeat, Haden taking the unusual command to walk backwards with some complaints.

Never moving my eyes from the enemy, we reverse through the encampment where not long ago, we killed all the sleeping warriors. At the last moment, and with Hereman and Ordheah still facing the enemy, who haven't moved, I turn my back on them, and encourage Haden through the gate, flung wide open to enable us to move quickly.

'Come on,' I call to my two remaining men. They follow, and I hear the slam of the gate being closed, and the crash of the iron bars being placed into position.

I seek out Jarl Guthrum and Ealdorman Sigehelm, under heavy guard, and rest my eyes not on Jarl Guthrum, who I know is a bastard, but on Ealdorman Sigehelm, who I suspected was allied with the enemy, but now have confirmation that he is.

I dismount, and leading Haden, I walk towards Ealdorman Sigehelm. I don't quite know what I'm going to do to him, but I'm not given the chance, for King Alfred's there, eyes wild and furious, with a blade to hand that he uses to stab him. I startle at the cry that rips from King Alfred's lips, astounded by the flood of blood pooling on our enemy's chest, and only just manage to grab the outraged man before he does the same to Jarl Guthrum.

'It's one thing to kill your treasonous ealdorman,' I mutter into Alfred's ear, as he ineffectually fights my hold. 'But quite another to kill Jarl Guthrum. Stand aside,' I urge King Alfred, and finally sense the fight leave him, as Icel and Rudolf ensure his blade is dropped to the ground.

Jarl Guthrum looks from me to King Alfred, and a slow smile spreads on his lips, one I'd love to wipe from his face.

'Well, that's an interesting development,' he comments. 'Very interesting, indeed.'

'Take him to the crypt,' I direct quickly. 'Make sure he's secured and no one is to have access to him without me there, or without my say so. See it done,' I order Ealdorman Ælhun. He inclines his head towards me, and quickly, four of his warriors surround the Viking raider jarl with Commander Wulfsige leading them.

I watch Jarl Guthrum being led away to the crypt, as the grey hint of dawn forms on the distant horizon. I bite my lip. Jarl Guthrum is far from an ideal prisoner. In fact, I'd rather he was dead than my captive. As he's still alive, I need to keep him that way or the enemy will seek vengeance against me.

I look to Pybba, and he offers me a grimace of apology, as he runs his hand around his neck. Next, I seek out Hereman, who grins broadly, pleased with his role in all this, as well as Ordheah and Oda, and then I look to King Alfred. Wild-eyed, but evidently still weak from whatever ailment he's suffered, he watches Jarl Guthrum with a hunger that surprises me. King Alfred would welcome Guthrum's death. Perhaps, I should have allowed him to kill the Viking raider. But no. Jarl Guthrum's end must come in battle, and not through any sort of ritual execution.

From without, I hear the roar of outrage from our enemy, and I meet Icel's unhappy gaze.

We're all together once more. Well, most of us. But how long that will last, I simply don't know.

I didn't expect our sneak attack to end in such a way. Now I really don't know what to do. Ealdorman Sigehelm's dead, but we've yet to find Lord Æthelwulf, and that, despite having Jarl Guthrum as our prisoner, worries me. It really fucking does.

* * *

Later that day, when the sun's risen, with Icel and Pybba at my side, I gain entry to the crypt. I'm grateful now for the archbishop's enthusiasm in showing the crypt to us. Yes, it might stink of decay, but it's also secure. There's one way in, and one way out.

I know Abbot Kynebert's been moved to a different room. Jarl Guthrum, while our prisoner, has been provided with warm clothing and hot food. We don't want to kill the bastard through neglect.

'Ah, King Coelwulf,' he greets me in his insufferable tone. 'This is a fine place. I've been praying since you brought me here.' My eyes flash to his neck, but the cross he wore has been removed. We can't have the bastard keeping hold of something that could be used as a weapon.

'Tell me,' I question him, 'how all this came about? How did you meet Ealdorman Sigehelm?'

'Who, the dead man? He came to me. Offered me his aid in securing Canterbury and killing you. You really don't make friends easily do you, my lord king.' I'd grimace at that understatement, but I didn't come here to exchange barbs. I need answers.

'When was this?'

'A month ago, when we were at Winchester.'

'So, he came to Winchester?'

'Yes. Him and a few of his warriors.' I consider this. Surely that would have been when Gardulf was there, or perhaps not. I've lost track of the passage of time. Alfred was a prisoner for over two weeks. I believe another three weeks have gone by since I left Old Sarum, so perhaps Gardulf wasn't at Winchester then.

'He didn't ask for anything other than Kent?'

'No, and he only promised to help me kill you, not King Alfred. I think he quite likes that ineffectual bastard.'

'And Lord Æthelwulf. What of him?'

'Oh Lord Æthelwulf is all talk and no substance.'

'Then where is he?'

'Lord Æthelwulf?'

'Yes, Lord Æthelwulf, he was with Ealdorman Sigehelm.'

'Was he? It's the first I know of it.' I can feel my temper fraying with Jarl Guthrum's dismissive replies. Icel menaces beside me, growling, but Jarl Guthrum merely appraises him and turns back to me.

'What do you plan to do now? You're surrounded, you must know that.'

'What do you plan to do now?' I counter.

'Wait for you to be overwhelmed. It won't be long. We vastly outnumber you.'

'You don't, Jarl Guthrum. You don't.' A flicker of uncertainty on his face is the only sign I might have penetrated his calm exterior.

'Well, yes. I'll need to find myself some new warriors. That was very underhand for Mercia's honourable king, and the man who likes to project an image of such righteousness.' Pybba coughs at Jarl Guthrum's words, but they do pierce me. I don't like to kill men who are ill or sleeping.

'I've been taught a few things by my enemy,' I counter, and Jarl Guthrum cracks a smile.

'So, how will you get out of this alive?' he presses the point.

'I came to ask you questions,' I counter. 'We're seeking Lord Æthelwulf.'

'Well, he's not here, is he?' Jarl Guthrum retorts.

'This is a waste of time,' Icel grumbles. 'He's not going to tell us anything. We should kill him.'

'Perhaps,' I muse, not moving my gaze from Guthrum's. He's doing a remarkably good job of looking unconcerned by Icel's threat. I'm not sure I'd be quite so calm.

'It would do you no good,' Jarl Guthrum bluffs. 'The other jarls have their objectives. As with your man there, the loss of me won't stop them. They won't even worry if you do kill me. They still mean to have Canterbury.'

'Do they now?' I question. 'I believed you were the Christian, not them.'

'Jarl Anwend's eager to have vengeance for the death of his son.'

'He drowned, it was nothing to do with me.'

'I don't believe he sees it that way.'

I shrug my shoulders. 'I know what happened. You weren't there. Neither was Jarl Anwend, and I doubt many others survived their dip in the River Severn to inform him of the truth.'

'He still means to seek vengeance against you.'

'And what of the others?'

'They'll do as they're told,' he dismisses my question easily, but I know how the Viking raider jarls work. They won't hold to Jarl Guthrum's objective now he's been captured.

'Even Jarl Halfdan?'

Jarl Guthrum can't prevent the swift look of fury that touches his cheeks. 'Jarl Halfdan holds Wareham.'

'Does he now?' I muse, infusing my voice with the same insuffer-able tone Jarl Guthrum was employing earlier. 'So, there's Jarl Anwend and who else? Is Jarl Oscetel with you?'

'He is, yes,' Jarl Guthrum affirms too quickly for my liking.

I absorb this information. I've not been told Halfdan holds Wareham.

'And if Halfdan isn't at Wareham?'

'He's at Wareham. I assure you of that.'

'But just, for a moment, pretend he's not at Wareham. Where then might he be?'

'What do you know?' Jarl Guthrum capitulates.

'I know there are no Viking raiders left west of here. I know Wareham and Winchester are in the hands of the Wessex ealdormen.'

Jarl Guthrum laughs, darkly, only for his expression to falter.

'That bastard,' he rages, and now I'm the one smiling.

'It seems I'm not the only one with some really shit allies,' I suggest. Pybba coughs at my side, perhaps recalling me to the fact I shouldn't be commiserating with my sworn enemy. Momentarily, Jarl Guthrum looks furious, but then a smile splits his face.

'You know, King Coelwulf, if we weren't on opposite sides of this, I think I'd quite like you.'

'A pity I can't say the same,' I retort, but only because Icel would have my stones on a platter if I didn't. Somehow, and despite everything, I think I'd rather have Jarl Guthrum as an ally than King Alfred.

'Now, what do you suggest we do?' I ask conversationally. 'Will they pay for you, as you tried to make us pay for King Alfred.' Jarl Guthrum winces at my question.

'Jarl Anwend's already lost his son trying to rescue me.'

'He has, hasn't he. I doubt he has another one to spare?'

Jarl Guthrum assesses my tone, and then shakes his head.

'They won't pay for me, but neither will they wish to lose more warriors to rescue me.'

'So, a stalemate?' I counter. 'We won't let you go, and they won't fight for you?'

'Perhaps,' he muses. 'Although, I might know a little more about your Lord Æthelwulf.'

'Might you now. What do you know?'

'My freedom for the information,' he counters. I find myself nodding along, as though I'll agree.

'The problem with that is that I don't know if the information is worthwhile having.'

But Jarl Guthrum's gaze bores into mine.

'I assure you, King Coelwulf. You'll want to know what that fucking cunt is up to.'

I startle at his command of my tongue, but then realise, I know how to swear in Norse as well. It speaks of many fights to the death with my enemy.

I nod. I do want to hear about Lord Æthelwulf. And, as I've been thinking, Jarl Guthrum isn't much use to me as a captive, and I sure as fuck can't kill him.

'We have an agreement. Tell me about Lord Æthelwulf.'

Jarl Guthrum looks surprised.

'That's it. That's all you want for my freedom?'

'Oh no, you can start to earn your freedom by telling me about Lord Æthelwulf, and then, when we let you go free, you and your little friends can fuck off to Ireland. You're not welcome on this island. Not now, and not ever again.'

Jarl Guthrum looks pained, but we're at something of an impasse.

'I'll do as you suggest,' he agrees. 'All the better to fight another day,' he counters, and I acknowledge that with a dip of my head.

'Now, tell me about Lord Æthelwulf, the little shit.'

Chapter Thirty-Two

We watch Jarl Guthrum convincing his allies to leave Kent, and only then do I turn to King Alfred.

'Hold Canterbury until Archbishop Æthelred returns.'

'My lord king,' he begins, all bluster and bugger all else.

'What remains of your force will be here as soon as the enemy are gone. Hereman informs me there are a lot of them. They'll keep you safe. I need to contend with Lord Æthelwulf.'

'What will you do to him?' King Alfred questions.

'What would you have me do with the treasonous little fucker?'

'I. Well, he's my brother by marriage.'

'He is, yes. Shall I return him to you?'

I see him swallow. 'Will you want him anywhere close to you after he tried to sell you to the Viking raiders in exchange for their support in proclaiming him king?'

'Well.' But he has no answer. I stride towards him, and grip his shoulders. They're surprisingly firm for all he still lacks the build of a warrior. Maybe Pybba has made some improvements to him although they still can't be seen, only felt. Or is it that he's lost weight while unwell?

'Stay here. Protect Canterbury. Ensure the Viking raiders leave, and then, when Archbishop Æthelred returns, take yourself to Winchester and start to rebuild. You need better defences and warriors. Reward your loyal ealdormen. Earn yourself some bloody respect.'

Without waiting for him to offer more, I stride to Haden, who's waiting for me, close to the now open northern gateway. I sweep a quick glance over Canterbury. I hope never to see this bloody place again. It's far from a good defensive location. I don't understand why it's so fucking important to Christians, but I don't need to know either. That's for Archbishop Æthelred to understand. Certainly, I've met more than my fair share of tricksters within its walls. Archbishop Æthelred can deal with the traitorous abbot. King Alfred can contend with Ealdorman Sigehelm's tarnished legacy. I need to return to London.

* * *

Hemming finds us before we reach the shallows close to Laleham Gulls. He and his horse don't look to be in the best condition.

'My lord,' he hurries to me. It's taken two days to reach here, travelling fast. With each beat of Haden's hooves, I've named myself a bloody fool. I can't say the others have been any kinder.

'Tell me,' I question, while he turns to join us, although I slow our pace.

'I was unable to get within London. I don't understand it.' His young face is flecked with concern.

'I do,' I advise him. 'But we have a plan.'

'To do what?'

'Break into London.'

'Break in?'

'Yes, that arse Lord Æthelwulf has taken advantage of our distraction to take London for himself.'

'How do you know that?' Hemming questions, eyes wide with shocked outrage.

'One of the Viking raider jarls told me.'

Hemming's face reflects his evident confusion.

'Tell me, how's the river?'

'Shallow today, or it was earlier.'

'Good. We need to get across.'

'And then what?' Rudolf questions. This, as always, is the problem.

'We've somewhat worked against ourselves,' I muse. 'I take it the repair work will be complete?' I direct this to Icel.

'I imagine so. We've been gone for many weeks.'

'Hum,' I mutter, but then allow a slow smile to spread across my face.

'It seems, we might need to try one of our old tricks.'

Icel looks at me without understanding, but Rudolf chuckles.

'Oh, I like that, my lord, I really bloody do.'

The shallows at Laleham Gulls are thankfully, exactly that. Without pausing to reacquaint ourselves with the innkeeper and his sharp-tongued wife, I lead Haden over the wide expanse of the river with the water barely touching his knees. From there, I direct the horses, not towards London, but instead to the woodlands Egbalth and the other London traders told us about. Or at least, in that direction. I hope we find the charcoal burners. We have need of them.

I acknowledge without Egbalth to aid us, this might prove tricky. The smell of woodsmoke reaches us on the wind, and I call my warriors close.

'We need to be bloody careful with these people. They don't know us, and we need them a lot more than they need us.'

'Ah, my lord king,' a voice calls, and I turn, astounded to see Egbalth and Cata standing there, Cata doing the talking, as she must. 'We wondered how long it would be until we saw you again.'

I gasp and then a slow smile spreads across my face.

'You knew to expect us?'

'We did, my lord king, yes, although I doubt anyone else did.'

'Then you know what my warriors and I need to do?'

'We do, my lord king, and we're ready for you. Now come. It's important you meet those who mean to aid you. You'll protect them, with your lives, and they'll do the same for you. I assure you Lord Æthelwulf isn't beloved by the people of London.'

'Then they're my kind of bloody people,' I grin. I dismount and step forward to greet Cata and Egbalth and the others who flood from beneath the trees. I face many men and women, wearing good clothes against the chill wind, and they smile and greet me. They're not at all the sulky lot I anticipated meeting, and I'm grateful I don't need to convince them to help us.

'You won't be sodding going first,' Icel fumes, but I turn to face him, gripping his wide shoulder with my right hand.

'You mean to bloody deprive me of this, do you?'

'Well,' he huffs.

'This is the stuff of legends,' I comment and reluctantly he needs.

'I'll have your word, my lord, that yours won't be the next line added to the tales of Coelwulf's war band.'

'Oh, you have my word on that,' I assure him. I'm grateful I don't need to tie Icel up to enable me to play my part in reclaiming London. I'd have done so, had he not capitulated so quickly. Mind, the following dawn, as the grey light of the coming day starts to grow across the far horizon, I can't say I'm as pleased to be taking part.

There are ten cartloads of heavy soil making their way to London, the improvements ongoing despite Lord Æthelwulf taking control of London in my absence. No doubt, his sister adds her voice to his and for that, my aunt will be furious. I will, when this is contained, allow her to determine on a punishment for Lady Ealhswith. I won't even bid her be kinder than she might have wanted to be. King Alfred will also have to deal with his recalcitrant wife, and I've promised him she'll not be welcomed within Mercia ever again.

Before the carts leave the safety of the trees, my warriors and I are forced to bury ourselves beneath the cold, and stinking soil. And, it's bloody cold. The soil heaps, already cut by the people who work as charcoal makers, are festooned with white frost as I'm joined by Icel, Rudolf, Pybba and the rest of my warriors to decide who'll escort who.

'We need our weapons as well,' Rudolf complains, shivering because he's refusing to wear his good cloak and risk it being irrevocably ruined.

'There's no need to state the bloody obvious,' I complain. My gaze is on Ealdorman Ælhun who looks uneasy at our intentions.

'We'll open the gates as soon as we're inside, and then you can join me.'

'It should be me who goes, my lord king, not you.'

'But Ealdorman Ælhun, my warriors and I have experience at this. We employed a similar ruse to break into Northampton. We know what to do.'

'Do you?' he demands, only to sigh. 'Of course you do, my lord king. I shouldn't question you. I'll do as you say. My warriors, and Kyred's men will be ready to support you as soon as the gate's open.'

'Good. Tonight, London will be ours once more.'

He inclines his head, but doesn't go far. I eye my warriors. They all look cold, and our task hasn't even begun.

'Right men. You know what we have to do. Stay quiet as we gain entry into London. We allow ourselves to be taken to the destination of the soil. Hopefully, by then, the warriors Lord Æthelwulf has with him will have lost interest and we can emerge from our hiding places and begin to restore London to our leadership.'

'Aye, my lord,' Icel rumbles. I catch myself eyeing him, waiting for him to offer a caution or a complaint. When none is forthcoming, I consider what I've forgotten. There must be something. His refusal to comment or complain that this is a shit idea is more unsettling than if he told me I was doing the correct thing.

'Nothing to add, Icel?'

'No, my lord. I'm even looking forward to it. I hear mud is good for the skin.' I gasp at his statement, amazed to see a broad grin on his face. 'Come on, my lord. Let's get on with this.'

'As you wish,' I agree. 'You know who you're with, and you know what to do. I wish you all good luck.'

'And hopefully we won't be too wet and stinking when we get within and give ourselves away.'

I grin at Rudolf.

'I never realised you enjoyed following my orders so poorly.'

He startles at that, opening his mouth to argue, but quickly subsides.

'You know that old phrase, 'the blind leading the blind."

I narrow my eyes at him.

'I'd much rather be blind with our king, than with bloody King Alfred,' Hereman announces firmly.

'Then come on my blind friends. Let's get on with this.'

For all that, I don't enjoy finding a hollow for my body beneath the weight of the soil and stones. The mud is indeed freezing cold. I bury my weapons first, shield to one side, spear to the other, but then there's no more putting off the inevitable. I lie down amongst the dank aroma of soil and rotting leaves, and Ealdorman Ælhun comes to cover the rest of me. He ensures none of my body can be seen, although a small hole is left to allow me to breathe, a handy twig placed there, so, if need be, I can wiggle it around when, or rather if, the soil moves. I don't want to give myself away by choking.

'Are you sure about this, my lord king?' he questions.

'I am, Ealdorman Ælhun. I really bloody am, and anyway, it's too late now. My warriors are all covered as well.'

My warriors are split between the ten carts, two of us in each. Beside me, I have Hemming, because he's slight and otherwise, the cart would be too heavy with all the mud for the oxen to pull. Icel didn't like it, but if both of us had been within one cart, it would have been too obvious, and would probably not have moved no matter the effort put in by the oxen.

Reluctantly, Ealdorman Ælhun covers my head, and with a juddering and shaking of wooden cart and wheels, the driver encourages his oxen on. Egbalth is beside him. I argued against that, but Egbalth was determined he'd be the means for us to gain entry. Without him there, he stated, through Cata, the gate wardens would be too suspicious of the ten cartloads arriving at the same time.

With the creaking cart moving off, I wince, aware sharp stones bite into my body, intermingled with the soil. I should have thought of that before lying down. It's impossible to do more than move my head a little to ensure I get enough air. Closing my eyes, I reconcile myself to being uncomfortable, biting back my pain when the cart travels over uneven ground, shaking my entire body. I hear Icel's shout of pain from behind me, and allow a little smile. At least I'm not the only damn fool suffering.

My grin lasts for as long as it takes for my body to grow cold and unresponsive, and for the air I'm breathing to become hot and tainted with the rich earthy smell of the freshly dug soil. And then my previous good cheer falls even lower as the cart comes to a halt. I know we've not travelled far enough to be within London. Then I hear the sound of voices, and grimace, even though the action allows mud to fall onto my lips.

'What's this?' the voice calls, and I immediately recognise Lord Æthelwulf. I know a moment of fear, but it seems Cata has once more been expecting this turn of events.

'My lord. This is the new soil for within London. It'll allow the settlement to be self-sufficient,' Cata calls to him.

'Will it now,' he muses. His voice comes even closer, and I try to not breathe or give myself away in any other small way. 'Tell me, I've heard reports of mounted enemy warriors nearby. Have you seen any riders?'

'West Saxons, my lord? Not at all.' Cata's words are smooth. I consider if Lord Æthelwulf will correct her and say he's seeking Mercians. It appears not, although for long moments, I'm uncertain. I can imagine the narrow-eyed look on the bastard's face. How I'd like to emerge now and stab the traitorous git but it's not time. Not yet.

'Be about your business,' Lord Æthelwulf instructs quickly. 'We'll seek out the enemy.' I almost breathe more deeply, but the cart still hasn't moved. 'I'll send four of my men with you, to ensure you're allowed entry without any fuss.'

'My lord, you're most kind,' Cata oozes, but I don't welcome this new problem. 'We'll be on our way,' she announces, and immediately, I feel the cart move off. I strain to hear if Lord Æthelwulf has also gone, but a sudden drop for the cart has me gasping with pain and trying not to cry out. The ground's far from smooth. Why, I consider, is there no road to take us to London? I might have to put right that oversight.

Chapter Thirty-Three

It takes a very long time to reach London. I might almost think it had taken all of the daylight, but as I hear the shouts of voices demanding to know what's happening, I appreciate there's still daylight.

Now comes the difficult part. We need to get within London, and to the home of Gayadore so my warriors and I can warm up and prepare to infiltrate London. First, we must secure the gates and allow Kyred and Ealdorman Ælhun within. Then, we need to make our way to the bishop's complex and safeguard my aunt before doing anything about Lord Æthelwulf and his warriors. I'd really like to be the one to kill him, but I doubt I'll get the opportunity. Already, I know his sister will try and intervene. It would be much bloody easier if she weren't here, but of course, Lord Æthelwulf's intentions are exactly why she's here. I consider if she suspected his plans towards me? I might have to ask her. King Alfred has bid me be gentle with his wife and children. I didn't exactly agree to his demands.

The welcome creak of the wooden gates opening washes over me and the oxen is once more encouraged to move on as Lord Æthelwulf's men arrange safe passage for the carts. I hope they move off quickly. The animal's movements are almost insignificant but they're so much stronger than horses for this duty that I entirely understand why they've been given the task. My thoughts turn to Haden. I hope he's behaving himself. I was in two minds as to whether Ealdorman Ælhun should bring the horses or not. In the end, I decided he should because we might need them. I don't know how many have turned in favour of Lord Æthelwulf. I'd hope not many, but I really don't know. Lord Æthelwulf has something about him. It doesn't appeal to me, but there are always those swayed by honeyed words and fuck-all intent.

As I hear the cart wheels rattling over the remnants of the stone road, I allow myself a grin of triumph, only to wince again. It feels as though my teeth are being rattled loose. It's most unpleasant. Eventually, the cart comes to a stop, but still I wait. I hear others drawing close as well, and eventually, Cata murmurs, 'It's safe to come out, my lord king. Those fool men have gone.' It takes more effort than I'd like to win free from the mud, but I manage it, pleased to inhale clean smelling air, even if I'm still bloody cold.

Hemming almost skips upright and I glare at him as my cold limbs struggle to get upright. I pull forth my shield and sword, and then slowly ease myself off the back of the cart. I look around, but it seems there's no more interest in the arrival of the mud. Not even Gayadore emerges from her hut. I'm surprised by how much soil has been brought within London, as I look around me. Egbalth and Cata have been true to their word. They've been busy performing this task while I've been absent in Canterbury. I'm grateful to them. I'll thank them, once we've dealt with Lord Æthelwulf.

'Stay low, my lord,' Icel growls. His face is brown with mud, and his beard, speckled with grey, is wholly dark once more.

'A bit of mud does you good,' I offer him appraisingly, but follow his command, and hunker down, with the cart ahead of myself, so no one looking this way can see me. Not even those I see dotted around the top of the fort. That also seems to be habitable again, for which I'm grateful. Hopefully the rats have all been killed.

'My thanks,' I murmur to Egbalth and Cata who stand close to me, their eyes surveying everything. 'We need to wait for the light to start to fade,' I remind everyone.

'In the meantime, we can make ourselves useful by shovelling the soil,' Icel comments. I glare at him, but he's probably right. We're all pinched with cold. Some physical exertion will warm us and make us ready for the coming fight.

'Very well,' I agree. 'Be my guest,' I direct Icel towards the collection of spades waiting in the soil that's already been brought to London. He grimaces, but sets to the task quickly enough. One by one, he's joined by the others, Hemming, Rudolf, Hereman, Lyfing and Sæbald, to name the few closest to me. Only Pybba doesn't offer to help, and none of us would argue with him about that. Easy enough to grip a seax or sword with one hand, but a shovel? That's not going to be possible. Even I set to, allowing the movement to warm my sluggish body, wishing I wasn't so bloody chilled. But, we're within London. We might have used an old trick to accomplish it, and we might still have to reclaim London in my name, but at least we've begun to counter Lord Æthelwulf's ridiculous efforts to take London, and possibly Mercia from me. I always knew him to be an arse. In this, he's proven he could have been competent had he not been so concerned with his own ambitions.

But ambitious men are, at least, often easily overwhelmed. He undoubtedly thinks more of his skills than anyone else does.

I'll enjoy watching his face when he realises how little he's achieved, and how much he's lost.

* * *

Eventually, we're all warm, and the soil has been taken off the carts. As the light begins to fade, I turn to my warriors.

'Right, now we need to take the gate and allow Ealdorman Ælhun and Kyred within, and then we can descend on the bishop's complex.'

'Are we to kill 'em or incapacitate them?' Pybba questions.

'Depends if they get bloody near enough to you to kill. We can take them as captive, if they're Mercians. It would be a shame to kill Mercians, even if they're not very loyal.'

'And if they're West Saxons?'

'Again, it depends on how good they are at fighting. Kill 'em if you need to. I'm not going to tell anyone that it's better to keep cowards and disloyal bastards alive.'

'How rousing,' Icel intones, but I shrug.

'What would you have me bloody say? We're not going to have time to ask them if they're loyal or not. In this, their actions must speak for their intentions.'

For a moment, Icel holds my gaze, and then nods quickly.

'You're correct, my lord. Men who are loyal to Mercia will be hesitant to attack us when they know who we are.'

I meet the eyes of every single one of my men then, from Rudolf, to Hereman to Lyfing and Sæbald.

'Stay alive, for fuck's sake. This would be a foolish way to die, and I assure you, we'd all struggle to find something respectful to say about you in our scop song.' My words lack heat but I mean them, all the same.

'Don't worry, my lord,' Wulfred calls. 'We wouldn't want to live with that fucking reputation. But promise us you'll do the same, or we'll revisit the shame on you threefold.' I meet his eyes, offering a quirk of my lips.

'You all heard Wulfred. He promises to sing shit about us until he meets us in the afterlife if you die here, today. That should be incentive enough to stay alive.'

And with that, I turn and shoulder my shield and move out, aware I'm flanked by Icel, Pybba, Hereman and Rudolf. From down by where I assume the quayside is, lights are being lit, but here, we must rely on the fading light of dusk. I hobble a little, my left leg still failing me on occasion, but aside from that, I feel ready for this fight. There have been a few things I've not allowed myself to consider, one of them being what's happened to my aunt, the archbishop and Gardulf, but soon, I'll have all my answers. I don't know what Lord Æthelwulf hoped to achieve with his outrageous takeover of London, but I can well imagine.

Honestly, I've spent the last eighteen months defeating Mercia's enemies, and what do I find but that the one I should have been fearing was a bastard Mercian dressed in sheep's clothing. I'll enjoy watching him suffer, I really will.

In no time at all, I can sense the fort at my back. We've encountered few people, and all of them have greeted me with relief on their faces and have been cautioned to silence. Eagerly, I've listened to them hurry to get away from the coming fight. But I wouldn't be surprised to discover many of them supporting us once the gate's secured and Ealdorman Ælhun and Kyred's forces have been added to the few men I have.

Pressed tightly to the wall of the fort, I allow my eyes time to adjust to the darkness. I look upwards, seeing the clouds moving quickly. I think it'll be a cold night, and one I hope to spend around a hearth rather than outside. I pray it's that easy.

Ahead, I can sense London's gate has been closed. I look to Icel, who leads us, but he doesn't glance at me, focusing on the gate. I could have sent Rudolf to scout the area and he'd have told us how many men Lord Æthelwulf had, but it doesn't matter. However many warriors he has, we need to overwhelm him and take back London.

Abruptly, a flare of light erupts. I narrow my eyes against the sudden glow. In its dancing flames, I see four warriors on gate duty. I hear them as well, complaining about the cold and generally moaning, as all guards are likely to do. I've been there. I've done it.

'My lord, you stay here, and I'll take Hereman, Rudolf, Wærwulf and Lyfing to overwhelm them.' Unhappily, I allow Icel to direct the men as he wants to do. I'd sooner be the one to attack but Icel might be correct. This could go very wrong, very quickly, and I shouldn't be risked.

With the shush of drawn metal, I watch the five of them slide along the wall of the fort, Pybba at my side.

'As quiet as a mouse,' he whispers, as Hereman kicks a stone, drawing the attention of one of the watching guards, but only one, because the other three are too busy laughing at some lewd joke. The single guard shakes his head, dismissing the noise and turns back to his allies, hunkering close to the fire. That's all the invitation my warriors need. Quickly, far more quickly than even I think is possible, the four guards are apprehended, hands around mouths as opposed to seaxes in the back, and they're dragged towards us. I appreciate then that Icel means to have the men kept under guard within the fort. It's a good idea.

As they hurry back, I turn to Pybba.

'Shall we?' I question him.

'We very much bloody should,' he confirms, and now the rest of us move to remove the wooden bars and open the gates. Pybba pokes his head through the space, and immediately rears backwards. I'm ready to defend him, but it seems Kyred and Ealdorman Ælhun are as keen as we are. They already ride through the gate, the sound of the rest of the warriors audible as the clank of metal and the stealthy movements of men who aren't used to having to be quiet. And so, not fucking quiet at all.

'We're in,' Ealdorman Ælhun announces with satisfaction from his horse. I see where our horses are being controlled by warriors under the orders of Commander Wulfsige. I don't go to Haden. I'm not sure horses are the answer here. Not yet.

'We are. Now, we must find Lord Æthelwulf.'

Although it's only possible to see in the glow from the fire, I know the number of men I have at my command has just quadrupled. We're still not a large force, but we should be large enough to take control of London.

'We close the gate,' I instruct Gyrth and Wærwulf. They move to secure it once more.

'I need four of you to remain here and be the guards,' I direct to those close to me. Of course, this is the least desired part of our endeavours. None of my warriors will want to stand here while the rest of their allies get to do the real work. Luckily, Kyred steps in to help.

'I'll have four of my best men on guard duty. I take it they're to allow no one within and to keep the horses safe inside the fort building?'

'You take it correctly. Even if they're crying for their mothers and saying they're loyal Mercians. They can wait until there's light enough to assure ourselves of the truth of those assertions.'

'My lord king,' Kyred inclines his head respectfully, and moves to direct his men accordingly. I'm aware of a scuffle coming from within the fort building, and furrow my forehead, but almost immediately, Icel steps outside and directs his steps towards me, shaking his head angrily.

'What's the matter?'

'Nothing,' he grunts, but I'm not so convinced. There's a shimmer of blood on his cheek and I consider which one of the bloody stupid fools thought to try and have a fight with him. I can't imagine it ended well. For them.

'We've done the easy bit. Now, we progress towards the bishop's complex, keeping close to the wall to our right,' I point where I mean, but we've already discussed this. My warriors know what's expected from them. 'No one is to fall in the bloody Walbrook,' I admonish, and content the gate's secured and guarded, and the horses being tended to, I lead on, only to trip over yet another stone.

'Steady there, my lord,' Pybba catches me before I fall and I'm grateful to him. It wouldn't have been my finest moment if I'd ended up on all fours, my knees hitting the hard ground, reawakening the pain in my left leg.

'My thanks,' I offer, and look with a little more care at where I'm going. But, as we move further and further away from the sentry fire at the gate, I realise it's going to be very difficult. I halt, Pybba just stopping from walking into me.

'Is Rudolf there?' I call softly.

'I am, yes,' his young voice pipes up.

'Then you can lead. I can't bloody see enough.' He rushes forward, and manages not to comment on my poor eyesight, to strike out with more confidence than I felt. Quickly, we're making good progress. London, despite Lord Æthelwulf taking it from me, is thrumming with its usual busyness. The smell of cookfires is rife, as are the voices of men and women returning home from a day conducting their business. We don't want to alarm them, even if they would support me. It's for this reason we make our way towards the bishop's complex using the wall at our right. Few people live to this side of the Walbrook. I'm not surprised. It smells dank even if those we spoke to told me the water wasn't the best for drinking.

More than once, I gaze upwards at the bright moon, shivering at the chill wind sending the cloud scudding across it. I'm reminded of the terrible winter we endured last year, forced to fight to keep Mercia safe, when any good warrior should be roasting his stones before a huge hearth fire. I'd hoped not to spend as much time outside this dark time. Whether I'm to have my wish or not very much depends on what happens with Lord Æthelwulf.

Drawing nearer to the bishop's complex, there's more light available to cast the buildings into sharp relief. Here is where it's going to get trickier. We must find my aunt, the archbishop and Gardulf, and I also promised to ensure Lady Ealhswith was safe. I've also told King Alfred I won't harm his children. I hope I can bloody keep to that promise.

When we can clearly see the walls surrounding the bishop's home, as well as the guards watching the entranceway, I pull Rudolf to a stop, and hunker down. I'm curious to see what the guards will do. They won't know we're within London. As such, they've no cause to be especially vigilant, just like the guards at the main gateway into the settlement.

We're hardly quiet as we hold in place, wood and metal bouncing off stone and dirt ground. I'd growl a warning, but that would be even noisier, and so give us away while trying to stop the daft bastards from doing just that. Instead, I scrutinise as the men stand a desultory watch, which quickly deteriorates into little more than a game of chance with some handy pebbles and a clay jug.

These men are more like fools than guards.

'Icel, Hereman, Sæbald and Lyfing, go and apprehend them. Don't kill them unless there's no choice,' I whisper my command. The four men strike out, bending low so as not to be seen by any moonlight catching on metalled shield, blade or byrnie.

Not that the four guards are paying any attention. Instead, their cries of dismay or triumph ring out, only to be cut short when my warriors emerge from the gloom and capture them. I hear the scuffling of feet, and a few muted cries of dismay. Then the heads of my warriors pop up in place of the four guardsmen. I'd recognise their thick skulls anywhere.

Unfortunately, this time our approach hasn't gone unnoticed.

'What's all the bloody noise?' an aggrieved voice shouts from inside.

'A rat,' Icel calls, in his deepest tone.

'Well kill the bloody thing,' the disembodied voice from within calls once more, and I scowl. I'm sure that's Lord Æthelwulf. But would he really be on guard duty? I can't see it. He's more likely to be within, roasting himself before a huge hearth and eating the produce of the Londoners, having spent the day assuring himself there are no Mercians about to attack him.

I grimace at the thought, and then suppress my own gasp as something rears up from the river bank. I turn to look at it, and then chuckle darkly. It's just a dog, no doubt chasing the bloody rat Icel just referenced.

'Come on,' I urge my warriors in a hoarse whisper, and now we move towards the entrance. The bishop's complex isn't as well-defined as that at Canterbury, the walls of its exterior are really made up of multiple buildings. All the same, we sidle along them, until I reach Icel.

'This should be bloody fun,' he mutters, already peering inside. I look where he does, and find the courtyard we visited only recently alight with many braziers. The sound of the monks at one of their night services floods the air, their prayers dull but persistent. It covers my rapidly beating heart and my ragged breath, and hopefully, the noise of my fellow warriors getting into position.

'This has felt too fucking easy,' I mutter unwillingly to Icel. He fixes me with a stern look.

'Aye, my lord, you're not wrong.' His agreement proves I'm correct to be worried. I bite my lip and then meet Icel's appraising gaze.

'Well, fuck it, we're here now,' I state, and he flashes me a quick grin.

'Aye, my lord, we are. Now, let's find that bastard and get this over and done with.'

I nod, and then indicate he can go ahead of me. Better that than us both trying to fit through the same gap and failing miserably.

He grins once more, and leads on. I'm right behind him, my fellow warriors behind me.

We emerge into the enclosed space, brilliantly lit with braziers but remarkably silent. There are no warriors there. There's no one, not even the voice we heard call to the others.

I narrow my eyes, considering if our arrival is truly a surprise or if the bastards knew to expect us.

And then I have my bloody answer, and I don't like it. Not at all.

Chapter Thirty-Four

Wherever they've been hiding, they chose well.

Abruptly, the court yard fills with warriors bedecked in iron and carrying shields and spears, or shields and seax, or shields and axes, all of them pointing at us. I turn towards the entranceway we've come through, but already those to the back are being forced inside at the point of a spear, angry shouts accompanying the action.

'Bollocks,' I huff, turning to meet my enemy, the pestilent arsehole, Lord Æthelwulf.

He's festooned in the finery of a king, including warrior garb to cover his chest. I'm grateful Mercia's warrior helm is far from here, being kept safe by Bishop Wærferth of Worcester, for if not, Æthelwulf would be strutting around in it looking like a prized prick. I mean, I can't say I look good in it. It would be impossible to do so. It's far too ostentatious, but Lord Æthelwulf has made a fucking good effort to look so bloody ridiculous.

'Ah, King Coelwulf, the second of his name. You took your time. I was thinking I might need to leave the bloody gates open for you.' As he speaks, Lord Æthelwulf comes through his line of warriors, but still stands, protected by them, as others move amongst us, taking our blades. Icel roars like a wounded boar and out of the corner of my eye, I see the poor warrior given the task, startle backwards. I'd chuckle if I weren't so fucking angry.

How have I allowed this? Lord Æthelwulf is an arsehole but in this, he does seem to have known my thoughts far too easily.

I look for my aunt, but she's not being held under guard by Lord Æthelwulf where I can see her. She must, however, be nearby. He better not have imprisoned her like the bastard Viking raiders did. I will kill him if he has. Once I'm free once more.

'Nothing to say, King Coelwulf?' Lord Æthelwulf's tone is jaunty. I feel my fists clenching. I'd love to knock that smirk from his smug looking face.

'Why are we under attack?' I finally speak. 'I'm Mercia's king. I should be welcomed here.'

'Come now, King Coelwulf. We both know that's not how this will unfold. You abandoned Mercia to aid King Alfred in Wessex, a kingdom not beloved by the Mercians, and now I claim it in your absence.'

'What, all of it?' Rudolf demands, his voice high with outrage.

'Yes, all of it. Even now, my warriors and messengers are busy securing Tamworth, Gloucester, and Worcester, amongst other places.'

'I wish you bloody luck with that,' I mutter arrogantly. I notice he doesn't mention Northampton. There's no chance he'd ever get within Northampton's firm walls. He must know that. He's visited the place. All the same, I don't believe his arrogant assertion. I also don't want to believe the bastard.

'You and what fucking army?' Icel taunts, finally relinquishing his hold on his sword, but only in such a way the warrior who takes it falls on his arse in a crash of iron and twisted legs. I eye the warrior, allowing my rage to build. I'm angry at myself for finding myself in this position. I'm furious Lord Æthelwulf has done this to me. If it was the Viking raider jarls, that would be one thing. But bloody Lord

Æthelwulf. He's such an arsehole. I'm fucking embarrassed for myself. To think I had to hear of this deceit from sodding Jarl Guthrum.

'Me and the one I have, filled with warriors from Wessex and some of the Viking raider jarls. If you spend enough time with them, you know, they're quite pleasant chaps. I mean, a bit blood-thirsty, but who isn't these days?' he shrugs.

'You've allied with the enemy?' I query, keeping my voice deceptively light even while my ire builds. I don't give a fuck how many blades the other bastards have. I will end their lives with my bare hands if needs must.

'I have a little alliance with Jarl Guthrum, yes. He's leant me a few of his allies while you've been busy pretending to protect Archbishop Æthelred. He's here as well, you know. You really did send me some rather delightful hostages.'

I wince. I was adamant Archbishop Æthelred sought sanctuary within London. I promised him he'd be safe here. I didn't expect such deception from Lord Æthelwulf. Evidently, I bloody should have done. At least he still lives. That's some consolation.

There's a scuffle behind Lord Æthelwulf, and Archbishop Æthelred is escorted forwards by some Viking raiders. Gratefully, I see my aunt is with them. If the archbishop looks confused at what's happening, my aunt is far more assured. Her clothing is immaculate, and her poise as confident as ever. However, I really wish people would stop fucking apprehending her. It's not doing much for my image as a warrior king. All the same, I'm overjoyed to see her. She looks well. She looks like my aunt. That pleases me. Gardulf is also there, his face filled with black rage.

'We've sent for your nephew, young Æthelred as well.' Now I see Lady Ealhswith emerge from the church's doorway. Whatever religious ceremony was being undertaken, it was merely a ruse. I could almost admire Lord Æthelwulf's bloody preparation and attention to detail. He evidently saw right through our ruse.

'And what do you plan to do to us?'

'Oh, kill you. Bring the current ruling line of Mercia to an end, as it should have been done many years ago. For this whole century, it's been ruled by men with little ambition and only the most tenuous of claims to the kingship.'

'And what, you'll be king in my place?'

'Of course. I have a very secure claim,' and now Lord Æthelwulf looks like an even bigger turd as he sticks his chest out and adopts a stance I must assume he believes is kingly. He looks fucking constipated to me.

'Through who and for what?' Icel demands. 'I know those with a claim to rule Mercia. I assure you, you bag of wind, your family name isn't on there.'

'I'm a member of the ancient ruling family of the tribal kingdom of the Gaini.'

'Are you now? And where the fuck did they rule? Consult your histories, you fucking arsehole, no one even knows who the Gaini were.'

Lord Æthelwulf's face flushes angrily. I chuckle. Icel is his usual charming self, and yet, he's confident as he speaks. Whoever the fucking Gaini were, their ruling line is so out of vogue not even the Gaini know who they were.

'They were once kings of Mercia.'

'They fucking weren't,' Icel counters. 'The Gaini are a name, conjured from a dream, by those who thought they should be more than they are. The Gaini are piss and wind, nothing else. You've no right to Mercia.' As he speaks, Icel stamps forward, the man pointing his spear at his chest, hurrying backwards to keep up with him. I'm not stupid enough to think Icel's this angry. He's playing for time. He's working to create something we can exploit to win back our freedom.

'I confess, Lord Æthelwulf. I've never heard of the Gaini either,' Archbishop Æthelred astounds me by announcing confidently. I turn my head, trying to assess our current position. My warriors have all been deprived of their blades, but you can take a blade from a warrior, and his shield, spear and war axe, but that doesn't stop a warrior from being a bloody warrior. We all have different skills we can employ. And, we're all far stronger than those who're trying to make us their subservient.

'Respectfully, Archbishop Æthelred, no one asked for your bloody opinion. Someone help here,' and Lord Æthelwulf indicates where Icel is almost within jabbing distance of him. 'You can't allow the personage of your new king to be threatened in such a way,' he calls, but his voice wavers fearfully. I'd be scared were glowering at me in the same way.

'What sort of fucking warriors are you?' I jibe, and Lord Æthelwulf's twisted face glares at me.

'One who's brought Mercia's previous king to his knees. You won't be leaving here alive,' he announces, again strutting like a cock in a hen house.

But, of course, a cock in a henhouse has an enemy. When that enemy decides to attack.

'You'll kill me,' I ask, amusement thrumming through my voice, showing no fear. I won't let him take my life, I really won't. I'd never live with the bloody humiliation.

'Yes. You'll be tried for crimes against your kingdom, and for denying your rightful king.'

'By who and what bloody army?' Icel derides once more, moving his fists so the men trying to keep him away from Lord Æthelwulf startle with shock.

From nearby, although I'm not quite sure from where, I hear a sound. I don't believe Lord Æthelwulf's heard it yet. If he has, it means he knows about it, and expects it. But if he hasn't? Well, I'd welcome what I suspect might be about to happen. I realise Icel and I need to keep him talking. While he's talking, and posturing and being an arrogant arse wipe, he won't be paying attention to anything else.

'My army. I've over two hundred warriors here. Jarl Guthrum is also bringing some ships, as is Ealdorman Sigehelm of Kent, to the quayside.'

'No, they're bloody not,' I counter aggressively.

'Of course they are. We've an agreement. An honourable agreement.'

'Do you, now?' I muse, walking forward, using my hands to force the pointing spears away from my byrnie and chest. I dismiss the men as though they're children playing at being warriors. The men, unsure about what to do, allow me to move with more freedom than they should. But, Lord Æthelwulf gives no new instructions, his eyes on me. He shows no fear. He will shortly.

'Remind me, again, Lord Æthelwulf.'

'King,' he interrupts me quickly. I smile condescendingly.

'Remind me, Lord Æthelwulf, when exactly did you make these 'arrangements' with your allies, and when exactly did you leave Canterbury?'

'What?' he questions, his chest deflating a little. I stand directly before him. I could reach over the shields and kill him here and now with my bare hands. I probably should do so, but I know no fear. Lord Æthelwulf's confident he's succeeded. He really couldn't be more fucking wrong.

'When did you leave Canterbury? You don't seem surprised to see me here. So, what, your allies were to let us live just for you to kill me here, in London?' I lift my hands to indicate the interior of the bishop's complex and smirk as Lord Æthelwulf veers away from my presence.

Confusion swamps his hateful features. I see him trying to make sense of what I'm implying.

'You ran from Canterbury and left it in the hands of Jarl Guthrum,' Lord Æthelwulf states, endeavouring to reclaim the narrative, chin defiant.

'Did I? Do you see any form of injury on my warriors, aside from those we already had when we last saw one another? Did we rush here, or did we take our time and arrive by stealth?'

'You ran from Canterbury, chased by the enemy. You spent two days heading north and crossed at Laleham Gull shallows in a hurry.

Jarl Guthrum's in control of Canterbury, with his allies, and Ealdorman Sigehelm of Kent. King Alfred's dead from wounds gained while fighting the enemy because you didn't protect him, as promised.' As he says this, Lord Æthelwulf looks towards his sister, who stands, chin raised, her face ashen in the flickering flames. I'd shake my head at his audacity in declaring his brother by marriage dead when he evidently yet lives, but Lord Æthelwulf's not finished bragging yet. 'And you'll be dead soon too, in retaliation for your failure to safeguard my bereaved sister's husband, and your oath. As such, I've crafted an alliance with our enemy, for the good of every-one.' Now he sounds sanctimonious, and I feel my rage pool around me. 'Wessex will be ruled by Jarl Guthrum and his allies. Mercia will be mine, until such time as my nephew can rule here,' he jabs a finger towards his chest while speaking, as though such wild entreaties will make it true.

'Ah,' I say, the sound soft so he has to lean forwards to hear me. 'I do believe, Lord Æthelwulf, traitor of Mercia, that you might not be entirely up to date with affairs in Canterbury and Wessex as a whole.' I'm aware of others listening carefully, their violent intentions slackening along with the grip on their blades and shield as they realise Lord Æthelwulf might have been lying to them. No doubt he came here and told them all it was my bloody fault King Alfred was dead, and in that way won the support of his sister, and a few others. A pity, really, he didn't stoop to ensure everything happened as he thought it was going to happen before progressing. A pity for him, but not for me.

I sense Icel preparing. I detect all of my warriors waiting for the right opportunity. I even see my aunt smile with pleasure, despite everything. She begins to shuffle backwards to stay out of the way of what will come next, taking Gardulf with her. My aunt knows me, and my warriors, far too well. Archbishop Æthelred's forehead is furrowed with confusion.

'The bastard traitor, Ealdorman Sigehelm, is dead,' I inform Lord Æthelwulf, lifting my voice so all can hear.

'King Alfred of Wessex isn't dead,' I continue quickly, seeking out Lady Ealhswith's face in the crowd, and watching a flurry of emotions cover her pale face. Next, I turn back towards Lord Æthelwulf. 'And Jarl Guthrum doesn't hold Canterbury, but rather King Alfred, who is very much alive, and very much busy praising his fucking Lord God for saving him,' I finish. As I do so, my warriors surge forwards, a great roar erupting from their throats. In that split moment, I see panic, fear and abject terror cover Lord Æthelwulf's face.

I reach for him, eager to have him in my custody, while my warriors use fists, elbows and knees to attack their enemy who've allowed shields and blades to loosen in their hands with every denial of Lord Æthelwulf's lies.

Lord Æthelwulf holds my gaze for a moment longer, and then the fucking coward pushes the two warriors protecting him towards me. They lose their balance and fall in a clatter of wood and metal.

Likewise, my balance deserts me as well, and when I'm standing once more, Icel to my right and Hereman to my left, I can't see Lord Æthelwulf, but there are a lot of frightened warriors facing me. Only a few with a backbone, mind. I snatch a seax from one of them, and surge into him with my forehead. He emits a half-strangled cry and crumbles to the ground as blood erupts from his nose. I spit the taste of him aside, lips curled in disgust.

I look for my aunt, but she's disappeared, as has Archbishop Æthelred, but I don't fear they've been taken. No, my aunt with years of experience, will have removed the archbishop to ensure he survives this. As I seek my next target, I hear a surge from where we entered the bishop's complex. I risk a look, but those who've come through behind us, aren't there to fight against us. No. The people of London, led by small Egbalth on his donkey, and tall Cata at his side have come to aid us.

'Find fucking Lord Æthelwulf,' I growl at any who'll listen. 'But first, let's take these bastards down.'

And all hell breaks loose.

Chapter Thirty-Five

The fighting's nasty. The Viking raiders that Lord Æthelwulf has brought to London aren't wanting to give up quickly, and because they're mingled with Lord Æthelwulf's force, the fighting's bitter.

They stand little chance of success against my Mercians, but there are some aspects in their favour.

We're in a very confined space. We're hemmed in between the church, the bishop's hall, the monks' dormitory and any other bloody building that might be there, including the stables.

There's also not much light. Braziers had been lit, but of course, in the midst of the combat, some have been knocked over or extinguished, possibly by falling bodies, and the moon's obscured by clouds. The air's filling with smoke.

And, of course, Lord Æthelwulf's disappeared. Somewhere. And I bloody want him, not these others.

I stab towards one of the enemy warriors, but the strike veer alarmingly downwards, sheering off his shield without making an impact.

'Bollocks,' I explode.

My next blow goes awry as well. I curl my fist and punch the arsehole fighting me. His shield veers up to protect him and I wince at the pain in my knuckles from hitting it and not him. My fury fuels me.

I reach out, knuckles pulsing and bleeding, and force my weight on the rim of the shield. A growl from the man who holds it and the bloody thing lowers to enable me to punch him. I aim for his neck. My knuckles already bleed, and where there's no sense, and all that shit.

He falls immediately. I snatch the blade from his hand and standing upright, stab both blades I now have towards the next warrior who thinks to fight me. He offers me a sly grin from behind his shield, eyes hooded behind a black-iron helm, his shield held before him. He's a bastard Viking raider if ever I saw one.

'*Skiderik*,' I growl and he chuckles. But not for long. While I stab towards him with my right hand, I bend and rip the shield from the gargling man who first faced me. With it in my hand, I march towards my enemy, closer and closer, until our shields are touching and he can't land a blow on me but Icel can certainly stab into his side, and does so.

'Arsehole,' Icel complains. The enemy shield falls. I finish the job with a slice through his neck which severs the talismans clacking in his hair.

'Where's the fucker gone?' I growl.

'We kill these first,' Icel pants. I'd argue with him, but Lord Æthelwulf's two hundred men do appear to be reasonable warriors. Already, I hear the cries of some cut down by the enemy.

'Come on you fuckers,' I direct to the next two warriors. The West Saxons waver, and that's their undoing. While the one waits for the other to attack me, I turn into him, seax jabbing towards him, and slice open the cheek of the one, before using my elbow to knock into the nose of the other. Both are bleeding and I've barely broken a sweat.

'Where's Lord Æthelwulf gone?' I menace, but neither replies, too frightened, and both gasping in pain. 'Tell me, or I'll fucking kill you,' I offer deceptively calmly, but neither says anything. Unwilling, but realising the necessity of killing men who should be fighting for King Alfred as opposed to fighting me, I end their lives with efficient jabs into their necks. I can't still their beating hearts with a punch through their chests for they both wear good byrnies. My blade comes away wet, dripping and stinking.

'Who's fucking next?' I direct towards the warriors who are still to join the fight. Some of them are pressed up against the building behind us. The bishop's hall. No doubt they intend to get within and defend themselves that way. It won't do them any bloody good. I'll fire the damn building, if I must, and make reparations later.

Beside me, I'm aware of Pybba and Hereman scything their way through the enemy as well. We leave a trail of the dead and dying, but hopefully, none of my men. To the rear, the Londoners are ensuring none can escape.

'Come on,' I roar at the next foeman. He assesses me, and then inclines his head respectfully.

'Men will sing of my battle prowess,' he suggests but I shake my head.

'No, they fucking won't,' but the warrior is a skilled fighter. He's light on his feet, and has a good seax in his right hand, and a good shield in his left.

He easily diverts my first blow. With the second one, I get a little closer to him, but then he thrusts his shield almost into my face. I veer backwards. I don't fancy losing any teeth today. Not to battle these arseholes.

I evade the strike. He comes closer, a grin visible on the part of his face not hooded by his helm. He thinks to win far too easily.

Next, I direct a blow towards him. He immediately moves his seax to counter it, but I stab back and redirect my strike towards his exposed side. My blade plunges into his left arm and I offer him a quirk of my eyebrows, which of course, he can't see beneath my helm. As he reacts to my strike, I thrust my shield towards his face. A tumble of teeth scatter to the floor. My seax impales him below the chin, right up into his mouth. For a moment, I see the fear and pain on his face, but then he slumps in death.

'Arsehole,' I growl, lowering his body and wiping my blade on his trews.

The next warrior I face is also a Viking raider.

I eye him. 'Why are you bloody doing this?' I ask. 'Jarl Guthrum and I are allies once more. You die for a man who'll never be king of Mercia, and for what? There'll be no songs of your death. There'll be no gold and silver for you to win.' Whether he understands me or not, and I suspect he does because he shudders at my words, it doesn't stop his approach.

He's all arms and legs, more akin to when Rudolf first learned to fight. But that makes him lethal. I turn aside, holding my shield before me. It takes multiple blows from his blades, all of them heavy and serving to exhaust him further.

I wait, looking sideways as I press against him, ensuring my warriors are well. Pybba strikes a man's hand from his arm effortlessly and then impales him through the neck. Rudolf fights his enemy with dogged determination, and a damn sight more skill than he possessed this time last year.

'Have you finished?' I question the man before me, lowering my shield. He's red of face and sweating, his features cast into shadows and light by the braziers, the smell of roasting flesh starting to flood the air.

'Good,' I murmur, and using my shield to protect me, I slide along his side. At the last moment, as he's turning to counter me with a slug-gish arm, I slide my seax beneath his shoulder and impale him. The thrum of falling blood is a delightful noise.

Now I'm at the barred doorway to the bishop's hall. Icel's there ahead of me, and Hereman, who runs at the door as though that'll force it to open.

'I didn't know you were a fucking battering ram?' I direct to him, but Hereman and Icel have seen the problem. The pair bend and hook their arms around a dead man, wearing a helm. Grabbing his legs I aid them. He's far from rigid in death, but the peak of his helm does a lot of the work for us. The door, never intended to withstand such force, fractures open, and we drop the dead man to land in a flood of lifeless limbs and useless iron.

The scene I'm greeted with is perplexing. The monks seem to have been secured within the room. Now, they pray on their knees, backs to us, while the warriors of Lord Æthelwulf are frantically trying to hew themselves the means of escape through the wooden wall opposite the entrance. They've gathered together any heavy object they can find to hammer against the wall, but of course, they've not thought to use a dead body. They're effectively cut off, or at least, they are until someone, screaming wildly, and with a three-legged stool before them, runs at the wall. It finally splinters, the man staggering with the action. Others are quick to use their hands to pull the wood away.

'Come on, they can't escape,' I order my men. I'm uncertain where this will lead the enemy. I'm unsure where Lord Æthelwulf has gone, although I can bloody imagine easily enough. He intends to escape. A pity really we didn't scuttle all the ships, but thought merely to gain entry into London from the landward side.

'Bloody come on,' I urge my men, already at the gaping hole. I feel a rush of cold air on my face, and shudder. Squinting left and right, and then ahead, Icel crashes into me, and we both nearly fall to the ground.

'Out the bloody way, my lord,' Icel demands. I growl low.

'Get Rudolf. We need him.' Rudolf emerges next, pulling splinters of wood from his byrnie, while he looks where I just did.

'This way, my lord,' he asserts confidently, and rushes left. I follow on behind, relying on Rudolf to warn me of any hazards. Quickly, the smell of the river grows around me. Lord Æthelwulf intends to escape by boat. I need to get to him first.

In no time at all, thanks to Rudolf's confident steps, we surge into the retreating enemy. I grab the first man, and with seax to his throat, I roar into his face. 'Where the fuck's Lord Æthelwulf.'

'Ah,' a high pitched squeal answers me. I shake my head, and stab him through the chest.

I grab another of the bastards.

'Where the fuck's Lord Æthelwulf?' I demand once more. Terrified eyes look at me. I see the man swallow.

'A ship,' he gasps. 'A ship on the quayside.'

'Bollocks,' I roar. 'The quayside,' I shout to Rudolf. I plough my way through the collection of warriors. They're not important. Not right now. It's Lord Æthelwulf I need. He can't escape. He really fucking can't. Not after what he tried to do.

I thrust the enemy warriors to the ground, confident Kyred and Ealdorman Ælhun will gather them quickly together, and follow my young friend. It's lighter here. I realise the inhabitants of London have thrown open their doors, despite the lateness of the day and the cold breeze. I see more thanks to the spluttering hearth fires illuminating the road I follow.

Rudolf's far ahead, the heavy tread of Icel's feet echoing back to me. Pybba stays close, as does Hereman.

'I wish I was a younger man,' Pybba huffs from my side.

'Just run. Don't even fucking think about it,' I instruct him, but my chest is tight as well. I've been bloody cold for so much of the day, and then very warm, and now I'm hot again. My healing leg hasn't appreciated the change in conditions.

Ahead, I see Icel disappear. I follow on, dashing through the gate and onto the quayside, panting heavily.

I look all around and then hear the sound of fighting. Warily, I walk onto the wooden quayside where I first met Egbalth. I squint into the darkness, for the moon remains obscure. I can see little, but the odd shimmer of blades reflecting in the light from hearth fires.

'He's got a fucking boat,' Icel roars, and I sense a shape, out there, on the water, rather than see it.

'Stop him,' I shout at the same time, hoping Rudolf can do so.

'I'm bloody trying,' I hear on the cold night air. 'I could do with some bloody help,' Rudolf rejoins, only for the sound to be abruptly cut off, preceded by a splash of something heavy hitting the water.

'Rudolf?' I call, gathering my legs beneath me to move even faster, even though I can't really see where I'm going. I hope I'm running in a straight line but I'm not at all convinced.

'Rudolf?' I roar. 'Icel, where's Rudolf?' I shout, worry infecting my voice.

'I'm bloody looking for him,' his words are as reassuring as a wet fart. After all our trips to and from Wessex, after the many trips across the shallows at Laleham Gulls or Lechlade, I can't believe Rudolf's fallen into the bloody river with all of his warrior gear on. He'll fucking drown. I can't have it. I won't allow it.

'Bollocks, Rudolf,' I call, crashing into a stationary Icel, and only stay upright by sheer bloody luck, as Icel and I grip one another tightly, endeavouring to stay on the thin wooden boards that are the only thing between us and the slurping water near our feet.

I hear splashing, and the very unwelcome sound of oars slicing through the turgid River Thames.

'Rudolf,' I shout, fear turning my belly leaden as I look all around, unable to see more than an arm's length in front of my nose. Shit, not Rudolf. I fear the worse, the desire for vengeance against Lord Æthelwulf evaporating like water on the hottest day of the summer.

'Rudolf, where are you, you little shit,' I bellow, bending to blindly grope forward, along the thin edges of the wooden planking.

Pybba's shouting as well. Hereman runs towards us, a brand in his hand, so bright I have to squint away from it.

'Rudolf,' I roar, and all I can hear is my heart thudding in my body. I hungered for Lord Æthelwulf, but as so often the case, I had absolutely no intention of losing another of my warriors in exchange for vengeance.

'Rudolf, where the fuck are you,' I don't deny that my voice cracks as I bellow for for my former squire. I have my hand in the water, reaching out, as though I'll be able to find him in such a way.

'Rudolf, you little shit, stop pissing about,' I cry.

'Lost your little friend, Coelwulf?' Lord Æthelwulf's goading voice, carrying to me from whichever shitting boat he's managed to fall into drives me to rage. I stand, run forwards, as though I can reach him, only to trip over something I don't see on the quayside. I lose my balance, flailing forward, landing upside down, flipped onto my back by my efforts to stay on the wooden quay, all the air knocked from my body. I look upwards, the moon finally clearing so I can see more than in front of my face. I see Rudolf's face in the shape of the moon, and remember all of his bloody questions and piles of pilfered treasures from the enemy, and the words of the scop song thrum through my ears, in time to my thudding heartbeat.

Not another one. Fuck, not another one to add to the long list of men I've lost in my time as Mercia's king, and before that, the ealdorman of Kingsholm. I feel my lip trembling, my grief threating to undo me more than any fucking deceit by that bastard Lord Æthelwulf, a man as loyal as a whore. The words fill my head, my senses, and I see all those I've lost as though they stand looking down on me, accusing me of failing.

"A man of the Hwicce,
  He gulped mead at midnight feasts.
  Slew Raiders, night and day.
  Brave Athelstan, long will his valour endure."

"Beornberht, son of the Magonsæte.
  A proud man, a wise man, a strong man.
  He fought and pierced with spears.
  Above the blood, he slew with swords."

"A man fought for Mercia.

Against Raiders and foes.
Shield flashing red,
Brave Oslac, slew Raiders each seven-day."

"Hereberht was at the forefront, brave in battle.
  He stained his spear, and splashed with blood
  A thousand and more before Halfdan's men
  His bravery cut short his life."

"A friend I have lost, faithful he was,
  After joy, there was silence
  Red his sword, let it never be cleansed
  A friend I have lost, brave Eoppa."

'A blood bath and certain death for his foes
  Brave Siric's bravery will endure forever
  Although he was slain, he slew
  And he will be eternally honoured.'

'Swift in the struggle
  It grieves me to leave brave Eadberht
  He was foremost in battle
  The enemy feared him, and in turn, he shamed them.'

"Sturdy and strong, it would be wrong not to praise them.
  Amid blood-red blades, in black sockets.
  The war-hounds fought fiercely, tight formation.
  Of the war band of Coelwulf, I would think it a burden,
  To leave any in the shape of man alive."

. . .

'Bitter in battle, with blades set for war
Attacking in an army, cruel in battle
He slew with swords, without much sound
Edmund pillar of battle, took pleasure in giving death.'

Just as grief threatens to undo me, to remind me of all I've lost and can never have, a sopping wet Rudolf leans over me, water streaming from his face to land in my mouth, so I'm coughing, and laughing and trying to breathe, all at the same time.

'I'm sorry, my lord. The bastard escaped. He threw me in the water, fucking cock.'

I reach up and grip the back of his head, pulling his forehead level with mine, feeling the coldness of his face against my hot one, and not caring. Not at all. I've lost too many of my men in recent months. I can't countenance losing Rudolf, even if it means that snake Lord Æthelwulf has escaped me on this occasion.

'Don't you worry, young Rudolf. We'll get the bastard. We'll get him.' And so spoken, I gaze upwards once more, the moon haloed around Rudolf's head. I know that however much I hate Lord Æthel-wulf, I won't be risking my men to hunt him down and kill him. No. I don't plan on ever leaving the relative safety of Mercia again. Not for anyone. Not ever. I'll adhere to my alliance with King Alfred, but I'll hold Mercia, and he'll have Wessex. And, if he wants, I'll let him build a bridge over the River Thames, and in that way, he can believe he has a claim to a small part of London. But nothing else. Mercia is mine. I'll not risk losing her again. Or any more of my fine warriors. Not unless they fight to keep Mercia free from the Viking raider bastards.

I might, I consider, send Jarl Guthrum to hunt down Lord Æthel-wulf. I'm sure he'd enjoy doing that. And, in such a way, I'd keep two of Mercia's enemies far, far away from her. I might enjoy that. A little bit of peace. A tiny moment of calmness in the chaos that's ensued since King Burgred, the first and only of his name, sold Mercia to the Viking raiders.

'Where the fuck have you been,' and Pybba hauls Rudolf upright, and on Pybba's face, illuminated by Hereman's brand, I see all my fears laid bare, and I don't fucking care.

I vowed to protect my warriors, and only then Mercia, and only then Wessex.

I need to remember that.

I must always remember that.

Only in that way can I avoid being deceived by men who lack all morality, and who hunger for the same as I do. My warriors, all of them, are the men to trust, and the men to fight beside. And all of them, every single one of them, are proud Mercians. And that's how we will prevail against all who threaten Mercia, be they the enemy Viking raiders, or traitorous Mercians who should be more loyal.

Cast of Characters

Coelwulf's Warriors

Æthelred – a youngster adopted by Coelwulf's war band. He is his nephew.

Ælfgar – one of the older members of the war band

Athelstan – killed in the first battle in The Last King

Beornberht – killed in the first battle in The Last King

Beornstan – one of Coelwulf's warriors

Cealwin – one of the older warriors from Kingsholm, first appears in The Last Shield

Coelwulf – King of Mercia, rides **Haden**

Cuthwalh – one of the older warriors from Kingsholm, rides **Aart**

Edmund – rides **Jethson**, was Coelwulf's brother's man until his death. Brother is **Hereman**. Dies in The Last Seven.

Eadberht – one of Coelwulf's warriors, now dead

Eadulf – one of Coelwulf's warriors, now dead

Eadfrith – one of the older warriors from Kingsholm, first appears in The Last Shield

Eahric – one of Coelwulf's warriors, rides **Storm**

Eoppa – rides **Poppy**, dies in The Last Horse

Gardulf – first appears in The Last Horse – Edmund's son, rides **Kermit**

Goda – one of Coelwulf's warriors, appears from The Last King onwards, rides **Magic**

Gyrth – one of Coelwulf's warriors, appears from The Last King onwards, rides **Keira**

Hemming – son of Beornberht, a young warrior from Kingsholm, rides **Perry**

Hereman – brother of Edmund, rides **Billy**

Hereberht – dies at Torksey, in The Last Warrior.

Hiltiberht – a squire

Ingwald – one of Coelwulf's warriors

Icel – rides **Samson**

Leonath – first appears in The Last Horse, rides **Petre**

Lyfing – wounded in The Last King

Oda – one of Coelwulf's warriors

Ordheah – one of Coelwulf's warriors

Ordlaf – one of Coelwulf's warriors

Oslac – one of Coelwulf's warriors, dies in The Last King

Osmod – one of the older warriors from Kingsholm, first appears in The Last Shield

Penda – first appears in The Last Horse – Pybba's grandson

Pybba – loses his hand in battle, rides **Brimman** (Sailor in Old English)

Rudolf – was a squire at the beginning of The Last King, rides **Dever**

Siric – now dead

Sæbald – one of Coelwulf's warriors

Tatberht – first appears in The Last Horse, normally remains at Kingsholm. Rides **Wombel**

Wærwulf – speaks Danish, rides **Cinder**

Wulfstan – rides **Berg**

Wulfhere – grandson of Tatberht, rides **Stilton**

Wulfred – one of Coelwulf's warriors, rides **Cuthbert.**

The Mercians
    Bishop Wærferth of Worcester
    Bishop Deorlaf of Hereford
    Bishop Eadberht of Lichfield
    Bishop Smithwulf of London, dies in The Last Seven
    Bishop Ceobred of Leicester
    Bishop Burgheard of Lindsey
    Ealdorman Beorhtnoth – of western Mercia
    Ealdorman Ælhun – of area around Warwick
    Ealdorman Æthelwold – his father, Ealdorman Æthelwulf, dies at the Battle of Berkshire in AD871.
    Ealdorman Wulfstan – dies in The Last King
    His son – (fictional) dies in The Last King
    Werburg – (fictional) his daughter
    Ealdorman Beornheard – of eastern Mercia
    Ealdorman Aldred – of eastern Mercia
    Lady Cyneswith – Coelwulf's (fictional) Aunt

Within London
    Egbalth, trader
    Cata, trader
    Gayadore, trader
    Brother Matthew, a monk

Within Canterbury
    Archbishop Æthelred of Canterbury
    Abbot Kynebert of St Augustine's Prior
    Nothbalth, messenger
    Father John, monk
    Father Jerome, monk
    Ælfric, warrior

Viking raiders
    Ivarr the Boneless – dies in AD870
    Halfdan – brother of Ivarr (above)
    Guthrum - one of the three leaders at Repton with Halfdan. Baptised as Æthelstan in The Last Viking
    His sister, who dies outside Northampton
    Oscetel - one of the three leaders at Repton with Halfdan
    Anwend – one of the three leaders at Repton with Halfdan
    Anwend Anwendsson – his fictional son
    Jarl Sigurd – dies in The Last King
    His wife, now dead

The royal family of Mercia
    King Burgred of Mercia
    m. **Lady Æthelswith** in AD853 (the sister of King Alfred of Wessex)
    they had no children
    Beornwald – a fictional nephew for King Burgred
    King Wiglaf – ninth-century ruler of Mercia (827-840)
    King Wigstan - ninth-century ruler of Mercia
    King Beorhtwulf – ninth-century ruler of Mercia
    King Coelwulf II – ninth-century ruler of Mercia from AD874 (the main character)
    Coenwulf – his older brother, died 10 years ago
    Lady Cyneswith – his aunt

The royal family of Wessex
    King Alfred of Wessex
    m. **Lady Ealhswith**, a woman of the Mercian royal family in AD864
    Æthelflæd, their older daughter, born c.866
    Edward, their older son, born c.974
    King Æthelred of Wessex, Alfred's older brother, died 871.
    m. **Lady Wulfthryth**

Æthelhelm, their son
Æthelwold, their son

The West Saxon Ealdormen
Ealdorman Bucca – appears in charter S345 without location
Ealdorman Cuthred - of Hampshire
Ealdorman Eadwulf - of Somerset
Ealdorman Garulf – appears in charter S345 without location
Ealdorman Wulfhere - of Wiltshire
Ealdorman Sigehelm – of Kent

Misc.
Eanulf – Mercian warrior
Kyred – oathsworn man of Bishop Wærferth of Worcester
Turhtredus – Mercian warrior
Wiglaf (now dead) and Berhtwulf – the names of Coelwulf's aunt's dogs, Lady Cyneswith
Wulfsige – commander of Ealdorman Ælhun's warriors

Places Mentioned
Canterbury, in Kent
Ermine Street, ancient roadway from London to Lincoln, and York.
Gainsborough, in north-east Mercia.
Grantabridge/Cambridge, in eastern Mercia/East Anglia
Gloucester, on the River Severn, in western Mercia.
Gwent, one of the Welsh kingdoms to share a border with Mercia.
Gwynedd, one of the Welsh kingdoms to share a border with Mercia.
Hereford, close to the border with Wales, on the River Wye
Icknield Way, ancient roadway from Norfolk to Wiltshire

Kingsholm, close to Gloucester, an ancient royal site

London – more strictly the twin settlements of Lundenwic (a market site) **and Londinium** (Roman ruin) **at this time**

Northampton, on the River Nene in Mercia.

Old Sarum, in Wessex

Powys was one of the Welsh kingdoms to share a border with Mercia.

Repton, important Mercian mausoleum. St Wystan's was the name of royal mausoleum.

River Avon, in Warwickshire

River Granta/Cam, runs from Cambridge to King's Lynn (East Anglia)

River Great Ouse, running from South Northamptonshire to East Anglia

River Nene, runs from Northampton to the Wash

River Ouse, leads into the Cam/Granta, runs through Bedford (Bed's Ford)

River Severn, in the west of England

River Stour, runs from Stourport to Wolverhampton

River Thames, runs through London and into Oxfordshire

River Trent, runs through Staffordshire, Derbyshire, Nottingham and Lincolnshire and joins the Humber.

River Welland, runs from Northamptonshire to the Wash

The Foss Way, ancient roadway from Lincoln to Exeter

The Portway, ancient roadway in Wessex

Torksey, in the ancient kingdom of Lindsey, part of Mercia

Warwick, in Mercia.

Watling Street, ancient roadway from Chester to London

Winchester, in Wessex

Wareham, in Wessex

Worcester, on the River Severn, in western Mercia.

Historical Notes

King Alfred was the last of four brothers to be king in Wessex, with another brother dying before he could become king. With historians starting to focus more on events in Mercia during the ninth century as opposed to believing Mercia was merely eclipsed by the West Saxons, this might well mean a rethink of how Alfred and his brothers interacted with one another, and their father. There's already a suggestion there might have been some sort of rebellion against their father's rule by the older brothers.

I'm always uncovering new information when researching this period. And sometimes, I have to include it, even if it might contradict an earlier, or later reference. So, despite my original thinking that Londinium was largely abandoned during The Eagle of Mercia Chronicles set in the 820s and 830s, I've discovered they believe the bishop of London might have lived within the walls even then. I've included that here.

I've spent more time than I care to admit trying to decipher how my warriors could cross the River Thames. I've found a fascinating article about it. This implies Lechlade was the place to cross although there has long been a belief it might have been possible to cross at

Laleham Gulls. It is also made very clear that the River Thames would have been more, not less, navigable in the winter. I've also spent much time endeavouring to decipher when/if there might have been a bridge over the River Thames. Certainly, the Roman-era bridge had long since disappeared at this time.

There is no mention of an Ealdorman Sigehelm of Kent at this time. I've created him using the father of Lady Eadgifu (Edward the Elder's third wife) as a basis, as their family was closely tied to Cooling, and indeed, Lady Eadgifu was embroiled in a long running conflict about the property for much of her life.

Readers of Icel's earlier stories will know he's spent much time in Canterbury, but I really wanted to take Coelwulf there as well. There is no indication the Viking raiders wanted Canterbury at this time but later attacks there allowed me to place one there. As did Jarl Guthrum's alleged conversion to Christianity, known to have taken place a few years later.

For those who are reading the Eagle of Mercia Chronicles alongside this series, yes, I am very much enjoying making use of Icel's earlier experiences in these later books. I hope you're also enjoying some of the Easter eggs scattered throughout the text.

In the course of writing this book, I was able to visit Old Sarum and Winchester, and wow, Old Sarum is so impressive. I also visited Stonehenge, which I found less impressive (and so I allowed Coelwulf to be a less than enamoured with it), and hence why our lovable giant, Hereman, tries to topple the stones.

Coelwulf will return. Soon.

Thank you for reading.

Bonus Short Story

Gardulf

The sound of the fighting's overwhelming as I trip through the rear of the trees. I know I'm bleeding from my belly wound, but not copious amounts. All the same, I feel weak. It's better to hide away here and evade the enemy. In time, I'm sure, my allies will come for me.

When I wake, sometime later, there's no sound, and the sky's darkening. I blink grit from my eyes and try to sit up straight. I'm concaved around my wound. I place my hand over it, but it doesn't come away bloody. That's a result.

But I can't hear my allies. I can hear almost nothing. I reach for the nearby tree and haul myself upright on one of the handy branches, wincing as I do so. My body's cold and unresponsive. I shouldn't have allowed myself to sleep. I shouldn't have abandoned my allies like that.

I reach for my seax, pleased it remains on my weapons belt, and turn to decide which way to go. In the gloom, it's impossible to determine which direction will allow me to leave the trees and which will simply push me deeper. I consider where my horse, Kermit, is. It would be so much easier if he were here. Then I wouldn't need to walk.

For a moment, fear prickles along my spine. I'm alone. I know it. Wherever my allies are, they're not here. They can't have been taken prisoner by our enemies, I consider, only for a worst thought to overshadow that one. They can't have been killed. I won't allow that. My father would be fucking furious if he thought I'd abandoned my lord king because of a paltry wound, only for Coelwulf to die.

'Bollocks,' I exclaim, licking my lips and tasting nothing but the salt of my exertions. I need water. I need food. I need to know where Coelwulf and my allies are. And my horse. I would never expect Kermit to leave my side willingly.

'Fuck, I should never have skulked away,' I mutter to myself, eager to hear something above the silence of the grave. And then I do. It's faint and could be the shush of leaves overhead, but I think it's a stream. I lick my lips again and realise I must reach the water. In the darkness, I can risk walking to wherever the water is. If I don't do that, I'll have to sit here and wait for some daylight before I do anything.

Not that it's as easy as I think it'll be. No sooner do I take a staggering step forward than I can hear nothing above the harsh bark of my breath and the shuffle of my feet.

I realise with a crushing sense of failure this isn't going to work. Tears sting my eyes. Fear makes me weak—fear for my friends and my king, and anger at myself. For long moments, I stand and just breathe, and then, when I realise crying will get me nowhere, I resume walking. Every so often, I pause and listen for the flowing water.

The night remains quiet. There are a few scampering animals and the odd bat, but nothing terrifying, well, other than being alone in West Saxon land with Viking raider bastards potentially surrounding me. Fuck, I hate them all. My desire to kill Jarl Guthrum for what happened to my father often threatens to overwhelm me, but I know killing him in exchange wouldn't heal the grief of losing my father. Edmund was a bastard to me. But I loved him, and I miss him. To atone for what befell him, I need to banish every bastard

Viking raider from Wessex, Mercia, what remains of the kingdom of the East Angles, and Northumbria. They all need to burn in a special kind of hell reserved for fucking bastards.

My steps never falter. It's not too dark to see, provided I'm careful. I don't want to lose an eye to a random branch, but my helm should ensure that doesn't happen. I can smell the water the next time I stop to catch my breath. I lick my lips again, grimace, and hurry to move off.

I step in the water before I realise I've found it. An icy cold splashes up my leg, and I move backwards, feeling for the river bank with my feet. Only then, when I can be sure I won't get any wetter, do I bend and scoop water into my mouth. It tastes of freedom, and I drink greedily until I finally feel sated.

The tree cover breaks beside the stream. I look up at the moon and stars overhead. There's little cloud cover, but as much as I can see, I still can't determine how to reach my allies. I want to go back to the site of the fight. I want to reassure myself that while they're not here, they're also not dead.

I bend and drink more. I'm tired, and my belly growls hungrily, but it must be content with water. For now.

There's little more to do until it's light. I drag myself to dry ground, and with the comforting shape of a tree trunk at my back, I close my eyes. If I sleep now, in the morning, I'll find my allies, or so I reassure myself. It's better to sleep now than scrabble in the dark, not knowing if I'm turning in circles.

My eyes close. I breathe deeply, and then I know no more.

When I wake, there's a hint of daylight. I've not slept for long. I can tell by the effort it takes to open my eyes, but I need to piss, and my wound's pulsing painfully. I gasp as I lurch to my feet.

'Bollocks,' I exclaim, dizzy with pain. I'm reminded of when I was last wounded. I wish Lady Cyneswith were here to help me, but she's not. And, if I want to live through this, I need to sort myself out.

On tottering legs, I move clear of the stream and fumble to release my stream into the undergrowth. It sounds like rain. When I'm finished, I take myself back to the water and bend low, wincing and gasping again, sweat beading my forehead to drink until I'm full. Then, I dunk my face into the water, first removing my helm. I watch the water turn pink and consider what else I've wounded. My head feels fine. Then I realise, I have a cut on my hand. In all my fumbling, I've knocked the scab from it, and now it bleeds.

I sit back on my legs. I must check my wound. I haul on my byrnie. It comes free. I can see the pink edges of a cut and the crust of blood over it. I bite my lip. Should I clean it and risk cracking the scab or leave it? Unsure, I pass my wet hand over it, shivering as the cold water runs down my belly beneath my trews.

What I need to do is move. I must determine if King Coelwulf lives and where my allies might be if they're not amongst the dead, which I hope they're not.

Fighting the pulsing pain, I force myself to my feet, shrug my byrnie on once more, and move back through the trees. As the daylight grows, I see more and more. The woodlands are ancient. The thickness of the tree trunks attests to that. There are some well-worn paths beneath the trees, but I don't know where they lead. I follow the one, I hope, will take me north to where I believe yesterday's fight took place.

Quickly, I'm sweating again, but I don't remove my byrnie or helm. If there are enemies, I will defend myself. The woodland creatures intrude on my hearing. Soft scampers and the occasional crack of wings assure me that despite evidence to the contrary, I'm not alone.

I survey the growing plants but don't know which ones are edible. I'll have to go hungry. And then, ahead, I hear voices. I stop, sheltering behind a tree and peer all around me.

The voices aren't Mercian or West Saxon. They're the bastard enemy, and they sound furious. I don't want to be discovered by them. I'll not die on the edge of their blades. But the voices come no closer. I peer forward, thinking I see the road up ahead. I don't know how many Viking raiders there are, but I might struggle with any more than one, and even with one, I know I'll be putting myself in an impossible situation.

So I wait. The day drags, and my legs tire, but I dare not move. If the sun glints off my helm or seax, held in my hand, then the enemy will be upon me, and I won't discover what I need to know.

Eventually, the voices drift away, along with the sound of hoof-beats. Still, I wait. And then I wait some more as well. I only step free from my hiding place when I've heard nothing for so long, I'm almost asleep again.

Carefully, eyes everywhere, I emerge from beneath the trees. The view before me brings a wolf grin to my dry lips.

'Fuck me,' I exclaim. The pile of enemy bodies is vast. My allies have done this. I know it.

I move forward, eyes everywhere, but all I see are dead men with long, dirty hair and trinkets in their beards or around their necks. There are no Mercians here.

Whatever the Viking raiders I heard were doing, they weren't moving the dead. I consider if they'll leave them here to rot and grow maggot-infested. Already, the buzz of flies is loud, and during the night, an animal with sharp teeth has helped itself to some tender bits while the birds have taken the eyes of most of the men. It's a grim sight but one that brings me joy.

Still, it doesn't tell me where my allies are. But I know they won't be here. They'd have killed the Viking raiders who came here if they were.

I turn, looking both ways along the road. Which way should I walk? I will have to walk. No spare horses are waiting to aid me.

I bend and eye one of the bodies, noting the shield abandoned on the ground, just within touching distance. I also examine the dead, realising there's an opportunity here to do something that should aid my king and Mercia.

With a grimace, I bend and help myself to the shield, wishing it didn't weigh so much. Then, I move closer to the dead man and take the chain from around his neck, which shows some lump of silver that might be supposed to be a raven eye or hammer; I can't truly tell.

I tie it around my neck, and decision made, turn towards where Icel said Winchester was.

I don't know where my king or horse is, but I do know where the bastard enemy is.

It might take me days to reach it but I'll go there, and discover all I can about the Viking raiders intentions. And then I'll seek out the Mercians.

I don't know where they'll be, but from the angry mutterings of the Viking raiders I saw earlier, I know one thing. They still live. Until I find them, I'll discover all I can, and that way, I'll have my vengeance against as many of the enemy bastards as possible.

I look up and grin.

If my father could see me now, he'd be proud of me.

I know he bloody would.

What to read next?

I hope you've enjoyed Coelwulf's newest tale. If you'd like to keep reading about Saxon England, and Mercia in particular, then please consider this series of interconnected titles, which I term 'The Tales of Mercia.'

Gods and Kings (Seventh century)
   Pagan Warrior
   Pagan King
   Warrior King

The Eagle of Mercia Chronicles (Earlier ninth century)
   Son of Mercia
   Wolf of Mercia
   Warrior of Mercia
   Eagle of Mercia
   Protector of Mercia
   Enemies of Mercia
   Betrayal of Mercia

The Lady of Mercia's Daughter (Tenth century)
    A Conspiracy of Kings

<u>The Earl of Mercia Series (End of the tenth century)</u>
    The Earl of Mercia's Father and subsequent titles (please note, perversely, I began this series first).

Enjoy

Meet the Author

I'm an author of historical fiction (Early English, Vikings and the British Isles as a whole before the Norman Conquest) and fantasy (Viking age/dragon-themed), born in the old Mercian kingdom at some point since AD1066. I like to write. You've been warned! My first non-fiction title is also now available.

Find me at mjporterauthor.com. mjporterauthor.blog and @coloursofunison on twitter. I have a monthly newsletter, which can be joined here. All subscribers will receive a free ebook short story collection.

https://dashboard.mailerlite.com/forms/699265/105452112446489757/share

Books by M J Porter (in chronological order)

<u>The Dark Age Chronicles</u>

Men of Iron

Warriors of Iron

<u>Gods and Kings Series (seventh century Britain)</u>

Pagan Warrior

Pagan King

Warrior King

<u>The Eagle of Mercia Chronicles</u>

Son of Mercia

Wolf of Mercia

Warrior of Mercia

Eagle of Mercia

Protector of Mercia

Enemies of Mercia

Betrayal of Mercia

<u>The Mercian Ninth Century</u>

Coelwulf's Company, stories from before The Last King

The Last King

The Last Warrior

The Last Horse

The Last Enemy

The Last Sword

The Last Shield

The Last Seven

The Last Viking

The Last Alliance

The Last Deceit

The Tenth Century

The Lady of Mercia's Daughter

A Conspiracy of Kings (the sequel to The Lady of Mercia's Daughter)

Kingmaker

The King's Daughter

Non-fiction title

The Royal Women Who Made England: The Tenth Century in Saxon England

The Brunanburh Series

King of Kings

Kings of War

Clash of Kings

Kings of Conflict

The Mercian Brexit (can be read as a prequel to The First Queen of England)

The First Queen of England (The story of Lady Elfrida) (tenth century England)

The First Queen of England Part 2

The First Queen of England Part 3

<u>The King's Mother (The continuing story of Lady Elfrida)</u>

The Queen Dowager

Once A Queen

<u>The Earls of Mercia</u>

The Earl of Mercia's Father

The Danish King's Enemy

Swein: The Danish King (side story)

Northman Part 1

Northman Part 2

Cnut: The Conqueror (full-length side story)

Wulfstan: An Anglo-Saxon Thegn (side story)

The King's Earl

The Earl of Mercia

The English Earl

The Earl's King

Viking King

The English King

The King's Brother

Lady Estrid (a novel of eleventh-century Denmark)

Fantasy

<u>The Dragon of Unison</u>

Hidden Dragon

Dragon Gone

Dragon Alone

Dragon Ally

Dragon Lost

Dragon Bond

<u>As JE Porter</u>

The Innkeeper (standalone)

<u>20th Century Mystery</u>

The Custard Corpses – a delicious 1940s mystery (audio book now available)

The Automobile Assassination (sequel to The Custard Corpses)

The Secret Sauce (coming soon)

Cragside – a 1930s murder mystery (standalone)

9 781917 374156